National Cash

by Marcello Antonius Versace Tino

Thompson and Prince

Copyright 2011 by Marcello Tino
Publisher: Thompson and Price, Ithaca, New York
Distributors: Amazon.com, Ingram Book Company, Baker
& Taylor

ISBN – 13: 978-0615588933 (Thompson and Prince)
ISBN – 10: 061558893X

Library of Congress Code Number: 2012930662

Key Words: American Literature __ Historical Novel __ Political Novel __ 1960s __ Student Activism __ Feminist Movement __ Civil Rights __ Counter Culture __ Vietnam __ Sex __ Drugs __ Rock and Roll __ Revolution __ Quantum Physics and the Human Mind.

Acknowledgement

I've been a very lucky man. The one person who I love the most loves my writing, my wife, Lorraine. For better or worse, I couldn't have written it without her. I dedicate this book to Lorraine, the children of the 60s, my brothers and sister who have died, some with broken hearts and broken dreams; and to those who survived, I hope this book will bring them back to when they were giants. To a new generation I hope this book will inspire, and this time we will break through to the other side.

Chapter One

Sonny Versace was in his room at the Chelsea Hotel in New York City; and he was looking at his own image in a windowpane where he saw himself as a projection and reflection in glass, his vague image a portal for his spirit that had traveled through time. It was a portrait of a young radical who had fought in a Second American Revolution where the children of the 60s became giants and took on the corporate Leviathan, overthrew two presidents of the United State, nearly toppled an Empire, and stood at the doors of eternity where Zen met quantum physics and everything was possible. But now it was 1973, the beginning of the end; and his image was fading.

When Sonny realized that he had lost the war against the Leviathan and its biomechanical symphony of harmony conducted with a swagger stick, he retreated deep within the caverns of New York City. Now, he was an exile in his own country; and he was looking through the pane at his own worse nightmare. Sonny opened the French doors; and he stepped out onto a wrought-iron balcony with a floral motif that overlooked 23rd Street and a modern day Inferno where he could hear the eternal combustion music of the city streets, the blare of cars imitating trumpets, and the constant thump of base reality. Across the street there was a dead hippie who looked like a filthy rag doll, his legs hyperextended and his back against the wall. Next to the dead hippie was a shopping cart filled with all his worldly possessions stuffed into black plastic garbage bags. He had a guitar in his lap, and his mouth was open as if he had sung his last song. The guitar had no strings.

Sonny stared at the prophet of change, and he heard a siren grow louder and louder until a blue and white ambulance appeared, and it parked near the body. Sonny watched the paramedics place the dead troubadour into a black plastic body bag that was similar to the garbage bags in the shopping cart. They then placed him on a gurney, shoved him into the ambulance, and drove away through the swarming sounds of chaos to the stainless steel silence of the city morgue. Sonny closed the doors on the stone gargoyles of capitalism that lurked on the rooftop nearby, and his room was as quiet as a cell in an ancient monastery, but then the phone rang.

"Hello."

"Sonny, it's Josh. We have a shipment coming in."

"When?"

"One o'clock."

"I'll see you at the warehouse."

Sonny hung up the phone; and when he entered the bathroom, a few cockroaches scurried down the drain back into the underworld. He splashed his face with cold water, toweled himself off, and walked back into his room that was furnished sparsely with a king size bed, a nightstand, a dresser, and a chair. Stylistically, the furniture could be categorized as a good buy at a garage sale; but he had what he needed – anonymity, privacy, clean sheets, a telephone, high ceilings with decorative friezes and molding chipped and peeled, and a white marble Victorian fireplace cracked and yellowed with age, the hearth black with soot. It was a bit shabby, but Sonny loved the old lady. She was a twelve story red brick Victorian with brownstone trim, a mansard roof, and wrought-iron balconies that looked like the lace edging of a black silk slip made of cast iron.

She was built in 1883 as a cooperative that defined urban opulence at a time when the Chelsea was situated amidst what was then the theater district of New York City. Back then she was a jewel surrounded by opera houses, vaudeville theaters, brownstone townhouses, tenements, and tree lined streets. In the early 1900s she fell on bad times and went bankrupt. The new owners turned her into a hotel; and for many years she was a haven for the genius and the mad, the gifted and the handicapped, the unique and the commonly abused, the lauded and the ridiculed, the star and the lonely runaway who found shelter and quiet behind her thick fortress-like-walls and genteel poverty.

Sonny left his room and entered the hallway that was dimly lit to hide its desperate need for a new paint job. The stairwell was darker. The iron staircase with its mahogany banisters and wrought-iron balustrades glimmered with sinister echoes from a past of lost dreams. It frightened Sonny because he felt that the hotel was haunted by ghosts who mocked the decaying walls of the Chelsea as they lectured him in whispers. It was something about creativity and the origin of creation and a sentence that he could not understand or make out; but to Sonny the Chelsea was a universe of imagination holding out behind its crumbling walls from the gross babble of the world; and he was a resident of that alternative universe of multiple stories, characters living in each and every cell on every floor.

Sonny pressed the button to the elevator and like magic the door opened, and it took him back to a primitive world where coincidence became fate. It was going to be a good day for him; the omens were right; and, appropriately, Sonny shared the elevator with Sid Vicious and his girlfriend, Nancy, who greeted him as if he didn't exist. He was just another ghost.

Sid, who looked like he was on a very strict diet of heroin, wore a white tuxedo jacket with a white badly worn tuxedo shirt open to the waist exposing his tattooed image of the American eagle descending upon his genitals. His hair was bleached blond and spiked, and he looked like a punked out version of Frank Sinatra singing, *"My Way."* Nancy was made up to look like a cosmetically smeared Marilyn Monroe in skin-tight leather pants and a black leather jacket with chains dangling from the epaulets. Her breasts were large and dominating. They looked like they had just thrown open the doors to a spirit that was bent on destroying her doll like image.

The doors of the elevator slid open, and Sonny passed through to the lobby that was a gallery of starving artist who at one time or another turned over their imaginary space for real space. Sonny called the collection, *Life Against the Wall*, a place where the nonmaterial emerged from the material in the form of tinfoil, chrome, twisted steel, distorted figures, color and form peeking out of decay at the electric shock of wonder. Through the nightmares left behind for rent overdue, Sonny could see the rockets red glare, the bombs bursting in air, and a portrait of Jimmy Hendrix singing, "Oh say can you see."

Sonny walked out the front door of the hotel; and he moved quickly so as not to be followed, disappearing into the city and the people, the sidewalks and the cars, the trucks and the tall granite buildings. He felt the density and the massiveness of what it was like to be gray rock somber and hard. He felt what it was like to be the man who was approaching him, the weight of his wool topcoat, the confinement of his patent leather shoes that hurt his feet, the lines in his face that spelled out weariness. He could feel his hand on the man's brief case; and he could feel the woman who passed him by, her hair as it flowed across her cheek blown by the wind that enveloped her and everyone, a million billion fingers blindly feeling the shapes of everything as it swirled into blooms of scent, the smell of coffee.

Sonny could see his own image in the window of the coffee shop. He was wearing a brown leather jacket that was worn from years of use; and underneath his open jacket, he wore a black mock turtleneck sweater made of Marino wool. His jeans were the old style Levi's with a button-fly, and his sneakers were made of soft light tan Italian leather that felt wonderful on his feet. Sonny's face seemed to be defined by the darkness and the shadows of his features; but when he saw a little boy who was sitting next to his father in the coffee shop bite into a sugar doughnut, the powdered sugar spilling over his hands onto the table and his lap, Sonny smiled and his face lit up and his eyes were full of life as he savored the moment of pure innocence when sugar was worth more than a million dollars.

National Cash

The ground shook underneath Sonny's feet, and he knew it was time to go. He was at the corner of 34th Street and 7th Avenue at the Herald Square subway entrance; and he could hear the subway train pulling into the station, the hiss from the underworld as he hurried down the stairs. He ran to the turnstile, dropped in a token, and he was through the clanking turnstile and onto the train just as the door closed with a hiss.

Sonny sat down on a stained metal seat in the subway car that was decorated with graffiti written in an unreadable language that was screaming to be read. The only words he could discern were "Love" and "Fuck," two words for the same thing in a death struggle over meaning. Sonny listened to the steel scales of the metal snake scraping against each other; and he listened to the couplings, links upon links banging to the screams and moans of an ancient rune, steel grinding against steel.

Across the aisle an old man fitfully nodded his head in affirmation as if to say, "I believe. I believe that it will all soon be over." The train screeched to a jerking halt, the old man woke, looked around, saw that it was not his stop, and he again began to nod in prayer.

To the right of the old man sat an Irish Geisha girl from Brooklyn with bleached blond hair, caked on makeup, a pink plastic faux fur coat, black vinyl boots, and a green and orange beaded purse clutched between her legs. He and she and everyone else was pumping and bumping and jerking with the snake as it swayed in and out of itself. They all seemed to be in a trance, their eyes black holes devoid of feelings like a street hooker being banged by an overweight business executive in a wrinkled suit pumping away mechanically in a seedy hotel on a bed with broken springs. The biomechanical monster screeched to a grinding halt and hissed as its doors flew open to disgorge and gorge itself of people; and then once more satiated, it slithered its way through the subterranean consciousness of the Big Apple conjuring up memories of stories told.

It was 1931, and Sonny's father was eighteen years old, the youngest of five children. His mother had died giving birth to Joe, and his father raised them on his own in the midst of the Great Depression and Prohibition. Where there should have been love, there were breadlines, bitterness, resentment, and coal that the boys picked up from along the railroad tracks so as not to freeze to death at night.

Joe left home to look for work, and he found a job at the Endicott Johnson Shoe Factory in Binghamton, New York, a medium sized factory town in Upstate New York. Endicott Johnson was one of the first companies to advertise in Europe that the streets were paved with gold in America, but it didn't take Joe long to find out that this was no paradise. He worked on a machine that pounded leather, no safety devices. Pound, pound, pound, all day long, a thousand pounds of steel like a giant hammer pounded down on the leather.

Nearly blinded by sweat, Joe Versace could hardly see as his arms went in and out of the machine in-between the poundings. The better he got at the job, the faster the machine went. The constant pounding was jarring Joe's brains loose; and when Joe didn't keep pace, the sound of steel against steel rang through the factory bringing the foreman to his work station. The foreman, a burly man who wore his excess fat like money in the bank, would glare at him like he was a dumb animal that needed to be whipped.

Joe wanted to quit, but there were twelve million Americans out of work, a quarter of the population. He had seen thousands of men, women, and children standing in soup lines or living on the riverbank in shanty towns made of cardboard boxes and any other scraps that they could find in the city dump. He had seen pictures in the paper of the Dust Bowl and the farm foreclosures, thousands of farm families stranded on the roadside, their Model T Fords broken down icons of power and speed. Their clothes were unwashed tattered remains of a picture dream of America bought from a Sears & Roebuck's catalog. Pages upon pages of flowering dresses full of promises of Eden and pages upon pages of toys full of promises of Christmas were being used as kindling for a campfire to heat a can of beans for a family of five.

Joe felt trapped; but then one day Jackie Hines, a coworker at the factory, took him to a speakeasy during lunch hour for a drink. Sitting at the other end of the bar was a man with one arm. Jackie noticed Joe looking at the man and said, "You replaced him, Joe."

Jackie smiled; but then he got quite serious when he said, "You have to be careful on that machine. The guy down at the end of the bar got it when the power went off."

"When the power went off?"

"Yeah, when the power goes, the block drops no matter where it is in the cycle. His arm was crushed, and they couldn't get it out until the power came back on. It was bloody horrible."

Joe looked at the one armed man, the stump; and he thought to himself, I've got to get another job. He watched the man behind the bar who owned the speakeasy. He had a clean white shirt on; and he was smiling, laughing, bullshitting with his customers, and taking in the dough. Joe wondered where he got his booze.

All day long he wondered; and after work, he wondered more. He looked around his apartment. It was on the ground floor, and he had a private entrance. He could turn his living room into a speakeasy. All he had to do was take out the furniture and put in some tables and chairs with red and white checkered table cloths to brighten up the room. At Vinnie Morelli's speakeasy they used wicker and green glass Chianti bottles as candle holders for atmosphere. He would do that too. That's it, he thought, now all I have to do is find out where the guy gets his booze from.

Joe hid in the bushes behind the speakeasy night after night waiting for the delivery of moonshine. Then one night the bootlegger came, and Joe followed him from one delivery to another until finally he followed him home. Once he knew where the bootlegger lived, he started going to all the speakeasies, buying drinks, making friends, and getting to know everyone. They didn't know it yet, but they were his future clientele. Several months later when he thought he was ready, he drove to the bootlegger's home in the country. On the way he prayed to the Blessed Virgin Mary. She had to help him. How was he going to pray to her with stumps for arms? She had to talk to her son, put a good word in for him.

Joe pulled into the bootlegger's driveway and parked his car. The farmhouse was an old graying Victorian that was stripped of most of its white paint. The black Model T Ford that Joe had followed was parked next to a woodshed, and behind the house he could see a dilapidated barn. The hay in the loft told him that there was probably some cows around somewhere; and in the field the farmer had planted corn and wheat, quite a bit of it as far as Joe could see. He didn't see any clothes on the clothesline; and there were no signs of children about; but as he walked up to the front door of the farmer's house, six bloodhounds came running from behind the house barking and growling. One of the dogs, a redbone hound, was foaming at the mouth and shaking off spittle and saliva because he was so eager to bite Joe in the leg.

The bootlegger opened the door with a double-barreled shotgun in his hand and shouted, "Shut the fuck up!"

The dogs stopped barking, and now they looked at Joe like a scrap of meat that their master was about to toss them. The man was older than Joe. He looked in his thirties, and he was small but wiry with thinning blond hair and ice blue eyes.

"What the fuck do you want?" the man asked.

One dog chewed on Joe's shoes, and the redbone snapped at his ass; but Joe stood his ground and said, "I'm Joe Versace. I work at the Endicott Johnson factory in Binghamton. I'm opening up a speakeasy, and I want you to sell me your moonshine and maybe some labeled whiskey if you have it."

"How the hell did you find out where I live?"

"I saw you make a drop, and I followed you home."

The bootlegger cocked the shotgun; but Joe raised his arms in a gesture of surrender and said, "Now wait. Hold it. I didn't sneak up on you, and I didn't come here to steal from you. I came to talk business with you, face to face like a man."

The bootlegger thought for a moment then said, "Why should I sell to you?"

Joe thought for a moment, "Well, all I can say for myself is that I know how to keep my mouth shut. I take my own falls. I'm starting out small; but it ain't always gonna be that way; and one thing's for sure, I don't care if you shoot me right here and now; but I ain't going back into that fuckin factory."

The man laughed and said, "OK, I'll check you out; and if you're who you say you are, we'll do some business, cash on the barrelhead." He then extended his hand and said, "I'm Harry Kaiser."

The next day, Joe talked to his landlady, Maria Squillace. She had just thrown her husband out for philandering, and she had three daughters to feed. Joe promised her more rent, and he promised to be careful and discreet. He winked at one of the daughters, and Maria asked him if he had any brothers.

The same day he called his brothers Johnny and Tony and said, "Come on up to Binghamton. We're going into the booze business."

Sonny, when he was a little boy, didn't know what being "in the booze business" meant. He didn't know that his father and his brothers started with a one-room speakeasy and ended up owning a string of speakeasies, a whorehouse, a still, and a brewery where they made their own liquor and beer. Sonny didn't know that after the Prohibition laws were repealed that his father and his brothers moved into gambling, loan sharking, and the fencing and warehousing of stolen goods. Binghamton was centrally located in

Upstate New York between Buffalo, Albany, and New York City. It was an ideal place from which to fence and move stolen property, black-market merchandise, and goods stolen from factory warehouses and hijacked from trucks.

Sonny knew none of this. As far as he knew, his father was a restaurateur who always wore a suit and spent most of his time in one or more of his restaurants. But one night when Sonny was six years old, he tiptoed down into the cellar where his father and his two brothers were sitting at a table near the furnace and the coal bin. The only source of light was the red hot coals from the furnace and a single low voltage light bulb that hung over the table from an electric wire.

Sonny heard his Uncle Tony say, "Al is getting out of hand. We can't let him say the fuckin things he's sayin."

Johnny the youngest brother, who was tall like Joe but had light blond hair and blues eyes, shrugged it off and said, "He gets drunk and shoots off his mouth. Al likes to play the big shot. He's a big fuckin blowhard."

Tony, who was short and chubby and had very soft features for a man who was so mean, pointed his cigar at Johnny as if to burn him for his stupidity and said, "He gets drunk and shoots off his mouth because he thinks he can get away with it. It's not one time or a few times. It's not booze courage. He thinks he's a big mobster now. Last night he pulled a gun in my bar; and soon he'll be showing it to you, Johnny; and he won't be just shooting off his mouth. He'll be shooting you."

Tony turned to Joe and said, "When he pointed his fuckin gun at me, you know what he said? He said, 'I don't give a fuck whose place this is. Al Melfadi does what he wants to do, when he wants to do it; and if you don't fuckin like it, Tony, you and your whole family can go fuck yourself.' "

"So what do you think we should do Tony?" Joe asked.

"Kill him."

Sonny watched his father hold the glass of homemade wine up to the light. To Sonny it looked like dark red blood with a blue flame around the edges surrounded by an ochre light.

Joe took a sip of the wine, studied the flame, and then said, "I think you're right. Every scumbag in the world will try to fuck with us if they see weakness. And there's no talking to Al. Sure, he'll say he's sorry; but as soon as his cock swells, it will be fuck you all over again."

"How are we going to do it, Joe?" Johnny asked.

Joe paused for a moment to think. It was so quiet that Sonny could hear the coals in the furnace hiss. Finally his father said, "When Al comes back, he'll probably be drunk. And when he's drunk, he thinks with his cock. I'll use Dolly Challier to set him up. The broad's got dancer's legs, a great ass, big tits, and everything she wears looks like fuckin underwear. She's the perfect setup."

Joe paused again, and Sonny could see the fire reflected in the glass of wine when his father said, "You know, she was gang banged when she was fourteen; and she never got over it. It rattled that poor girl's brain." Joe shrugged, "But it is what it is. Now, she's a crazy fuckin prostitute; but she's not stupid; and she loves money. She'll do it for a price and keep her mouth shut. And besides, she has a special incentive."

"What's that?" Johnny asked.

Joe laughed a laugh that seemed to come out of the

fire itself and said, "Al was one of the guys who raped her."

They all laughed; and then Tony asked, "Do you think Al will go for it?"

"Shit, yes," Joe said contemptuously. "I know Al will go for it. Fucking the same broad at the same time? That's being close for Al. That's like being a buddy. He'll love it. She can blow us while we're talking over old times." Joe laughed again and then got serious and said, "I'll talk to Dolly tomorrow and set it up. If Al shows up in any of our places, you call me; and then I'll call Dolly."

Sonny was very excited. He didn't understand most of the words; but it was a revelation for him to find out that his father was a cowboy like the heroes in the movies who killed the villains, people who tried "to fuck with them," as his father said. He didn't know who Dolly was except that it sounded like they were going to play with her like a toy.

A couple of days later, Sonny was playing soldiers; and his father was sleeping in the living room in a soft rose colored velvet chair. The phone rang, and his father woke up. He could hear his father say, "Call Dolly. She knows what to do. Buy Al all the drinks he wants. Tell him his money is no good. I'll be there in about an hour."

Joe hung up the phone, went to the bathroom, and drew a bath. When he came out, Sonny was hiding under the dining room table; and from there he could see his father dressing in the bedroom. His father was a big man, tall and lean with huge hands and veins on his arms and hands that seemed ready to bulge out of his skin. He had jet-black hair and sculpted features and deep-set gray blue eyes with long lashes that his mother said a woman would die for. Sonny also heard people say that his father was handsome enough to be a movie star.

Sonny watched his father put on a carefully ironed and starched white shirt with his initials embroidered on the breast pocket. He put on a pair of dark blue pin stripped pants, gray suspenders, a burgundy silk tie that looked like wine, and a pair of patent leather black dress shoes that Sonny had polished. His father then walked into the dining room and reached deep into the hope chest and pulled out a revolver in a shoulder holster. As he walked back into the bedroom, he strapped on the holster and then put on the double-breasted jacket to his suit. He looked in the mirror and adjusted his tie. He was dressed to kill, Sonny thought.

Moments later his father came out of the bedroom and opened the door to his daughter's bedroom. She was wearing her pink ballerina slippers, and she was up on her toes putting a pinup on the wall of a star ballerina suspended in air.

"Where's Sonny?" his father asked.

She turned and smiled but then went back up on her toes, deep in concentration, trying to balance the photo of the star ballerina. "He's in bed, Dad."

"Where's Tony?"

"He's out playing."

While they were talking, Sonny snuck into the kitchen, quietly opened the door to the porch, softly closed it, and snuck down the stairs into the darkness and the alleyway where his father parked his car, a black Packard that glistened in the moonlight like a monster with big chrome teeth. Sonny opened the rear door and got in the car. There was a dark brown blanket on the floor, and he slipped under the blanket and waited.

A few minutes later, he heard his father's heavy

footsteps on the stairs. Then he heard him walking through the alleyway, open the door to the driver's side of the car, and get in. Sonny could feel his father's weight in the car. He could smell his aftershave lotion; and a few moments later he heard the car start up, the motor throbbing as his father backed out onto the street.

The hypnotic sound of the motor, the motion, and the whoosh of cars going in the opposite direction put Sonny to sleep; but the feeling of a dirt road and the sound of gravel under the wheels of the car woke him up. Ten minutes later, Sonny's father pulled to a stop, and they got out of the car. Sonny waited a few minutes then peeked out the window.

They were in the parking lot of The Red Rooster, a roadhouse his father and his brothers owned way out in the country. Sonny got out of the car and walked quietly through the parking lot. He could see that there was a cockfight in the barn. He could hear the shouts, the beating of wings, and the screams of excited women. He went through the bushes and walked quietly around the old farmhouse to where he found an open window and a clear view into the bar. The bar was paneled with knotty pine, and it was full of people cloaked in cigarette smoke.

He could see his father at the bar talking to his Uncle Johnny who was bartending. There was a moose head over the bar and a petrified big swordfish that looked like it was in its death throes gasping for air amidst the swill of beer. On top of the upright piano there was a stuffed brown squirrel holding onto a broken limb looking wide-eyed at the horrors of human nature and a stripper on the dance floor dancing with a live boa constrictor that was writhing underneath the talons of a stuffed American eagle hanging from the ceiling. Sonny watched the snake flick its tongue into the stripper's open mouth as it tried to get in; and when she pulled it away, it wrapped its body around her leg and flicked its tongue at her bare breasts.

Sonny turned away, and he saw a well-dressed man in a gray suit and a black and gold tie come up to his father. They shook hands as if they were old friends who hadn't seen each other for awhile, and then they leaned their backs casually against the oak bar and watched the naked woman lying on the floor, bump and grind in a weird dance, the snake wrapped all around her with its head between her legs. Sonny had never seen anything like it. He looked over to the bar to see if his father was watching, and he saw a beautiful woman come up to the man who was with his father and put her arm around him. She began to rub his pants. She had long bright red hair, and she wore a short black silk dress with silk stockings and high heeled shoes that shimmered like silver. She had big breasts and big nipples that showed through her silk dress, and she made Sonny hungry.

Another woman appeared at the bar, and she must have just come in because she had an overcoat on. She was huge. She had to be as tall as his father and probably was heavier. She opened her arms wide, and underneath her armpits hung strings of homemade sausage and bottles of homemade wine. She gave Sonny's father a big bear hug lifting him off the ground; and when she put him down, she reached under her arm like a gorilla and grabbed links upon links of sausage. Her huge breasts were popping out of her dress.

"You want some, Joe?" she shouted so everyone at the bar could hear.

Sonny's father laughed and pulled out a roll of bills and stuck one bill down into her breasts and shouted loud enough so Sonny could hear, "Give it to Johnny. He'll put it in the ice-a-box."

She laughed, "I'll give it to Johnny all right." She reached into her coat and pulled out a twelve-inch meat knife and cut a string of sausage then plopped them on the bar.

That transaction completed, she turned to the man next to her seated at the bar, stuck a breast in his face, and grabbed one of her jugs of homemade wine by the neck and said, "How's about it, baby? You want some of mother's milk?"

The man laughed and shouted, "My Momma's jugs ain't filled with no Dago red, Anna."

Anna shoved him, "So much the worse for you, you skinny son of a bitch." She pulled out her knife again and cut the string on the bottle and set it down on the bar and said, "Give me a shot, Johnny."

She then turned to Sonny's father who was going out the door with the man and the woman, and she raised the jug of homemade wine up into the air. "Hey, Joe, this is for you, Sweetheart. Free from Anna."

Sonny was jolted into the realization that his father was leaving. He rushed through the bushes and into the parking lot. As he ran passed the barn, a man came out and threw a dead cock into a garbage can. There was another fight going on inside. He could hear the beating of wings, and he could see the giant shadows cast against the whitewashed walls splattered with blood. Sonny found the car, opened the back door, and crawled under the blanket.

A few minutes later he heard a woman's laughter, his father's rumbling voice, and the other man's laughter. They all got in the front seat with the woman in the middle. His father started the car, and they drove off. The woman and the man seemed to be playing with each other as his father drove over dirt roads further and further into the woods. Sonny saw Al's hand reach up and grab Dolly by the back of the head and push her down. He heard a zipper being unzipped; and then he heard Al say, "Listen, Joe, I'm going to be straight with you. Your brother, Tony, has a crocodile mouth and a canary ass. Without you he's nothing, and I told him so, but that's not what I want to talk to you about. I want you to come in with us. We have the Magadino family in Buffalo behind us, and they want to control all the fencing and distribution of swag in Upstate New York using the Triple Cities as a depot and distribution center. It's a natural, Joe. We're in a central location between Buffalo, Albany, Scranton, and New York City; and we want you to come in with us, to be part of our family."

"What's in it for me?" Joe asked.

"You can have all of Binghamton."

"I already have that."

"Listen, Joe, this is just the beginning. Together we can move out of the county. With your connections and mine, we can take over all of Central New York State and Western and Central Pennsylvania. There's a big hole here ready to be filled, and we can do it. It's simple. We'll consolidate your fencing and warehouse operations with our own. We'll share the profits 50/50, equal partners. You'll double your business in a year."

"Let me get this straight," Joe said. "You want to give me what I already have; and, for that, I will get half of my own business? And, you tell me I'll double my business, which means... Let me see. I only went to sixth grade; but...if I remember right, one plus one equals two. Oh, I got it. I'll have to work twice as hard as I do now to make the same amount of money. And...I will take twice the risk. What a fuckin deal. How can I refuse?"

"Look at it this way, Joe. You're a small business being swallowed up by a big corporation. It's the American way. Fight us, and you lose. Join us, and the sky is the limit."

Joe laughed and said, "Dolly, You better zip Al up. He's getting a big head."

Dolly sat up and said, "Jesus, Joe, where's Willow Creek? I'm so hot I might do you both right here." She hugged Al and said, "I love the taste of you."

"It's right up here," Joe said.

A few minutes later, Sonny's father pulled off the road, stopped the car, and they got out. Sonny peeked out the window. He saw Dolly leading them down to a creek. She was holding her high heel shoes in her hand and was dancing along like a child. There was a grassy knoll near the stream; and she turned around and went down on her knees, her skirt went up over her thighs.

Sonny got out of the car and crept forward. He heard Dolly beg for Al to give it to her. Al unbuckled his belt and unzipped his fly. Then he grabbed his penis and held it out to Dolly. Dolly held it in her hand and said, "Lay back, baby. Enjoy it. I want Joe to fuck me from behind."

Al laid back on the knoll, and Dolly bent over and slipped him in her mouth. With her other hand she pulled down her panties. Sonny could see her bare ass in the moonlight. However, he couldn't understand what was going on.

His father was standing behind Dolly, facing Al. He heard his father say, "How do you feel, Al?"

"I'm in heaven, Joe."

Sonny saw his father reach into his jacket and pull out his revolver. The shot was like a lightning bolt. Al's head exploded spewing blood.

Sonny was horrified. He raced back to the car and hid under the blanket and cried. He stopped crying when they came back; and his father drove off, away from Willow Creek. They drove in silence. When they were back in town where the lights were bright, his father let Dolly out and then drove home.

When his father got out of the car, Sonny's mother was waiting for him. She was crying, "Sonny is missing!"

The backdoor of the car opened. He felt a hand pull the blanket away, and he heard his father say, "Oh God. No!"

Joe held his crying son in his arms, and he was crying too. He keep stroking his head and whispering, "I love you, Sonny. I would never do anything to hurt you. This was just a nightmare. You have to forget about it."

Sonny never forgot it. He was afraid of his father, and he didn't trust him. His father was like the Dick Tracy character, Two Face. One face was nice and sweet and the other side of his face was horrible and twisted. Sonny was especially afraid of his father when he came home late at night drunk. Sonny could tell he was drunk by the sound of his footsteps on the stairs, by the rattle of the door, the feeling of things being grabbed then squeezed then squeezed a little more, by the sound of a kitchen chair being dragged across the floor like a dead body, the smack of a glass against a bottle, the relief of a drink being poured. In the silence Sonny listened to the darkness move.

Out of the darkness his father's voice emerged. He hissed in a whisper, "Fuck you," then poured himself another drink and pondered over all the kinds of fucks there were. Each fuck was different, but they were all the same. Joe Versace only had a sixth grade education; but from his limited vocabulary, he had developed a sound fundamentalism, an economy of style, and a dramatic sense of musical composition.

Sonny listened to his father's version of Revel's *Bolero*. It was a bolero of fucks. From one simple fuck in the dark, a multitude of fucks emerged; and each fuck was dealt with in its own way; but the fucks kept coming on louder and louder, "Fuck" after "Fuckin Fuck" until Joe Versace hissed; and the Bolero began again; and the composition became more complex with varying textures, the fucks developing new ways of being fucks, the tempo picking up until the fucks achieved some kind of transposition and became "Fuckin Assholes."

In the darkness Sonny could feel Joe Versace tear away the niceties of the English language and turn it over on its ass before he finally filled in the naked truth with a final cataclysmic crescendo. Sonny heard his father walk out onto the porch. His voice soared over the rooftops. It was like an opera. His voice had all the qualities of a great tenor, and his range defined his territory. It was simple. "Fuck you all." Then came the final and ultimate question, "Who wants to fuck with Joe Versace?"

Silence. Not a sound. It was as if the world stood still and everyone had

died; but then Sonny heard his mother go to the screen door and whisper to his father in a hushed voice, "Joe, stop it. Someone will call the cops."

The flame in Joe's voice rose from the grease that Sonny's mother had thrown on the fire. "Who's going to call the cops? Nobody calls the cops on Joe Versace. I call the cops."

"Oh my God, the man has gone mad," his mother cried, and she returned to their bedroom imploring God for help while Joe Versace called the cops. He called them every fuckin name in the book, but they never came.

Sonny heard a shot and knew that his father had slammed the screen door, and he had come back into the house. He wanted to believe that the concert was over; but he knew that he was only in the eye of the storm; and this was just a prelude because, now, the Devil was going to enter the Queen's Chamber.

Sonny put his pillow over his ears. He had seen and heard one variation or another of this scene so many times before that he could visualize his father walking into the bedroom where his mother was pretending to sleep. His father turned on the light on the table next to the bed. The bedroom set was much too large for the small room, and there was only a small space in the middle of the room to stand. So there he stood, crowded between the bedroom set for the new house that never came and surrounded by wallpaper decorated with a life full of roses and magazine dreams.

Sonny could hear his father say, "I'd like to take off my pants and go to bed, but I can't."

Rose continued to make believe that she was asleep.

"You know why I can't?" he asked.

Silence.

"Because, if I take off my pants and go to bed, as soon as I close my eyes, you'll put your hands in my pants and steal my money."

That woke Rose from her sleep. Now she was ready to play fuck fuck with Joe Versace. "You throw your money away on your scummy friends," she began. Then she mimicked him taking a big roll of money out of his pocket and throwing his money around. "No, no, keep your money in your pockets. Nobody buys when the big sucker's around. Save it for your family, save it for important things. Don't be a sucker like me. Don't be a big jackass." She screamed, "Don't touch me!"

"Keep your hands out of my pockets."

Rose screamed again. Sonny's sister cried from behind her bedroom door. "Oh God, please stop."

Sonny cried too.

His brother cried, "Stop. Come on, Dad. Go to bed."

Rose screamed again.

They all cried, and their father stopped.

That's when their mother started. "Scaring your children like this, you should be ashamed of yourself."

"I should be ashamed? Why should I be ashamed? I'm not a thief in the night."

"So I'm a thief because I take your money and put it

in the bank where it belongs?"

"You're a thief because you're a sneak."

"Oh, I'm a sneak thief because I clean up after you when you're sleeping off a hangover. I'm the one who has to nurse you when you make yourself sick drinking trying to forget the men you buried. If you want a conscience, think about your family and forget about that shit. What is done is done. It's a hard world, and they had it coming to them. In your own words, 'a fuck is a fuck.' Don't ruin us with your drunken sentimentality."

Joe growled, "So you're the one who wants to fuck with me."

"Come on. Let's hear it," she shouted. "Let's hear the filthy mouth that stands in the way of me getting a new house."

"You fuckin American cunt."

"Don't you dare!"

Sonny could hear his mother running. The door of his bedroom opened, and his mother locked the door behind her; and Sonny pressed himself against the wall next to his bed clinging to his pillow.

Joe tried the door, and then rattled it so hard that the walls shook. "So I spend all the money. You fuckin bitch, what about the twenty pairs of shoes you own? What about that fuckin morgue you call a closet? I see a dress once, and it's dead. What about that drawer full of jewelry?"

"What about the future?" she said.

The door began to rattle again. Sonny's father was getting to the hinges as he shouted, "You haven't got no fuckin future, you bitch. I'm going to kill you tonight."

As the hinges were weakening, Rose spoke to Sonny in the dark. "I never should have let him buy me all those things. Your father is a good provider. He just doesn't have a sense of the future. He thinks the good times will last forever."

Sonny looked at his mother's eyes wild with fear and rage, and he knew they were both mad. He had to get out of there. He had to get away; but he didn't know how; so Sonny withdrew into his own universe where he was Superman; and he could not be hurt; or he was Captain Marvel who knew the secret word, "Shazam," that gave him the wisdom of Solomon, the strength of Hercules, the stamina of Atlas, the power of Zeus, the courage of Achilles, and the speed of Mercury; or he became Plastic man who could disappear by turning himself into an inanimate object. But then one day, when he was twelve years old, he found a way to transform his fantasies into reality, a way to protect his head from the bad people and become a hero.

Day after day, on the way to the Boy's Club, Sonny stopped at a sporting goods store and stared at a red football helmet, the real thing, not a toy helmet that children wore. Everyday for a year he stared and dreamed as if the football helmet were his crystal ball. When he looked into the future, he saw a stadium full of people cheering for him as he crossed the goal line, victorious. He could hear the marching band playing; the drums gave him goose bumps.

There was nothing that Sonny could keep from his father. Sonny had figured out that the difference between God and the Ruler of the Underworld was that God knew everything you said and did, but the Devil could read your mind. He knew your deepest and darkest secrets, and he could tempt you with your forbidden dreams. Sonny knew this because that Christmas under the spreading arms of a plastic Madonna and the pretty colored Christmas lights and the plaster of Paris wise-men bearing gifts, he opened a box; and there it was - the red football helmet. Sonny put it on; and he was off running, dodging imaginary tacklers, throwing the football through a swinging tire, exercising until his mother beat him with a broom to make him stop, eating twelve eggs for breakfast, and drinking four quarts of milk a day so that he could get big.

Wearing his red football helmet, he took off running through the alleyways of life, one, two, three, ring-a-lei-via, everyone was chasing him. They chased him in-between cars, around telephone poles, up stairways, and onto porches. He jumped into the bushes, and he ran through the park and around the merry-go-round then disappeared back into his crystal ball. They chased him in sandlot football, and they couldn't catch him. They chased him in high school, and they couldn't catch him. When he graduated, he was one of the best high school football players in the country, and he went to Cornell University on a scholarship. He was so happy. He was finally going to get away from home, and he was going to become an All American. How much more American could he get than that? He was going to be like everybody else, but better.

At Cornell, away from home, he felt like he was in Paradise. He joined a rich fraternity; and he lived in a large red brick Tudor mansion with balconies and decked patios overlooking the campus, the town, and Cayuga Lake. He ate in a paneled dining room with large pilot windows and a fireplace. He entertained in a living room with crystal chandeliers, a huge ornate fireplace, luxurious leather couches and chairs, light pouring through the ceiling to floor leaded glass windows. He had tea in the tearoom, and he made love to beautiful heiresses and blue-bookers that were rich in passion for a coming star.

It was all so dreamy being on top of the hill, a soft cushy cloud overlooking reality, detached. Everything was so crisp and clear. The buildings looked like they came out of history books or science fiction stories. The students looked like they came out of magazines. From far above the lake he could see wind filled white canvases dreamingly sail over the waters. Through the campus waterfalls cascaded over gorges deep in thought, running into brooks and streams, and pastoral fantasies. Best of all, his bedroom and study had corked floors and double doors; and he slept the sleep of someone never in fear of being woken up by footsteps in the night. When he wasn't sleeping, he was studying and day dreaming knowing that soon he would wake up and his dream would come true again when the leaves turned orange, red, then fall; and it would be football season again.

For true believers, football was not a game. It was a sacred rite as old as Mt. Olympus and the Roman Coliseum and as new as the modern cathedrals of America's true religion, the football stadiums where every Saturday and Sunday millions upon millions of Americans congregated to give up their individual consciousness to become part of the mass - a collective being that conjured up mythological heroes and their most primitive urges for victory.

For Sonny, he was the mass, the focal point of their collective consciousness, the apex of the primal roar that raised him up into another dimension where running with a football was an abstract art form, a living canvas of clashing colors, balance, and grace in the midst of violence and the brutal impact of reality that had to be avoided at all cost as he wove his way through all the monsters of his past.

One-on-one with the last defenders from the deep, he was the light bearer emerging from the black ink of every magazine and newspaper in the country, cameras flashing as he spelled out all his dreams in pure body language, vivifying the black ink with emerald green fields and blue skies, Paradise. But then he fell from grace. He blew out his knee against Navy, and it was all over. His dream was gone. Everything became nothing again, and he was back where he started, but worse.

That winter he discovered that his father was dying of one of the worst forms of cancer, a cancer that was eating him alive from the inside out. Sonny remembered standing at the side of his father's bed in the hospital watching his father stare at the crutches and then at his son. Joe had tears in his eyes. It was he who had bought him the red football helmet and watched his son tear off the wrapping paper and look into the box. Joe Versace never had a childhood; and, for that moment, he experienced pure joy in his life through the joy in the eyes of another. Sonny's father reached out to hug his son only to fall back and disappear into the dark pools of his eyes where the light receded to the furthest star beyond the sun; and Sonny could only watch helplessly from the lowest depths of hell encased in ice, indifferent to the fires that raged around him.

The metal snake ground to a halt. It hissed as its doors flew open, and Sonny poured out with the rest of the passengers like the off springs of some mad scientific experiment. Sonny was on the run again, but this time he was not running against

Harvard, Princeton, or Yale, Syracuse, or Navy. Now it was the NYPD, the DEA, and every law enforcement agency between Florida and New York as well as the Columbian Army, the Strategic Air Command, and the Coast Guard that monitored the air and the sea looking for little blimps on its radar to squish. Sonny wove his way through the wall of commuters, slipping from one reality world into another, and bursting onto the streets of New York into the roar of the city, the arena where he played in the middle of Spanish and Black Harlem, near the Met where Sibelius's *Seventh Symphony* was playing, a lone violin soaring above the towering harmonies, yearning for immortality while down in reality the streets were strewn with crushed wet brown cardboard boxes, discarded plastic bags, broken bottles of beer, and empty soda cans.

Turned over garbage cans lined the street, and Sonny's ears and nose were filled with the sound of roaring trucks and the smell of burning rubber. Across the street was a man with a pushcart selling used clothes draped over the side of the cart like corpses found on the street. Black and white and Latin faces were twisted by cultural and cognitive dissidence. Everywhere he turned he saw hostile stares, hunger, and despair.

Sonny stopped at a telephone booth on the street and called the warehouse. "Josh, it's me, I'm coming up."

"OK, I'll bring the elevator down."

Sonny walked from the corner to the warehouse. There was a window on the first floor of their building that wasn't there yesterday. Sonny didn't like it. Whoever was moving in was going to be able to look out onto the street and see everything that was coming in and out of the building.

Josh came down with the freight elevator. The building was a converted parking garage, and the elevator could lift cars and vans. It was perfect for them.

Josh was smiling, "Good morning, buddy."

Josh was small and slight; and he would have been considered frail with his wispy blond hair, even features, and vulnerable blue eyes, except for the fact that every move was precise and determined; and he talked with the assurance of a man who was talking to himself in the mirror. Sonny was sure that Josh saw a giant in that mirror, and he liked Josh for that.

Sonny smiled and said, "What's happening, Josh?"

Josh started the elevator. "We have three cars coming in today with about fifteen hundred pounds of pot."

"Is anyone coming to pick up?"

"Yes. CB, Sal, and Allen, they'll take it all."

"How much do we have left in the warehouse down South?"

"About six thousand pounds and we should receive that by the end of the week. So what happened with Charlie's brother? Do we have a deal?"

"I'll bring Ginny the sample after we finish up here today. Then we'll see."

"How much do you think he will take?"

"All of it. I hope. Two hundred and fifty dollars a pound."

"Cool. When do you think it will go down?"

"Ginny said that she would get the sample to him before she went to work. That means that we may be able to make the deal tonight. I'm going to push for ten in the morning tomorrow for the exchange. That means that you have to load the pot in the van and park it where I showed you on Pier 40. You think you can do all that before ten?"

"Why so early?" Josh asked.

"I want everyone there with a hangover praying to God for mercy, especially Charlie. He'll be far less dangerous then.

Josh smiled, "No problem."

The elevator creaked to a stop at the third floor; and when they entered the warehouse, Sonny watched Josh shut the steel folding security gate, lock it from the inside, and then swung the plywood doors shut.

Just the thought of Charlie, Larry, and the Genevese Family who had eyes and ears all over New York aroused Sonny's acute sense of paranoia; and when he looked at the large crack between the bottom of the plywood doors and the floor, it just made it worse. "Josh, we have to cover that crack up. Anyone can see in here."

Josh laughed. "Sonny, nobody is going to look through the crack under the doors when they go by on the elevator."

"You don't know shit about human nature, Josh. Everybody is curious about what other people have in their box. That's what New York is all about. I want to know if that Puerto Ricans downstairs are fixing hot cars in their garage. I want to know what the hell those guys are doing upstairs. Can they hear us talking business? What about the new guys on the ground floor? With that brand new window that they just put in, they can look out onto the street and see everything. We're supposed to be antique dealers and all that comes in and out of here are cars from Florida and Alabama with CB antennas."

Sonny looked around the warehouse. In front of him

he saw Josh's van parked in a space large enough for three or four cars. In the back, behind a wall of stacked plywood and sheetrock was the space where they stored the boxes of marijuana ready for shipment. To the right of Sonny was the workshop with a table saw, two radial arm saws, empty work benches, no tools or work apparent, wood bins with nothing in them but scraps of wood and boards with nails sticking out of them like booby traps. Like a cop, Sonny noticed that there was no sawdust on the floor.

"Josh, we're supposed to be antique dealers, and we don't have any antiques. We have a workshop and no sawdust on the floor."

"Who cares?"

"I care, and you should too."

Josh laughed, "Would you rather be unloading on the streets?"

"Are you kidding?"

"OK, then stop bitching and count your blessings. We have it made here. Come on. Let's sit down, and I'll bring you up to date."

They walked across the parking area to a small office that looked out onto the work space and the parking area. Sonny sat down at an old oak office desk, and Josh sat down on the threadbare soiled couch near a steel plate door that exited to the stairway. Another door led to a short hallway and the room where they packed and boxed the pot. Sonny looked at the empty desk, the empty room, the bare-brick walls of the warehouse that were cracking in many places where the mortar had crumbled and gravity had its way; and he realized that sometimes he looked forward to the paranoia just to fill in the empty spaces and mask the shabbiness of it all.

Josh took a sip from a paper cup, grimaced at the cold coffee, and put it aside where later it would be knocked over adding to the office décor – a pool of milky brown on poured concrete. Josh lit a cigarette, sat back, and crossed his legs like he was sitting in a board room on Madison Avenue. "Another boat should be arriving in Florida in the next couple of weeks."

"How much?"

"We have an option on half the shipment, fifteen thousand pounds."

"Sounds good."

"That's just the beginning, Sonny. When we get that boat out of the way we plan to invest in the next trip from beginning to end, double our money back on our investment with first option on the full shipment delivered as usual, three boats, sixty thousand pounds."

We're fronting all the costs?"

"Yes."

"Josh, you're talking about a million dollar investment and a six million dollar dope trip." Sonny intertwined his index and forefinger and said, "Billy's like this with the Columbian government. They'll pop this trip, sell the pot back to Billy, and he'll sell it back to us again."

Josh smiled and looked at Sonny as if he was crazy. "No, he won't."

"Why won't he?"

"Because we can buy it all and make life easy for him. We're his main buyers, Sonny. He fucks us, man; and he's out of business."

"Maybe he's going out of business."

"No way."

Sonny couldn't believe the confidence that Josh had in someone that he hardly knew. How can he be so smug, so certain? "How do you know, Josh?" Sonny asked.

Josh smiled knowingly. "There's too much money to be made."

"He can fuck us and do business with someone else."

"Why should he want to do that? We can move more pot than anyone else in New York."

"Maybe it's getting too hot for him down there. Maybe he wants to make a killing and get out. Maybe he wants to become a yoga master. I don't know, but neither do you. That's my point. You're working off a few good assumptions and then walking in blind. You don't know what's going on down in Columbia. It's not good business. It's a game of blind man's bluff."

Josh laughed and then said, "Hey, Sonny, if Robbie and Little Sheik were good businessmen, they wouldn't be losing money on every legitimate investment they make."

"So we should lose money too?"

"Listen, Sonny, let me worry about the money; and I promise you, by the time we're through here, you're going to have more money than you ever dreamed of."

"Josh, you know how I feel about the great movie in the sky, dollar signs floating down. The big picture looks good, but sometimes I think you paint pretty pictures because they make you feel good and safe."

The phone rang. Josh nearly jumped out of his skin. Sonny answered the phone, "Hello."

"It's Harvey," said the voice on the other end of the phone.

"Where are you?"

"We're a couple of hours away."

"How many cars?"

"Two."

"I was told there were three cars coming."

"They sent out a van, but I don't know where it is."

"A van?"

"That's what they told me."

"Where is it?"

"I don't know. They didn't come with us. Those suckers are on their own."

"Fuck." Sonny ran his hand through his hair in exasperation and gave Josh the 'I could kill you' look as he went back to talking on the telephone. "Harvey, can you be here by one?"

"Sure."

"Alright, give me a call when you come in."

"You got it."

Sonny hung up the phone and dialed another number.

Josh was anxious. "What's going on?"

"It was Harvey. They're on their way. They'll be here in about half an hour."

Josh's eyes lit up. The big picture was coming up from Florida. Sonny could almost hear Josh's calculator clicking off numbers that he quickly converted to pictures in the alchemy of money.

Sonny's observations of Josh were cut short when someone answered the phone on the other end of the line, "CB?" Sonny said.

"Yeah."

"Be here at two."

"It's there?"

"It's coming. I'll call you if there are any changes. Write off."

Sonny hung up the phone and laughed. "Write off. You know where I first got that? Remember when I got my first safety deposit box?"

"I remember."

"I go to the bank with twenty five thousand dollars in my jeans. This old fart at the desk in the safety deposit vault explains the whole thing to me. I go into a private stall and put the money in the box."

Sonny dialed another number and continued the story. "All the time I'm wondering to myself, what is this guy going to think when he sees me coming in and out of there with money? Will he know? Will he say something to someone?"

Sonny shrugged. "When I go out, I give him the safety deposit box, and he says to me, Right off."

They both laugh, but Josh was still trying to fill in the picture. "How many cars?"

"Two. He doesn't..." Sonny made his connection on the other side of the line. "Allen, it's Sonny. Can you be here at three? I'll call you if there's any change. Yeah."

Sonny dialed another number. He turned to Josh. "What the hell is the story on the van?"

"What van?"

"There's a van out there somewhere on its way to us."

"Robbie and Little Sheik probably put some pressure on Billy for more flow. He only has four cars running right now." Josh shrugged. "Robbie and Little Sheik probably talked him into sending a van with twice the load."

"It's risky, man," Sonny said; and then he made his connection again. "Hello, Sal, be here at three. I don't care if you're having trouble with your van. Go out and rent one. What do you mean, who's going to pay for it? I'll put a finger up your ass and loosen you up. Don't fuck around. Be here at three."

Sonny hung up the phone. "A van is risky on the road, Josh. Why the hell couldn't they wait?"

"We want to get this trip over with. I told you. The boat is coming in soon. We got to get ready for that."

"I don't like it. Everyone is in a hurry to fuck up. The cars are safe. They'll be lucky to get the van out of Florida."

"Don't worry. If they get busted on the road, it's all covered."

"Covered, my ass, the regular drivers won't touch it. They probably got some desperate son of a bitch to do it."

"It's covered."

"I don't like shooting craps."

"We're not shooting craps."

"You're shooting craps with other people's lives."

"It's not our part of the business. If they don't make it to New York, there's no risk to us."

Sonny took a long thoughtful look at Josh. He was changing again. Sonny thought back to the sixties when he and Josh were friends Upstate. Every day he had a new uniform on, a new hat – Josh the Plumber, Josh the Real Estate Brokers, Josh the Garage Attendant, Josh the Carpenter, Josh the Craftsman, and Josh the Florist playing his autoharp and talking to the plants. Josh went through identities and friends like a woman who was trying on new dresses and couldn't find one that fit. Now he was a capitalist and he didn't give a ship about anybody or anything except money.

Josh looked at Sonny and saw him staring. "What's the matter?"

"I'm thinkin about you. I'm thinking that the next time you try on a new identity, you might want to become a human being."

"Oh fuck you." Josh took out his calculator and began to play with it again.

Sonny picked up the Nikon camera with a zoom lens from the top of the desk and walked to the window. He looked out onto the street, adjusted the focus, and watched the rich and the poor all twisted together in a mass contortion, a traffic jam of bodies and steel.

"Hey, Sonny, listen to these figures. On the next trip our share is one million five hundred thousand. That's seven hundred and fifty thousand apiece and that is not counting what CB sells on the side for us. I bet we can make two hundred dollars a pound on what CB sells." Josh smiled and pressed some more buttons.

Sonny focused in on the chic people in designer clothes who walked by a man who looked near dead in the gutter. One couple stepped right over his body as they rushed to get a table with a view. It was a Kafkaesque scene in which murder glared in the steel light with dead eyes. Everyone seemed alive with fear, hatred, and despair, their faces, distorted by alcohol, drugs, mental illness, malnutrition, junk foods, cold cash, and a poverty of the spirit. They all looked like bland featureless zombies of the consuming dream. Sonny zoomed in to a picture of the bum in the gutter near the edge of the curb next to a pile of horseshit. There were New York State Lottery tickets strewn all around him, and one ticket was sticking out of the pile of horseshit like the Statue of Liberty.

Sonny lowered the camera, but then he saw a car across the street from the warehouse that aroused his suspicions. He zoomed in tight on the car. It was a late model, dark green, Ford sedan; and two men were sitting in it.

Josh was still working on his calculator. "On the big trip…Listen to this. Depending on the quality of what comes in…" Josh's face lit up as he figured it out. "We could make as much as six million dollars. What do you think of that?"

"I think the American Dream has become a one hundred and fifty million to one shot."

Josh was frustrated by Sonny's negativity. He put the calculator down and said, "Why don't you tell me something new."

"There's an unmarked police car parked across the street next to the bodega."

"What?"

"You heard me."

Josh got up from the desk and walked over to the window. He grabbed the camera and said, "Let me see."

He looked through the viewer, adjusted the lens, and said, "I think you're right. What are we going to do?"

"What are we going to do? We're going to sit here in wonderment, Josh. We'll wonder what it's going to be like when the cars come in from Florida with their CB antennas waving. And let's not forget the van. I can see it now. I bet it has a custom paint job with pretty pictures painted on the side panels, pictures of freaks, rock and roll, drugs, pot sticking out of the doors, dual exhausts, Beanie Babies on the dashboard, Leon Russell playing *Manhattan Serenade* on the tape recorder."

"Oh, yes, Josh, we'll wonder then. We'll wonder if the Puerto Rican in the garage downstairs with the hot cars has traded us off to the cops. And what can they see under the crack in the door? No antiques, no sawdust, just two assholes sitting in a box, sitting on a thousand pounds of pot, looking at numbers turning into the American Dream, things in the alchemy of money."

"Fuck you, Sonny."

"Fuck you, Josh."

The doorbell rang. Sonny's heart fell into his stomach, and Josh walked to the door and looked through the peephole. He then turned to Sonny who was still at the window and smiled. "It's the guy from upstairs."

While Josh talked to the neighbor from upstairs, Sonny continued to watch the Ford across the street. He took a few shots of it. A few moments later the car pulled out of the parking space, and Sonny zoomed in to take a picture of the license plate.

When Josh finished talking to the neighbor, he walked over to the window again.

"What did he want?" Sonny asked.

"He wanted to borrow a power-sander." Josh looked out the window. "They're gone."

"They pulled out a few minutes ago."

"Seriously, Sonny, what are we going to do if they come back?"

Sonny laughed and put his arm around Josh and said, "If they come back, or they are parked out here tomorrow, it's simple. You are going to curtsy, and I'm going to bow, and then we're going to close the curtain on this show, and we're getting the fuck out of here."

Josh smiled and said, "I'm hip."

Sonny could see that he had bummed Josh out. He smiled and grabbed Josh's calculator. "Hey, cheer up." He looked at the figures on the calculator. "We're rich."

Sonny then handed Josh his security blanket and said, "Come on, let's get to work."

As they walked back into the office, the phone rang. Josh picked up the phone. "Hello. OK, buddy. We'll be right down."

"It's Harvey and Bob," Josh said. "They're around the corner."

"I'll go get them," Sonny said.

Sonny entered the elevator; and as he descended slowly to the street, he listened to the sound of the pulleys creaking like an old man's joints and the cables straining on rusted wheels. The certificate of inspection on the wall of the elevator was dated 1956; and every time that Sonny pulled the lever to stop the elevator, he expected the cable to snap; and, if it didn't, he counted it as another good day in Paradise.

Sonny opened the steel doors to the outside world; and so as not to exude the smell of fear that cops could smell like dogs smelled your rear end, he focused on everything that was normal and beautiful in his environment. – the smooth soft textures of the clothes that a woman wore who passed him on the street, the graceful lines and folds of silk that flowed like a stream of water down her breasts and over her hips. One woman who was entering a bodega wore nearly all the colors of all the vegetables and fruit being advertised as today's specials: dark purple eggplants, green peas, California navel oranges, fresh tomatoes, and grapes. Holding her hand was her prepubescent daughter who was wearing a bright yellow T-shirt that featured a sketch of a little angel playing in a plot of white daffodils.

Next door to the bodega, Sonny saw an old man with a white mustache and swept back hair who had the distinguished look of a man who has lived for his family all his life. He was wearing a neatly ironed white shirt, tan khaki pants, and polished inexpensive black dress shoes. One hand was resting on the warm wool of a gray sports jacket draped over his arm. As he entered the neighborhood dry cleaners, the bell over the door rang like a hand held church bell that signaled to all the parishioners that it was time to kneel in worship of normalcy and a god who could find a rainbow in spittle with just the right change of light and perspective. Sonny turned the corner and walked to where the cars were parked. He signaled Harvey with a friendly wave.

Harvey got out of the car and extended his hand, "How you all doin?"

"OK," Sonny said. He shook Harvey's hand and then got into the car leaving Harvey standing on the street.

"How did the trip go?" Sonny asked.

"No trouble."

For a moment they just looked at each other and smiled and nodded their heads in approval. They were glad to see each other.

Sonny waved goodbye and pulled away. Through the rearview mirror he could see Harvey turn around and head for the diner on the corner for a cup of coffee. Harvey would watch his cousin Bob from there to make sure that everything stayed cool. Sonny knew very little about

Harvey. All he knew was that Harvey was a redneck that made five thousand dollars a trip and loved every dollar of it. He'd make this trip three times a week if they'd let him. He had a wife and a couple of kids in a mobile home somewhere down south in Florida or Alabama. Right now they're probably watching television on a brand new Sony Color TV waiting for Daddy to bring home the bacon. Harvey told Sonny that someday soon good old Harvey and his cousin Bob would have real homes, ones that didn't move; and then he was out of the business.

Sonny pulled Harvey's Mercury into the elevator. The car barely fit. The CB antenna was the last thing to make it in as it snapped its way into the elevator like a deep sea fishing pole. As Sonny took the elevator up to the warehouse he thought to himself, maybe someday Harvey and he will meet when this is all over. Harvey will invite him to his home, meet the kids, meet the wife, sit down and have a beer, have a good old time with some good old boys, watch the Sony, shake hands, fellow workers, soldiers who fought in the same war against poverty. Sonny imagined messing up one of the boy's hair in fond affection. They would all watch *The Brady Bunch*.

Sonny pulled into the garage, left the car with Josh, and went back down to the street. He looked around. The street looked cool, no one hanging around, no beat up stakeout cars, nothing out of place, nobody peeking through the new front window, no carpenters, nothing, nobody. Now all he had to do was pick up Bob's car.

When Sonny got back to the warehouse and parked Bob's Ford, he saw that Josh had the trunk of Harvey's car open; and he was unloading the green garbage bags filled with bricks of marijuana. Each bag held a brick weighing approximately thirty pounds apiece. The rear seats of the cars had been hollowed out to increase the load capacity, and there was about five hundred pounds packed in each of the trunks. Sonny and Josh had the cars unloaded in ten minutes. Josh vacuumed the trunks of the cars, and Sonny lowered the pressure in their pneumatic shocks. The pneumatic shocks in the rear enabled the car to run level with a heavy load. State Troopers loved to see you driving with your ass hanging down South. It was an open invitation to take a peek and see what was inside.

Half an hour after Sonny pulled the two cars into the warehouse, he had Harvey and Bob on the road again and on their way for another five thousand dollars.

"You all take care now," Harvey said waving goodbye with his CB swaying, Florida bound.

Sonny raced up the stairs to the warehouse looking for the shadows in the darkness, the unexpected surprise appearance of danger lurking in the shadows of the stairwell. He rang the bell, and Josh let him in and locked the door behind them. They went to the back of the warehouse to the room behind the office where they boxed the marijuana. In the room there was a compressing machine to compress the garbage, several stacks of unfolded cardboard boxes, a large box of garbage bags to repackage the pot, a hand roller, a cutting machine for the tape, a banding machine, and a digital scale. They had an hour to repackage, grade, weigh, and box the thousand pounds of pot stacked in the middle of the floor. Josh popped a tape by The Eagles into the tape player, and Sonny heard them sing,

Desperado, oh, you ain't getting' no younger
Your pain and your hunger,
They're driven you home
And freedom, oh freedom
Well, that's just some people talking
Your prison is walking through the world all alone.

Sonny took a deep-sea boning knife and sliced into the double wrapping of green garbage bags. The talcum powder, which kept the smell of the grass down, poured out from in-between the two bags. Josh and Sonny looked at the product. They had three grades for Columbian pot – gold, multi-mix, and green garbage.

Josh was disappointed by what he saw. "It's a multi-mix. I hope it isn't all like this."

Sonny looked more closely at the brick. Josh was right. It was a mix of gold, red, brown, and green. "You want gold, Josh?"

"Yes, I want gold."

Sonny began to cast magic spells over the bags and said, "I have to get paid extra for this."

"Hey, buddy, if you can make gold, it's a bonus."

Sonny had handled so many bricks and packaging jobs that he could almost tell through the wrapper whether it was gold or not. The gold was firmer with lots of resin to hold it together yet more shapely and full of well-formed buds. He felt the package and then looked at Josh and said, "This is it."

Josh's eyes lit up.

Sonny cast another spell and sliced the package open to reveal green pagoda shaped buds with golden hairs and touches of lavender that smelled like frankincense. The leaves that swirled around like a nest to protect the buds were drying up and turning into the color of sandalwood - Columbian Gold, the top end of the marijuana trade.

"What did I tell you," Sonny said. He began to cut open other packages while he chanted, "Gold, gold," conjuring up expectations that were reasonably well fulfilled. It looked like a good load.

Josh pitched in; and the room glowed as they cut, graded, repacked, boxed, and weighed the gold, green, and multi-mix of rainbow dust that filled the room. Breathing in the dust, Sonny was getting stoned. Sonny could see by Josh's eyes that he was stoned too. You couldn't help but be stoned. Their arms and hands and faces were caked with rainbow dust. The resins seeped into their pores and then into their bloodstream. The air was thick with color. They got higher and higher with every breath. It was one of the few fun moments on the job, the pot of gold at the end of the rainbow.

Sonny looked over at Josh, and they smiled at each other. They were experiencing something that very few people experience. They were on the ultra-high end of the drug world that was the low end of where Sonny had been.

Sonny remembered going back to school after his knee blew out and his father died. It was a bitter winter of skeleton trees, icy fingers, and broken limbs. It was mournfully cold. He remembered walking along a gorge that had turned into gagged and frozen falls. The wind howled; and broken crystals of snow whirled about forming drifts and frozen waves, the ground crackling as he walked. He watched his shadow on the snow and followed an icy stream into a frozen garden of natural ice carvings from which he could watch the light reflect upon a frozen mirror.

Sonny remembered sitting on a stone bench and crying his heart out amidst the frozen indifference. Everything seemed lost; and yet deep inside of him all the depression, anger, and rage seemed to be compressing in upon itself like a black hole that was giving birth to a new sun on the other side of reality, an empty page full of anticipation and the longing to find an object of illumination, something that would give shape to the darkness and rekindle his imagination.

That spring he found that spark of light amidst the ashes, the sub particles, the photons, the space debris of forgotten dreams; and he found it in a place that he never imagined that he would find it; but it was probably the first place that he should have looked in his youthful quest for meaning.

He found it in a lecture room at Goldwin Smith Hall listening to Professor Burnham and Professor Lowe debate the nature of politics. Professor Lowe argued that politics was all about power and who controlled the political decision process. The facts of life about politics in America were that it was all about influence peddling, buying votes, special interests, convenient coalitions, and manipulation. It was a hodge-podge of compromises that destroyed ideals and made the quest for reform an exercise in futility that rivaled the follies of Don Quixote.

Professor Burnham, on the other hand, believed in the power of an idea to transform reality. "It was the idea of an idea that was discovered by the Ancient Greeks," Burnham said. "And it was this discovery that gave Western Civilization its unique dynamics and creative capacity for change."

"It's not that ideas never existed before," Burnham quipped. "They did, but nobody knew what they were, much like nobody knew, at one time, how women got pregnant. In both instances, it was a major advancement in the evolution of consciousness. One thing led to another, and bang! You have a baby, and this baby gave birth to all the ideas that followed. Linked together they formed the intellectual matrix of our civilization. In fact, you and I wouldn't be here in this lecture hall today if it were not for that baby born in the cradle of Western Civilization, a place called Ancient Greece in an era we call the Golden Age of Pericles."

Professor Burnham paused, suspending what he just said for the students to absorb. Sonny marveled at his great sense of pace and his timing. It was like watching a great broken field runner; and Burnham made his break for daylight just when he should have made it, just when you could hear a pin drop.

"It's all about the power of an idea to define and transform reality," he said. "An idea whose time has come is one of the most powerful forces in nature. An idea whose time has come can break all the windows and bursts open all the doors to the temple of reality and bring a breath of fresh air to the dark stodginess that Professor Lowe calls the facts of life but are merely a rationalization for the status quo."

Immediately, Professor Lowe began to plug the gaps in his defense. For Sonny, Professor Lowe was like a defensive genius in football. He kept throwing facts at Burnham to stop him from breaking away; and Burnham keep dodging him, enveloping reality with a vision beyond.

49

National Cash

Burnham called it the Enlightenment; and Sonny called it breaking in the clear because, at that moment, thinking and running with the football became the same thing for him. Later, he would describe it as the moment when his ass and his head came together; and he was thinking with his whole body. This was the feeling that he was running to. It was the feeling that a great artist has when color and form take on a life of their own shaping passions and perceptions never seen before; and a great writer becomes the symbols that cast spells and conjures up characters and stories that come out of the darkness into the white light that separates into a prism of color, landscapes, faraway places, vivid images that come to life in the mind, on a screen, and in the theater where a great actor gives himself up to become someone else totally possessed by the magic. It is the same magic that the mathematician feels who becomes one with his numbers and feels the mass and weight and velocity of the stars and the planets and the gravity of black holes and negative space. This was the feeling that Sonny had when he looked into the crystal ball of his red football helmet, and he created a star, and this was the feeling that he was still running to.

Sonny graduated from Cornell University, and he went on to graduate school for his doctorate in American Studies at Syracuse University. He loved the tranquility of dozing off in a comfortable leather chair in the Maxwell School of Public Affairs and Citizenship Library surrounded by tomes upon tomes, each book a doorway to the DNA coda of our collective knowledge and memories. He felt like a monk in the monastery of the mind seeking wisdom and enlightenment; and his heroes were no longer the football stars of his early childhood. They were scholars and writers like Hegel and Spengler, Jean-Paul Sartre and Ernest Cassirer, James Joyce and William Faulkner, Hemmingway and Fitzgerald.

Sitting in the library with a book on his lap, the window open, the smell of spring mingled with laughter and voices in the quad; Sonny dreamt of becoming a professor, pleasing his mother, and writing books that would be read from generation to generation. But, the more he learned about America, the more his dreams were turning into a nightmare because, like many of the children of the 60s, he realized that they had been fed lullabies, lies, false gods, and heroes; and behind *Howdy Doody*, John Wayne, *Father Knows Best*, and the pretty Madison Avenue pictures and consumer totems that promised a breast in every bottle of beer, there lurked the dark side of the post war promise of *Happy Days*. It was the story you never saw on TV or read in a magazine or newspaper or heard on radio. It was the untold story of racism, gender bias, lack of opportunity for the poor, class privilege, and an imperial foreign policy fueled by an industrial military complex, greed, and vampire capitalism.

For Sonny the phenomenon that all these evils mutated into was the cancerous growth of the corporate state and global corporatism. It was spreading throughout all of America's institutions, including higher education, where it was turning American's children into chits on an IBM punch card to be manipulated and processed by a faceless bureaucracy. This knowledge industry was mass producing minds and shaping the life forces and dreams of America's youth to conform to the needs and the insatiable hunger of an amoral biomechanical organism that Sonny called the Leviathan.

In the beginning, Sonny and students like him thought that they could reform the universities from within and make academia live up to the ideals of higher education. They looked to their teachers for help and leadership; but, except for a courageous few, they all turned out to be timid well paid pieceworkers buried in narrow niches with titles for headstones in a graveyard of knowledge where the only common denominator was money.

No longer did Sonny believe in his teachers or what he could accomplish as a professor in the learning industry. He ceased believing in the liberal political philosophies that his teachers taught him. For Sonny, the whole notion that the system could be pragmatically and incrementally reformed from within without significantly altering the power structure or challenging the fundamental values of the system died with John F. Kennedy and a bullet in the head. Tweaking the system was not going to change anything except to ameliorate the excesses of legalized crime. America was in need of systemic change that Sonny believed would only come with a true democratic revolution of the people. Power to the People was an idea whose time had come.

Sonny remembered the day that he left the university. It was the beginning of football season; and the trees were ablaze with a glorious autumn death of red, yellow, and orange leaves amidst evergreen trees looking down somberly at the winged angel like leaves floating down to their doom. The fallen leaves created a mosaic of colorful impressionistic tiles along the path that Sonny was following across the Quad to a neo-classical building with the columns and tablatures and the wings of an ancient Greek temple. Hints of ancient Greece and Rome were all around him in the sandstone, granite, marble, and Georgian red brick that was seeping with youthful hormones and rebellion.

Somehow amidst the slow creeping takeover of academia by Corporate America, the children of the 60s were able to see beyond the myths and lullabies and pry open the tomes of forgotten knowledge and let lose the ghosts and spirits of freedom that poured out of the darkness, new and old words mutating into a new generation that was now filling up the Quad, preparing for a mass demonstration against the War in Vietnam. The police lines were forming, and the state troopers were wearing riot gear and helmets with faceless dark visors that gave them the appearance of dark plastic medieval knights with sword-like-nightsticks. Over the entranceway of the Palladian rotunda of Hendricks Chapel hung a large orange banner with bold white letters that read, "Go Orange!"

Sonny entered Maxwell Hall, and he walked to the classroom where he was the TA teaching a course on Public Affairs and Citizenship. When he entered the classroom, he could see through the window that the Quad was now filled with thousands of students; and he could hear the chants, the words of freedom like a ghost fire raging across America. Civil war was beginning to find tinder in the dreams of youth turned to anger and outrage.

"In the last lecture," Sonny said, "I concluded by saying that no matter what party you belong to, Democrat or Republican, there are no real choices to make or issues to be resolved in an election because all the important issues had been bought up before the election begins.

Democratic institutions in this country are controlled by big money interests, giant corporations, and the major economic organizations and professionals that serve these interests. They do this essentially through campaign funding, the lobbying of Congress, the control of mass media and education, revolving door regulatory boards, and the issuing of oral promissory notes to public officials, both elected and appointed, backed by historical precedent, that they will all make millions of dollars after they leave public service working for their masters. In fact, the actual casting of ballots is becoming a meaningless formal ritual designed to ratify the selection of candidates who have already won the one-dollar-one-vote fund raising contest."

In the background, Sonny could hear the ancient Greek chorus in garbled notes of freedom breaking through the windowpanes crackling like a growing fire

One of the students raised his hand and said, "But is there anything new about this, Professor Versace?"

"No, Mark, you could say that this is the way it has always been; and, up to a point, you would be quite right. Unrestrained capitalism has led us down this road before; and we have seen the amassing of great wealth and power in the hands of a few during the era of the robber barons of the late eighteen hundreds and the early twentieth century; but during the Great Depression and the post war years of the 50s, the avarice of unrestrained capitalism was somewhat mitigated by the New Deal that for a time created a balance between big government, big business, and big labor. However, with the growth of the American empire, American corporations have become transnational corporations that are extending their tentacles across the globe. This cancerous growth of global corporatism and vampire capitalism feeds off of cheap and child labor and threatens to dwarf the nation state and usher in a new Dark Ages of Corporate Feudalism and Fortress America."

The roar outside grew louder. Sonny shouted over the language that was in fragments burning at the altar of mass fervor. "We are creating a monster. I call it the Leviathan, others call it the Golem or the Devil, and some call it a society gone mad. It takes on many forms in the labyrinth of lies we create to hide from the truth. However, no matter what form it takes it is still all around us and about us because we created it out of our own individual greed and narcissism. It came out of the dark depths of our collective unconscious, unrestrained by reason and empathy; and, now, it has a life of its own, and the monster grows."

"How do you combat a powerful force like that?" Janet Smith asked.

We have to become the Giants of Democracy with millions upon millions of heads. You cut off one head, and there are millions more, each a cell that contains the whole. Only then will we be able to take on the Leviathan in a battle of Titans."

Sonny went about the room and opened up all the windows. "Listen to the Greek Chorus. They have the answer."

The bell rang ending the class, and the room was flooded with the sound of the student demonstrators chanting, "Power to the People!"

The next day, Sonny left Syracuse University, and he became the Johnny Apple Seed of the Revolution going from campus to campus, lecturing where he could, speaking at rallies and demonstrations, hanging out where students gathered in pubs and parks. Wherever Sonny went, he found fertile soil for the seeds of freedom in the youthful rebirth of a nation that reoccurred with every new generation. Freedom was a native plant that began to grow wildly everywhere, and it all seemed to be coming together.

Sonny remembered being so high that he was tripping out into the spaces between the electrons of the stars where about 10 million neurons and 23 trillion synaptic connections formed the galaxies of his mind. He was at the threshold where the world of logical sequence disappeared into a world of metaphors, associational patterns, and archetypal imagery and symbols that broke down the Aristotelian teleological world built on the syllogism of deductive reasoning and inductive logic. It was the world of the ever present now stripped of its past and future. Life radiated with immediacy and pulsated with its being. It was a world of magic where you could cast spells with words that would conjure up images; and in conjuring up images he could be transported into a reality beyond the walls of material possession. It was the world of the artist and the poet, the Buddhist monk and the magi. It was the creativity behind every great idea, the metaphor that burst into a star. It was consciousness. It was the world of the quantum mind, and Sonny was one of the billions upon billions of receivers and focal points – the billions upon billions of eyes of a universe in quest of itself. But now? He had to get stoned to convince himself that he was in Paradise again when, in fact, he knew he was sitting on a pile of shit.

Sonny looked around. The room was a mess; but somehow, stoned as they were, he and Josh were able to clean up the seeds, loose pot, torn garbage bags strewn about, and the talcum powder that dusted the floor like a thin layer of snow. They bagged the garbage and put it in a large box that was banded and set aside for disposal. Garbage was the tell tale clue when dealing in large quantities. How to get rid of the garbage was no easy task. It was a business in itself, and Josh had worked out a deal where he could drive the garbage out to the pier where it was then loaded onto a garbage barge and dropped into the ocean at a garbage disposal site.

Using a handcart, Josh rolled the boxes of garbage to the exit door; and now with everything boxed, he looked relieved. Sonny thought about the absurdity of it all. They were in the middle of Black and Spanish Harlem. They were in a neighborhood where murder was committed for a dime, and mental patients poured out of hospitals as refuge on the streets. They were in the middle of one of the biggest drug operations in the city; and they could be a headline in the *Daily News* and a promotion for any cop, any day, anytime; but, now, according to Josh, they were just another box in a city full of boxes. This was supposed to make everything cool. This was Josh's big innovation.

Sonny laughed.

"What?" Josh asked.

"I was just thinking…"

The phone rang.

It was the first pick up, and the boys came and went. Josh was happy and smiling, and Sonny was worried.

"Josh, it's four o'clock. Where's the fuckin van?"

"I don't know, but I have to run some errands. I'll be right back."

Sonny, who was still thinking about the van, paid no

attention to Josh.

Josh took the records and waved goodbye. "See you later, buddy."

Sonny found himself alone in the empty warehouse, and then it dawned on him, where the hell was Josh going, and why did he take the records with him?

Time passed. It was four thirty; and there was no van, no Josh. Sonny began to get the funny feeling that Josh had left him holding a bag of shit. "That little fuck."

The phone rang. Sonny picked it up, and on the other end of the line he heard someone say, "We're here."

"Who the hell is this?"

"I was told to call when we came into town. We're lost."

"You're driving the van?"

"Yeah."

"Alright, where are you?"

"At a Hundred and Eighth Street and the Avenue of the Americas."

"Great. You're in the middle of Harlem. Get your ass out of there right now."

"Should I ask directions?"

"No, head south and white. You know what I mean?"

"Yeah."

"OK. Keep on the avenue. As the numbers lower, you're getting warmer. When you get in the eighties, you're home. Give me a call, and I'll come pick you up."

"I'm on my way."

Sonny hung up the phone and thought to himself, God damn it, where's Josh? That fuckin driver is in Harlem, and he's lost. I hope my directions were clear enough. The driver sounded scared as hell. He may get lost again. Sonny shook his head. There was nothing he could do but wait and resign himself to the fact that this was going to be just another fucked up deal. Sonny remembered a friend of his once saying, "Life is a mud puddle. Splash around in it, and all it does it get a whole lot muddier."

Sonny laughed and ran through has game plan – lock up, pick up the van, run it around a little, make sure no one is following you, and then come back here and unload a thousand pounds of pot by yourself. And be careful. This one is hot and shaky.

The phone rang again.

Sonny grabbed the phone, "Hello."

"I'm at Broadway and Seventy Ninth Street."

"What do you look like?"

"A black van with Florida plates."

"Alright, I'll be there soon."

Sonny hung up the phone. Take some time, he thought to himself. Don't let him know how close you are.

Sonny double checked the warehouse to make sure everything was locked, and then he walked down the stairs. On the street, everyone looked like a cop. As he walked, he changed directions several times, reversed his field, stopped to tie his shoe, and looked around to see if anyone was following him. He didn't see anyone, so he headed down Broadway looking for the van.

There they were. He spotted them on the corner – a black van, custom painted with a scene of a desert sunset airbrushed in bright colors onto each side panel. Two chrome mufflers were sticking up in the air like smokestacks, one on each side of the van. The hood to the engine was open.

Sonny stopped at a fruit stand and watched. There

were two of them, a guy and a girl, freaks, two sore thumbs sticking out in a crowd like their mufflers, all smoked up. The young man in his twenties had long hair and a beard; and he was busy working on the motor, or seemed to be. Maybe it's just an excuse for parking in a no parking zone, but maybe it's for real. Sonny wondered how the hell they made it this far.

Sonny stopped at a fruit stand, bought two apples, and walked over to the man who was looking at the engine. "Is this piece of shit ready to go?" Sonny asked.

"Are you the guy I called?"

"I wish I weren't, but…" Sonny smiled and took an apple out of the bag and handed it to the man. "Welcome to New York."

Sonny also handed an apple to the girl with penciled eyebrows sitting behind the wheel of the van, and then he opened the door of the van for her to get out.

Sonny got into the van. "What's on the tape?" he asked.

"*Sympathy for the Devil.*"

Sonny laughed then asked, "Do you two know what synchronicity is? The man and the girl looked at him blankly; and he laughed again, "Alright, there's a coffee shop across the street. Go have some coffee. I'll bring back the van when I'm done. Stay there until you see me pull up right here in this loading zone, then get out of here."

Sonny pushed the tape into the player, and studied the man and woman for a moment. It's over for them, he thought. He could see the relief on their faces.

Sonny waved goodbye and drove off. He drove around for a while to make sure no one was following him. He wove in and out of traffic, shifted gears, changed speeds, stopped as if to park then took off, turned left, and caught a few lights just right. He looked into the rear-view-mirror one last time and then pulled up to the warehouse. He was in luck. The elevator was waiting for him.

He pulled the van in and took the elevator up to the warehouse. The warehouse was empty and quiet. No Josh. He was alone with a long way to go. He opened up the van, and the smell of cheap perfume washed over him. Sure enough the van was packed with garbage bags filled with marijuana, no boxes. A shabby rug hid the evidence and a couple of rock and roll guitars and an amplifier were thrown in for effect.

"I don't believe this."

Sonny worked fast. He had to haul a thousand pounds of marijuana into the back room. When he was finally done, he was perspiring, and his clothes were wet. Then he remembered the twenty pounds of pot that he was bringing Ginny as a sample. He opened several boxes until he found the multi-mix he was looking for. Then he quickly weighed out twenty pounds and put it in one of the black plastic garbage bags.

The doorbell rang.

He waited.

It rang again. Cops could be behind that door. They could be outside, all around the warehouse. Fuck it. He threw the bag of pot in the van, and he drove the van onto the elevator, locked the gate, and descended into the whatever with the doorbell still ringing. The elevator stopped. Cops could be on the other side of the iron doors, blocking his way, guns drawn.

When Sonny pulled open the garage doors, he was blinded by the light that hit him like the muzzle flash of a gun;

but there was no one there, no cops, just the normal chaos he lived in that sounded like a lullaby. Sonny climbed back into the van and drove around the corner to where the man and woman were waiting for him at the diner. He pulled into the loading zone, and the man and woman came out of the diner and approached the van.

Sonny got out of the van, handed the man the keys and said, "Next time, get a haircut, shave your beard, look neat." He looked at the girl. "Buy a new dress, something nice, and paint this van white for purity, no pretty pictures, and no more fuckin smokestack lightning."

Sonny dangled the garbage bag of pot that he was holding by the neck in the face of the man like it was a severed head and said, "And no more fuckin bags of pot like this. Get yourself some boxes. We're a respectable business around here. Got it?"

The man smiled and said, "With my first pay check."

Sonny laughed, hailed a cab, threw the bag of pot in the back, and gave the man and woman the peace sign. As the cab drove off into the traffic, Sonny sat back in his seat, sighed and said to himself, "God, I love New York."

Chapter Two

The black Jamaican cab driver wore his dreadlocks coiled up in a colorful knit cap that he wore like a hairnet of metaphors that conjured up memories for Sonny of being in Jamaica at night when the moon was full, and the dark golden orb of the moon lit up a jungle plant with finger-like-leaves reaching out to touch a pale yellow boa coiled around the Tree of Life as insects rubbed their antennas together in tone with the music of the spheres. He was there to buy ganga; and after the drug deal went down, Sonny and the Jamaicans gathered around a bonfire burning with laughter and a bottle of rum glowed like ambers. A joint was passed hand-to-hand by thin artistic fingers, just like the fingers sticking out of the frayed wool sweater that the cab driver wore under a severely worn black leather jacket.

Sonny had earlier taken some pot out of the garbage bag filled with pot, rolled a joint, and handed it to the driver who now passed it back to him as they listened to Bob Marley sing, *No, Woman Don't Cry*. The cab driver, as he listened to the music, held the steering wheel of his car like he was holding a woman's hips; and he drove her like a lover leading his lady through an intricate tropical dance that was accented by a beat that he would play out with the brakes of the car. When he came to a red light he taped out a subtle rhythmic change until the light changed; and then he was off again, taking his lady on a spin through the Big Apple. From time to time, he would look into the rearview mirror and stare at Sonny through oversized black horn rimmed sunglasses and smile like a long lost brother.

"So, what are you doing here, man?" Sonny asked as he watched the dance of cars flashing by as if he was whirling across a crowded dance floor below a spinning globe of tiny mirrors.

"I'm in a Reggae band, man. And we're gonna rock this town with solid shit. Dig?"

"What's the name of your band?"

"The Chillin Brothers."

"Cool. I like it. I like Reggae too. It's sort of like one of those old time lawn mowers that you had to push. You could just push it along at your own rhythm, no hurry, no fuss; and it kind of made a cool sound, like music is everywhere."

"Yeah, man. That's it. Cool," said the cab driver staring into the rearview mirror like light reflecting off of the moon. "That's what Reggae's like. It's like gravel slipping off a shovel when you dig the earth. You're right on, man. Music is everywhere. You just got to listen."

Sonny inhaled some more pot and let the marijuana light up his mind with a world of similes. "Like, dig this," he said. I'm lying on a beach, chillin out, listening to a transcontinental portable radio, searching for music. I couldn't get anything, but then I got this sound. It had a great beat; and it just kept repeating itself like the lawn mower, but with a syncopated beat that kept rolling over on itself like hammers playing on steel drum in a calypso band, but deeper, heavier with this pounding bass like in a rock and roll band. Dig?"

Sonny took another hit from the joint and then began to sift through the sands of time. He could feel the heat of the sun, and he reached out and turned up the portable radio . "I was grooving, man. I could make up songs to it, and they all sounded cool no matter what I played in my head. I was an electric guitar soaring over the waves, and the cymbals were the ocean crashing into the shore and slipping away. I could hear the sandpipers playing flutes and the ocean waves booming like a supersonic airplane breaking the sound barrier. I was there, man. I was riding the vibrations. I was part of the song. And then I realized. I was listening to the fuckin motor of a freighter somewhere out in the ocean."

Far fuckin out," the Rasta said.

Sonny saw that they were nearing where he wanted to go. "Hey, man, you can let me off up here."

The Rastafarian pulled over, smiled, and asked in a high-lit reef off of an ending beat, "How's the player going to close this session out?"

"You got a bag up there?"

"What sort of bag?"

Sonny smiled and shrugged.

The Rasta looked around at the seat, the floor, and then reached down and came up with the kind of brown paper bag you would get if you bought a sandwich at a deli. "I got this."

"Let me have it." Sonny reached into his black plastic garbage bag and felt the buds and seeds and the sticky resin that exuded from the leaves. The smell of pollen filled the air as he pulled out about an ounce of pot and stuffed it into the bag and handed it back to the cab driver saying, "Keep the change."

The door of the cab squeaked like an old barn door when Sonny got out of the cab; and as he was walking away, the Rasta stuck his head out the window and shouted, "You come and see us, man, The Chillin Brothers, Tuesday night at The Ocean Club."

Sonny stood for a moment on Wall Street to absorb the moment. Wall Street reminded Sonny of how civilizations built upon the foundations and ruins of past civilizations transforming old temples into new temples for the new gods. He remembered standing in the middle of Saint Peter's Cathedral in Rome and looking up at the massive dome, marble columns, and vaulted ceilings and realizing that he was standing in the middle of a Roman palace; and the Pope was the last Roman Emperor. All the statues of the apostles and the saints were merely the old gods transformed into the new gods, the same as the old gods. "Saint Anthony, Saint Anthony, come around. Something is lost and must be found." This was a chant that Sonny's mother taught him to recite when he lost something of value, and it was a chant that obviously went back much further than the birth of Christ.

Here on Wall Street the temples of Ancient Greece and Rome and the churches and palaces of the Renaissance, the Baroque, and the Romanesque all came together in a Neo-Babylon of architectural styles. In some instances different styles came together in one building, each layer a different period like the stratification of rock formations. Rising high above the temples of old were the modern temples of the New World - architectural monoliths that reduced the gods to abstract mathematics and the cold efficiency of calculus and simple geometry in the service of alchemy. In the background, Sonny could see the Twin World Trade Towers, a symbol of the redundancy of power, childlike in its lack of adjectives.

For the believers, this was the center of the universe where God dwelled and converted all values into one denomination – Money. And like the ancient religions, whose secrets were hidden in the runes and the hieroglyphics of a secret language, the secrets of Wall Street were hidden in a numerology that had to be translated back into its human figures to reveal the truth of the Eucharist. Money was blood, Capitalism was human sacrifice, and Wall Street was a modern Aztec temple, a blood bank where all the surplus blood was stored, traded, and circulated amongst the Puritan elect, the priests in suits and the prophets of money that basked in the blood of the lamb. This is my body. This is my blood. At the corner of Broad and Wall Street, Trinity Church loomed with its Gothic spire and jagged edges that looked like a sacrificial knife.

As Sonny turned onto Broad Street, he realized that he was one of those selves being sacrificed to the system. He was like a corpuscle of blood streaming through the veins of the Leviathan. He and the other human selves shared cell walls and impulses that became the circuitry of information, the data banks and the computerized DNA of a monster that lived under the bed of reason.

Ginny lived only a few blocks from Wall Street in one of the few Dutch Colonial Revival townhouses remaining on the street. The brick townhouse with Flemish bonding, sandstone trim, and twin stepped gables that ascended a deeply slanted blue gray slated rooftop reminded Sonny of a Rembrandt painting with its ruddy earthen tones and dormer windows that reflected light like golden gilders that were polished in the night. Sonny could conjure up the sounds of seagulls and the smell of dead fish, the sound of horses and wagons full of lumber and grain. He could smell the spice ships and the horse manure and the flapping of sails and the sound of ropes and wooden pulleys. He could see the burghers wearing large brimmed black felt stovepipe hats and dressed in black silk breaches, black woolen socks, and black silk waistcoats worn over pure white linen shirts with broad white collars that draped over black winged capes. It was a picture of moral certitude and smug smiles filled with muted money.

Sonny could smell the hot dog and mustard and sauerkraut and bun that the food vendor was preparing at his stainless steel food cart that was parked on the sidewalk. He could smell the fumes from the bus as it passed by, and he saw a pigeon that looked like it was a refugee from an oil spill as it stood perched on one of the telephone wires that slashed the sky like a knife. Sonny knew something of the history of the house. It was built at the turn of the century, and Ginny's father bought it in 1950 for her mother who was then pregnant with Ginny. Her father, who was a stockbroker, committed suicide in 1960; and her mother remarried one year later. Her father had left the house to Ginny; and when she legally came of age, she sued for legal possession of the house, won the suit, and threw her mother out. Several years later she converted the four-story townhouse into an apartment building, and she kept the first floor for herself.

National Cash

As Sonny walked up the stairs to the entranceway, he could see that the townhouse was in disrepair. The stone stairs were badly cracked and the iron bracket that tied the wrought-iron railing firmly to the wall of the townhouse had broken loose and the railing swayed to the touch like a little old lady with rolled down nylons and varicose veins. When Sonny looked up he could see that the grout that held the bricks in place was crumbled away, and many of the panes of glass in the sidelights and the transom that framed the carved oak door were cracked and in need of replacement.

Sonny rang the buzzer on the intercom for Ginny's apartment; and they communicated through the static that was like the sound of electronic snow that appeared on old-time TVs when the programming went off late at night, just before you went to sleep.

The lock on the door snapped open, and Sonny entered what had once been the reception area of the townhouse. A mahogany stairway with sensually rounded handrails and fluted balusters curved gracefully towards the entranceway like the train of a wedding gown. The navel was veiled in garlands, and the inlaid foot treads led up to the second floor and the mysteries beyond. To Sonny's left was a large floor-to-ceiling pocket-door that had once been the entranceway into the living room. Above the wainscoting, the walls were covered with gold linen wallpaper that once again reminded Sonny of Rembrandt and his search for light like a miner digging in the dark for nuggets of the spirit. At one time, the gold must have glittered in the light of the gas wall sconces, but now the crystal lampshades were gone and the wallpaper was peeling back at the edges revealing cracked plaster and water stains.

The THC in the marijuana that Sonny had absorbed through the rainbow dust and the joint he had smoked in the cab had triggered his most primitive senses and enabled him to sniff out life like an animal that could read history with his nose. Sonny could smell traces of the past like an archeologist digging in the muck. He could smell cut-stemmed-flowers in a mist of a Cuban cigar and an expensive perfume that smelled like scented rain water that had passed through the hands of an iris and flowed downstream into the folds of a silk gown. He could smell patent leather and black shoe polish, starch and virgin wool, pine oil and brass and silver polish buried deep under the smell of steak being cooked in a badly ventilated apartment somewhere on the second floor. He could smell the remains of pizza and cheap wine and stale beer intermingling with the incoherent smell of unrelated body odors that cancelled each other out like badly mixed paint that turned into brown muck.

Sonny smelled incense and sugar donuts, and then saw Ginny at the other end of the hallway standing at the doorway to her apartment. She looked at the garbage bag in Sonny's hands and asked, "How did you get here?"

"I took a cab."

Ginny's eyes widened a little. "Nice packaging job, Sonny."

"We have a date to do our laundry together, don't you remember?"

Ginny laughed and said, "Out of sight." She then gently pushed Sonny into an apartment that had been the living room in the original house and had opened up to the hallway through the large floor-to-ceiling pocket-doors that were now sealed. This room must have been quite grand at one time. The ceiling had to be at least fourteen feet high, and the moldings formed an elegantly curved arch along the edge of the ceiling that was ornate but not overdone. There was a hole in the center of the ceiling where, in all probability, a crystal chandelier had once hung. Light poured through the four floor-to-ceiling-windows that looked out onto the street. Many of the lead framed windowpanes were hand poured and original to the house, and the new and old glass together formed a quilted vision that fragmented and diluted the edges of the reality outside the house making it more like an impressionist rendering of a street scene rather than the Wall Street of today. The light that passed through the quilted optics of the windows formed a colorful mosaic of light across the oak floors made of shipboard planks, the kind that the Dutch and English colonists used to make the hulls of sailing ships. The fireplace was framed with two slender, fluted, marble columns that supported a white marble mantle that was cracked and veined with hairline fractures. To Sonny it looked like the entranceway to the ruins of an ancient Greek temple dedicated to the goddess of the hearth.

Sonny put the garbage bag down and felt relieved of the burden of fear. For a moment he could remain still in the eye of the storm and enjoy his life full of tranquility fringed with terror. He sat down on a comfortable, dark brown, leather couch that was torn in places, the cotton stuffing sticking out of the seams like an old stuffed cow on a child's bed. Across from the couch and the coffee table were two brown leather chairs, and the whole set looked like it belonged in a man's study along with the Cuban cigar that he smelled earlier. The coffee table was covered with books that were stacked like a house-of-cards. Half of the house had fallen into a pile of dead tomes. The flayed pages of Euclid's logic were draped over Kant's *Critique of Pure Reason*; and far below that, at the very bottom of the beginning was *The Book of the Dead* by Evan Wentz, a book of translations of hieroglyphs and spells that began the long line of immortal bed time stories. Balanced on the very top of these words in rune was a book entitled *The White Goddess*, a book about a time before the reign of Zeus when women sacrificed men to fertilize the earth with their blood and give birth to the flowers of creation. It was a time like now when Jesus became Dionysus after a long day at work drowning himself in cheap red wine looking for a Mary Magdallene in a topless bar to swallow him up in her soil. Also on the table was a scale that Ginny used to weigh the pot. On the record player Dr. John was singing,

> *I been in the wrong place,*
> *But it must have been the right time.*
> *I been in the right place,*
> *But it must have been the wrong song.*
> *I been in the right vein,*
> *But it seems like the wrong arm.*
> *I been in the right world,*
> *But it seems wrong, wrong, wrong.*

While Ginny was busy weighing the pot, Sonny continued to look around the room. Three life size papier-mâché figures made out of ticker tape and stockbroker's slips were suffused with the light that poured in through the windows like a theatrical stage light. A father, mother, and a prepubescent daughter were sitting at a small table drinking tea from antique Chinese porcelain tea cups that were white and decorated with tiny hand-painted red roses barely in bloom. The family looked so frail that if the window were opened they would probably blow away.

In the middle of the floor was an oil painting on an easel. It was a study in color and form; but Sonny couldn't figure out whether the darkness or the bare canvas was swallowing up the colors or if the colors were coming out of the darkness or the light. He didn't even know if Ginny believed that the painting was finished or not, though he did know that the painting was in the same state when he was here six months ago. The palate board and the splashes of paint on the board were partially mixed into hardened swirls of color; and the tubes of paint that were scattered all over the wrinkled tarp on the floor looked the same as they did before when he was here. It was as if her creativity had become petrified. Maybe that's it. Maybe it is done. Maybe it's a portrait of a dead art.

Sonny studied Ginny's round soft features and long jet-black hair. Her velvet eyes were the dark violet color of the horizon at the edge of the ocean at sunset, and they defined the mysteries of her trans-Mediterranean beauty that seduced the seer into the warm darkness that you had to feel to understand. Sonny remembered when he first met Ginny. She was in an all-girl rock-and-roll band called the Curlicues, and they were playing at the Electric Circus.

The Electric Circus was on Saint Marks Place between 2nd and 3rd Avenues. The building that housed the Circus was actually three neo-federal houses that in their many transformations had been joined together and converted into a community ballroom and community hall that was then bought by the Polish National Home Society to house Polish organizations and activities, dances, and weddings. Sonny remembered when Stanley Tolkin rented the dance floor and the downstairs basement and converted it into a bar that he called The Dom, which is Polish for "home." He then advertised five-cent beers and the whole East Village converged on the new hot spot that went through several more mutations before it became the hottest spot of all, The Electric Circus.

The Electric Circus was the light hearted tribal bonfire around which the children of the 60s danced and stripped themselves bare of all the inhibitions of their traditional middle class values and the social and cultural icons of the previous generation. They exposed themselves to the quantum nature of their psyche and the infinite possibilities of alternative universes where they could try on new identities to see what fit an emerging spirit that wore glitter and black vinyl, purple suede jackets and leather pants, silver and gold hip huggers, miniskirts and linked plastic discs, bell bottoms, cowboy boots, and army fatigues. It was a circus of consciousness, a tribal dance to the repeated beat of rock and roll, jugglers juggling day-glow balls, and a woman trapeze artist in leopard tights soaring overhead amidst strobe lights and laser beams under the fragmented images of a deconstructed America flashing across the walls and tent like ceiling; and this was only a prelude to the Grateful Dead coming on stage and singing *Dark Star* after Ginny and the Curlicues finished their opening set.

Ginny was the lead guitar in the band and she was quite good, but she was only part of the multiple images that had no single focus because once you focused you became a part of classic physics and the party was over. Sonny was later to discover that music was not Ginny's only talent. He saw her again several years later at a poetry reading in the basement of Saint Marks Church. He especially liked one of her poems in which she wrote about dancing between raindrops. Later as he got to know her more he realized that the poem was a self portrait of a deep sadness that she always avoided by going from one thing to another without having to confront her own tears.

Ginny was so cool back then, the model hip-dealer, writer, artist, musician, and women pioneer of far out spaces; but then she just stopped doing everything, except pot and playing poker with Tarot cards. Ginny loved to gamble but even now all that seemed to be left of her love for gambling was the discarded ways to play – discarded crafts and art, discarded stories and knowledge, half woven weavings, little wows here and there taken from the top of the dock, discarded. Ginny was a victim of the sixties. She was a victim of a society the killed its own children, killed its own dreams, and killed its own future.

When Ginny finished weighing the pot, she turned to Sonny and asked, "Is it all like this?"

"Yes or better."

Ginny rolled a joint, lit it, and took a hit of the pot, savoring the taste and smell and the quality of the high like a wine connoisseur. "Not bad, Sonny, I think that Larry will go for this if I give Charlie the go ahead."

"Cool."

Ginny studied Sonny for a moment, and she watched him study her like a princess in the shadows of a veiled palace somewhere in the Old Testament where Jewish Sibyls told men their fortunes. "Are you sure you want to do this, Sonny? I know what Charlie will tell his brother. He will tell him that you're cool, which means to Charlie that you're not a cop, and he can kill you. No problem."

Larry was Charlie's brother, and he ran a smokehouse for the Genevese crime family in Harlem. Ginny had told Sonny that Larry wanted to find his own sources for pot. What should make the deal attractive to Larry was that the pot that Larry was able to purchase in Harlem was of a lower quality than what Sonny could sell him at a lower price. Every month Sonny and Josh had to weed through their shipments of marijuana, and often they would end up with hundreds of pounds of lower grade pot that they could not sell to their high end consumers. They had to get rid of it. It was just stacking up in the warehouse. This could work out for both Larry and Sonny. Larry could increase his profit margin substantially without arousing the appetites of the Genevese family. Pot was, for the most part, under the radar of the Mafia, too bulky, not a large enough profit margin, too small to eat unless you put the meal right under the tiger's nose and he realized that he could feast off of an established drug network that generated millions of dollars of revenue a year.

"Two questions, Ginny. "One, is Larry a good enough businessman not to kill the goose that lays the golden egg? Two, can he control Charlie?"

Ginny thought about it for a moment then said, "Yes, Larry is a good businessman. If he made a move on you, the Genevese's would get wind of it; and they would come in to take the butcher's choice, leaving Larry with far less than he would be making off of you. Charlie, on the other hand, is a big question mark. Larry uses him for his wet work; and he gives him small jobs here and there; but, for the most part, he tries to keep him out of the rest of his business. Charlie is too impulsive. But Charlie complains to his brother all the time that he doesn't give him enough of the action. He wants in."

Ginny gestured towards the pot and said, "This is a bone that Larry will throw Charlie's way, but he'll have Charlie on a short leash. Will it be short enough?" Ginny shrugged then she took another hit of the joint and disappeared again behind the mist of her veiled palace.

Sonny got up to leave.

"What about this?" She pointed to the pot. "I haven't paid you yet." Ginny reaching into her ruined house of knowledge and pulled out a German edition of *Das Capital* by Karl Mark. She opened up the lid of the book, and Sonny could see that she has cut out a secret compartment just large enough for what had to be forty one hundred dollar bills, four thousand dollars to be exact.

Ginny smiled, "Now this is a packaging job, Sonny."

Sonny laughed, "I wonder what Karl Mark would say about this?"

Ginny without hesitation said, "He would say that it was a primitive but effective example of unrestrained capitalism?"

Sonny laughed and took the money and the book then said quite seriously, "Thanks for reminding me how far I have fallen." Sonny pointed to the twenty pounds of pot on the table, "There's another twenty pounds in this for you as a finder's fee if the deal with Larry goes down right."

Ginny was pleased, and she was all business now. "If Larry wants the eight hundred pounds, will you meet with him and Charlie tonight at Dante's?"

""Sure."

"Where can I reach you?"

"I'll be in my room. You have the number."

Sonny walked out of the townhouse onto the street and was once again conscious of being a single point of consciousness, a single nuclei amongst millions of eyes and nuclei that formed the Leviathan. He felt so alone, like a star that had to feed off its own light and travel millions of miles just to touch something, and that something was his many selves that were cyborgs, part organism, part mechanical technological mutations that had evolved beyond DNA and the slow process of organic evolution.

Sonny hailed a cab and raced through the asphalt arteries in a hard shelled delivery system propelled by exploding gases, gears, pistons, and pulleys that had replaced ligaments and rotating joints. Stone and concrete and steel beams made up the skeleton and bones of the Leviathan. Plastic replaced skin, and the electronic circuitry and digital information and data processing made up its nervous system. All he had to do was plug himself into the Leviathan, and he could see around the world through television eyes, his visual and auditory neurons extending into outer space allowing him to talk to anyone, anywhere, as if they were one part of his mind talking to the other. Attached to its mutant parts, a self could travel faster than the speed of sound, move mountains, hold back the oceans, telescope its vision and see millions of miles into outer space, or contract itself into a microscopic eye that could see into its inner space where the inner world met the outer world and an atom became a star that could blow up the world by simply pushing a button.

As part of the Leviathan, he was more powerful than any of the ancient Greek Gods; but there was a price to be paid for being a demigod. He had to give up his infinite possibilities to become like the cells in his own body capable of being programmed into organs and tissues, fingers and arms that served the food, drove the cab, exchanged currency from one self to another while selves turned into eyes supervising the flow of blood in response to impulses and commands from the many synapses that administered the social organism and managed the different functions of its mutant parts, all directed by the collective mind made up of the many specialized faculties that were increasingly divided and subdivided into specialized functions and perspectives, knowledge fragmented so that the only common denominator was money. That was the lifeblood of the Leviathan that poured through its arteries and veins turning humans into things, cyborgs in the service of a monster that feed off its own body parts

Sonny understood why this powerful social organism was flawed in its evolution and its mutation from the organic to a non-organic lifeless form. In an organism, each cell contained the whole. In the Leviathan, nothing contained the whole. In DNA, the microcosm and the macrocosm are the star in a single cell, the universe in each and every single part. In the Leviathan, the brain can't feel its toes; and the head is detached from its asshole.

The cab driver pulled to a stop in front of the Chelsea Hotel, and Sonny entered the lobby then took the back stairway to his room. The dark mahogany handrails and the ornate black wrought-iron balusters and panels of the stairway mirrored the ornate floral design of the black wrought-iron exterior balconies. The stairwell itself was an art gallery of paintings and descending light coming from a skylight far above. This was the double helix of the Chelsea in which each canvas was a doorway to an alternative reality, and each floor was part of a multileveled story about the Titans of light and darkness. Sonny was near the bottomless darkness where flickers of light looked like they came from a bonfire where homeless shadows gathered and stared out into the nothingness where everything began.

Ghosts and shadows lurked in every canvas; and as Sonny ascended, the light intensified. Flesh was revealed and exposed when layers of darkness slipped away like a satin sheet. Golden flakes of light appeared through dark green leaves; and above that, a vivid blue sky and pure white light fragmented into vivid abstract colors and shapes free of the earthen brown far below and the darkness of the Nether World.

Sonny entered his own canvas, and he locked the door behind him, safe for a moment within his single cell, safe from all the other realities. He stripped off all his clothes and took a long hot shower then crashed on his bed exhausted. When Sonny fell asleep, he dreamt of a time when he was a child, and he was sick with a fever. He was burning up. His mother put him in her bed surrounded by flowering wallpaper; and then she called his grandmother who came and sat by him smelling of what all old people smelled of, death and decay, like a fallen tree covered with moss. Sonny watched her take small glass jars out of her purse, jars like the ones she had in her cellar full of fruit preserves, the jelly he liked, especially the strawberry preserves made out of the strawberries that they would pick from secret places in the woods. He knew what she was doing; she had done it before. She was casting a spell to rid Sonny of evil spirits and the bad thoughts of others. The Italians called these evil spirits the malochia or the evil eye. It was believed that a person who possessed the evil eye could cause sickness with their evil thoughts. Children were especially susceptible because the evil thoughts could spread through their body like a virus causing illness and even death. It was her job to cast out these evil spirits that were infecting her grandson; and she was doing it with a ritual that had been passed down from one generation to the next, its origins going back to ancient times, long before the Christ child was even born.

Burning with fever, Sonny watched her pour holy water into a white porcelain saucer, and he listened to her chants. He watched her then unseal the next jar and pour salt from the Bay of Naples upon the water where the earth took form. He could feel a mass of darkness exploding from the depths, and he heard the roar of the ocean from the mountaintop. She unsealed the third jar, and she dipped her fingers into the golden oil and sprinkled the waters with fire from the blazing sun. She unsealed a final jar full of lava soil. Buried in the soil was an herb shaped like a tear. She stripped it bare then pierced its heart, and its soundless cries gave breath to the formless form of the spheres of life. Through the blood and the stream of fire that passed through the underworld of the spirit, he saw into the darkness. He could see a silhouette of a tree near the tip of a mountain, the moon between the branches, the stars beyond, and he could hear a baby goat crying. He heard its heart beat like wings seeking golden orbs in the dark deafening blaze, pier amidst the cave, the baby goat cried again. Then he heard footsteps and saw hands reach out, a man's hands, large and strong, trying to reach the baby goat at the edge of the precipice. He realized in his dream that he had become his grandfather, and his grandfather had become him. But he was not only his grandfather. He was the goat, the stars, the stones, the moon that made the jagged rocks look like frozen lightning bolts.

The little goat was perched up on the edge shivering with cold and fear; and as he snatched the little goat away from the edge of the precipice, he could feel the goat's little heart ready to bolt into the air and flee. He could hear his mother in the music of the night, the chimes of silence, and the whirl of hymns. The little goat bolted down the mountainside through the moonlight to the milky way of its mother's tit where Sonny saw ancient Greeks drawing lines between stars and lightning passages flashing from shade to shadow. This must have been what it was like, he thought. This must have been the origin of the first idea. He took his finger and traced a line from one star to another, from one point to another; and in his mind he formed the constellations, the sigils within the decans, the magical seals that unlocked the mysteries that led into a path between trees, down steps into terraced fields and a village of stone built into the mountainside.

Sonny's grandfather entered his home, a living room that was dark except for a candle burning on the table. He undressed and blew out the light. In the darkness he could smell the sweet smell of his children sleeping. He could smell his wife, the flowers of the night; and he could still feel the light within him as he crawled into bed, and his wife embraced him enveloping him in her warm darkness. He began to paint the ceiling of her womb with murals of ecstasy, the strokes of the brush painting fingers reaching for God, a universe of stars exploding with light. His wife moaned and cherubs touched the walls with feathered wings. She felt pink and blue as dark lines filled her with new colors, golden fires, a lightning bolt igniting new constellations in which every mother is a Madonna, every father a Joseph, and every son a God.

Sonny woke up; and half asleep, he wondered which was the real world, the world of 20/20 vision or the primordial world of no barriers between the past and the present and the future that he had just passed through in a sequence of perceptual visions from Cézanne to Gauguin. Was reality merely a prescribed way of looking at things? Sonny was drifting back to sleep again when the phone rang.

"Hello."

"Sonny, it's Ginny. Can you come to Dante's?"

"Is the deal on?"

"I think so."

"OK. I'll be there."

Sonny dressed and took a cab to Dante's in SoHo, the nightclub that he created and owned with his partners in crime. Dante's had a façade of jet-black marble with tall pillar-like-columns of darkly tinted glass that reduced the life inside to the movement of light and shadows. The towering entranceway doors were clear glass and modern, devoid of any value judgments. Above the entranceway was a tall neon sign that spelled out in bold red letters the name of the nightclub. The building itself was a ten-story, stone-faced, neo-classic office building with pilasters and pediments framing the windows. Horned cornices crowned the rooftop; and entablatures divided each story to give the impression at night of ancient catacombs layered one upon the other, the windows - dark chambers within which the past was buried.

Dante's was not The Electric Circus with its carnival atmosphere and its carefree belief in the liberation of the spirit from the past. The 60s were dead. The Electric Circus was closed, and America was trying to find a way to warm itself in the cold world of friendly fascism. Dante's was that new hot spot and that hot spot was Hell. It was early in the evening; so there was nobody outside the club; but later limousines would be double parked all along the street; and there would be a line of customers four blocks long eager to bare witness to the decline and fall of the American Republic, eager to play their part in the collective madness that was a composite of their individual greed that took on a life of its own and became a being that some people called the Devil.

Outside the club, two of the bouncers lounged near the entranceway waiting for the masses to descend upon the demilitarized zone that they would be patrolling. Joe was a black ex-middleweight boxer with a shaved head who was wearing a short well-tailored black leather jacket, a black silk T-shirt, black leather pants and black cowboy boots tipped with silver. Joe's standard look for the customers at Dante's was the look of a black panther at the zoo, completely bored because it wasn't his feeding time. Jim, the other bouncer, was a two hundred and eighty four pound bear of a man with a blond beard and a shock of blond curly hair that stuck out of his John Deere cap. His eyes were sky blue; and like the sky they seemed to envelop you, yet had no single focus. Jim wore a red and white plaid hunting shirt, blue jeans, suspenders, and tan Timberland work boots. They both wore all the right labels to conjure up all the racist fears of a class B movie. The white kids were afraid of Joe, the stereotypical black bad ass from Harlem; and the black kids were afraid of Jim, the stereotypical red neck shit-kicker from Bonnie Town U.S.A.

Actually, they were pretty nice guys. Joe was an ex-middleweight fighter with a record of fifty-four and four, but he never got a title shoot because Joe would never throw a fight. He retired from boxing, and now he worked construction during the day and then worked at Dante's as a bouncer during the night. He had three children, and he was a religious man. Jim, on the other hand, was a farm boy from Alabama. He played defensive line at the University of Alabama and came to New York to become an actor. From time to time, when there was trouble, Jim would wade into it like a grizzle bear while reciting the lines from a Shakespeare play that he was working on at the Actor's Studio. Sonny found it amusing to watch Joe and Jim interact. Jim never stopped talking and Joe never talked, but every once in a while Jim would get Joe to smile and sometimes he'd actually laugh, but then he would realize where he was, and he would retreat back into his bad ass Black Panther role.

Sonny walked into the main floor of Dante's, and the first person he saw was Tom behind the bar. Tom, who was six foot four and weighed well over two hundred pounds, had a face that looked like it had been formed out of the rugged mountains of Greece and the steep waterfalls that flowed over jagged rocks down into deep pools of Ancient Greek mysteries, the New Jersey Turnpike, Seaside Heights, hoagies, and Bucknell University where he was a political science major and a star basketball player who came to the Rome of the World, New York City to make his mark. Tom was a revolutionary turned bartender/drug dealer who made enough money behind the bar and on the street to feed his appetites for good food, good wine, beautiful women, world travel, a good book, and a well turned phrase. Tom believed that he was a descendant of the Ancient Greek Gods and that his destiny was to rule the world someday. Dante's, working for tips, travelling the world, breaking the law, studying human nature down and dirty, roaming the streets of New York and becoming a connoisseur were all training for the day when his time would come. Tonight, Tom was alone in the main room of Dante's, a God in waiting.

It was only nine o'clock, and the place would be dead until eleven, but then it would be mobbed wall to wall. Sonny liked this time of night at Dante's because he could talk to the most interesting people who came into Dante's, the people who worked there. Sonny sat down, and Tom poured him a Martel's cognac with a back of soda then poured himself a drink. They toasted then Sonny sat back in the bar chair and took in the main floor of Dante's that was called The Turf Exchange. Dante's had been a speakeasy during probation, and then it became quite popular in the forties and early fifties as an upscale bar and restaurant, but in the sixties it fell on bad times and closed down after years of serving fifty-cent shots and cheap meals. However, despite all the changes it went through, the original design and décor of the bar had been well preserved; and with some restoration and embellishments, the dark mahogany bar now looked like an altar to Dionysus with hand carved garlands of flowers and columns of fennel stalks entwined with grape vines and crowned with pinecones. The front bar was over a hundred feet long, and the back bar was so vast that you could stock a liquor store with all the bottles that were on its shelves. The background lights built into the shelving and the spots from the ceiling made the spirits glow like magic potions that promised to send you to another world where you could be that genie that lies within, the wish that was never fulfilled, the word that was never spoken, the dream, the giant that lurks within each of us that comes out roaring with a joy and a rage and a sorrow that has no object.

The centerpiece of the bar was a black and white engraving of Milton's *Paradise Lost*. Lucifer and all the other gods who had fallen to the one and only god gathered at a temple that they had carved out of golden veins of ore found deep in the earth to form massive archways and golden Doric pillars, architraves, cornices, and freezes. Diamond and crystal and ruby lanterns were aflame with the reflected light coming from the molten core of the earth. Sulfurous smoke bellowed around Lucifer who stood at the top of the stairway to Hell where the many gods and goddesses, satyrs and nymphs, stories and myths had fallen, cast out by the one single author, the one book, the word made flesh in black and white, all their colorful glory reduced to shades and shadows receding into the darkness of oblivion.

Large black and white linoleum tiles gave the floor a touch of art deco as did the 50's Retro booths upholstered in black vinyl with red piping that gave the softly rounded edges a sensuous sheen. The tabletops were black onyx with chrome trim; and the two rows of double booths ran parallel to the bar, separated by a mahogany and glass partition and etched flowers. On the back wall above the booths were three large paintings in gold gilded frames bathed in a magical liquid of light.

The painting on the left side of the wall is a painting of Dionysus and Selinus riding in a chariot surround by satyrs, nymphs, and naked men and women who are in a riotous frenzy brought on by wine and the coming of Selene, the goddess of the moon. The chariot is being pulled by two-bull-like-chimeras that are the color of the dark brown earth. Selinus, Dionysus's fat and debauched teacher, is seated like a baby in lion's fur, his stomach distended from gluttony; and a naked nymph is pressing her breasts against his leg while another is pouring him wine from a womb like jug. He is blind drunk like a snake that can only see heat and feel his skin against another.

Dionysus, who is driving the chariot, is the son of Semele, who, like the Virgin Mary, was a mortal who mated with Zeus in an immaculate conception. Dionysus is naked except for a crown of grape leaves; and his naked body is the perfect male figure as conceived by a woman, muscular but feline in repose. His face is a perfect balance of gentleness and strength, beauty and danger like a big cat with soft paws and sharp claws who purrs, enchanted by the appearance of the goddess who has come to tuck in the sun. The reins of the chariot are slipping from Dionysus's hands as a satyr with the hindquarters, hooves, and the horns of a goat, is pulling Dionysus from the chariot into a feast of hands grabbing everywhere for flesh – lips consuming the immortal seed, men and women wallowing in the furrows. Dionysus roars with laughter; and with one massive sweep of his arm, he wipes away a soiree of flutes and mathematical harmonies coming from the white light of an Apollonian temple of Platonic logic.

The painting on the right side of the wall is once again a painting of Dionysus. He has the same subtle features and form, and he is wearing the same crown of grape vines, but now he is wearing a dark red cape over his bare chest and a lion skin loin cloth that trails off like a tail. In his right hand he holds a crown of thorns made out of stars over the head of Ariane who radiates in a pure white light, a blue silken watery robe falling off her shoulders revealing her naked breasts the color of milk. Ariane has reached out and given Dionysus the thread that she had given Theseus to find his way out of the labyrinth of lies that we create to hide from the truth that the Minotaur eventually gores us with, killing us with our own deceit. The thread leads to her womb as it did then, but Dionysus will not betray her as Theseus did. He holds up the thread to the heavens; and it is like a sliver of lightning in his hand, immortalizing her love in the stars forever.

The centerpiece of the three painting is a painting of Beauty and Life naked and helpless in the arms of nymphs dressed in the black habits of nuns. The radiant light of Beauty and Life in human form is being devoured by the darkness and is so finely done that the pose blurs gender and caused Sonny to see three figures in one – Nature in the form of a beautiful woman raped and dead, Dionysus helpless and weak under the Tree of Life, and Jesus Christ being taken down from the cross. This is the true holy trinity, the secret coda woven through classical Western religion and erotic art.

Beyond the bar and the rows of booths and the paintings was the dance floor, and above the dance floor was a giant video screen upon which millions of sperm were racing for one egg. Superimposed over the sperm race was a horserace that came in and out of focus, two horses nose to nose at the finish line. Like America, only one sperm won the race while millions of others smashed into the wall like atoms in a cyclotron creating bursts of light across the dance floor.

"Sonny, I saw an ad on TV today. It was really interesting," Tom said. "In the ad you see a picture of what seems to be a college campus. It's a pastoral scene with modern towers in the background. The voice-over says something like this, 'Many people feel that American corporations are ivory towers, cut off and removed from the reality; but here at Money Corporation we're down to earth and in touch.' "

Tom laughed and said, "What I find incredible about this ad is that an American corporation could suggest that American corporations have become ivory towers; for in fact, it's true. They have become insulated from reality." Tom leaned forward and whispered in a conspiratorial manner, "What's the lesson?"

"They have feet of clay?"

"That's right," Tom said. "All we have to do is control the streets; and we can take over this country block by block, neighborhood by neighborhood." Tom spread his arms and looked up at the ceiling. "As the bricks fall from above, we'll catch them and build from below; and when the final brick has fallen, the final brick will be laid."

The door opened, and Sonny could hear the composite sound of millions upon millions of voices and the nervous system of the Leviathan buzzing like billions of electronic insects, a metamorphous of protons filling the air with images, words, and sounds, stereos and TVs and radios all playing simultaneously in a symphony of Babel. Horns blared and engines roared to the constant drone of tires against asphalt and trillions of mini-explosions of gas and air compressed into a cylinder head, thrusting up and down like a steel penis, coming over and over again in a chemical mechanical orgasm, its heart pumping pulsars.

Sonny looked up when he heard the door open, and he saw Ken White, the floor manager, walking towards him like a soldier reporting for duty. Ken was an ex-marine and playwright from the Beat Generation who had been thrown in the brig and wrote an award winning off-Broadway play based on his experiences. He looked at Sonny and Tom, tilted his head to the side, and gave them his Cheshire cat smile then reached over and squeezed both their shoulders like he was about to give them a loan of knowledge that had to be paid back. "How are the generalissimos doing tonight? Are you preparing yourselves for the hordes from Brooklyn, Queens, Harlem, and the Bronx that will invade us?"

He emphasized each borough as if each group would be the most formidable foe that they would ever have to face. "This you can be sure of," Ken said as he paused and smiled again. "They will come."

Tom poured Ken a Stolichnaya on the rocks, and Ken took his drink and the racing form, and he went to the other end of the bar where he could be alone to drink and read under one of the hanging green glass cabaret lights that lined the bar. Ken didn't write anymore. He had only one interest and that was the track. He went every day and bet everything.

Sonny watched Ken sitting under the bar light reading his racing form, sipping his drink; and every once and awhile his legs would swing like a little kid sitting at his desk waiting for the bell to ring, waiting for school to get out so he could go see the horsies run, place a bet, take a chance, win. Fate and luck were important factors in Ken's life. He wrote a play that he had no hope of doing anything with, and it became everything to him, and everything that he had intentionally written since then had become nothing to him. No matter how much you do, fate, on any day, can win the race. That's what Ken had learned from life; so he studied his racing form looking for a winner, reading in between the lines, looking for lady luck, wondering what the weather conditions would be, will it rain or shine.

Dave Sharky, who worked with Tom behind the main bar, walked into Dante's marching to the same old beat that Ken marched to; and he looked like he had just woken up, plunged his long brown hair into a cold shower, thrown on his rumpled blue jeans, hand-made moccasins, and a badly faded orange and green plaid shirt that looked like a relic of Christmas past and a broken marriage. His features were a cross between the molten ore that spilled out of the mold onto the floor of a Buffalo steel mill and the arid features of the Texas panhandle and too much heat and not enough water, too much booze for a tall lean cowboy without a horse whose fiery character was tempered on the frozen battlefields of North Korea. Dave, like Ken, was an ex-marine, and he had been one of The Chosen Frozen from the Chosen Reservoir who had been immortalized in Marine folklore. The Chosen Frozen were the twenty five thousand Marines who were trapped at the Chosen Reservoir when over a million Chinese crossed the border into North Korea to fight the Americans. Dave was one of those Marines who had waged a continual battle in thirty degree below zero weather; and when he peed, he had to pee in his pants - the pee frozen to his leg as he marched home in retreat with over two hundred thousand Chinese trying to cut him off. Dave, after all these years, was still marching. He marched with his broad shoulders back, and he moved as though his shoulders hung from a coat hanger, the rest of his body dangling loosely as he slid along, still afraid of the frozen waters, never letting his feet get too far off the ground.

As Dave marched down the bar he spoke like an ancient master of the oral narrative who sat at the campfire of the gathering tribes and told stories passed on from generation to generation in the Homeric tradition, his voice echoing in the empty cavernous bar. "I have seen the Titans and they are here." He pointed to the floor, and he walked on as he said, "Shipwrecked in this graveyard for giants."

Ken looked up from his racing form and smiled. He then grabbed Dave by his shoulders and said, "Are you ready for action, Sir?"

Dave saluted and the two marines who had marched down many roads now marched together down to where Sonny and Tom were stationed. Ken and Dave came to a halt, and they looked at Tom and Sonny as if they were new recruits. Ken confided in Dave. "They conspire to conquer the world."

Dave looked at Sonny and Tom; his eyes were round

with shock. "I have heard rumors in the street," he said. "Organ grinders pass messages and old ladies cry."

Ken smiled, "I told them that Brooklyn, Queens, and Harlem invade tonight."

"And don't forget the Bronx," Dave said as he wagged his finger. "They come with greased back hair and razors dangling from their neck, charms to make you sleep." He ran his finger across his neck as if to slit his throat.

Ken was pleased. This was the living theater, the real play, the real off-off-Broadway. "I went to see Robbie today," he said. "Get this scene. Robbie is lying in his bed as fat as Claudius, shaving coke from a rock the size of your fist. We snort a couple of lines, and then he says to me, "Ken, you're not doing anything for me at the bar.""

"I say to him, 'why should I? There's nothing to do.' "

Dave laughed, and he was about to say something, but Ken raised his hand to indicate that there was more to the story; and said, "We snort a couple more lines. And Robbie says to me, 'Sharky is too old for Dante's.' "

Dave's eyes widened. "What did you say to that?"

"I said to him," 'So...he ain't no Shirley Temple.' "

"And what did he say to that?" Sonny asked between fits of laughter.

"He didn't say anything. He just wouldn't give me any more coke."

Amidst the laughter, Tom leaned over, and he asked Sonny if Robbie could really fire Sharky. Sonny, who was cradling a glass of brandy in his hand that was shaped like a woman's breast, took a sip of the dark amber and said, "No." He was about to take another sip of his brandy when he heard the door open and Charlie shouting, "I want more money!"

He turned to see Charlie and Ginny walking in the door. Charlie was one of the bouncers, an ex-heavyweight contender who had put Jose Torres out of business and got knocked out in the fifth round by Floyd Paterson. Now he was in Robbie's custody facing charges of manslaughter and bank robbery. Charlie was in a huff and puff, and Ginny's eyes were shining and her pupils were dilated. She was obviously very stoned; but it wasn't on life; or, at least, it wasn't life as seen through the prescribed lenses of society. Judging from the smile on her face, what Ginny saw was more like what a baby saw when it looked up at the mobile over its crib for the first time.

"This white bitch won't give me no money," Charlie said. "I gotta have money from my women."

Charlie gestured threateningly at Ginny. "Give me some money, Bitch."

"Go fuck yourself, Charlie."

Charlie laughed, "See what I meant that Jew bitch won't give me shit."

Tom poured Ginny a drink and said, "Ginny, don't give Charlie money."

Ginny looked at Tom in disbelief. "I'm not going to give that Nigger any money," she said; and then she turned away and floated off by herself knowing that they were all looking at the same thing, her ass.

Charlie turned to the boys and said, "Robbie is just like her. I told Robbie, 'I want mo money.' "

"Robbie says to me, 'Charlie, you're my friend.' "

"I say to him, 'Robbie, I want money.' "

"So he hands me some of his stepped on shit. 'Here,

Charlie, have some coke.' "

"I want money," Charlie said, pounding his hand with his fist. "I want money!"

"So, Robbie says to me, 'Charlie, if it weren't for me, you'd be in jail.' "

"I told him I don't want to be no mother fuckin slave. I want money."

Charlie then looked at everyone in disbelief. "He tells me he's going to fire me if I keep askin him for mo money." Charlie laughed. "I told that mother fucker he can't fire me. Because if he fires me I go to jail for life; and if I'm going to jail for life, I might as well kill his mother fuckin ass. It's all the same thing, right?"

Sonny looked at Charlie and smiled to himself. Some people thought Charlie was dumb, but he wasn't dumb; he was just hard to understand. Sonny also knew that he'd been in New York City too long because Charlie was beginning to make sense to him.

Charlie saw Ginny walking down the aisle towards him, and he said, "Those fuckin Jews are all alike. They'll give you anything but money."

Ginny walked past Charlie completely ignoring him.

"Ginny, baby, why won't you give me some money?" It was almost a plea. When he didn't get a response, Charlie chased after her; and when he caught up to her, he whispered something in her ear. They both laughed, and Ginny put her arm under Charlie's arm and her hand on his bicep as they disappeared into the backroom.

Dave shook his head in disbelief and said, "Charlie Butter Knife Watkins, prize fighter, bank robbers, murderer, and bonded slave." Dave assured everyone. "It's true," he said. "The judge did tell Charlie that if he lost his job he'd throw him back in jail." Dave laughed at the implications for Charlie and Robbie. "Until death do us part."

As the laughter echoed through the bar, Ken retreated back into his racing form. Dave settled down to some serious drinking. All the employees came in. The hordes began to invade. Ken and one of the bouncers handled the door, and Charlie patrolled the floor. Ginny waited tables, and Tom and Dave took care of the bar. All the staff took up their positions. The music grew louder and louder. The dancers knew Ginny. They knew all her moves. She seemed incorporated into their dance. Twenty or thirty of the regulars formed a line and discoed in unison as Ginny weaved in and out, never spilling a drop, never breaking a glass. Tom and Dave choreographed their moves behind the bar featuring a sleight of hand act where money disappeared with every sweep of the bar mop and glasses tinkled in rhythm to the music as they made the drinks. Charlie walked the floor giving lectures on brute force. Charlie carried a butter knife in his pocket, and after a few blunt stabs, you'd get the point. Charlie Watkins would kill you with a butter knife, that's what kind of guy he was.

The wall of dancers grew and grew. Time and again Ginny would plunge back in and find her way through the chaos; but after a while the wall became so great, the hordes so numerous, that Ginny gave up the fight and stood back and watched the show. At some point Ginny went back into the crowd and never came back, dancing with whoever it was who stood in her way. All the floors to the club were open now, and New York poured into Dante's full of sexual expectations and dark desires that flourished in the underground world of New York City's subconscious mind where sperm and fertile eggs were stirred up, shaken, then poured over ice only to be stirred up again and again by the constant beat of the drummer, the fingering of keys, the guitar player hitting chords that vibrated through the dancers in a rock and roll ecstasy of one climax after another like a never ending lover.

In the background, on the giant video screen above the dance floor, amidst pulsing lights and laser beams, the history of carnal knowledge flashed in clips upon the screen – the first kiss ever filmed in 1896 followed by the first kiss to steal away a husband in *Kiss Me Fool*, the camera focusing on a touch of silk, a bra strap, hair gone wild, and a necktie like a hangman's knot gone loose followed by the first open mouth kiss by John Gilbert who slipped his tongue into Greta Garbo's mouth in a close-up of flesh tasting flesh that dissolved into Humphrey Bogart taking Lauren Becall into his arms as she fell back into the abyss, and he followed her into the bare décolletage.

On the dance floor, a ballerina from the Met performed one pirouette after another, dancing in and out of the lines of kids from the boroughs doing *Onward Christian Soldiers* to a disco beat. Also on the dance floor were members of a mime troupe who were each trapped in an invisible glass cage agonizing over their individuality as they tried to reach each other and the mass of humanity that was moving in and out of one another, caught up in the flow, hypnotized by the beat, the mix, the melting pot of New York.

Sonny shouted to Tom, "Have you seen Charlie's brother?"

"No, but Josh is here."

"Where?"

Tom shrugged.

Sonny motioned for Tom to come closer, and he shouted in his ear merely to whisper in the chaos of sound, "That deal may be on with Larry, either tomorrow or the next day. Tell Sharky."

Tom nodded, and Sonny put down the drink that he had barely touched and gave Tom the peace sign as he turned away and began his search for Josh in the deluge.

Sonny walked down stairs to The Ballroom, the next level of Dante's Inferno. The Ballroom floor was covered with holographic tiles that gave the impression of dancing on fire, the flames licking the dancers with passion. A tall female model was formally dressed in tails and top hat, her stark white hair slicked back like a man's, her lips cherry red. Her tongue a flame entered the mouth of an equally tall black model with pink full lips and long jet black wavy hair, the back of her skintight black and silver sequin gown plunging to the crevice of her ass. The finger nails of her dark mahogany hands were painted pink, and they dug into the neck of her lover as she tasted the heat.

The room itself was made to look like Lucifer's temple carved out of a diamond mine deep in the earth to form massive archways, Doric pillars, cornices and friezes made of blue kimberlite with green olivine grains, purplish red garnets, and diamond dust and gems that sparkled as a remnant of a volcanic ejaculation millions of years old. The walls were covered with glow board and then layered over with a mosaic of shattered mirrors that formed a silk, moon-lit web of images amidst strobe lights and laser beams reflecting off of the tiny mirrors of an old time giant ballroom globe light that spun slowly, hypnotically, creating a sexual collage of broken images and shattered genes.

On the dance floor, men were dancing with men; and women were dancing with women; but they all seemed to be dancing with themselves, groping wool and silk and nylon and plastic skin, tasting each other, molding each other's lips like life-like three dimensional dolls that said everything that you wanted them to say; but they were all saying the same thing. They were saying that they wanted to fuck themselves. That was the fatal flaw of capitalism. It was a prism cell of narcissisms that no one could escape from in a society devoid of love and empathy where everyone lived in individual cells isolated from one another, trapped in the body of a Leviathan without a heart or a soul that treated them as human resources, like coal and oil to be burned up and discarded.

The bar that spanned one wall of The Ballroom was composed of sheets of colored glass that formed a green and yellow and blue mist from which a half naked woman emerged like a bronze age Amazon warrior wearing a bra and thong that looked like inlaid armor, fluid silver and gold. Two snakes entwined themselves around her forehead and stared out at the lust with diamond eyes. Above the bar hung a lithograph of Saint Sebastian tied to the Tree of Life, like Jesus Christ, hanging limp from the crucifix of limbs, feminized, androgynous, pierced with phallic arrows.

To the right of the black and white lithograph of Saint Sebastian with his long black hair hanging down like the leaves of a weeping willow was a painting of Dionysus. Dionysus was lying in a death-like-repose, asleep in a dream whose roots reached down to the core of the earth and into its inner sun. The branches of the tree spread out over his head into a blue ocean of sky, and Dionysus's hand seemed to be reaching out to touch a lily pond of white vaginal flowers, the water still as a mirror reflecting the forest and the naked light of the nymphs that hovered around their fallen hero like a halo. His mother, Selene, who had conceived Dionysus in her own image of a man like Zeus had conceived Athena, reached out to her son and cradled him in her arms like Jesus Christ was cradled in the arms of Mary at the tomb of her womb dreaming of when the sun would rise again.

A guitar screamed in agony and the drummer pounded the drum like someone pounding on a door trying to get out while Jimmy Page, the lead singer for Led Zeppelin, shouted, "Love;" and the word echoed and reverberated through the cavernous temple and fell into the abyss to ignite the flames that danced under Sonny's feet.

Above the paining of Saint Sebastian, Dionysus, and Christ; lurked a massive relief of the Minotaur with his human like body emerging from the granite and the diamonds and its hard volcanic core. He was bulging with power, his head crowned with horns. His huge arms held up the ceiling; and his bull like visage with flaring nostrils glared down on the sinners. Sonny mused over the folly of imagining that God would ever forgive us for crucifying everything that was good and loving and caring and creative in life. The more likely story is that we are condemned to die over and over again until we realized that we crucified ourselves.

Sonny made his way across the dance floor to the

portico that seemed to be carved out of solid granite. Two rows of Doric columns with diamond dust cornices formed the portico and the screen to the colonnade beyond where silhouettes of undetermined gender disappeared into one another and the carnivorous darkness, the only light coming from the paintings on the wall, a sequence of nudes in which the female form is always captured, exposed, looking somewhere else or inward at a secret place all her own, or at her own reflection in the beauty of nature, the crystal clear water pouring over granite worn away, smooth like a woman's legs opening up to sunlight reflecting off of the mist like gold, naked in her dreams, vulnerable to the predatory eye of rock hard objectivity that sadistically enjoyed binding her by her panties as she made the hardness soft and turned the rock into shifting sands pulled down into the undertow of an ocean of passion, the white light of her purity folding into a silk fabric revealing her breasts.

Naked women were immersed in sweets of all kinds, desserts and cakes, frosting smeared over their faces and legs, their breast, their lingerie looking like cellophane and colorful wrapping paper and fine woven cotton candy that you could eat, nipples like pure brown chocolate Kisses. A woman stripped bare stood with her arms behind her head like a prisoner of war exposing her breasts.

Sonny saw kind and gentle souls, who in another culture would have been monks and priests and priestesses who had evolved to a higher spiritual level beyond carnal and material lusts and possession being led like slaves downstairs to The Bitter End where the narcissism of capitalism degenerated into the sadomasochism of fascism.

At the entranceway to The Bitter End, Sonny observed

Tommy, a young buffed up gay African American bouncer who monitored The Ballroom and The Bitter End to make sure everything remained fun and games. Tommy was wearing a skintight black T-shirt, old fashion Levis that you folded up to a desired length, and old fashion black and white high-top Converse sneakers. "Glitter" was spelled out across his chest in silver sparkles; and he wore a silver ring in his nose and a ring of thorns tattooed around both biceps. Sonny felt that Tommy, like many of the new generation, had pierced and mutilated himself in an unconscious anticipation of the sadomasochism that they would have to endure in the New World Order.

When Tommy saw Sonny, he smiled and said, "Hi, Sonny. Want to dance?"

Sonny laughed and said, "No, I'm looking for Josh. Have you seen him?"

"I think he's downstairs."

Sonny frowned and then walked down the cavernous stairway to the labyrinth of dungeons and web like mirrors and streams of molten lava and pulsing lights that gave only a glimpse of the men and women who were being tied up with brightly colored ribbons, submitting to bondage and humiliation, striking poses that mirrored the poses of a crucified Jesus, the pierced body of Saint Sebastian, the fallen Dionysus, and the sexual pornography that revealed the true nature of hard core capitalism that identifies everything that is good, kind, and empathetic as feminine and therefore weak.

Near the exit to The Bitter End, a long line of people waited to be punished for crimes unknown. One woman was lying over the Devil's knee; her skirt was up; her panties were down; and, as she was being spanked like a little child, she whimpered through her tears, "I was bad. I was bad."

As soon as she got up another woman was grabbed and pulled down over the Devil's knee, and she passively let him pull down her silk pants as she moaned in the ecstasy of innocence in search of sin. In the light she looked red hot and on fire.

Sonny looked down the line. There was Josh waiting his turn. Sonny walked up to him and said, "Have you seen Charlie's brother? Has anyone talked to you about tomorrow?"

"No."

Sonny looked at the line and then at Josh and said, "What the fuck are you doing here?"

Josh smiled. "I'm going to confession."

Sonny shook his head in disbelief and said, "I'm getting out of here. I'm going up to The Executive Suite; and if I don't see him there, or I don't see anyone else who knows what going on, I'm going home."

Sonny left Josh to be born again and walked out of The Bitter End, passed The Ball Room, up the stairs to The Turf Exchange, and then up one more flight of stairs to The Executive Suite. The doorway to the Executive Suite was a circular steel vault door; and the room inside was a black void with what looked like poured molten gold floors and pillars that glowed green, violet, blue, and orange then disappeared high up in the ceiling-less ceiling. From the ceiling hung thin invisible holographic plates that gave the impression of hundred dollar bills floating down from the void above and then disappearing like bubbles created with a child's plastic wand. In the four corners of the room were islands of black leather couches and chairs, cocktail tables, green and gold free standing torcheres, and paintings where all the eroticism and passion of nature and the human form were abstracted and transformed into two dimensional techno-mechanical shapes and splashes of paint that muffled the human cry for help like Andy Warhol's can of Cambell Soup and the cubes of Picasso flesh. Above the bar floated a huge golden dollar sign, a hieroglyph of the snake in the Garden of Eden coiled around The Tree of Life.

On the dance floor murder, fraud, prostitution, and white-collar crime danced with Exxon and IT&T, movie stars and punk rockers with pierced body parts and shaved heads, half naked models wearing price tags and the children from the main floor honored for the depths of their vices. Want-to-be victims and perpetrators swarmed the entranceway waiting to get in.

Holding the masses at bay were two giant bouncers and Peter Tattoo, the floor manager and the house coke dealer. Peter, who was a Yale graduate and a Hell's Angel, tied his long silver-white hair back in a ponytail; and he wore black eye liner, motorcycle boots with steel toes, black Levis, and a black leather vest with a winged death head insignia on the back. Barbed wire tattoos coiled around his bare arms; and on the back of one hand he had tattooed his motto, *Never Give An Inch*. In that hand, he carried a club like cane with a weighted pure gold handle that he used for crowd control. If that didn't work, Peter had a choke wire wrapped around his head like a bandana, throwing stars in his breast pockets, and a .38 Colt in an ankle holster.

Peter spotted Sonny coming through the crown and said, "Hey, man, how you doin?"

"Great, if I could find Charlie's brother."

"He's not here. But how do you like my crowd?"

"When it comes to trash, Peter; you're a fuckin poet."

105

Peter nodded his head in approval and said, "I take that as a real compliment, Sonny."

"You should." Sonny walked away; and as he crossed the dance floor to get to the bar, the twins came up to him. The twins were beautiful, but they got off on being like "*The Two Faces of Eve*," identical but opposite, changing identities, yet still the same woman. They were The Good Girl and The Bad Girl. Good Girl had done her blond wig up in pigtails with red bows; and she was wearing a pleated red and black tartan mini skirt, white bobby socks and black penny loafers, a white dress shirt with a matching red and black plaid tie, and a black cashmere sport jacket with a school crest on her chest with the motto, "Know Thy Self."

Bad Girl was dressed in black spiked high heel shoes, black sheer stockings, and a black web like silk slip that posed as a mini dress and revealed her black lace bra, panties, and garter belt. Her body was sprayed with gold sparkles, and her jet-black hair was teased and frozen in a wild whirl that made her look as if she was in the middle of having sex, straddling her lover, pumping away, her hair turning into Medusa's snakes.

Simultaneously they both said, "Hi, Sonny."

"Hi, girls, where's CB?"

"We tied him up in the bathroom," Bad Girl said.

The twins each took one of Sonny's arms. He looked from one to the other and said, "Doesn't he get confused?"

"He likes it like that," Good Girl said.

Bad Girl smiled, "We do too. Come on, Sonny, dance with us,"

As they danced, Good Girl and Bad Girl undulated around Sonny, coming in and out alternatively, whispering in his ear.

"I'd love to cook and sew and clean house for you, Sonny."

"I love to be sexy. I want you to desire me, baby. I'll take it any way you want to give it to me, Sonny. You can tie me up."

"I want you to give me babies, Sonny. I want to be a Momma."

"I'm a whore, Sonny. I want to be fucked by everyone. When you kiss me, you'll be kissing your best friend."

When Bad Girl put her hand on his crotch, and Good Girl lifted up her mini skirt to show him her pure white panties; Sonny put up his hands up and said, "Wait a minute, I give up."

He spotted CB coming towards them, and he shouted, "CB, save me. Get me away from these witches."

CB, who was tall and lean and in his late twenties, had styled his hair in an Afro; and he was wearing an apple green polyester suit with flaring bellbottom pants and wide lapels. Underneath his jacket he wore a flaming red dress shirt with a broad collar that was partially unbuttoned to reveal a hairy chest and a gold chain with a gold coke spoon for a medallion.

CB put his arms around the twins and said, "Come on, girls, leave Sonny alone. Go stick pins in somebody else."

Simultaneously, the twins said, "Bye Sonny," and they walked away weaving in and out of each other, undulating through the crowd until they disappeared.

Sonny smiled, shook his head in disbelief, and said, "How do you do it? How do you handle them?"

"I don't. I just let them do their thing." CB laughed and

said, "They're absolutely out of their minds. You should see my loft, Sonny. What they have done to it. It's furnished with new wave furniture, all slanted in weird angles and painted in weird colors. We got Al Kapp and Andy Warhol originals on the walls; giant crayons, toys and games from the fifties all over the place; and the bedroom is decorated in Spanish Harlem Modern with a giant picture of Elvis painted on black velvet hanging above our bed."

CB was going on about the girls and their schizoid sense of interior decoration when Sonny saw his Beatrice, but her name wasn't Beatrice. Her name was Miranda Delano Hewitt, and she was the woman he loved and lost somehow near the end in a haze of alcohol and drugs, about the same time he lost everything else he cared for and believed in. Friends had told him that she was back from Kenya and the Peace Corp, and she was living in Ithaca, but he never thought he would see her here. She was so out of place. The women around Miranda were models and actresses and women wearing thousands of dollars of clothing and plumage like rare birds of Paradise in a gilded cage; but Miranda, who was without any makeup and wearing simple street clothes, actually glowed in contrast to the vampires of consumption around her.

Sonny walked up behind Miranda and recited a stanza from *The Divine Comedy*, "I am left with less than one drop of my blood that does not tremble for I recognize the signs of the old flame burning."

"Sonny!"

Miranda spun around and hugged Sonny in a way that reminded him that Miranda was as small as his mother, and he marveled at how much love and warmth could be generated by just touching her skin that was radiating with sunshine.

Miranda looked at him searchingly. "Where have you been? I heard you were an exile in Canada. Then I heard you were sick, and then I didn't hear anything. Why haven't you called me? Where are you?"

Miranda searched Sonny's dark and veiled eyes for the little boy who was hiding somewhere inside. She looked around Dante's and said, "You created this. Didn't you?"

Sonny smiled and asked, "How do you like the capitalist version of Dante's Inferno?"

"It's brilliant, but why?"

"I was stoned, and I was counting money, and I came up with a residual tale."

Miranda laughed and said, "Are you going to the funeral for the 60s?"

"What funeral?"

"Didn't you get an invitation? Robin organized it. It's in Ithaca at The Sunrise Farm Cooperative. Next Saturday."

"I haven't opened my mail in a week."

Miranda squeezed his hand, affectionately, "You have to come. I'm leaving New York City tomorrow. I'm living in Ithaca now. Say you'll come."

"Yes," he said, "and when I come, we will meet for the first time as we have always met, over and over again, from one life time to another, always falling in love, forever."

Miranda looked at him with eyes the color of green that you could only find in a Gauguin painting and said, "Yes."

Sonny felt reborn, and he was about to say that he loved her when Charlie and Ginny came up to him. Charlie shouted in Sonny's ear, "Come on, man. We got the meet with Larry."

Sonny frowned and turned to Miranda, "I have to go."

"Me too," she said. I have friends downstairs waiting for me." She looked at Charlie then turned and disappeared much as she had appeared, an apparition, a vision that Sonny wasn't sure was real.

Charlie was watching Miranda as she walked away and said, "I think that chick digs me."

Ginny laughed and said, "Charlie, that girl looked at you like a vegetarian looks at a cold bucket of Kentucky Fried Chicken."

They all laughed, and then Sonny asked, "Where?"

"At the smokehouse," Charlie responded.

Sonny, Charlie, and Ginny left The Executive Suite and walked down the stairs and through the main floor to the exit. Sonny stopped at the bar and told Tom and Dave to be ready to go to work tomorrow. Ken was at the door collecting money as people came in. He held up his hand to a couple that was at the door and said, "Five dahllurs."

The man looked in and said, "What do you have?"

"A lot of assholes like you. Do you want in or not?"

The man took out his wallet. Sonny waved goodnight to Ken and left with Charlie and Ginny. They picked up a cab outside the nightclub, and Charlie gave the cabby directions to Larry's smokehouse in Harlem. Along the way, they drove past loading docks and discarded boxes and warehouses closed for the night. The dazzle of nightlife was replaced by pouring rain. A gallery of street lights created splashes of electric color against the rain of black. Shadowy figures appeared and disappeared along with the streaks and flashes of illumination created by passing cars and red tail lights, bright and bobbing on broken streets. Sonny could see his own reflection looking out the window of the cab, looking through the dark pillars and walls of New York that formed shadows of meditation in the night. Through the rain Sonny could see a beggar washed ashore in America, asleep in a pool of debris, clinging to the curb at the foot of a wall of concrete. Looking up in search of the sky, Sonny got a glimpse of the moon forming a sick halo around the torch-like-top of the Empire State Building.

The cab disappeared into the foliage, and the winding ways of Central Park then reemerged in the darkness of Harlem. They pulled up in front of an old four-story brick building with a doorman standing under a dimly lit canopy. When they got out of the cab, Charlie slapped the giant doorman on the back; and the doorman opened the door and smiled like a little boy would smile at the school bully who had just been nice to him. They walked up a flight of stairs to another entranceway where Sonny was frisked for a gun, and Charlie whispered in Sonny's ear, "They think you're a mob guy. That's the only white that comes here."

When the two security guards with bald heads and a lot of tattoos and bulging muscles were certain that he wasn't packing, they let him into the main floor of the club that was dimly lit with smoky silhouettes. A jazz quartet was playing, and the spotlight was on a soloist playing a baritone sax. He sounded like he was playing his brassy cock in the middle of a traffic jam. The crowd was sedate, well dressed, and pleasant. Everyone had left their troubles and their hardware behind. Only the music was allowed to honk. Sonny, Charlie, and Ginny sat down at a table and ordered drinks. The coke was laid out on the table for them to buy, and the waiter rolled them a joint. It was a pleasure to be in a smoke house like this where everything was open; everything was available for a price. It was all on the table for their enjoyment.

The drinks came, and Charlie leaned over and said, "See, man. What did I tell you? No bogymen in this story, Sonny. Everything is cool."

A man came to the table and whispered in Charlie's ear. Charlie motioned to Sonny to follow him; and they all got up from the table and walked through the after-hours nightclub past the gaming tables. Sonny could hear the roulette wheel turning, the cards being shuffled, the dice turning over and over again and again proving that Newton was wrong. There was still a chance.

Sonny entered an office that was tastefully furnished with contemporary modern furniture. The rug was a hand woven wool abstract painting of orange, green, and brown geometric patterns on a black background. One wall was covered with a bank of TV screens from which Larry could view everything that was going on in the smokehouse including the cash registers and the exchange of money, every penny.

Larry, who was sitting at a large executive style teak desk, was wearing a light chocolate colored double-breasted suit with a darker brown dress shirt and a gray brown tie. The only jewelry that he wore was a solid gold Rolex wristwatch and a simple gold wedding band. Sonny liked the fact that Larry had good taste and an aesthetic sense of how all the pieces fit together to make up the big picture.

But Sonny had no illusions about Larry and the four men playing cards in the background or the three hundred pound, six foot eight bodyguard who was pouring a glass of champagne with nimble hands the size of a baseball glove. They were all killers; and everyone was packing a piece, even Ginny was probably packing a small but effective twenty-two in that little gilded purse of hers. The only one who was not carrying a gun was Sonny.

Sonny could see that Larry was watching him inspect his place; and when their eyes met Larry asked, "What do you think?"

Sonny smiled and said, "I think that nobody spills anything on your carpet, except maybe blood if they get caught stealing from you."

Larry laughed and got up from his desk and extended his hand and said, "It's good that you could come. Sit down, man. Relax."

Larry gestured to his bodyguard, and the man handed Sonny a glass of champagne. He then laid out massive lines of coke for Charlie and Ginny who joined the four men sitting around the coffee table playing cards. Ginny took a sip out of the glass of champagne that had been poured for her; and then she took out her Tarot cards and began dealing her version of poker where the hearts were cups, the clubs were wands, the spades were swords, the diamonds were pentacles, the jacks were knaves, the aces were knights, and the twenty two Tarot trump cards were the prophesies.

The bodyguard finished up by laying out a line for Sonny on the silver tray and placed it on the serving table next to Sonny's chair along with a freshly open bottle of champagne. Then all three hundred pounds of him disappeared into the lurking darkness behind Sonny. Sonny took a sip of the champagne, looked at the label, Brut Cuvee Angeline 1er Cru. He smiled in appreciation and said, "Larry, you've been around the Italians too long. I've never been so graciously intimidated in all my life."

Larry laughed and said, "Don't flatter yourself, Sonny. The Italians are the only people I know who grab their balls more than we do, so let's cut the bullshit and get down to business. That sample you sold me was cool. Ginny tells me you got eight hundred pounds more of same quality that you want to unload."

"What I have Larry is a gold business. This multi-mix you got, I send back if I can't unload it easy at a reasonable profit."

Larry smiled. "If the price is right, I can make it easy for you, Sonny."

"What about the Genovese family?"

Larry shrugged and said, "What about them?"

"You work for them. If they find out that you're buying from another supplier, we're both fucked."

Larry laughed. "For sure, brother."

Charlie, who was listening to their conversation, gulped his champagne then said, "I told you, Sonny, you don't have to worry about anything. I'll protect you."

Sonny laughed and turned to Larry for comic relief. "Talk to me."

"Don't worry about the mob, Sonny. All we're doing is jiving between the lines a little."

Sonny appraised the situation. He could pretty much read Larry's mind. Larry wanted this to go down easy. He wanted Sonny to feel secure in dealing with him.

Larry knew over the long run they could both make a lot of money, and he could make a hell of a lot more if he could find out where the warehouse was located with all that gold. The risks were obvious to Sonny. If he did business with Larry, he would bring the Mafia and the Harlem gangstas into play. For what? Why was he trying to read Larry's mind, the cards, and the Jungian synchronicity of it all?

Sonny could hear Ginny calling out the cards. The symbolic archetypal imagery and numerology of the human condition was being laid out on the table – The 3 of Hearts and the Lord of Abundance, plenty, success, pleasure, sensuality, eating and drinking, pleasure and dancing, and new clothes – The 10 of Spades and The Lord of Ruin, undisciplined warring forces, ruin in all plans and projects, disdain, insolence and impertinence, yet mirth and love of overthrowing the happiness of others – The 10 of Diamonds and The Lord of Wealth, completion of material gain and fortune, but nothing beyond except old age, slothfulness, heaviness, dullness of mind and then eternal death unrelieved by any natural transcendence – The 2 of Spades and The Lord of Peace Restored, strength through suffering, pleasure after pain, sacrifice and trouble yet strength arising from the symbol of the rose as though pain itself has brought forth beauty.

As Ginny read the cards everyone in the room was being transformed into the mythological archetypal characters symbolized by the cards. The Ace of Clubs appeared as a winged warrior riding upon a black horse with a flaming mane and tail. Beneath the rushing feet of his stead were warring flames of fire. He was active, generous, fierce, sudden and impetuous; and he was being opposed by The Ace of Spades, a winged warrior who was mounted on a brown stead that was racing across dark driving clouds. He was active, clever, subtle, fierce, delicate, courageous, and skillful; but if he was ill dignified, he could be deceitful, tyrannical and crafty. They were in contention for the loyalty of The Queen of Clubs who was wearing a crown and sitting on a throne beneath which water was flowing and lotus flowers could be seen. Upon her crown was an Ibis with open wings; and though she was wearing silver chain mail armor under her aqua marine blue cape, her face was dreamy. According to the cards, she was imaginative, poetic, kind, coquettish and good-natured yet not willing to take much trouble for another. She was much affected by the influence of others and was therefore dependent and unreliable and unpredictable as she dealt

Sonny watched the Ginny as the Queen of Clubs deal out The Foolish Man who through his ideas, thoughts, and spirituality strived to rise himself above the material. He was followed by The Hanged Man, Fortitude, The Devil, The Hermit The Magus; and somewhere in the hole card lurked Death – transformation and change in search of The Wheel of Fortune and the one thing that was certain. The universe loved to gamble. It loved pure randomness, the surprised mutations, and the unlimited possibilities for creativity where cause and effect relationships were merely the table upon which to gamble.

Sonny grabbed the rolled-up-one-hundred-dollar bill lying on the silver tray and snorted a line of coke. He then brushed the coke from his nose and said, "O.K., let's play. Two hundred and fifty dollars a pound. Non negotiable."

"OK, Sonny. How do you want it to go down?"

"I'll meet you on Pier 40 at 10:00 AM, tomorrow."

Larry winced. "Why so early?"

"I know the parking lot. Nobody is there at that time of the day."

Larry nodded in agreement and said, "OK, that's cool, so how do you want to do this?"

"I'll be on the top level on the far side of the parking lot in a gray 1971 Volvo station wagon. You bring the money, Charlie, and your bodyguard. I'll be there with the pot, Tom, and Dave. Charlie and your bodyguard can take the pot and me anywhere you want to go. Tom and Dave will take you and the money and hold you until everyone is satisfied. Then we all can go home."

Larry smiled, "It's nice to know that you trust me, Sonny."

Sonny laughed. "I don't go down no dark alleyways with nobody," he said. Then he smiled, "Especially on our first date."

They both laughed, and Sonny got up. "Well, I guess that's it."

Larry stood up as well, and they shook hands to seal the deal. Charlie started to get up, but Sonny motioned for him to stay and said, "Enjoy. I'll see my own way out." Charlie wasn't about to leave the coke and that was good. He would be less dangerous with a hangover. They all will be less dangerous in the daylight than they are now in the dark, Sonny thought.

Sonny left the club and took a gypsy cab home. As he walked into the lobby of the Chelsea Hotel, he could see Bill, the resident poet sitting with two drag queens. Sonny walked up to the front desk and waited for the desk clerk who was on the phone. He wanted to pick up the mail that had been collecting in his box for a week. He stood there and watched the lobby scene as he waited.

Bill was dressed all in white as usual. His metal crutches hung on his arm, and his artificial leg beat time to the poetry that he was reciting.

> *"Whirling weaving wandering eye*
> *Give back my vision of mind.*
> *Me her here?*
> *Who am I?"*

Bill stopped. "See, it's in the vowels. Listen." He gritted his teeth and turned red.

> *"Oh wicked eyes that crystallize*
> *Break through your icy pain.*
> *We are born on a cross of prismatic light.*
> *When we meet,*
> *We disappear."*

Bill stopped again and said, "See, now it's in the consonants. The vowels are female and the consonants are male. You can get your sex fucked up by messing up your vowels and consonants. You can keep your manhood like I do by building tension around your jaw when you're beginning to feel weak. Feel your consonants."

Bill tensed his jaw to show them how it was done. He turned fire red, and he looked aflame with his own pain as he reached into his white purse for a cigarette.

One of the drag queens laughed and said, "Bill, I

think you're right. Someone is always trying to get their consonant in my vowel."

Bill spotted Sonny at the front desk and wobbled over. "Sonny, come and join us," he said. "I'm reciting some new poems tonight."

"No thanks, Bill. I'm tired. I have to get some sleep." Sonny noticed a gash on the side of Bill's head. "What happened to your head, Bill?"

"I was mugged last night."

"Jesus, that's too bad. Did the police catch them?"

"Nah, it happens all the time. I'm mugged at least once a month."

"What do you mean?"

"I'm lame and fair game."

"Isn't there anything you can do?"

"Yes. I'm going to remain white and pure and keep on writing poetry." He whispered in Sonny's ear, "I'm going to teach all the sensitive, kind, gay people how to fight back against evil. I'm going to teach them about consonants."

"The hard line?"

Bill smiled. His face was red with pain, "Yes, the hard line, the firm set jaw of revolutionary poetry."

Sonny grabbed his mail from the desk clerk and quickly sorted through it. There it was - the invitation to the funeral. He affectionately patted Bill's cheek and said, "Good night, Bill."

"Good night, Sonny."

Sonny rode the elevator up to his room, took a hot shower, and then collapsed onto his bed with the French windows open to the sounds of chaos. All he could think about was Miranda; and when, for a moment, he touched a bit of Paradise.

It was 1969, and Sonny was driving into Berkeley from the University of Washington where he had been participating in a seminar on global corporations and the death of the nation state. He came to Berkeley to visit Eban Sinclair, a friend from Cornell University who was a graduate student at UC. Eban was a member of SDS, one of the more powerful political activist groups in the country. Sonny had met a few students at the University of Washington who he thought had potential as campus leaders, and he wanted to pass their names on to Eban as potential recruits and future organizers on campus. Sonny also wanted to talk to someone who would know about SDS and where it was going.

When Sonny stopped his Ariel motorcycle for a traffic light on Telegraph Avenue, he saw a young man with shoulder length dark brown hair crossing the street. He was carrying an aluminum framed olive green backpack; and he was wearing brown leather sandals, blue jeans with multi-colored patches, and a tie-die T-shirt with red, yellow, and purple bursts of far out colors.

"Where's the campus?" Sonny asked.

The young man stopped in the middle of the intersection and pointed straight up Telegraph Avenue. He then smiled and said, "Welcome to The People's Republic of Berzerkley."

Sonny laughed and then formed a V with his middle and index finger and his palm facing forward, the universal sign of peace in the 60s and a symbol of the oneness that bound together the youth of America. The light changed, and Sonny cruised up the tree-lined road and then parked near Sproul Plaza and the entranceways to the Berkeley Campus. From what Sonny could see as he walked into the Plaza, the architecture on campus was a blend of Beaux Arts and a modern cubist style that glorified concrete and glass. The Student Union to his left was one of those gray slabs of concrete; and to his right on the opposite side of the Plaza, was a grand stairway that led to a granite Romanesque building in the Imperial style of Rome that housed the administrative offices. At the far end of the Plaza he could see Sather Gate, a steel and bronze clad Beau Art gateway to the campus with ornate floral trim in the style of the French Baroque era; and beyond that, in the background, towering over the treetops, he could see the landmark clock and bell tower that resembled the Campanile de San Marco in Venice.

Sonny stopped for a moment to appreciate the fact that he was standing in Sproul Plaza, the Fort Sumpter of the student Free Speech Movement. He then walked over to some students sitting at one of the tables in front of the Student Union building. "Can any of you tell me where the Unit One Dorms are?"

A beautifully suntanned girl with blond frizzed hair who was wearing a bright orange halter top, low cut blue bell-bottom jeans, sandals, and purple Granny sunglasses smiled at him and said, "Go down Telegraph one block and take a left on Durant. Then go two blocks to College Ave. You can't miss it."

Sonny gave them the peace sign then walked back to his motorcycle. He found Durant Avenue and College Ave and then Derful Dormitory, a dorm that looked like all the other dormitories in the complex of cheerfully painted prison blocks named after famous alumni. Sonny entered the dormitory, and he was immediately immersed in a collage of smells. There were hints of hamburgers, French fries, ketchup, a pizza with mushrooms and sausage, and a meatball sub to go. These smells mingled with the smells of laundry bags filled with dirty clothes that were being washed in a swirling pool of testosterone thinly veiled in deodorant, shampoo, and the vaguely respectable smell of used textbooks, smudged paperback books, and ink. Sonny could hear a typewriter clicking away and music coming out of one of the suites when the door opened and closed to the sound of Pink Floyd singing,

> *"We don't need no education*
> *We don't need no thought control*
> *No dark sarcasm in the classroom*
> *Teacher leave them kids alone."*

Sonny found Suite 104, but printed on the door in bold black letters was, Resident Counselor. Sonny looked at the scrap of paper where he wrote down Eban's address, and he wondered if he had the right building. The idea of Eban being a dorm councilor seemed preposterous to him, but he knocked anyway

The door opened, and Eban appeared wearing a black French beret in the style of Che Guervara, beat up unlaced brown combat boots, black jeans, and a white T-shirt with a black and white image of an AK 47 assault rifle printed on the front, along with the blood red caption that read - PIECE.

Sonny looked at Eban, then at the sign on the door

again and said, "Resident Counselor? You got to be kidding me."

Eban smiled. "Hey, I'm the main man in this cell block, Sonny. You need toilet paper. No problem. You need someone to intercede with the screws. I'm your man."

Eban spread his arms and embraced Sonny, "How you doin, brother? It's good to see you."

"It's good to see you too, Eban."

"Come on in, man." Eban gestured towards the couch, "Sit down. Relax. Do you want a beer? It's ice cold, and I loaded up in anticipation of your eminent arrival."

"Sure. It's been a long trip on that old Ariel of mine." Sonny dropped his backpack on the floor, and he sat down on the couch and watched Eban walk across the room to a mini refrigerator. Eban had been the president of his graduating class in high school and a star wrestler who wrestled at one fifty, but now his crew cut had grown into wild locks of blond hair, and he didn't look like he could make weight anymore. The lean meat-eating wrestler had been transformed into a sturdy brown rice and beans Buddha with wire rim glasses.

Eban, like many of the young students who joined the new left and other progressive student organizations was an above average student with an above average intelligence who majored in the humanities. In the new world order of the knowledge machine, the humanities were viewed, at their worse, subversive; and, at their best, the new Sherwood Forest for the neurotic dysfunctional children of the rich. Eban was one of those poor lost souls who majored in comparative literature and minored in philosophy; and after reading all those books about all those different kinds of people from all those different kinds of place and different eras of history, he was transformed from a beer guzzling, panty raiding, petal-to-the-metal teenager into a maturing young man who was developing a sense of empathy. Eban had learned how to walk in other people's shoes and hear their cries for help. This was a malady of the heart that the knowledge industry was desperately trying to cure by making it clear that becoming a human being just didn't pay. The money was in manipulating people and nature as objects and numbers to be converted into money.

Eban popped the top on a can of Budweiser beer, handed it to Sonny, and said, "Welcome, brother. My casa, your casa." He then sat down in a red beanbag chair and pulled out a joint from his breast pocket. He raised an eyebrow inquisitively and then smiled as he waved a joint of marijuana back in forth in front of Sonny's face to tempt him with the forbidden fruit of their generation.

"Absolutely," Sonny said.

Eban lit the joint, took a drag on it, and then passed it to Sonny who also took a hit, holding in the smoke until he felt it wash over his body like a massage. Sonny sat back on the couch and looked around the room. Like most dormitory furniture the desk, chair, bookshelves, and couch were made out of thick slabs of oak bolted together so as to withstand the nuclear blast of generations upon generations of invading teenagers. The upholstery on the couch could best be described as brillo-wool or possibly woolen chain-mail. The prison cell appearance of the room was softened by a large picture window that looked out onto a rather pleasant view of the campus and the wooded area along Telegraph Avenue. A worn Persian rug covered the cold hardwood floors; and two beanbag chairs, red and black, added a touch of comfort. The coffee table looked like it endured years of disobedient children, a fact confirmed by the empty coke cans that should have been thrown away, the large ashtray full of cigarette butts, and a mound of melted candles of all colors that looked like a psychedelic lava flow. Next to Eban's desk, Sonny saw a large pile of the *New Left Notes*, a SDS newsletter; and his bookshelves were stacked with political pamphlets. On the wall were posters of Mao, Che Guevara, Malcolm X, and two SDS posters. One of the posters called out in bold letters, RESIST! Another read, DON'T MOURN, ORGANIZE.

Sonny took another drag off of the joint, and then he looked at Eban incredulously and said, "Dorm Counselor? How the hell did you manage that?"

"It's part of the University's efforts to coop the movement with the creation of student and faculty councils, promises of more diversity, and better food and housing. It's all window dressing. But fuck it. I'm through with this fuckin place. There's nothing we can do here anymore. SDS is going to the streets, man. We're going to become the vanguard of the New American Revolution."

"So what I heard is true. A group of you have taken over the leadership of SDS, and you're advocating guerilla warfare and a Marxist Revolution."

"You're fuckin A, man. We've tried everything, Sonny; and we got nothing to show for it. We tried to reform the universities, and all we got was window dressing. We fought for civil rights, and we got tokenism. We've organized massive antiwar demonstrations, sit-ins, and teach-ins; and all they've done is to intensify the war."

Eban got up and went to the refrigerator to get two more beers, and he stopped in front of the bookshelf filled with stacks of pamphlets. He picked up one of the pamphlets and said, "Let's see what we got here, *Racism and Imperialism*". He threw the pamphlet at Sonny and picked up another. *"The New Labor Class,"* He threw that at Sonny too. Then he went through the pamphlets like they were cards in his hand, *"The Myth of the Domino Theory – A Guide to Student Activism – The University, Agent Orange, The CIA and Beyond – Environmental Melt Down – The Cost of Imperialism – The Selling of America."* He discarded all those pamphlets and then said, "And here's one by you, Sonny."

Eban tossed that one at Sonny. Sonny looked at the title, *Mass Media and The Consumer Culture of Primitive Totems: The Devolution of America.* Sonny laughed, and Eban put Dylan's album *"Subterranean Homesick Blues"* on the record player, and Sonny listened to Dylan sing,

> *"Look out kid*
> *Don't matter what you did*
> *Walk on your tip toes*
> *Don't try "No Doz"*
> *Better stay away from those that carry around a fire hose.*
> *Keep a clean nose*
> *Watch the plain clothes*
> *You don't need a weather man to know which way the wind blows."*

Eban handed Sonny another beer and then sat down

and said, "Sonny, we've tried to speak truth to power." Eban paused and a dark sadness passed across his face. "All we got for that, man, is clubbed, gassed, shot, and fuckin murdered. We're not taking it anymore. Fuck them. We're fighting back!"

"With what army?"

"All revolutions started with a small dedicated cadre, man. We'll unite with our black brothers in this country, and we'll become a vanguard army that will recruit from the billions of poor people in the world who are rising up against American imperialism and its capitalist racist institutions."

"Your black brothers? "They threw you out of SNCC because you were white, and now the Black Panthers and other radical black organizations like them are advocating Black Nationalism and Separatism. We're doing nothing to unite the black and white workers of America. That's the problem."

"Fuck the hard hats," Eban said. "They're the praetorian guard of a global system of oppression, and they'll pull the trigger on their fellow workers for a fuckin pickup truck, a six-pack of beer, a TV set, and a recliner chair."

"Right," Sonny said. "And the brightest and most opportunistic of the black working class will be cooped into the system; and they will be getting off the *Freedom Train* in Old Greenwich, Connecticut; and the rest of us will be getting a round trip ticket back to nowhere, courtesy of our black brothers in BMWs."

"For sure," Sonny said. "The system is brilliant in the way it divides and conquers and alienates the working class from itself. But, the point is that everything is changing. With globalization, American corporations aren't American anymore. They'll go anywhere there is cheap slave and child labor, and they'll abandon the American white working class in the near future. They don't need us anymore, and we need to make Americans aware of what is happening to them and what will happen to their children. You're right. We do need to leave the campuses. We need to knock on the doors of working class families, go to the union halls, their workplace, the malls, the bars, the sports fields where their children play, the VFWs and the American Legions, everywhere we can find them. We need to explain to them how they are going to be fucked too. All of us."

Sonny took a sip of his beer and took a drag of the joint and passed it back to Eban, then said, "Another thing. You say we tried everything, and we failed. That's not fuckin true. In the beginning, when SDS was founded, we believed that how you make a decision was as important as the decision you make, so we became a direct and participatory democracy. And... because of that we were open and free; and, we were flexible and diverse. Wherever we were we could take the immediate issue important to that group or community and use it to open up the discourse to the broader issues. That's what the universities never got. The issue was never the issue with us because we were able to take almost any issue and connect it to the civil rights movement, the student free speech movement, and the antiwar movement; and we could take all three movements and connect them with one another and the broader issues of the evils of corporate globalism, imperialism and vampire capitalism. We got millions of people to think about things they never thought about before...and... we got them to act on things they never thought they could do anything about."

"Now you want to give it all up?" Sonny shook his

head in disbelief. "For what? Soviet or Chinese Communism? That's your alternative? That's progress? The only thing that has changed in those two countries is that the Communist Party in the Soviet Union replaced the old aristocracy; and in China, the Communist Party replaced the old Mandarin class. Otherwise, nothing has changed. The old boss is the new boss, the same as the old boss. No, man, the old models of capitalism, socialism, representative democracy, and communism are all seriously flawed. We need a new vision of an alternative social, political, and economic structure to replace the old. We're getting there; but we're not there yet. We're not ready for a revolution. America is not ready for a revolution."

"American is never going to be fuckin ready for this, man," Eban said." There's no reforming America. This isn't about evil in America. It's about America being evil, man. There's no hope for America, Sonny. America is fuckin over."

"I can't believe that," Sonny said. "It's like giving up on your family because they're fucked up."

Eban laughed and said, "That sounds like an abused child talking." Sonny laughed as well; and then Eban stood up, and said, "But, I know something that we'll agree on, brother."

"What's that?"

"Pizza, man, I'm starving."

Sonny laughed, "Me too. Do they have any good pizza in this town?"

"Yeah, there's a pizza place called La Val's, man. It's not bad. The closest thing you'll get to New York pizza here."

Sonny stood up and spreads his arm. "I'm ready."

Sonny and Eban drove to Val's in Eban's red 1961

ragtop Volkswagen Beetle; and when they arrived at Val's, they sat down at one of the tables and ordered a cheese pizza with pepperoni and two mugs of beers. Val's was like many campus type pizzerias/Italian restaurants/ take-out joints. It was crowded with tables and chairs, beer signs, and a take-out counter. A black and white menu board over the counter listed a huge selection of food all derivatives of one another and the smell of garlic, onions, cooked tomatoes, ground beef and pork, and the smell of burnt flour, cheap wine and beer. Behind the take-out counter was a large black and white blowup of an aerial photo of the UC campus; and near the entranceway, Sonny noticed a poster calling for students to join in on the building of People's Park. "*Let a Thousand Parks Bloom,*" it said.

Sonny pointed at the poster. "What is that all about?"

"The university purchased and then tore down a block of low rent apartment buildings as a buffer zone between poverty and the university. The DMZ zone, as we call it. It was allowed to degenerate into a muddy parking lot and a garbage can for trash and abandoned cars. Recently, some student activists got the students and the community behind an effort to clean up the area and turn it into a park for the people. It's become a happening. They even got fraternity and sorority kids volunteering and the local businesses and building contractors and landscape artists have contributed plants, building materials, and skilled labor."

"That's great, man."

"Yeah, like it's going to change anything," Eban said dismissively.

"You know, Eban, sometimes it doesn't matter how it affects them. Sometimes we have to do things just to remind ourselves about who we are."

Eban bit into a slice of pizza, wiped his lips and chin with his hand, then took a swig out of his mug of beer and said, "I dig, man; but you wait and see. They're not going to let them even have a small piece of Paradise. Paradise is private property in America, and you have to buy your way into Heaven."

After they finished eating, they drove back to Eban's room, argued politics for a while more, and then gravitated towards the youthfulness upon which their politics soared. They talked about the girls that they knew, the fun they had at Cornell, drank more beer, smoked more pot; and watched Laugh-In on TV. Somewhere between Laugh-In, the nightly news, and a trip to the refrigerator for a can of coke, and a bowl of potato chips; Sonny, exhausted, fell asleep on the couch.

The next morning he woke up, took a shower, and left a note for Eban who was still asleep. Sonny fired up his Ariel, and he drove down Telegraph Avenue to Bowditch Street and Dwight Way where he was told that People's Park was located. There were hundreds of people there; and as Sonny cruised around weaving his way slowly through the crowds of people, he saw a hand made sign nailed to a tree that read, *People's Park*; and below it was a table where he could volunteer.

One of the students tending the table had dark bushy hair that was puffed out into waves and curls of anarchy. He was wearing black penny loafers without any socks, tight black tapered jeans, and a black T-shirt with a message scrolled across his chest in white letters that read, *Don't Trust Anybody Over Thirty*. With his wire rim glasses and his pale delicate features that seemed to be oblivious to California sunshine, the student looked like a cross between Bobby Dylan and a Russian Trotskyite trying to escape the tragedy of a Dostoyevsky novel; but when he spoke, he was obviously only several semesters of well-attended English literature classes away from Brooklyn.

The girl seated next to him at the table was wearing a green Rigoletto style wide brimmed felt hat with a white ostrich feather as a plume. A white cotton Mexican riding blouse was unbuttoned to reveal a royal blue T-shirt with silk screened yellow daisies blooming on voluptuous breasts.

She smiled at Sonny and asked him, "What can you do?"

Sonny smiled in response and said, "I know how to use a pick and shovel, dig a hole, pound a nail, cut a board..." Sonny shrugged, "I got hands."

The girl stood up and said, "Gotcha. Follow me."

Sonny followed the girl through the park that was forming out of the debris, and he was amazed by what they had done. Sod was being laid down on a massive scale. Bushes, scrubs, trees, and flowers were being planted everywhere. Sonny saw a mason creating a brick pathway; and near the pathway he saw a sign that read, *The People's Garden* which was a plowed plot of land where people were planting seeds for organic vegetable in natural compost. In the background they were building what looked to be a sheltered stage/bandstand for future plays and concerts.

The girl stopped in front of a long line of people who were passing squares of sod from hand to hand. "Here's your helping hand," she smiled and said. "Step in anywhere. You are now officially part of The People's Park Commune."

Sonny looked around for a place in the line, and then he saw her. She was small and built like a gymnast with well-toned graceful muscles that turned every movement into an athletic dance like water patiently wearing away rock. She was dressed simply in a white spaghetti strap T-shirt, sand colored cutoff jeans with frayed edges, and light tan leather John Deere work boots with white turned down athletic socks. She had a beautiful tan, and her breasts were small but beautifully shaped like prepubescent buds of unknown gender blooming into a woman that he wanted to shape with his lips. Sonny was amazed with how much space she took up for a little person. She seemed to radiate the space around her with a light from within.

There was a moment pause in the line; and when someone stepped out, Sonny saw his opportunity. He slipped into the line next to her, but she didn't notice him because she was having a conversation with the girl in line next to her. Then the human conveyor belt started again.

She turned, and she was like a shaft of light, a portal to Paradise in People's Park.

"Hi, I'm Sonny."

She seemed stunned for a moment like she thought she might know him, but she couldn't figure out from where. Confused, she said, "Yes, it is a nice day, isn't it?"

"No, no," Sonny said laughing. "My name is Sonny."

She laughed as well and said, "Oh, I'm sorry. My name is Miranda."

As Sonny passed the piece of sod to Miranda he asked, "Do you go to UC?"

"I just graduated."

"What now?"

"I'm going to Cornell for a Master's degree in feminist literature, and I'll be working part-time for the National Organization of Women as a regional organizer."

"Wow. I graduated from Cornell. I'm going back there when I leave here."

"What do you do?"

"When I graduated from Cornell I went to the Maxwell School at Syracuse University for my Ph.D. in American Studies. I taught for awhile at SU; but now I'm a sort of itinerate scholar. I go from campus to campus and try to infect the body politic with democracy. I sort of cough on people and hope they catch the virus and pass it on."

Miranda smiled and said, "A kind of germ warfare. That's cool. Maybe you can start a nation wide epidemic."

"I hope so."

A young man with long blond hair and a beard wearing blue denim overalls, no shirt, work boots, and a carpenter's belt came up to Miranda and said, "Miranda, David and I have to go to class. We could use your help with the stage."

Miranda turned to Sonny and said, "Do you know anything about carpentry?"

"I was a carpenter's assistant one summer. You tell me what to cut, and I can cut it without wasting wood."

Miranda grabbed his hand and said, "Come on, you're hired."

They walked over to the stage where a wood sign stuck in the ground declared in rainbow colored letters that it was *The People's Theater and Performance Center*. Next to the stage there was a table saw and piles of wood. The frame of the stage/bandstand was constructed, and they were laying down the floorboards. Steve, the student who had asked Miranda for help, turned his carpenter's belt and tools over to Miranda. As Miranda put on her tool belt, she pointed to the table saw and said, "Can you handle that? I'll tell you what I need, and you cut it."

Sonny shrugged and said, "Sure, I'll need a measuring tape, a pencil, and a square if you have one."

The student, who was leaving with Steve, handed his carpenter's belt and tools over to Sonny and said, "This stuff belongs to the commune, Sonny. When you're done, you pass it on to whoever takes your place or put it in the carpenter's box over there."

As the student walked away, he gave them the peace sign and said, "Up the revolution," and then he disappeared into the park.

Miranda smiled and said, "Let's get to work," and then she joined the carpenters on the stage and started calling out measurements.

Sonny looked around. Everyone was working to the sound of The Band singing, *"Take a load off Fannie, take a load for free."* Sonny smiled. They had turned work into play, and at times it looked like a playground where you worried that the children running around would bump into each other or fall off of the jungle gym and get hurt but nobody did. He loved it. He love working communally with his brothers and sisters. This had always been a concept of his, an ideal, an abstract idea that he wrote about; but now he was living the dream, and at the center of that dream was Miranda. He couldn't take his eyes off of her. He was enchanted by Miranda; and when she smiled at him or touched his hand as he passed wood to her, it was like his mommy smiling at him and telling him he was doing a good job; but his mommy almost never smiled at him like that; and he never seemed to be able to do anything that would make her happy; so he was sucking up her smiles like California sunshine.

They worked for hours, and then a cowbell rang. Miranda came over and said, "Come on, let's go eat."

Three picnic tables were full of all sorts of vegetables, rice and bean dishes, the distinct smell of curry, a big pot of vegetable chili; and nearby, a hippie wearing an Uncle Sam hat and coat was grilling hot dogs and hamburgers. In the background Peter, Paul, and Mary were singing,

> "*Carry on my sweet survivor,*
> *Carry on my lonely friend.*
> *Don't give up on the dream,*
> *And don't you let it end.*"

Sonny served himself a black bean, corn, and red pepper salad, a hamburger, and a cup of cider. Miranda filled her plate with chicken curry and rice, a fresh green garden salad, and a glass of ice green tea and honey. They found a tree to sit under; and when Miranda gave Sonny some homemade bread from her plate she said, "So, what is Ithaca like? I was only there for a couple of days. The campus is nice, and I loved the view of the lake."

Sonny smiled. "It's ten square miles surrounded by reality."

"Do you have someplace to live?"

"Not yet. I can't decide whether to sign up for a room in a graduate residential dorm or find a place myself when I get there. What do you think?"

"I'll help you."

"Really?"

Sonny smiled, "Sure."

"Do you have a place to stay?" Miranda asked.

"I have a friend here in one of the dorms. I guess I'm going crash on his floor." Sonny didn't mention that Eban had a couch, and he gave Miranda his best lost-dog look. All he didn't do was wag his tail and lick her hand.

"You can stay with us. We have lots of room."

"Who's us?" Sonny asked, fearing the answer.

"I live in a commune. Everyone is cool, and we always have guests." She smiled and looked at him like she just asked him if he wanted a cookie with the promise of more.

"Far out, that sounds great, Miranda, all I have to do is pick up my backpack from Eban's dorm room."

"Splendid," she said as she got up. "I think we better get back to work. Don't you think?"

Sonny wanted to say, "Miranda, I'm not thinking at this point. I'm just going with the flow, and it feels great;" but he just got up and said, "OK, I'm ready."

They worked for several hours more, and then they walked over to where Sonny parked his motorcycle. Miranda loved the old Ariel; and when she straddled the back seat of the bike and wrapped her arms around him, he felt her breasts against his back and the motorcycle throbbing before it roared off down the road. Sonny smiled to himself thinking, "Now this is what a motorcycle is all about."

He pulled into the dorm parking lot; and when he went up to Eban's room to pick up his backpack, Eban looked out the window, saw Miranda, and said; "I understand, brother. The first and most important guy rule, pussy before friends."

They both laughed, and Sonny rejoined Miranda who suggested that they take a walk along Strawberry Creek. As they walked along the path that followed the creek through the campus, they held hands; and it was like they had always been together. They talked about their childhood, and they talked about their hopes and dreams for the future. They walked hand and hand through the Romanesque arch of Hearst Bridge, and Sonny felt so comfortable with Miranda that he wondered if we all fall in love with the same person over and over again from one lifetime to another. Maybe love is the Adam and Eve of matter and antimatter that constitutes the fundamental core feeling that created the universe at the beginning of time and continues to hold it together and illuminates reality with its magic, a touch, a first kiss that turned their lips, their love into a link across time and made them feel like they were a part of an impressionistic painting, the abstract rays of light fragmented by coastal redwoods and giant Eucalyptus trees speckled with dots of pink rhododendrons, wild currents, and ferns. A white egret seemed like a winged anchor to a reality that flowed over a blue crayfish that crawled through the green gold water that glistened in the sun; and when they finally stopped kissing Sonny looking into Miranda's eyes and said, "Wow. So that is what lovers mean when they say, 'I will love you forever and ever.' "

Miranda looked deeply into Sonny's eyes and said, "Do you think you could love me forever?"

"I already have."

"So you think we've loved each other from lifetime to lifetime?"

"Yes."

"Well then how come we don't remember?" Miranda asked as she took his hand and led him further down the path.

Sonny laughed. "That wouldn't be any fun. It's like... Well, what if from lifetime to lifetime we remember the first time we saw a sunrise or a sunset? That wouldn't make any sense. It's better that each time is the first time so that each time we experience the wonder of it."

"So you're saying that we've been in love forever, but we're meeting for the first time, but each time we meet we fall in love all over again."

"Yes, and each time it's more spectacular and more beautiful than before."

"I like that," Miranda said. "But what about other guys that I have been attracted too?"

"They're all cases of mistaken identity."

They both laughed and walked on so totally and completely enchanted with one another that they didn't notice that the stream was polluted by sewage runoff from the football stadium and the pathway was carelessly neglected by a university that had no aesthetic sense when it ran steam pipe lines across the creek in total disregard for its natural beauty. Miranda and Sonny didn't notice this because they were in the world of infinite possibilities and a world of what could be.

Later in the day, they drove to the commune where Miranda lived in an old Victorian house on Sutter Street. Some of the young people there were working in the communal kitchen where they were cooking food for their evening meal and baking whole wheat bread for People's Park and a free food kitchen run by another commune called Provos. Provos, like the Sutter Street Commune, were off springs of the Digger movement which believed that everything should be free.

Other members of the commune were working in *The Free Print Shop* where they were printing out the latest edition of an inter-communal newspaper called, *Kaliflower*, a paper that describes itself as a "flower growing out of the ashes of this currant age of destruction."

The front page of the paper had a green and purplish gray floral sketch of a woman who seemed to be emerging from nature with heart shaped lips. The title story on the front page was *Lousy Dreams*; and it read,

> *"A specter is haunting San Francisco – communal capitalism. People who rob their brothers from 9 – 5 and then come home to love and share with their <u>selected</u> brothers. Are they the vanguard of a New Age?*
>
> *THE WHOLE WORLD IS YOUR FAMILY. The things you create have nothing to do with money – DESTROY THE MYTH. Security as love and faith in your brothers and sisters is coming thru the door – MAKE PROPHETS NOT PROFIT."*

Sonny looked up from the newspaper, and he loved what he saw in the commune, but he wondered if he would ever be a part of it. Would he ever shed the excess baggage of his violent past? Sometimes he felt like the Roman fighting for the Christians. If he was victorious he would never become part of the world he was creating. Even the students around him, who were trying so hard, had their own excess baggage to overcome. Most of them were from upper middle class families, and they grew up in the insular environment of homogenous suburbs. From childhood they were taught to compete for the top in an American Darwinian society of winners and losers where money was the way to keep score. Often the nucleus of their family life was split by divorce; and love was betrayed at its core. Many of their hopes and dreams came from the negative space in their lives, the void that was being filled by dreams of the future and the dreams that they were living now. Sonny wondered if they were the prototypes of a cultural evolution of humankind or were they condemned to failure. Would they ever enter the Gates of Eden and live in the Age of Aquarius where *"Peace will guide the planets and love will steer the stars,"* or were they trapped in a society closing in on itself like a snake eating its tail?

As Sonny was musing over his fate, Miranda, who seemed to glow with goodwill, grabbed his hand and swept him up in her enthusiasm. Sonny signed and went with the flow. He helped her carry boxes of freshly baked bread out to a Volkswagen van that drove off to deliver the bread to the soup kitchen. They joined the others for their communal dinner. Everyone was friendly. Some of them were curious about Cornell and where he had been. After awhile they figured out who he was. They had seen other activists like him come to the campus to organize or lecture or speak at meetings or just hang out, tune in, and pass the word on.

Herbie, who looked like a stoned hippie rabbi,

pointed to Sonny and said, "He's one of Tolkein's Rangers. He's a member of the Brotherhood of Hope who roams the borders of the empire looking for cracks in the wall." Everyone seemed satisfied with that. Sonny now had an identity and a place in their community. He was now baptized with a new name, and he was born again as the "Ranger."

After dinner Miranda and Sonny helped with washing dishes, and Sonny tried to remain cheery, friendly, and entertaining; but he was becoming weary of the effort. He was tired, and all he really wanted to do was be alone with Miranda. Miranda, who was watching him as much as he was watching her, sensed his weariness. She made him stop and put the pot away that he was washing; and then she took off her apron, whipped his hands with the towel she was using to dry the dishes and said, "Do you want to take a shower before you go to bed?"

"I'm going to bed?" Sonny asked.

"Yes."

"Where?"

"With me, silly."

"Oh, then I guess I'd like to take a shower. Sonny smiled. "And the other thing... I'd really like to do that too."

"OK, follow me."

Sonny followed Miranda up the oak stairway with tapered balusters and an ornate newel with hand carved rosettes. The stairway and the floors of the hallways squeaked so much that Sonny imagined that the house was being held together by the bold colors of the walls and the trim on the moldings, the vivid purple and blue and the orange that glowed like a Tibetan temple that vibrated to the mantra tremors of the Saint Andreas fault. As he walked up the stairway and through the hallways, he also marveled at the beauty of Mirada's body. It was one of those bodies that men watched at women's Olympic gymnastics meets, or went to the ballet for, or watched a beautiful woman figure skater just to get a glimpse of her ass as she leaped then whirled revealing the glory and beauty of the human form on cold hard ice.

When they get to Miranda's room, Sonny leaned his backpack against the wall near the door, and Miranda put a Joni Mitchell album onto her Sony stereo player. Miranda's room had bare oak floors, and it looked like they had been recently refinished. The walls were painted yellow and the moldings and window frames were painted a medium range bright garden green. The ceiling was high in the Victorian style, and the upper panes of the bay windows were stained glass causing red, orange, yellow, and blue speckled bands of light to dance with the silver moon across the floor. A giant rubber tree acted like a blind for the bay window, and it made it seem as if he were looking through a jungle forest out at the city lights and into the night.

On one side of the bay window, there was an old fashioned art deco green velvet stuffed chair, and next to it was a Tiffany type stained glass standing lamp that was dimly lit with bright stain glass flowers. On the other side of the bay window was Miranda's antique brass poster bed with rainbow sheets and a white down comforter. An artist's drafting table served as a desk, and the book shelves that were made with 2 x 8s and cinder blocks were full of books on art, literature, anthropology, and other assorted topics and subject matter.

Browsing through the books he saw *The Feminine*

Mystique by Betty Friedan, *Thinking About Women* by Mary
Ellmann, *Coming of Age in Mississippi* by Anne Moody, *Male
and Female, And A Study of the Sexes* by Margaret Mead. He
also saw books by Mircea Eliade and Camus, both of whom he
loved. On Miranda's stereo record player Joni Mitchell was
singing,

> *"Sisotowbell Lane*
> *Go to the city you'll come back again*
> *To wade through the grain*
> *You always do*
> *Yes we always do*
> *Come back to the stars*
> *Sweet well water and pickling jars*
> *We'll lend you the car*
> *We always do*
> *Yes sometimes we do*
> *We have a rocking chair*
> *Someone is always there*
> *Rocking rhythms while they're waiting*
> *With the candle in the window*
> *Sometimes we do*
> *We wait for you."*

Miranda watched Sonny while he browsed through
her bookshelf. She watched the way he moved. Like many
outstanding athletic men, Sonny moved gracefully like a big
cat; and when he turned away from the bookshelf and stared
at her, his eyes were like dark pools that she could get lost
in. Miranda smiled and handed Sonny a large white cotton
towel that she had pulled out of a drawer and said, "The

bathroom is through that door, Sonny. I'll be back in a minute. I need to sign you in and inform my chatty girl friends that this is definitely a Do Not Disturb night." Miranda kissed Sonny on the check and then disappeared down the hallway.

Sonny flipped the light switch on in Miranda's bathroom. The source of the light were two Victorian gas lantern style brass sconces with cream colored shades on each side of a large oval mirror with a gold gilded frame that hung above an old fashioned white porcelain pedestal sink. The soft light poured over the violet walls and the black and white checkered tiles. An art deco style 1950s glass brick shower stall glowed transparently from the refracted soft cream-colored overhead shower light.

As Sonny was undressing he noticed that unlike most women's bathrooms that he had seen, there were very few signs of the usual array of makeup, perfume, and other concoctions that were a total mystery to him. Sonny did smell the slight scent of frieze; and on the shelf above the towel rack, he saw a squeeze bottle of oil of aloe and white jar of coconut cream. On the sink next to a small metal container of bees wax balm that Sonny imagined she used as an all-purpose lip-gloss was a plastic container of Dr. Bronner's Peppermint Soap.

It was identical to the container of Dr. Bronner's Peppermint Soap that Sonny had in his hand along with his toothbrush and a towel. For many of the children of the 60s, Dr. Bronner's was the Swiss camping knife of cleanliness. Sonny used it to shampoo his hair, shower and bath, brush his teeth, and wash his motorcycle and his dirty clothes. In the shower the downpour of warm water soothed his muscles that had been strained by days of riding a hard sprung scrambler motorcycle and working in People's Park. The excitement of everything new had kept him going, and now it was his passion for Miranda that energized his young body and made him feel renewed.

The shower door opened and Miranda appeared naked and said, "I thought you might need someone to scrub your back."

They kissed and washed each other all over like they were being baptized and cleansed of all the sins and all the people who ever touched them. They were reborn again, anew for one another; and when they went to bed, they began to disappeared into one another; and love became two black holes dancing around each other in a cosmos becoming one, swirling into the darkness that swallowed up all of life, compressing it into the gravity of its nothingness until it burst out on the other side a newborn sun.

In the aftermath, they both stared at one another as if they were looking at their own reflection, and they touched each other gently as if they were discovering themselves for the first time. It's hard to say who closed their eyes first. Maybe it was the candle light going out flicker by flicker as they drifted down into the depths of the ocean like they were floating on a gentle wind spiraling down to the bed of the ocean where a volcano was forming.

Sonny and Miranda woke up to shouts, and there were so many people running around that the house seemed to be shaking like they were in an earthquake. Miranda opened the door of her bedroom and asked, "What's happening?"

"They're tearing up People's Park!" someone shouted.

When Sonny and Miranda went down stairs, it was chaos. Everyone was leaving for the park. It seemed that the police had come in the night with a construction crew and built a chain link fence around the park; and, now, they were bulldozing Paradise.

Miranda was ready to rush out of the house like everyone else but Sonny said, "Wait, I'll be right back."

Sonny ran up the stairway to Miranda's room, and he dug out two bandanas, two pairs of motorcycle goggles, a pairs of leather gloves, and a water bottle. He stuffed them into his daypack, threw it over his shoulder, and ran back down the stairs.

Sonny found Miranda on the front porch watching people pour out of the student apartments and heading for People's Park. When Miranda saw Sonny she grabbed his hand and said, "Are you ready to face the beast?"

Sonny smiled. "As ready as I'll ever be." He also said to himself, "And I'm exposing myself, like I never should, all because I'm crazy about you."

They joined the crowd that grew and grew as they got closer to People's Park. By the time they got to the park there were over a thousand students and local residents outside the park shouting at the city and campus police who were behind the chain link fences that closed off the park. In the background was the tank like clatter of the bulldozers as their steel tracks tore up the new laid sod. A ton of steel slammed into the ground, its steel blade digging up *People's Garden* and then plowing ahead running over newly planted apple trees. Thousands of more students came marching down Telegraph Avenue towards the park chanting, "Take Back the Park!"

Sonny saw Eban who was dressed for battle in combat boots, cargo pants, a leather jacket, and a UC Football helmet leading a group of students bent on tearing down the fences. Seconds later, tear gas was thrown; and then rocks and bricks were thrown in retaliation.

Sonny opened up his daypack, and he wet down the bandanas with the water from his water bottle and gave one to Miranda along with a pair of goggles. Miranda, despite the chaos about her, laughed and said, "You certainly came prepared."

"I've been here before."

Miranda put the bandana over her face like an outlaw from a Hollywood western; and so did Sonny. The goggles protected their eyes, and the leather gloves allowed Sonny to pick up a canister of tear gas that was rolling down the street in front of them and throw it back at the police. All around them there were shouts of anger and rage. A car was set on fire, and a National Guard jeep sped by spewing out a white cloud of smoke screen gas that mingled with the black clouds of tear gas to form snakes of toxic vapor. Behind the smoke screen, hundreds of deputy sheriffs wearing riot gear and carrying shotguns joined the local police.

Sonny turned to see Miranda take off her T-shirt so that she could grab a tear gas canister that was in the middle of the street. Sonny stopped and watched Miranda, bare breasted, throw a perfect pass into the middle of group of cops; and he wished he had a camera to capture her naked courage; but then Sonny heard shots. The deputy sheriffs who were wearing gas masks and were armed with shotguns were firing into the crowds of people.

Sonny saw someone on a rooftop get hit; and Sonny grabbed Miranda and shouted, "Run!"

Miranda put her T-shirt back on, and she and Sonny

ran up Telegraph Avenue towards the university that had been Miranda's parents away from home that had now turned against her. They saw a student go down, shot in the back while running away. His back was riddled with shotgun pellets. Several students stopped to help him. Sonny was shocked. It looked like double-o-buckshot. Double-o-buckshot could tear through a car door at close range.

Sonny turned to see who was pursuing them when he saw a deputy sheriff wearing a gas mask, a riot helmet, and flack jacket run up to Miranda and grab her by the hair. He was ready to smash Miranda in the face with his baton when Sonny grabbed the club by its business end, swirled the deputy around, and smashed him with a football style forearm shiver across the jaw sending him sprawling to the pavement. Sonny now had the baton in his hand; and when he saw the deputy reach for the revolver in his side holster, Sonny cracked him in the head sending his gas mask and riot helmet flying.

Sonny looked down at the deputy's face. His smug piggy eyes looked as if they were hidden behind the movie screen of his own mean minded perverse projections. Sonny heard his father's voice say, "So you like to beat up on women with your wooden dick, you fuckin cock sucker. Here, see if you get off on this."

Sonny grabbed the T baton by the opposite end and swung the handle in between the officer's legs and into his groin causing him to squeeze his legs together in agony with the wooden baton sticking out like a penis. Sonny picked up the revolver that had fallen to the ground, and he raised it. He could hear Eban saying, "Do it, Sonny. Show the son-of-a-bitches that they're not the only ones who can shoot people. Start the revolution right here and now. One shot will do it!"

Miranda grabbed Sonny and shouted, "Stop!"

Sonny turned and stared into Miranda's eyes, and he became himself again. "Look," Miranda said.

He looked down the street, and he saw more cops emerging from the clouds of black smoke. Sonny threw the gun away, and he and Miranda turned and ran off down the street. They cut up an alleyway that led into a parking lot that exited onto a side street; and they were able to get away by following the labyrinth of connected backyards, driveways, and side streets to Miranda's house.

When they got there, they immediately washed out their eyes, took a shower, and scrubbed off the residue of tear gas from their bodies. Rumors and news was pouring in. Hundreds of students were admitted to the hospital suffering from head traumas, shotgun wounds, and respiratory problems brought on by being exposed to the tear gas. Hundreds more were probably injured but didn't go to the hospital in fear of being arrested. James Rector, the kid that Sonny saw get shot on the rooftop, was in critical condition from shotgun wounds. Another student was believed to be permanently blind; and many others were riddled with shotgun wounds on their heads, necks, backs, and legs. It was also confirmed that many of the deputies in the sheriff's office were using double-o-buck shot. There was talk of sit-ins, boycotts, rallies, and outright violence. There were calls to all the other communes and political activist groups. Meetings were being set up, but nothing was settled though it was clear that they would march on the park again tomorrow.

National Cash

That night Sonny and Miranda made love with a desperation that came from a near death experience where every gene shouted out for survival. Sonny growled like a big cat when he came, and his growl turned into a guttural purr, the vibrations sending Miranda into ecstasy as his hands like paws caressing her, his claws contracted as he licked her breast, her nipples, his lips touching the very sensitive tips of her existence.

She looked up at his muscular silhouette. In the background she could see the moon ringed with stars and the red, yellow, and blue lights from the stain glass dancing on the tongue like leaves of the rubber tree. She felt like she was being licked all over by the moonlight, the stars, the jungle like tree, and the beast within who was staring at her with dark pool like eyes.

"Who are you?" she asked.

"I'm you," Sonny said.

The next morning Miranda, Sonny, the students of UC Berkeley, and the residents of the city woke up to discover that they were being invaded by thousands of National Guard troops; and the City of Berkeley had become the first American city to ever be occupied by an American Army since the Civil War. At first, everyone just wandered out onto the streets to watch the spectacle of what seemed to be an endless convoy of trucks and jeeps rumbling through the city, a drab green metal centipede that belched smoke, spite fire, and had a thousand marching feet.

They watched People's Park being turned into an army campsite and a place to park their trucks and jeeps next to the bulldozers. Barricades of barbed wire were set up, and the streets that accessed the park were closed and guarded by soldiers with rifles and fixed bayonets.

A few makeshift signs appeared. One read, *Welcome to Uruguay*, and another read, *"Join Us."* A student dressed as Jesus Christ was carrying The Cross of Private Property and Capitalism, and a sign hanging from his neck read, *All of This for Two Acres of Paradise?*

The next day there was a meeting at Miranda's house that was attended by representatives from all the communes in the Berkeley area. The agenda was to discuss possible political actions and elect representatives to a steering committee that would be made up of all the political action groups on campus for the purpose of determining a strategy for a unified action. Because of the curfew and the suspension of habeas corpus, it was decided to hold the campus wide steering committee meetings in Oakland. Already several meetings on campus were broken up, and the participants were arrested. Everyone was on edge and fearful that at any moment their door could be broken down in a warrantless raid, and they would all be arrested. Many of the students were very angry. They had seen friends and fellow students beaten and shot. Some of them called for a massive confrontation, even violence if necessary.

At this point, Miranda stood up and said, "We can't become them. We have to beat them in the spirit of People's Park. I propose that we surround them. We create a People's Park everywhere in the city. Wherever there is a green space, we plant flowers. We become terrorists and attack them in the night with love and care. Let them fear their mother's touch. That is our greatest weapon against a patriarch that wages war against its own children."

Miranda's speech was met with applause, and it seemed

that she had planted the seeds of an idea that spread from house to house, dorm to dorm, organization to organization. Flower power would surround the war machine and smother it with love.

The battle lines were drawn, and every night the student terrorists attacked, planting flowers in all the parks and any and every available green space in the city. Some of Mother Nature's more aggressive warriors dug up slabs of sidewalk and replaced them with flower gardens. Others were repairing the cracks in the asphalt and concrete roads by ripping them up and planting patches of violets, red and yellow geraniums, pink and orange tulips, sunflowers, and marijuana plants. Other students blocked off roads with strips of sod seeded with flowers and full-grown plants and grass. It was the Flower Children's version of barbed wire, and signs were planted to warn of the dangers ahead. One sign read, *"Beware! Flower Zone."* Another read, *"Beware! This Area is Mined with Seeds of Love."*

Sonny was trying to do his part by calling all his connections at all the universities that he had visited to get support for the People's Park Movement. He was also helping to write leaflets and news releases along with eyewitness accounts and photos to be sent to newspapers throughout the nation so as to let people know what was happening at Berkeley.

When Miranda walked into her room, Sonny was talking on the phone to a friend of his at the University of Oregon about organizing a rally and coordinating it with a press release. "Listen, Dave," Sonny said. I'll send you the news packet. Yes, we're living in a police state here; and if we don't do anything about it, we're the future. Thanks, brother. Up the revolution."

Sonny hung up the phone and turned around to see Miranda dressed all in black. Her face was blackened with wax shoe polish; and she was holding two flower pots, one filled with yellow daisies and another with red, white, and blue tulips. She smiled and said, "Are you ready again to take on the Beast?" She held up the two flowerpots. "This time we are fully armed."

Sonny winced and then asked, "Where are we going?"

"Into the heart of darkness."

"I was afraid of that."

Miranda handed him one of the pots, took out the can of black shoe polish she had in her pocket, and painted streaks of war paint on Sonny's face. She laughed, and said, "There. Now you're ready."

When they went down stairs, there were over twenty members of the commune armed with flowers and dressed in dark clothing ready to go. They were organized in pairs and fours, and they each had a destination. When they were outside, Sonny turned to Miranda and said, "Where they were going?"

"The Park."

Sonny smiled. "Why did I ask?"

"Come on," Miranda said. "Follow me."

So like a good puppy in love, Sonny followed Miranda into the war zone. They kept to the side streets, backyards, and alleyways, and away from streetlights. If they were caught by the National Guard patrols, they would be immediately arrested for violating the curfew. If they were caught by "The Blue Meanies," who were the off-duty cops that roamed the streets looking for students, they would be beaten. On campus, the students in the dormitories had synchronized their radios to the campus radio station and put their speakers in the window so as to fill the air with an eerie electronic tribal music that vibrated throughout the city turning it into an instrument of suspended tension as Paul Simon sang,

> *"Hello darkness, my old friend.*
> *I've come to talk to you again,*
> *Because a vision softly creeping*
> *Left its seeds while I was sleeping,*
> *And the vision that was planted in my brain,*
> *Still remains,*
> *Within the sounds of silence."*

Hidden within the sounds of silence, Sonny could feel the Leviathan. It was there. He was right. It did come out of the depths of the darkness from our collective unconscious, unrestrained by reason and empathy, and now it had a life of its own. He could feel the evil, the vibrations of its breath creating an atonal resonance, its sharp steel claws scratching the electrified air. As Miranda and he were standing in the dark shadows of an alleyway next to a boarded up Indian restaurant; he could feel it all around them. Many of the stores were boarded up in response to the occupation and the student sit-ins and protest marches; and Berkeley looked like a ghost town except for the music and the students who were now banging garbage can lids together like shields as background percussion to the Rolling Stones singing, *"War, children, it's just a shot away."*

Miranda was ready to bolt across the street when

Sonny stopped her. He could hear what sounded like drum sticks banging together, and then he saw them. Two Blue Meanies were walking down the middle of the street banging their nightsticks together to the beat. The Blue Meanies were wearing their blue uniforms without an identification tag, and their faces were hidden behind Halloween masks. One was Frankenstein, half human, half machine with electrodes sticking out of the side of his head, his face made of cadaver skin crudely stitched together. The other was Wolf Man, half human, half animal, blood dripping from his fangs. They approached a darkened entranceway to a building, and a skull appeared out of the darkness with lifeless eyes. Then a Devil Clown appeared who had crazy eyes and was laughing at the sadistic fun of playing hide-and-go-seek with the children.

Just as Sonny was going to suggest that they try to cross the street further down the road, three students appeared from Parker Street armed with what looked like marijuana plants. They were about to plant them in a pothole in the middle of the road when all four Blue Meanies came running out of their hiding place. The students saw them coming, dropped their plants, and ran back down Parker Street with the Blue Meanies in pursuit.

Sonny didn't know who the students were, but they looked athletic, and they could run. Sonny doubted that the Blue Meanies would catch them; so he turned to Miranda and said, "Let's go," and they ran across the street and disappeared into an alley and then into the back lots and trees. It was so dark amidst the trees that he could barely see Miranda who was carrying the yellow daisies like a candle light in the dark. They crossed Regent Street on the run, and Miranda once again led him through the darkness. She opened the gate to a backyard fence, walked across a lawn and up the stairs to the back porch of a very large old house and knocked on the door.

The door opened, and it was Herbie, from the commune. Herbie smiled and said, "Hi, Miranda. Hello Ranger." We've been waiting for you.

There were four students in the apartment, Herbie, Archie, Heather, and Jennifer; and Sonny guessed they were couples. As they passed through the kitchen to the living room, it was obvious that the house, like so many student apartment buildings, had been broken up into as many apartments; and the landlord had done as little as possible to maintain what had once been a beautiful turn of the century home with tall ceilings and a broken down marble fireplace in the living room. The cracks in the ceilings were covered over by a false ceiling of Styrofoam squares that were water stained, and the deteriorating plaster walls were covered over by fake wood paneling. The furniture looked as if it was donated by a parent who had cleaned out their mother's house after she went to a nursing home or died. The furniture was expensive but worn and not really of antique quality, but it created a cushioned generational presence that was comforting.

On the walls were quality copies of two famous posters. One was an art nouveau poster by Alfon Mucha of a beautiful young girl growing out of floral lines and a plant motif, her golden hair a living light shaped by a crown of white daisies. She was holding up a drawing board with a heart in the middle that was threatened by the thistles of stupidity, the thorns of genius, and the blossoms of love. The other poster was *The Kiss* by Gustave Klimt, a poster where straight lines and rectangles embraced swirls and circles, and white light was transformed by the mysterious shapes of darkness into the Sun God kissing Danae. The two lovers were surrounded by a golden Byzantine aura and a mosaic of brilliant impressionistic colors slipping down like a silken gown into a bed of flowers on the edge of an escarpment where lesions of love were rooted in the impenetrable amidst the fall of naked transparency.

The windows were decorated with hanging plants, and the living room floor was covered with pots of flowers – daisies, petunias, geraniums, tulips, and even large sunflower plants. "I see," Sonny said. "This is a munitions dump."

Miranda smiled and set down her plant on the floor and said, "Come, see."

She knelt down next to the large front window and cautiously pushed the curtain of orange and green scrolling Indian mandalas aside just far enough so that Sonny could see that they were on Dwight Way, directly across the street from People's Park, the chain link fences, and a wooded area at the edge of the park. Some troop trucks and jeeps were parked near the fence and beyond that was a bivouac of troop tents.

Herbie, who was standing behind Sonny said, "We created a diversion earlier, and we were able to cut part of the fence with wire cutters. It's held together now with garbage ties. See, the post to your left, near the trees. See how it sticks out a little at the bottom? We didn't do such great a job there. We had to hurry, but so far no one has noticed."

"I see," Sonny said.

Miranda grabbed the pot of red, white, and blue tulips;

and Sonny grabbed a pot of yellow daisies from the munitions dump. It was decided that they would rely on Herbie, Archie, Heather, and Jennifer to watch out for the police and the military patrols. Miranda and he would hide in the hedges outside, and Herbie would give them the go ahead by blinking a flashlight, just like in a black and white late night spy movie.

Miranda and Sonny left the house; and as soon as the latch on the front door clicked shut, Sonny knew there was no return. Being outside again was particularly eerie because everything all of a sudden seemed so normal. The music had stopped, and all Sonny could hear was the electronic buzz of the street lights and the chirp of a cricket nearby. When he settled into the silence, he could see fireflies flickering about on the lawn and in the park.

The flashlight blinked in the front window of the house, and Sonny and Miranda ran across the street. They found the ties that held the lower end of the chain link fence together, untied them, and slipped through the opening with their plants. Using the trees and the parked army trucks for cover, Sonny looked around trying to figure out where he would plant his flowers. He saw a bulldozer parked near one of the trucks, and he decided that he would plant his pot of daisies in the exhaust pipe that was sticking up vertically, high above the engine block of the bulldozer. He turned to tell Miranda, but she was gone. He then saw her crawling towards the dark olive green tents. There was laughter from one of the tents, and several of the tents were glowing from the lanterns within.

The flap of a nearby tent opened up like a bat taking flight, and a soldier appeared. He was walking straight to where the trucks were parked, and he seemed to be walking straight towards Sonny, but then he stepped into the darkness nearby, and Sonny could hear him unzip his pants and pee so loud that it sounded like a waterfall in the darkness. When he was done, the soldier retraced his steps and disappeared back into the tent. Miranda reappeared from the darkness, and Sonny was trying to figure where she was going when he saw it.

Some soldier had stuck a bayonet into a small tree next to the nearest tent and hung a battle helmet from the bayonet to use as a water bucket. Above the helmet he had hung a mirror. He probably was using it to brush his teeth, wash his face, and shave. Miranda reached up and pulled the helmet down and planted the red, white, blue tulips in it. She then hung the battle helmet turned hanging plant back up on the bayonet.

Miranda snuck through the darkness back to where Sonny was standing, and she was flushed with excitement. Her eyes nearly glowed in the dark like a wild animal at night. Sonny smiled and said, "I don't believe you. I'll be right back."

Sonny kept low and used the trucks to screen his movement. He climbed up onto the bulldozer, reached up and planted the daisies in the exhaust pipe, and then hurried back to where Miranda was waiting for him between the troop trucks. They were about to retreat back the way they came when a match flared, and they were looking into the face of a soldier who was lighting a joint of marijuana.

The soldier, who was an African American teenager hiding his age behind a mustache and long sideburns, took a toke from the joint and then handed it to Miranda and said,

"You two are crazy, man. They catch you here, and you are truly fucked."

Miranda took a toke off the joint, handed it to Sonny who said, "Where you from?"

"I'm from Oakland, man; but I've been goin to San Francisco State College part time and doin this National Guard shit to stay out of the draft. Dig?"

He looked around to see if anyone was coming and then said, "This is all weird shit, man. I don't even know what the fuck we're doin here." He took another toke out of the joint that Sonny handed him and said, "You got to go, man. They be changin sentries soon, and some of these crackers would love to beat on you. You all Niggers to them."

"I'm hip," Sonny said. "Come on, Miranda."

"What's your name?" Miranda asked.

"Ronnie Wright."

Miranda hugged him and said, "Thanks, Ronnie Wright."

They were about to leave when Ronnie said, "Wait." He took a sheet of folded up paper out of his shirt pocket, wrote something on it, folded it back up, and then handed it to Miranda and said, "Now get the fuck out of here before we all get caught."

Miranda and Sonny disappeared back into the darkness. They slipped through the fence and crossed Dwight Way without being spotted; and once they crossed Telegraph Avenue, they ran like hell, stoked by what they had just done. They burst into the front door of the commune laughing; and when they were safely in Miranda's room, they frantically took off one another's clothes and made love in celebration of their triumph. Miranda opened herself up like a flower, and they were like the Gustave Klint painting, *The Kiss*. They both fell off the edge, a golden aura of falling flowers and bright bursts of color that crashed down to the rocks below and the swirling waters that were like hands that carried away particles of the impenetrable.

After they came together, they laid in bed, their arms around each other, looking out the window at the golden moon and the stars beyond, the orange, green, and blue lights of the stained glass fusing into each other, dancing on the tongue of the tropical leaves, the last drops of a sparkling potion of passion that lingered to be savored.

"Oh, I forgot," Miranda said. She got up and looked through her pants and pulled out the folded sheet of paper that the soldier had given her. She turned on a light, sat cross-legged on the bed next to Sonny, and read it. She then handed it to Sonny who read the leaflet.

To Our Fellow Students

The Nation Guardsmen are not pigs. They are young people and teenagers like us who just want to have a good time, a life of their own, and a future to look forward to.

Most of them, like us, do not want to go to Vietnam. That is why they are in the National Guards, but now they are occupying an American city because we wanted to build a public park and turn a neglected trash ridden mud hole into a little bit of Paradise for all.

National Cash

To The National Guardsmen

Talk to your brothers and sisters here. Find out what is happening, man. Resist when you can and get hip. There is no compromise with the rich old white men who want you to go to far off Vietnam to fight an imperial war or turn your guns on your fellow citizens here at home.

Trust no one over thirty. Trust us, not them, and join the Movement. Resist anyway you can, and, remember, we are fighting for you. We are fighting for all young people in the country. We want Peace not War. We want Love not Hate. We want a future that belongs to us, not them. People's Park was built for you.

Across the page was Ronnie Wright's handwritten message shouting out, *"Help!"*

"Wow," was all Sonny could say. It was one of the leaflets that he had written.

"We can't let him down," Miranda said.

"No, we can't," Sonny said. Sonny kissed Miranda, who turned off the light, and they snuggled up dreaming of all the things they would do only to wake up the next day to discover that James Rector had died in the night at 10:12 PM while they were planting flowers in People's Park. He died of acute heart failure resulting from double-o-shotgun wounds in the stomach, spleen, pancreas, kidney, and portions

163

of his large and small intestines. A silent mourning descended on the campus and the city, and there was a memorial scheduled for James Rector to be held that afternoon in front of the administrative offices at Sproul Hall. After that there was a rally scheduled in Sproul Plaza for a campus wide referendum on People's Park.

Everyone was apprehensive. They had already torn off the mask of friendly fascism from the face of Ronald Reagan to reveal the monster within. Now there were rumors of tanks parked at the Marina; and today Sonny and Miranda and thousands of other young students were going to lay their bodies and lives on the line and bare witness to the fact that America was murdering its youth, not just the kids in Berkeley, nor just the dreams and hopes of a generation, but the youth of a nation. The past was murdering the future, forever; and America was turning in on itself and becoming a closed society.

Earlier that morning, a house meeting was called at the commune to discuss what was happening and what they were going to do. Information sheets were passed out and experiences were shared to help people prepare themselves for what could be a violent confrontation. After a silent prayer for James Rector, the meeting was adjourned with an announcement that they were having homemade pizza for lunch and all the Coca Cola they could drink. With a cheer they rushed into the dining room and devoured the pizza and coke like children at a birthday party with hopes of cake in the end. For the moment they had forgotten all their fears and were absorbed in the pleasure of what they liked.

After lunch Miranda and Sonny went to her room and dressed for the memorial and rally. They wore long sleeve shirts and layered clothing, running shoes, motorcycle helmets, and goggles. In their daypacks they put a bandana soaked in vinegar, bottles of water with baking soda to cleanse their eyes and hands, and a clean hand towel and a bar of soap in a plastic bag. On their wrists they printed the phone numbers of legal aid services and lawyers who had volunteered to help them. Everyone had written down their parent's phone numbers and their home addresses in the house directory in case they couldn't make bail or they were hurt badly. They also had to sign out if they were going to the rally, and they had to sign in or call in by dinnertime, or it would be assumed that they were missing in action.

At the meeting, Dave Wycoff, the commune's representative to the People's Park Steering Committee stressed that above all else there could be no violence. He warned that the police may try to provoke them, and they may try to seed the crowd with agent provocateurs. "If you see them, stop them," he said. "They would love to portray us as a violent mob; so, no matter what, remember, we have to keep to our principles. This is about love not hate, peace not war."

This was very hard for Sonny. He had never in his life turned his back on a fight and to stand there and take a beating was against his very nature. Yet, he had to do it, whether he wanted to or not. He had to follow Miranda and give love and peace a chance.

Miranda and Sonny helped set up the first aid table in the dining room, so they were late leaving for the rally, but even then there was still a large flow of people walking up Telegraph Street to get to Sproul Plaza. When they got there, things were worse than Sonny had imagined. The students in Sproul Plaza were ringed with Nation Guard troops wearing gas masks and carrying M-1 rifles with fixed bayonets pointed at the students. Behind the masks were teenagers with their own individuality, but now they were non-human parts of the machine. They had no minds of their own. They were the hands and arms and legs of an organism whose brain was somewhere else up in the chain of command.

Miranda was about to enter the Plaza when Sonny realized that it was a trap. He grabbed Miranda and said, "Stop. Look. They're letting people in, but they are not letting them out. See." Sonny pointed to a couple who were trying to leave, and the Guardsmen were holding them back.

"There. Look," Miranda said and pointed to another group of students. "You're right. They are holding them back there too."

"It's a honey pot," Sonny said.

He was about to warn people when he heard the helicopter overhead. White clouds of tear gas descended upon the students in the Plaza below causing them to panic as the troops closed in. The gas was like nothing Sonny had ever experienced before. Even with a bandana and goggles on, the gas was seeping into his eyes, mouth, throat, and nose. It felt like he had just swallowed an extremely hot chili pepper. His eyes were watering, but he could see students running in every direction. The air was full of screams. He heard someone cry out that they were blind, and he saw other students wandering around disoriented as the troops and the police closed in. People were being beaten and arrested while they were still holding their throats gasping for air from the effects of the tear gas. Sonny saw one student bent over vomiting from the effects of the tear gas get smashed in the back with the butt end of an M-1 rifle by a faceless Guardsman with plastic bug eyes and gills for a mouth. He watched the student go sprawling to the pavement vomiting all over himself as a young coed stood by horror stricken, her eyes full of tears as another faceless Guardsman grabbed her by the hair and dragged her off into her own horror story.

Sonny turned to look for Miranda. Miranda was helping a girl who was shaking her hands hysterically like she was trying to shake something evil off, but she couldn't because it was all around here. She was a tall and lean girl with long blond hair and pleasant features; and she was wearing white shorts and tennis sneakers and a bright green T-shirt with bold bright red letter that read, *Surf's Up*. She even had make-up on. She obviously had no idea of the danger that she was in by coming to the Plaza, and now her whole body was covered with rashes and blotches of red. They had to get her out of there.

Sonny came up to Miranda who was trying to calm the girl; and at the same time, wash her eyes out. "Are you all right?" he asked Miranda.

"I'm feeling nauseous, and I'm having a hard time breathing."

"How about her?"

"That stuff temporarily blinded her, but at least now she can see."

Sonny put his arm around the girl's shoulders and asked, "Can you run?"

The girl nodded, and Sonny said, "OK, we're running down this road towards college town, and we keep going until the air clears."

Miranda grabbed the girl's hand and said, "Come on, Susie, let's go," and they all started running down Telegraph Street along with thousands of students who had broken out of the Plaza. When they got near downtown Berkeley, Sonny took off his goggles and mask; and he immediately started coughing, "Jesus, they've gassed the whole god damned town. Come on, let's keep going."

They kept running, and as they neared the commune, the air began to clear and the effects of their exposure began to wear off. They were all exhausted, so Miranda made them stop at a gray two story stucco house with green trim that had an outdoor water outlet. With the clean hand towels and soap that Sonny still had in his backpack, they all washed their hands and faces thoroughly. Sonny rinsed his mouth out and then took a drink of fresh water, and he felt much better.

A middle aged woman, who was wearing a cotton dress with a floral pattern and had her hair tied back in a neat bun, came out onto her front porch that was decorated with hanging plants of red geraniums flowers and said, "My God, what happened?"

"We were gassed," Miranda said.

"Where?"

"On campus."

"Good Lord," the woman said, "and it carried all the way over here. I had to close the windows, and my daughter called me. She is a nurse at Cowell Memorial Hospital; and the tear gas was so intense there that it interrupted operations, endangered patients with respiratory illnesses, and put many of the nurses out of commission. One patient had to be put in an oxygen tent, or he would have died." She looked at Susie who looked totally miserable, and said, "Do you need anything? You could come inside and wash up properly, and I could wash your clothes for you."

"Thank you, that is very kind," Miranda said, "but we live nearby, and we have everything we need there. If we come into your house, all we're going to do is contaminate it; and it's going to be a mess for you to clean up. It's like someone poured cayenne pepper all over us."

The woman thought for a moment and then looked at Susie again and said, "Wait." She went inside and came back with a plastic squeeze bottle and handed it to Susie and said, "My daughter, the nurse, told me that if I broke out with a rash or anything that I should us this. You treat it like a sun burn, and this should work."

"Thank you," Susie said, holding the bottle like it was the cure to all her misery.

The woman took one last look at Miranda, Sonny, and Susie before she went back into her home. Shaking her head in dismay she said, "You're just children. If that stupid man in Sacramento who I voted for had just been patient, he could have simply waited for you kids to graduate; and the day to day realities of life would have defeated you; but now look." She smiled. "You won't forgive him. Will you?"

Miranda clenched her fists, "Never!"

The woman shook her head again then closed the door behind her; and Sonny, Miranda, and Susie walked the rest of the way back to the commune. When they got to the house, the dinner table was set up for them. There was a box of surgical gloves to wear and garbage bags to put their contaminated clothes. There were bottles of antihistamines, aspirins, milk of magnesia, and skin lotions for burns. There were also stacks of clean towels and individually wrapped packages of soaps.

Sonny, Miranda, and Susie went up to her room, stripped off their clothes, and they each took a shower. Miranda gave Susie an antihistamine, and then Miranda and Susie went in search of clothing for Susie. Sonny took some milk of magnesia for his stomach and changed into clean clothes and then fell back on the bed thinking that maybe Eban was right. Maybe not now, but sometime in the future there would be a truly bloody civil war; and he must ready himself because he was never going to stand by again and watch innocent people be brutalized like they were today.

As he was lying in bed he watched Miranda and Susie running all about, coming in and out of the bedroom, going into the bathroom, trying on clothes. Susie had called her friends who lived nearby, and she was going to go there. Later, hopefully they could drive her back to her dorm. All her clothes were contaminated, so now the fun seemed to be in getting her dressed to leave. There were giggles and laughs. They seemed totally oblivious to him.

He heard Miranda say, "What do you think?"

Susie was wearing a plum colored silk spaghetti strap T-shirt and a light tan Western Indian style leather vest with long leather tassels along the sleeves and the hem of the vest. She was also wearing a matching tan leather belt tied together by large brass decorative rings and long leather laces hung low below her exposed navel and her low rise light blue bell bottom pants with holes in the knees. Peeking out of the bellbottoms were nomad sandals and pink toenails. On her head she was wearing a mauve colored silk scarf, gypsy style, with one end of the scarf draping down over her shoulder. Someone had airbrushed violet flower petals, transparent like sexy silk lingerie around her cheeks and eyes to blend in with the dark purple mascara and violet eye shadow that highlighted her sky blue eyes with flecks of green. A wild white daisy that was pinned to her golden hair brushed the violet flower petals on her cheek and made everything seem real.

"She looks beautiful," Sonny said, and it was true. Miranda had turned the sorority girl from San Diego into a beautiful hippie girl, and now Susie had forgotten all about the ordeal that she had just gone through. She was beautiful again and all was forgiven.

She hugged Miranda and said, "I love you," and then she turned to Sonny who was standing up now, and she hugged him so tight that he could feel her breasts against his chest. He could smell lilacs when she said, "And I love you too." She looked like she was about to kiss him, but then she stopped, turned to Miranda and said, "Well, I guess it is time to go, Miranda. I'll bring the clothes back as soon as I can get into my dorm room. Probably by tomorrow, I would think."

She then looked at Sonny in the same way she looked at him when she was about to kiss him and then whispered in Miranda's ear, squeezed her hand, and then she was gone.

"What was that all about?" Sonny asked.

"What?" Miranda asked.

"The whispering."

"Oh, she said that you were gorgeous, and she was never going to forget you. You're her hero for life."

"Oh, come on. You did more for her than me."

"That's true, but she won't want to fantasize about

me when she masturbates at night. She is going to want you."

"What are you talking about, Miranda."

"She is going to marry Mr. Right. He'll probably be good looking and be a corporate CEO or a high tech type; and they will have a beautiful home in Marin County or Silicon Valley; but every once in a while, when she is feeling particularly depressed about her totally scripted life, you will come to her in her fantasies at night while she is sleeping next to her husband; and you will make love to her in ways that her husband could never do because you are free, sensitive, and courageous. You are everything she could never be and feel secure. But, she can have her life long affair with you, and no one will ever know."

Sonny laughed and said, "You are weird, Miranda. Or maybe I just should say that you're a woman and the two terms are mutually inclusive. Would you do such a thing?"

Miranda grabbed Sonny's arm gently; and as she was leading him out the door she said, "Of course not. I have my fantasy man, and he's quite real."

Sonny paused at the door, thought for a moment, smiled and said, "Miranda, that is quite flattering, but why is it that I hear Homer saying to Ulysses, 'Beware Ulysses, you are in the grasp of the Sirens, and you are beyond your depths.' " Sonny kissed Miranda passionately then whispered in her ear, "And I don't care."

Miranda laughed, and they both went down stairs to see if everyone got back safely and to hear the latest news. Bob Ward and Rachel Swartz were in the emergency room being treated for respiratory complications, but it was expected that they would be released soon. The hospitals were overflowing with students and Berkeley residents suffering from tear gas related symptoms and bruises and concussion suffered from the beatings they took at the hands of the local police and the Guardsmen. Judging from the relatively small number of arrests, it would seem that the police were content with inflicting suffering and pain. In many instances, they just left students in the Plaza seriously injured without giving aid. They just walked away like bullies in a schoolyard. However, they went too far this time. They not only gassed Lowell Memorial Hospital, but they also gassed Jefferson and Franklin Elementary School where it caused many tears and enraged parents. The hospitals analyzed the tear gas used in the gassing of Berkeley, and it was reported that it was, as Sonny suspected, CS tear gas, a gas developed for Vietnam and outlawed by the Geneva Convention.

By the next day it was decided that these acts of brutal sadistic stupidity had turned public opinion their way, and it was time to organize a massive march on People's Park. They would call on the whole community and students throughout the state to join them.

Sonny and Miranda talked things over, and they decided that he should go on the road and plant seeds again. This time the message would be come to Berkeley and join the march on People's Park. Sonny was certain that the roads were going to be carefully patrolled, and campus police and law enforcement in most campus towns were going to be looking for "outside agitators," so Sonny decided to use a disguise that he used before when he was going from campus to campus. Sonny rented a four door white Ford sedan, and he hung up a three-piece suit and a tie on a coat hanger above the back seat door. He wore kakis, brown cordovan shoes, a button down white dress shirt; and he casually hung an olive green herringbone sport jacket over the front passenger seat. On the front passenger seat, he also placed an open briefcase that featured Oxford University Press stationary; and in his wallet, he stuffed some Oxford University Press business cards conspicuously next to his driver's license.

Miranda trimmed his hair and put nonprescription wire rim glasses on him and said, "There. You look like a defrocked professor looking for a new career in publishing."

"Thank Archie for me," Sonny said. Archie Cowen was an English Literature Instructor at UC and a member of the commune. He loaned the clothes to Sonny for the trip, and Eban gave him the stationary and the business cards.

Sonny kissed Miranda goodbye, and he went on the road going from campus to campus. He had posters hidden in the car that he put up in conspicuous places, and he placed ads in the local campus newspapers announcing the march. He visited with local student activists and even reached out to fraternity and sorority organizations that were surprisingly supportive. Reagan had fouled the nest and violated the traditional sanctuary of the university, and even the most conservative of students found this a threat to their own well being. Somehow they understood that Reagan had attacked youth itself.

Sonny drove day and night, and he went as far south as Arizona and as far north as Oregon. When he got back to Berkeley the day before the march, Miranda immediately put him to bed, made love to him, and then took him out to dinner for pizza and beer at La Val's where she told him all that was happening while he was gone.

"Things got bad after you left," she said. "We tried to march on downtown, but they broke it up. They arrested over four hundred of us, and they put everyone on the Santo Rita Prison Farm. It was awful. They made everyone lay on gravel all day long and treated us like we were Viet Cong prisoners of war. But once again they went too far. *The San Francisco Chronicle* wrote a front-page expose demanding an investigation into the mistreatment of the students. Then the Berkeley City Council voted to encourage the Regents to allow them to rebuild the park, and students voted in a referendum overwhelmingly for People's Park in the largest voting turnout in the history of the university. Out of almost fifteen thousand votes we received nearly thirteen thousand votes. We also created a People' Park Annex on Hearst Street. It's a mirror image of the original. And... nine thousand students from all around the state conducted a peaceful protest in front of the State Capitol Building in Sacramento against the seizure of People's Park and the occupation of the City of Berkeley."

Miranda hugged Sonny and said, "I'm sure you had something to do with that. Now people are coming to Berkeley from all over to march on People's Park tomorrow. They estimate that there will be over thirty thousand people marching. And get this. Two sweet old ladies donated thirty thousand daisies for the march, and the Quakers have come in to organize the march and train marshals to insure that the march is peaceful."

Miranda hugged Sonny and said, "You made this happen, Sonny. Many people are here because of the work you've done."

Sonny smiled. He didn't really know how much he

did. So many people were doing so many things simultaneously that it was hard to determine who did what except that they were all of one heart and somehow that caused everything to converge into this moment of truth.

After dinner, Miranda said, "I want to show you something. Let's go to the park."

"What about the curfew?" Sonny asked.

"They're in retreat."

Sonny fired up his motorcycle, and they drove towards People's Park. Sonny was a bit nervous. He was wondering what Miranda was getting him into now. He did notice though that things seemed different. There was a noticeable absence of cops and Guardsmen on the streets, and he could no longer feel the presence of evil in the air nor could he see the strange glow that Berkeley took on at night during the occupation, as if it was being seen through the eyes of something that wasn't human and ate light. As they neared the Park, Sony felt like he was tripping. It seemed like he was driving his motorcycle into a milky way of flickering stars, and then he realized that thousands of students and Berkeley residence had surrounded People's Park in a candle light vigil. There was no sound at all. It was as if the universe had stood still for a moment just to listen to itself breath. Sonny felt totally refreshed and hopeful.

The next day it was bedlam. Everyone was converging around the People's Park Annex for the march. The marshals were giving orders through megaphones and herding everyone in. Sonny and Miranda were in a vanguard of over fifty motorcycles. Sonny saw some Hell's Angels amongst the motorcyclists, and he wondered what they all must look like to the National Guardsmen in the park - thirty thousand people descending upon them like a tsunami wave of humanity with flower children running along the edge of the marchers handing out daisies, putting them in the hair of policeman who were standing by smiling, totally overwhelmed, now merely spectators to something so vast that it could swallow them up like the back tow of the ocean.

Like a tail, the marchers left behind grass sod where there had been asphalt and concrete, and bare breasted girls showered the sod with flower seeds. Overhead, a helicopter was flying with a banner trailing behind that read, *LET A THOUSAND PARKS BLOOM.*

When they reached the park on Dwight Way the flower children stuck daises into the barrels of the Guardsmen's rifles and weaved flowers into the chain link fence creating a tapestry of color as the sound system on a flat bed truck blasted out the Beatle's singing, *"All You Need is Love."*

Maybe love could conquer all, Sonny thought. Maybe Miranda was right and women should take over the leadership of this country and care for it like a family, everyone related to one another in the pursuit of the common good, beauty everywhere. All the children in the world would become our children, and Mother Nature would embrace all, making sure that every child had its place in the sun.

Behind the park fence Sonny saw a Guardsmen waving at him, and he realized that it was Ronnie Wright. "Look, Miranda," Sonny shouted. "It's Ronnie."

Miranda waved to Ronnie, and he held up the combat helmet with the potted red, white, and blue tulips. Ronnie had saved them.

Sonny was swallowed up by the massive goodwill that pervaded it all, and it was the first time in his life that he ever experienced the pure joy of the spirit of life that was magnified by each and every one of them. Sonny listened to John Lennon sing, and the words vibrating throughout Berkeley, a message to the generations to come.

"You may say I'm a dreamer,
But I'm not the only one
I hope someday you'll join us,
And the world will live as one."

After the March on People's Park, Miranda and Sonny prepared to leave Berkeley for Ithaca. Sonny made some calls, and found an apartment. He was familiar with the building. Some friends of his had lived there, and he knew the landlord. The third floor apartment was on Eddy Street next to the old entranceway to Cornell, and it overlooked the city and the lake. Miranda and Sonny packed up her things, and they arranged for a moving company to deliver her stuff to Ithaca in two weeks. When everything was arranged, Miranda said her tearful goodbyes to her friends with pledges of eternal friendship, jumped on the back of Sonny's Ariel motorcycle and off they went, super tramps making love to America.

They made love in the golden green grass of Big Sur with the ocean playing its symphony of waves and crashing symbols, the percussion of water against sand and the booming of the bass. The sun turned the peaks of the waves into silver, and their bodies glistened waiting for the words of love that came over and over again. They came in Glacier Park amidst the verdant greens and gray and white veined stone cliffs looking down into mirror like pools of water that reflected the blue sky, the evergreens, the red and yellow wild flowers, and the snow peaked blue gray mountains. The motorcycle roared across Utah passed red stone memories sculpted over millions upon millions of year from long gone mountains and valleys and rivers, now immortal profiles of the beauty of death.

They roared across these ancient museums of nature at the peak of their youth. They were in love; and they felt immortal and free as their hair blew wild in the wind like filaments of light connected to the rays of the sun that touched their very being at every point, every moment, making them one with everything it touched, every grain of sand, words of green giving birth to hundreds of miles of golden cornfields.

When they arrived in Ithaca, they camped under a fragmented mirror of stars that flickered through a tapestry of leaves and towering trees that formed a cathedral of nature, the sounds of Buttermilk Falls echoing through the glacial gorges like a chorus as they danced naked around a campfire, the flames licking at their flesh as The Grateful Dead sang,

> *"Dark star crashes,*
> *Pouring its light into ashes.*
> *Reason tatters,*
> *The forces tear loose from the axis,*
> *Searchlight casting for faults in the clouds*
> *delusion.*

National Cash

Shall we go, you and I while we can,
Through the transitive nightfall of
diamonds?"

When Sonny and Miranda arrived in Ithaca, they moved into the apartment on Eddy Street, and everything seemed to be coming together. Sonny was in love, and the movement was gaining momentum. On October 15th the Moratorium to End the War in Vietnam was conducted throughout the United States. Hundreds of colleges and high schools were closed; millions of Americans wore black armbands; and people from all walks of life joined the marches, rallies, vigils, and teach-ins; but then on May 4th, 1970 at Kent State University, in the heart of America, without provocation, twenty-eight National Guardsmen fired on several hundred unarmed and defenseless students who were part of a peaceful demonstration protesting the war, ROTC, and the oppressiveness of the university.

Thirteen seconds later, four students were dead, and nine other students were wounded, one student paralyzed for life. Nineteen-year-old Sandra Scheuer, an honor student in speech therapy, lay dead, shot in the neck. Her only crime was walking across campus to her next class. Just a few hours before she was looking in the mirror and wondering if the new blouse that she recently bought was the right shade of green for the color of her hair. On the bed was a teddy bear that she had as a child. Just the touch of the fur reassured her that she was surrounded by people who cared for her.

Allison Krause was also an honor student, and she was barely twenty years old. Her father was a Holocaust survivor, and she believed that she was protesting Fascism in America. She had heard about the riots the night before in downtown Kent City, but it sounded more like a drunken brawl than a protest. Today, she thought the protest would be more sober and peaceful; but if the police tried to stop them, she was prepared to go to jail. If she was going to be a liberated woman she had to learn to stand up to power; and someday when she was old, she would tell her granddaughters how she had taken on the man in the name of democracy. Before she left her room she glanced in the mirror and wondered if she was really pretty, and she wondered if the boy who was sitting next to her in literature class would be at the protest. He smiled at her the other day, and she was a sucker for boys with blond hair and blue eyes. She also wondered where she was going to eat that night. She felt like Chinese.

An hour later, an M-1 rifle bullet that was designed to tear through a tree and kill Germans and Japs ripped through her body and tore up her wonder and she laid dead in a pool of blood. William Schroeder was nineteen, and he was an Eagle Scout who had won an Association of the United States Army award in history. He was walking across campus to class wondering if he was going to win an ROTC officer's training scholarship when he was hit in the back, the bullet passing through his vital organs exiting the other side leaving him bleeding to death with an expression of wonder on his face. What had happened to him? What did he miss? What didn't he know about his country, and what was Jeffrey Glen Miller saying when he was shot in the mouth. If you could read dead lips, the message was clear.

All the wonder of youth was gone. It had once existed between the lines where dreams were made and infinite possibilities dwelled, but now it was a place where nightmares roamed and the message was clear. It was written in blood. The killing of James Rector at People's Park was no mistake. America had become a Greek Tragedy where they were killing their own children, and the Furies were loose.

In the next four days there were over a hundred campus demonstrations per day involving half the colleges and universities in the country and over four million students. Ohio, Kentucky, and South Carolina declared all campuses in a state of emergency; and the National Guard were called in twenty four times at twenty-one universities in sixteen states. Five hundred and thirty six schools were completely shut down for extended periods of time with fifty-one of them closing down for the school year. In the first week of May, thirty ROTC buildings on college campuses were burned or bombed at the rate of four a day; and by the end of the month, there were no fewer than one hundred and sixty nine incidents of bombings and arson, ninety five of them occurred on college campuses and another thirty six targeted government and corporate buildings. At the peak of the uprising, there were over a million people who saw themselves as revolutionaries, and it was estimated that they were supported by as many as a fifth of the population, or approximately 40 million people. Then why couldn't they win?

The answer was clear to Sonny, but this answer was written in confusion. They had not got their message across to the vast majority of working class people in the country, and the generation gap had become a chasm that they had helped intensify by not developing a central vision that would bring the generations together and link the past with the future. They had not developed a clear vision of a workable and well thought out alternative economic and political system that would bring about a truly democratic society and support and nurture the emergence of the new quantum man. Sonny could see flashes of this vision, but he was only seeing the outer edges of the metaphors that he believed could become the starbursts of a new reality.

Sonny went back to his studies. He was convinced that he could find the answers, but was it too late? With the withdrawal from Vietnam, the movement had lost its momentum; and it was breaking up into its compound parts like a kaleidoscope of broken dreams. The revolution was over, and the dreams of millions of young Americans were stillborn, and what could have become an American cultural and political renaissance was dead, and the right wing counter-revolution had begun. He could see it in the money and the lobbyists pouring into Washington, the right wing think tanks and trade associations forming and the corporations merging and swallowing up all the information resources and means of communications creating the dream machines that churned out advertisements, movies, and TV shows glorifying greed and narcissism.

The Leviathan was emerging as a complex of giant corporations that were transcending the nation-state and creating a world of corporate feudalism that would usher in a new Dark Age with Fortress America being the castle-keep. He had seen it from the beginning, but no one listened to him. They had attacked the symptoms and not the causes. So here he was at the beginning again trying to figure out what he had missed. What was the answer to the answer man?

Sonny tried to go on, but like the movement, he was exhausted. He felt like he had lived the last five years with the same intensity that he had lived sixty minutes in one football game; and, increasingly, he relied on drugs to keep him going and to give him that feeling of euphoria he felt when he first broke away; but when the drugs wore off, he would often fall into moods of deep depression; and when he was in these dark moods, his relationship with Miranda changed. Miranda was no longer the reflection of his love. She became a projection of his doubts and fears, and he became convinced that she didn't love him anymore, and she had found someone else with a future. He wanted to talk to her about it, but he wanted so desperately to be her hero that he feared that she would see him as weak and love him less, so Sonny did what many lovers do when they think that they are going to lose their loved one. He began to look for flaws in her, reasons not to love her. They began to argue, and one day after a particularly bitter argument, he left and never came back.

He went on the road again, but this time his heart wasn't in it. He felt like he didn't have anything to say anymore; so he ended up crashing from place to place, staying with friends, getting lost in psychedelics looking for his lost vision. For awhile he felt like he was so high no one could touch him; but when he fell, he woke up with a blanket of snow on his chest; and he realized that he was a homeless person.

Lying there freezing to death, Sonny remembered one night when his father had stopped raving, and there was a lull in the fury. His father was on the other side of the locked door to his bedroom, and he said, "I know you think that I am evil and that I am the Devil; but, someday, you will thank God that the Devil is your father. Someday, you will call on me for help; and I'll be there for you even if I'm dead and buried because you are me and I am you. You're just the better part of me, Sonny; and, maybe, someday, you'll realize how much I love you."

Sonny stood up and shook off the snow. He had fallen asleep on a broken down couch on someone's back porch. He was very cold, and he did what his father predicted he would do many years before. He called on the Devil; and he could hear the Devil say, "Don't worry, I'll take care of this."

Chapter Three

The next day, Sonny drove with Tom and Dave to the Pier 40 parking lot. When he entered the lot, he drove up a ramp to the top tier that overlooked the Hudson River and then drove to the north side of the lot and parked his Volvo near where Josh had parked the van. Sonny sat back and took a sip out of a cup of coffee that Tom poured for him out of a thermos bottle. Now, all there was to do was wait for Larry to arrive. Sonny lit a cigarette and stared out at an ocean liner moored at the Cunnard boarding dock that looked like a beached steel-whale vintage 1955. Seagulls were flying all about screeching triumphantly when they found a breakfast morsel amidst the garbage along the shoreline. Sonny reviewed the plan and how the deal would go down; and then he turned to Dave who was in the back seat and said, "Do you have everything straight, Dave?"

"What's there to get straight? I shoot the son of a bitch if anything goes wrong."

Sonny smiled and turned to Tom and said, "You're the Greek philosopher, Tom. What would you call that?"

"I would call that a categorical imperative."

Sonny laughed then took in the view from the pier of downtown Manhattan, the Twin Towers, and the Battery. It was early in the morning, and a gray haze of jeweled trace particles, heavy metal, mercury, and pewter colored lead veiled lower Manhattan in an early morning blur. It was so quiet without the traffic that it reminded Sonny of one winter, several years ago, when New York City was hit by a severe snowstorm and the streets became impassible and traffic came to a dead stop. After awhile people came out of their apartments, and they looked around as if they had been in an air raid. For a moment, all the stress from being bombarded with sound day after day was gone, and it was like a small town. People looked at each other, smiled, and said hello. They looked up at the sky and saw the stars, but then the big mechanical plows came, and they pushed away the silence.

At this moment, it was like it was then. It was so quiet that Sonny could hear a radio playing somewhere near, and he could hear a couple laughing on the street. As New York woke up, Sonny could feel the city coming alive, one shower after another turning into a rainstorm punctuated by the rolling thunder of feet walking across wooden floors and up and down stairs and onto the sidewalk. Doors and drawers opened and closed, banging away like a drum beat on a hollow log. China and glassware and utensils clattered to the sound and smell of bacon and fried eggs, coffee brewing, and the sweet smell of butter and bread. The internal combustion engines that ruled the airwaves began to fire up along with the trains and planes and power plants that fueled the Inferno and spewed sulfur dioxides like volcanic ash forming a devilish halo above the city in the early morning light.

Sonny spotted Larry, Charlie, and Larry's bodyguard driving up the ramp and onto the top tier of Pier 40 in a black Mercedes. The body guard, who was driving, pulled next to Sonny's car; and they all got out of the car as did Sonny, Tom, and Dave. Everyone was serious. Charlie's eyes were red. In fact, there probably wasn't enough coffee in the world to fully awaken these Manhattan denizens of the night this early in the morning.

Sonny smiled and cheerfully said, "Good morning, Gentlemen," and then he got right down to business with an ice cold shower of reality. "Let's see the money."

Larry looked around, and Sonny could see what Larry was seeing. They were isolated on the far end of the parking lot. From where Larry was standing, he could see in every direction, and he could see anyone coming before they became dangerous to the exchange. There was an attendant at the far end of the lot, out of sight, but within gunshot range. It was broad daylight. Larry smiled then reached into the car, pulled out an attaché case, and opened it up on the hood of his car.

Sonny was relieved when he saw the money. A rip off was much less likely if there was real money flying around. Sonny checked the stacks of hundred dollar bills, and he was satisfied that it was all there. "OK, Larry," he said, "you go with Tom and Dave in my car."

Dave opened the door and waited.

Larry looked around. "Where's the pot?"

Sonny handed Charlie the keys to the van and said, "It's that white van over there."

Charlie walked over to the van and opened the rear doors. He got inside, checked it out, then got into the driver's seat of the van and shouted to his brother, "It looks like it's all here."

Larry turned to Sonny, "OK, man. I'll see you later."

Sonny got into the van with Charlie and Larry's bodyguard, and they drove out of the parking lot into the traffic with the radio playing. On the news station, Sonny heard that the solar arm on the space station, Skylab, was seriously damaged. He also heard that Howard Dean testified at a Congressional hearing that Nixon was involved in the Watergate break in, and Mayor Lindsay recently announced that New York City was near bankruptcy. An economist from NYU who was being interviewed about the state of the city's economy was saying that things were not as bad as they seemed because foreign money was pouring into New York City, infusing it with new wealth. Sonny thought that there should be a sign out there somewhere that read, *America for Sale*. There were even rumors around New York City that the Russians owned the Empire State Building. Soon someone would be buying the Brooklyn Bridge and shipping it to England.

Charlie reached over and began to search for another radio station; and as he scanned the bands he said, "This country is one big shit hole, Sonny. It's like a big fuckin buildin with no fuckin plumbin and a hol' in the middle of the flo' where ya all take a shit. The people on the top, day get no shit, man. The people on the next flo', they get some shit splattered on dem, and every fuckin flo' below them gets mo' and mo' shit until ya get to the bottom flo'. Dat's where the shit gets really deep, man. Get this. Just yesterday, a teenage mugger bit a eighty year old lady's finger off to get her wedding ring, and I read in *The Post* where dis unemployed woman, she boils her baby alive like some fuckin lobster. Now dats the fuckin news, man. Dat's the news from the fuckin streets."

Charlie found the station that he was looking for; and Sonny listened to Curtis Mayfield sing, *"we the people who are darker than blue"* from his album, *The New World Order.* As Sonny listened to the music, they drove passed Time Square and up Broadway where the garbage was piled high and litter was floating around like stray brain cells. Unlit neon signs looked like electronic test tubes in a Frankenstein laboratory; and many of the signs advertised the Japanese electronic invasion of cheaper, better, and smaller like the mutant electronic headphones that would soon replace ears.

Sonny watched shopkeepers pulling up steel shutters and rolling down faded awning, the bricks of the buildings looking wrinkled in the early morning light like an old man's skin. They stopped at a red light; and on the corner, a homeless woman was eating cat food out of a can; and her male companion was going through the garbage looking for deposit bottles. In the background, billboards advertised the movies, *Mean Streets, Live and Let Die,* and *Jesus Christ Superstar.* One billboard advertised *Oh Calcutta* a musical and theatrical revue composed of series of sex sketches. Sonny had learned recently from Leonard Melfi, one of the playwrights who had contributed to the revue, that the title was taken from a painting by Clovis Trouille, itself a pun on "O quell cul t'as!' French for "What an ass you have!"

As they drove through Central Park, Sonny remembered when he first came to New York City. The difference between hippies and most of the other young people who came to New York from all over the country was that hippies and the political activists of the 60s did not come to New York to make it. They came to change it and reform it into their grassroots vision of a more humane and organic city of flowers and gardens and parks amidst terraced mountains of stone. Sonny remembered how they turned rooftops and vacant and abandoned spaces into vegetable and flower gardens, and the East Village sidewalks and walls became floral murals that held out a promise of a greener future. Hippie carpenters and builders squatted in old and abandoned buildings, formed co-ops, restored the buildings, and created communes where people could live in Manhattan at affordable rents. They created health clinics and food co-ops for the poor, and Sonny dreamed of a time when automobiles would be banned from Manhattan, and the streets would become tree lined walkways and a mosaic of art. The greatest artists, musicians, and architects would construct buildings as monuments to the people rather than as monuments to corporations and money. It would be a city where, when the wind blew, it would vibrate like a symphony and everywhere you looked it would frame a visual masterpiece.

Charlie drove into the street level garage adjacent to Larry's club. He got out, came around the van to the passenger side of the van where Sonny was seated, opened the door and growled, "Get out."

Sonny got out of the van, and he ignored Charlie who was glaring at him through his bloodshot eyes. Larry's bodyguard unloaded the van, inspected the pot, and then weighed it. Finally, he walked up to Charlie and said, "It's solid, man."

Charlie grunted. He turned to Sonny and said, "All right, now what?"

"Let me have the phone, Charlie."

Charlie handed the phone to Sonny, and he called Tom and Dave at the hotel room where they were holding Larry. "Tom, it's Sonny. They're satisfied. Did you count the money? OK."

Sonny felt a gun in his ribs. Charlie pulled the phone away from Sonny and growled into the telephone, "Tom, dis is Charlie. I'm gonna shoot Sonny if ya don't let my brother go with da money."

"Fuck you, Charlie," Tom said in a matter of fact tone of voice, and then he shouted to Dave to get ready to shoot Larry.

Larry shouted into the phone, "What the fuck are you doing, Charlie?"

Sonny walked to the van. Larry's bodyguard was smiling, and Sonny and the bodyguard both shrugged. Sonny got into the van, and he started it up. The bodyguard opened the door to the garage.

Charlie was trying to talk to his brother. He was spitting all over the phone. He shouted at Sonny, "Wait a minute, Sonny."

Just as he was about to drive away, Charlie came up to the driver's side door. Sonny rolled down the window, and Charlie said, "Come on, Sonny. You got to tell me what I did wrong, man."

"You're kidding me, Charlie."

"No, I'm not. You owe me. I just saved your life."

Sonny laughed. "How did you do that, Charlie?"

Charlie spit in his ear and said, "By not shootin you, mother fucker."

"It would have been a mistake, Charlie."

"I know, man. That's why you got to tell me what I

did wrong."

"What did your brother say?"

Charlie mumbled something. He had his head down. Sonny leaned forward. "What did you say, Charlie?"

"He said I was a dumb Nigger."

Sonny burst out laughing. Charlie laughed too. He pleaded with Sonny, "You got to help me, Sonny, or I'll never get ahead."

"So tell me what you want to know," Sonny said. "Do you want to know how you could have ripped me off today, or do you want to know how you could have shot me and got away with it?"

Charlie smiled. "Both."

Sonny was still laughing. "But, Charlie you're the one who told me to never hip a lame."

Charlie was hurt. "That ain't fair, Sonny. You can't use my own shit on me."

Sonny smiled again and said, "What can I say, Charlie. You're my mentor." Sonny waved goodbye and drove away.

When Sonny got back to the Chelsea Hotel the phone rang.

"Hello."

"It's Josh. How did it go?"

"I'm alive, and I have the money. I'll be at the warehouse in about an hour."

"Don't bother. We're finished here. Have dinner with me tonight."

"When?"

"Any time you want, buddy."

"Where?"

"I don't care. Where ever you want."

Sonny thought for a moment and said, "How about Joe's? Nobody is there except Joe and the ghosts. I'll meet you there in about an hour."

"Why there? That place gives me the creeps."

"It makes me feel safe. I could drown you in the spaghetti sauce, and nobody would say a thing."

"What the hell are you pissed off about?"

"You didn't have to deal with Charlie, and where the hell did you disappear to yesterday?"

"I'll explain everything to you when I see you. I have some very good news."

"This better be good."

"It will be. I'll meet you at the graveyard in about an hour."

Sonny hung up the phone, took a shower, and changed into clothes that didn't smell of pot. When he left the Chelsea, he decided to walk rather than take a cab. He loved to walk in the city. It was dark now, and all the denizens of Hell were coming out to play, and the pace of life had quickened amidst clouds of bulbs and swirling tubes of color. It was a weaving incantation, the streets dancing with the plural verse of people who poured out of their boxes and into the streets, many merely to gaze upon one another, to gaze upon the extraordinary variety of faces, shapes, and costumes. Even the bricks and the blocks of granite seemed to vibrate and come alive with the human activity, the play, the incessant noise of cars, trucks, sirens and horns blaring, the music playing in the midst of a kaleidoscope of street entertainment. In The Village, under almost every street light, on almost every corner, a variety show played – a ventriloquist, a singer of blues, and an old woman who sang opera badly but got to meet people. A pantomime artist beckoned everyone to gather around the magic ring he was casting as he juggled balls and listened for applause. A Moroccan man with a red and orange turban hammered on an Autoharp with wire balls, ever so lightly, eyes closed, as a woman in a space suit sang. A man wearing green leotards, silver cowboy boots, and a pink cowboy hat was walking his Doberman pincer; and behind him came a Mad Hatter wearing an army surplus coat, tuxedo pants, and sandals. From his waist hung a long thin paperclip chain that skipped along beside him on the pavement and protected him from lightning bolts.

Little old ladies and little old men wearing dark sunglasses and baggy clothes shuffled by, probing the crowd with their bags and canes. Page after page of Macy's, Saks Fifth Avenue, Bloomingdale's, and Gimbel's paraded by as if on a fashion runway; and in-between the walking pages and labels, were children and women in tattered clothes unafraid in the relativity of values, the sociological schizophrenia that came to the City at night when all the human content came out of all the boxes to circulate amongst its many selves and reflect upon one another and the infinite possibilities of the human spirit.

Sonny thought he could hear a giant child laughing as he played with all his toys growing out of the voices, the sounds, the sirens and the horns, the cry of the automobiles and the constant drone of rubber against concrete, the variety show. Every sound blended into the sounds of a being that was being created in mass by each and every individual multiplied by millions upon millions of individual impulses, one plus one equals one equals a multiversity of people creating a monster in a box. Sonny felt the death rattle of a subway underneath his feet and imagined the gnawing of rodents and cockroaches on the blocks of boxes. He saw a bum asleep in a box gorged of its contents. He was curled up in a prenatal position shaking, jerking, haunted by the ghosts of goods forsaken. Sonny realized that the bum was prophetic; and soon, when this monster came of age, we would all become discarded toys amidst tumbling blocks.

Sonny walked into Joe's Restaurant, and Josh was waiting for him at a table near the window. Old man Stanzani was in the back of the restaurant sleeping with one eye open on a reclining lounge chair surrounded by enlarged photos and press clippings of himself. Joe Stanzani was a hero in the First World War, decorated for courage by the President of the United States and the King of Italy. There were pictures of Joe in his uniform, enlarged copies of his valiant deeds in print, and pictures of his certificates of honor.

Above Joe were two pictures in particular that touched Sonny. One was a picture of Joe's son and a write-up that said that his son was one of the top ten lawyers in America. The other picture was a picture of Joe's father sitting in front of his restaurant in Naples. Joe's father and his father's father and his fathers before that had been restaurateurs, and now Joe's son was a lawyer. America may be the land of opportunity; but there was no son to take over the business; and Joe would sit here in his place like his father did until he died and that would be the end, no more tradition, no more Joe's.

Josh looked at the old man and then at Sonny and said, "Boy, am I glad that you're here. I've been alone with the old man, his wife, and the waitress for a half an hour now. Nobody comes to my table, no one asks me anything. They just look at me."

Josh flinched when the old man called his wife. "Maria! Maria!"

The old man gave his wife an order, and then he closed his eye again. She talked to the waitress, and the waitress came over to the table. Without asking Josh, Sonny ordered for both of them. The waitress quietly took the order, and she left the table soundlessly. She whispered the order to Joe's wife, and she then sat down at the far side of the room and began to knit again.

Josh shook his head in disbelief and said, "What service."

"Josh, they're not here for you. They're here for him."

Josh looked at Sonny with a puzzled look on his face. "Why do you like this place?" he asked.

"It reminds me of home. I feel safe. Whenever I feel paranoid, I come here. The old man senses it. He'll get up from his sleep, come to the window, peek out, then lock the door, and close the metal gates on the windows. I can stay for as long as I like and drink coffee and read poetry. We never say a word to one another, but he knows. Didn't you hear what he said to his wife?"

"No. It was in Italian," Josh said.

"He told her to get a garbage can ready. They're going to have a guest, tonight." Sonny pointed at Josh.

"Come on, buddy," Josh said. "I'm sorry I didn't get back to the warehouse and help you with the van. I thought that I would drop the records off to Robbie and Little Sheik, and that would be it. But something came up."

"Bullshit," Sonny said. "You knew it was going to be shaky, and you split with your ass and the evidence."

"Man, are you paranoid. Robbie and Little Sheik wanted the records; and when I got there, I found out that we're going to have a party tomorrow to celebrate the end of the trip."

"The trip is over?"

"That's what I said, buddy. We're done until the next boat comes in and that may not be for another couple of weeks, maybe a month. A lot of things have been happening down South."

The waitress brought their dinner and a bottle of Chianti. For himself, Sonny ordered polsilipo, an Italian bouillabaisse with squid, mixed fish, cod, and clams cooked in a marinara sauce and served over garlic bread. It looked delicious. For spite, Sonny ordered Josh the spaghetti and octopus. A huge octopus tentacle was plopped on a mound of spaghetti.

Josh looked at Sonny in disbelief and said, "What is that?"

"It's an octopus, and if this story of yours isn't any good that tentacle is going to reach out from the plate and grab you by the neck and pull you into the sauce."

Josh shrugged. "There's not much to tell," he said. "Robbie went down South and looked at what was left in the warehouse. He turned it down. We're going to wait for a new load to come in."

"What's this about a couple of weeks? I thought the boat was going to come in next week."

"I did too, but it seems that there's a power struggle going on in Columbia over who controls the traffic."

"Between who and who?"

"I don't know." Josh peeked at the octopus.

"Are you hiding something from me?" Sonny asked.

"I don't know. I swear. All I know is that they're going to wait until things cool down. What the hell are you bitching about? Go Upstate. Relax. When the boat comes in, I'll get in touch with you, but until then enjoy."

Sonny looked at Josh suspiciously then looked at the octopus. Josh hadn't touched his meal. Sonny took the octopus and cut it up. "Here, eat," he said. "You look like you're starving to death. All you eat are those fuckin vitamin pills, tofu, and bean fuckin sprouts."

Josh smiled and said, "I'm famished." He tasted the octopus. "Oh boy, this is delicious."

Sonny poured the wine. He liked the idea of a vacation, and he began to warm up to the prospect. The idea of being able to get away from the warehouse and out of town and into the country made him forget about everything else. "What's this about a party?" he asked.

"Six o'clock tomorrow at Pier 12. You can't miss it. It's a hundred and twenty foot yacht called *The United States.*"

Sonny laughed and said, "A hundred twenty foot yacht called US?"

Josh laughed also. He liked the pun. "You got it, buddy."

"I'll be there," Sonny said. He raised his glass. "Time off."

Josh raised his glass as well. "For good behavior."

They ate with relish. Josh was in a good mood. He talked about how he could use the time to investigate new business ventures. He wanted to copyright the name, Sin Semilla, and merchandise a perfume in that essence. He needed a chemist to make the synthetic essence of the flower.

Sonny suggested that he bottle it in the shape of a seed. Sonny could envision the ad – a woman staring out of the symmetry of a clitoris shaped weed peeking through the stem where the buds of the female organs first appear. In the foreground would be a frosted seed shaped bottle laden with the pollen of essence – *Sin Simella*, the fragrance of a flower prolonged in the agonies of love. Sonny laughed.

Josh liked it. He wrote it all down on a paper napkin.

"Josh, what is going on down South?"

Josh looked up from the napkin, finished what he was writing, and then put it away in his wallet. "If you want to know, all you have to do is pick up the phone and call Billy. I'll get the number for you. You can join the list when the IRS subpoenas his telephone records."

"Is he hot?"

"No, probably not; but why take the risk? That's Robbie and Little Sheik's job. We have enough problems of our own."

"I don't like it."

"What's new? You don't like anything. Relax. We're nice and safe where we are. You and I are going to come out of this smelling pretty. Wait and see."

"Josh?"

"What?"

"Are you trying to sell me a perfume that smells like pot? And that is going to cure my paranoia?"

They both laughed and Josh asked, "Sonny, where are you going to go when you leave the city? I just assumed that you would go Upstate?"

Sonny reached into his pocket and pulled out the invitation to the funeral, and he handed it to Josh, "Want to come?"

Josh looked at the invitation and laughed, "No way."

He then looked at his watch and said, "I have to go. Have a good time at the funeral, and don't forget to keep in touch. Seriously, I need to know where you are. You know how it is; things can go down at anytime."

"Leave a message at The Palms or just send a letter addressed to Ithaca, New York," Sonny said. "I don't know where I'll be for sure, but you'll find me if you need me, and if not."

"Come on, don't be a prick. Let me know where you're at as soon as possible."

"Sure."

"Good. Listen, I have to go now." Josh extended his hand, and he said, "Don't forget the party tomorrow."

"I won't." They shook hands, Josh left, and Sonny remained alone with Joe, his wife, and the waitress. A thought flashed through Sonny's mind. I'm free with nothing to do. Sonny looked around the ghost house for the waitress. Old man Stanzani was asleep. Sonny paid the check and got up from the table and headed for the door. As he left, he took one last look. Who knows, Stanzani and family may be gone when he came back.

When Sonny got back to his room at the Chelsea Hotel, he lit up a joint, poured himself a Martels, and listened to the radio intermittently as he read Ernest Cassirer's *Philosophy of Symbolic Forms*. Sonny was a diehard Yankee fan, and George Steinbrenner had recently purchased the Yankees from CBS. On radio the sports newscaster was quoting Steinbrenner as saying that he would bring the Yankees back to their former glory days. The Yankees had obviously become a rich boy's toy; but if Steinbrenner could make good on his promise and bring back the days of Babe Ruth, Lou Gehrig, and Joe DiMaggio, Sonny was prepared to make this one concession to unabashed capitalism. When Sonny was finished reading, he marked his book, turned off the radio; and he laid back in his bed and watched M*A*S*H on TV. The last thing he heard before he fell asleep was the theme song at the end of the story.

> *Through early morning fog I see*
> *Visions of the things to be*
> *The pains that are withheld from me*
> *I realize and I can see*
> *That suicide is painless*
> *It brings on many changes*
> *And I can take or leave it if I please.*

Sonny woke up the next day, and he felt great. He opened his French doors and walked out onto the balcony. It was a beautiful day, and he let the sun pour into his room as he spent the afternoon getting ready for the trip Upstate. He organized everything then washed up and changed into a finely woven white Perry Ellis white T-shirt, a brushed gray and black loosely woven wool Armani sweater with a rolled collar, and a pair of worn Levi jeans and cowboy boots. It was too early to go to the party, so he decided to walk downtown to the village and SoHo to take his daily color bath at the many art galleries in the area.

When he got there, he was hungry and in need of a cup of coffee; so he first stopped in Vinnie's Café, one of his favorite places in SoHo. Vinnie's Cafe was a neighborhood hangout for what remained of the Italian neighborhood that huddled around St. Anthony's Church, Prince, MacDougal, and Sullivan Street. Though the price was right to sell out, and the rents were going up and up, and the children went to college, and they never came back; many of the old Italians refused to move away from their neighborhood, their block, the place where they were born. They helped build the city, and they were proud of it, so they walked around like little blocks of stone with legs looking for a place to rest their burdens. They shunned the newcomers as foreign and strange, but their insatiable curiosity would get the best of them, and they had to go to Vinnie's to take a peek out of the big picture windows.

Vinnie kept everybody laughing while he ruined their stomach. Today he was down on Con Ed, the gas and electric company.

"Ten years that meter has been fixed; and now that I'm here," Vinnie said, "they got to find out. They didn't find out when Tony was here. They didn't find out when Louie owned this place." Vinnie shouted over the counter. "Hey, Babe, remember Louie? This place was a dump when Louie owned it. Hey, it's a dump now, but at least ya got a fork to eat with. When Louie owned this place you had your hands and a piece of bread."

"Use the edge, he used to say. That son-of-a-bitch, do you think Con Ed would check his meter, and he's the one who fixed it? No, god damn it, they got to check mine."

Vinnie looked up to God. "What have I done to you?" Then he looked to Babe and said, "Where am I going to get the money?"

Babe shrugged. Vinnie put his hands together as if to pray, and then he began to gobble air. "What am I going to do, eat rosary beads?"

He looked up and crossed himself. "Look at my children." With an open hand he motioned to each child. Vinnie's youngest daughter was playing the pinball machine. She was plump and happy. His youngest son was playing in a box under the pinball machine. He was plump and happy. His oldest son was half asleep at the end of the counter, his head in his hand, a dishtowel thrown over his shoulder. He was plump and happy. JoJo was so plump and happy she could hardly make it through the aisles. Vinnie had pictures of all of them on a shelf above the back counter – JoJo sitting at a desk reading the Encyclopedia Britannica, Michael in a football uniform looking like Vinnie would like to look, and the other two children hugging each other and laughing.

Vinnie leaned down over the counter and stared into Babe's face to make sure he was listening and said, "Do you know why these kids are happy?" He raised his hands as if he were going to pull his hair out of his head. "They eat me out of house and home, that's why they're happy. They're like vacuum cleaners."

Vinnie imitated a vacuum cleaner. Babe held his plate. Vinnie looked at Babe in shock. "The whole refrigerator is gone," he said then smacked himself on the head. "What am I talking about? What refrigerator? You can't even get the food out of the bags."

His daughter JoJo waddled by. "You don't do so bad yourself, Dad."

Vinnie looked at her incredulously then at his fat belly. "Do you see this? Do you think this is from eating too much? You've seen those pictures of all those children starving in Africa." He put both hands on his stomach and extended it.

"This is the stomach of a starving father. They eat the food off my plate. Then I come here. Do you think I can eat this stuff? You got to be crazy to eat my food."

Vinnie's daughter JoJo came behind the counter and tried to get by her father. There wasn't enough room for both of them. He pinched her in the ass and propelled her by him then said, "Find a boyfriend; get married; get out of my house."

Over her shoulder she shouted back at him, "Oh no, I'm going to stay with you forever."

He looked around at everybody and said, "Do you see what I mean?"

"Hey, Vinnie, how about some scrambled eggs," one of his customers shouted.

"Like my brains, Eddie. Comin up."

Vinnie saw someone come in the door and shouted, "Hey, Johnny, long time no see."

Johnny looked around at everybody in disbelief. "Vinnie, I was here yesterday."

"Yesterday?" Vinnie asked. "Yesterday, I didn't have my new salad bar. Look over there, Johnny."

"Vinnie, I want some chic pea soup."

"Chic pea soup?"

"Yeah"

"OK. I'll fix you some chic pea soup." Vinnie headed for the kitchen. "All the time my customers say, 'Hey, Vinnie, how come you don't have a choice of salads. Salads are big.' I should listen to my customers. I never met a customer who knew what the fuck he wanted, but my children know what they want."

He spread his arms wide and shouted, "They want

everything."

Vinnie disappeared into the kitchen. Sonny looked at the salad bar. There was nothing in the pans. Sonny smiled, put the money down on the counter for his check with a generous tip, left Vinnie's, and wandered through the galleries, the vibrating colors that created new colors, shapes, and forms. He found one piece particularly fascinating. It was a sculpture made of slabs of steel and cast iron figures. The two rectangular slabs of steel looked like the skyscrapers that formed the outline of the New York City skyline; but they also looked like rusted tombstones that had been varnished and stained in what looked like mud and blood and fire and darkness. Both of these monuments to the death of the industrial age were torn open to reveal the raw ore and the granular texture of the molten lava that formed the core of the earth. Miniature cast iron people rusted out with the sins of mortality walked in military order across a steel beam that connected the two gravestones that were etched with the Ten Commandments. Many of the iron people had fallen into the graveyard to decompose and meld into the mangled cogs and springs and levers. A giant pink, plastic, dildo towered over the broken images heralding the triumph of the post-modern era and the schizophrenic deconstruction of the human mind.

Sonny checked the time. It was getting late in the day, and the sun was setting on New York City. It was time to go to the party, so Sonny hailed a cab that raced across town to Pier 12 where he saw the *United States* harbored at the dock. It was very impressive and very modern, a sort of art deco spaceship on water surrounded by towering buildings that seemed to be emerging from the sea at twilight. The lights on the top of the Empire State Building were shining brilliantly in the background.

Sonny boarded the ship and was about to join the party when he felt someone squeeze his arm. It was Robbie. Robbie was wearing a light brown Nehru style shirt with crème colored linen slacks and Gucci snakeskin shoes. He was short and wore a layer of baby fat like a child that had been fed on the nipple of privilege and coddled in a blanket of expectations. However, his mother's dream of straight A's and a law degree miscarried when he was thrown out of Columbia Law School for selling pot; but he still wore the smirk, the twinkle in his eye that said that he had the answers and that he was the smartest kid in the class.

Sonny noted that Robbie carried his head as if it was the only part of his body worth caring for; but to Sonny, Robbie's head looked like a balloon ready to float away except for the string being held by the child within, a balloon full of dreams of money, the center of his being that gave everything else meaning.

"Welcome aboard, Sonny, I'm glad you could come." Robbie extended his hand like a reptile seeking heat, and he looked at Sonny like he was a sequence of numbers to be calculated and evaluated as an asset to be converted into profit or a liability to be written off and liquidated. Robbie must have come up with an answer that pleased him because he was beaming with goodwill.

Sonny smiled, "This is one hell of a party that you're throwing here, Robbie." Sonny leaned over and whispered in Robbie's ear, "Am I paying for this?"

Robbie laughed, "No, man. This is not on company money. This is on me, and you haven't seen anything yet.

We're going to take a ride around Manhattan. We're leaving at sunset."

"Far out, I've never seen New York City like this before."

"Well, enjoy, man. You've earned the price of admission. Welcome to New York."

A couple came up to Robbie, and he turned to greet them; and judging from their eagerness, the big hugs, they probably came for the free coke. Sonny grabbed a glass of champagne from a tray being carried by one of the ship's catering crew; and as he did, he looked around the ship to see who was there. Most of the people there were customers from Dante's and dealers that they were associated with along with a smattering here and there of celebrities and Wall Street and Madison Avenue types. They all seemed stoned on coke, the ego drug of the 70s that feed their narcissism; and they all were dressed as if they were little children going to a Halloween costume party, the theme being *The Beautiful People*. Maybe Robbie and Josh were right, Sonny thought. Maybe money is alchemy, and it can turn base metal into gold.

CB was a case in point. He was standing nearby with the twin towers of femininity, Good Girl and Bad Girl, one on each arm. Good Girl was dressed to look like the Barbie doll version of Jackie Kennedy. She was wearing a sleeveless aqua marine knee length silk dress by Oleg Cassini with matching high heel shoes with bows on the toes; and her hair was done up in Jackie Kennedy's signature Bubble cut. To add to the costume party effect, she was wearing Jackie Kennedy style oversized tortoise shell sunglasses to hide her identity.

Bad Girl was dressed in the post apocalyptic style of

sadomasochistic punk, her hair spiked like some prehistoric animal with Cleopatra eyes. Sonny could see a black lace cone shaped bra with diamond nipples through her shear black blouse; and she was wearing skintight black leather bellbottom pants and black leather cowboy boots with silver inlaid pointed toes. The rear end of her bell-bottom pants was cut out to reveal her naked ass and a silver and diamond thong, and throughout her body artfully hand painted gold and silver scales appeared and disappeared into erogenous zones.

CB's costume looked normal compared to the girls. He was wearing a black silk shirt with balloon sleeves, a white silk scarf like tie, brown leather bell-bottom pants, cowboy boots, and a diamond in his ear. CB was one of the people at the party who would have been condemned to a faceless middle class existence, always plagued with complexion problems, always yearning for the world he saw in the window of his TV, except for one thing. He broke the rules. The front door of the American dream was locked, so he climbed up the fire escape. Now he was part of the illusion, the consuming dream, starring in his own X rated movie with the two Manhattan mutants from Brooklyn, center stage in his own mind, King of the Disco Dealers.

In the group with CB and the twins were Sam Gold, Margo Wayne, and the actors Joey Carbone and Barbara Ballard. Joey and Barbara were living proof that the media was the message. They were both small screen actors who were so much like the people who sat in their living rooms watching TV that they could have walked right out of the TV and sat down in the living room and watched themselves.

Joey was the archetypal working class guy from

Brooklyn who no matter what role he played – the plumber, the electrician, or the cop – he always played himself, the guy with a face of a man who had worked too hard and made too little money, broke his nose in a bar fight, and suffered from an on-the-job accident.

Barbara was the archetypal girl next door who could get away with almost anything because she was so damned cute and had perfect middle class breasts, not too big, not too small, just right for three kids and a ranch home. Today, Barbara was dressed in a white leather miniskirt and leather jacket with flaming red stockings, high heel shoes, and a flaming red blouse. Her auburn hair was teased; and she was wearing sunglasses like a movie star; but even now, with all the flashy clothing and glamorous make-up, she still didn't look like a big screen movie star. She looked more like the girl next door who desperately wanted to get out of small town America, so she went to New York City and became a hooker. Even her agent, who was standing next to her, looked like a pimp. Maybe this also was why she was so attractive to the average male viewer. He sensed that this beautiful girl was flawed; and if he could only get a date with here, he could get in her pants. All he had to do was tell her that she looked like a movie star.

Sonny had gone to bed with Barbara; but when he made love to her, he was put off by the fact that in her bedroom she had surrounded herself with mirrors so that she could see herself making love like she was in a movie; and when she came, she looked like she was coming to the camera, begging for a close up to catch the parting of her lips, the tragic gasp as she broke through the fourth wall.

Barbara saw Sonny; and she opened her arms to receive

him. "Darling," she said, "why haven't you called me?"

"I have but you were busy."

"No, I mean why haven't you called me when I wasn't busy."

They both laughed, and Barbara kissed him on both cheeks. Bad Girl kissed him with her voluptuous halogen purple lips, and Jackie Kennedy gave him her hand to kiss and said, "I'm slumming."

Sonny laughed, "So I see."

Barbara, always the perfect hostess, took Sonny's arm and said, "Sam, here, was telling us how he has the advantage over the average investor."

Sam Gold was a stock broker and the grandson of the founder of the prestigious brokerage firm of Marrow and Gold. He was also the banker for the big drug deals. Margo, who was at Sam's side and holding his arm possessively, was a professional model; and she was wearing a mini dress with angel sleeves. The dress was made out of silver and gold, coin sized metallic disks woven together with shear pink and silver and gold thread. She was also wearing a skull cap made out of the same material over her shaved head - the disks becoming smaller and smaller as they blended into the silver sparkles on her cheeks and eye lids. Pink silk stockings and pink spiked high heels shoes accentuated her long legs and height. With her button nose, puffy pink lips, and aristocratic pose she looked like the gene bank waiting for the right deposit, someone who would shower her with money on a pink cloud.

"It's really quite simple," Sam said. "The difference between me and the average investor is a difference in scale. If I invest, I can invest so much money that I can bet on a favorite and make millions of dollars on half a percentage point; but if the average guy were to make the same bet, he would make just enough money to buy a cup of coffee."

Bad Girl put her arms around Sam's waist and stuck out her diamond-studded breasts and said, "Let me get this straight, Sam. Are you saying that you have a dick the size of the Empire State Building whereas most men can barely achieve penetration?"

Sam laughed and said, "Yes, I guess I am."

Bad Girl put her arms around his neck and stared him in the eyes and said, "OK, baby, go ahead give me that intense dollar sign stare backed by a well-endowed bank account."

Sam took off his glasses and stared at Bad Girl like a potential investment; and Bad Girl swooned, bared her neck, and said, "Oh, Sam, bury your fangs in my neck and cover it up with a diamond choker, Tiffany preferred."

Everyone laughed and Joey said, "I got to get me one of those."

Good Girl, with an expression of disdain on her face said, "Where I come from, a million dollar penis is no big thing. And, besides, my man here has two of them."

CB put his arms around both of the girls and said, "Double barreled, baby."

Barbara gave Sonny one of her we made it in the back seat of your car cheerleader looks and said, "Now Sonny is far more frugal. I speak from experience. He will give you all you need and then a little more to give you a hint of what ecstasy it would be if he gave it all away. Then he pulls it out leaving you gasping, waiting for the sequel with just a taste of the preview on your lips."

Everyone was laughing at Sonny, and Sonny, who

was embarrassed, said, "OK, that's it. I have to get something stronger than this to drink and take whatever you all are taking to get caught up. I'll be back."

"It's down stairs, man," Joey said.

As Sonny was walking away, he saw Billy Trips working his way through the crowd. When Billy saw Sonny, he smiled and headed his way. Billy had long shoulder length wild blond hair; and he wore Indian moccasins with no socks, one gold earring, and a Grateful Dead T-shirt underneath a thousand dollar white silk Armani suit. Billy was wearing aviator sunglasses with mirror lenses, and he had a glass of champagne in one hand and a Cuban cigar in the other. Billy, like most hippies, liked to smoke pot; and like most hippies, he started out by buying pot by the ounce; but then he and his friends figured out that if they pooled their money, they could buy a pound and save money; and when they came back with the first pound, they discovered that their friends and their friend's friends wanted pounds too. It was like a chain letter; and Billy, being the entrepreneurial type, saw the opportunity; so he began to buy weight until finally he was buying and selling hundreds of pounds of pot.

As the competition intensified, Billy went further and further south in search of volume and price until one day, tripping on acid, Billy took a plane from Key West to Bogotá, Columbia. Nine out of ten hippies who went to Bogotá and asked the most likely Columbian where they could buy lots of pot ended up in jail or dead; but somehow Billy picked the right Columbian out of the cosmos of random chance where the Gods love to gamble; and, now, Billy was their main supplier; and he was no longer a hippie anymore. He was an outlaw businessman who lived in a world that had no laws, no contracts, no lawyers, and no government or law enforcement to protect him. He lived in the world of pure unregulated primitive capitalism; so one day, in his devolution, he decided to go all the way. He went to the Amazon, and now he lives in the Amazon jungle of Columbia, and he very seldom came to the states except for trips like this to see his buyers.

Billy put the cigar in his mouth and extended his hand, "How you doin, brother?"

"I'm cool, Billy. When did you get into the city?"

"I flew in yesterday."

"You enjoying yourself?"

Billy looked around. His face registered amusement and contempt. "You know, Sonny, everyone here is trying to be something that they're not; and they're all jerking themselves around with dreams of this and that; but they can shit in one hand and dream in the other, and you know what will come up first, man? Selling drugs is easy money, and they're all too lazy to do anything else."

Billy took a sip of his champagne and a drag from his cigar, and said; "Now, me, I got no pretensions, Sonny. I'm a dealer, and I like it. I like everything that comes with it – getting stoned, rock and roll, beautiful women, lots of money, a villa in Italy, a coffee plantation in Kenya, and a mansion in the Amazon. I'm not interested in all this high society stuff. I flew up here from Columbia to talk business, and all they want to do is talk bullshit."

Sonny didn't want to talk business with Billy. That was not his job, so he quickly changed the subject. "Billy, I want you to explain something to me."

"What's that, Sonny?"

"What do you like about the Amazon? Why do you stay there?"

Billy took a drag from his cigar, paused for a moment, and then he said, "Other than business, I love the jungle, man. It's full of life and death, and when you let yourself be part of it..." Billy paused for a moment looking for the words, and then he said, "It's like that Nietzsche book. It's beyond good and evil, man. It's like you become part of God, the real God, not the bullshit God. Dig?"

"Yeah, Billy, I think I do. I've been there myself, but I think you got your genders fucked up. She's not a God. She's a Goddess; and if you ignore her, she'll eat you. If you pause to admire her fabulous beauty, she'll eat you; and if you love her, she'll make you rich and fat and juicy and then she'll eat you." Sonny pointed at Billy.

Billy laughed. "You may be right, Sonny; but it's better than living around these ugly cock-a-roaches." He gestured at the partygoers. "They're all mouths and bellies."

Sonny smiled, "Maybe so."

"Listen, man," Billy said. "Why don't you come down there and work with me. Everything is changing, Sonny. You got the last shipment of Columbian Gold. We've moved out of the mountains. The army has raided all the fields up there. It's not safe anymore. The next shipment will be all Columbian Red. We can grow it in the low lands and the jungle, but the future is in cocaine, and I'm going to turn the Amazon into one big coca plantation. No more bulk, no more freighters, man; and the mark up is astronomical. Seriously, Sonny, think about it; and we'll talk about it again; but right now I have to find Robbie and get that asshole to talk business. I want to be out of here tomorrow and on my way home." Billy shook hands with Sonny; and when he pulled his hand away, he left an envelope of cocaine in Sonny's palm. "That's one hundred percent pure. Enjoy, brother."

As Billy was walking away, he turned back and pointed at Sonny and shouted, "Think about it, Sonny. That's Eldorado there." Then he disappeared into the crowd in pursuit of Robbie and "mo money" as Charlie would say.

Sonny heard the engines of the yacht start up, and he felt it slowly pulling away from the dock. He watched the New York skyline, its modern parapets and bastions of wealth and ease casting broken shadows of a colossus across the waves. The sunset crowned the glowing Empire State Building with brush strokes of orange, lavender, and deep purple that was being swallowed up by a groping and lonely darkness that ignited a galaxy of man-made stars, a living being of pulsating light dancing with its own reflection on the water like a Goddess in an undulating silk gown.

Sonny felt a hand on his arm; and he turned to see Ginny who was wearing a black silk ballroom gown with a sweeping full skirt and a strapless bodice trimmed with fantails of diamante across her breasts. She also wore micro-diamond hoop earrings and a white gold link necklace from which hung thirteen brilliantly cut diamonds in graduated sizes with the largest resting in the curvature of her breasts. Her black hair glittered with silver sparkles, and silver embroidered slippers peeked out from below her gown.

Ginny smiled and said, "Sonny, you look like you could use a real drink. Dave and Tom are at the bar."

Sonny laughed and said, "And you're the only person who came to this party looking like themselves."

"And who is that, Sonny?"

"A beautiful virginal Jewish Princess."

Ginny laughed, and then she took Sunny's arm, and said, "I wonder why I never fell in love with you. You're without doubt the handsomest man here, and you're the perfect Renaissance prince. We could have beautiful babies together."

"I don't think I'm dangerous enough for you."

"No, that's not it. You're a leopard amongst jackal and sheep. No, I think you're not hopeless enough for me. Somewhere along the way you would disappoint me by becoming fabulously successful, and then I would hate you for making me feel terrible about myself for being such a coward, and no number of beautiful children would cure me of my malady of the heart. I'm too selfish for that. Which reminds me, did you bring the money?"

"Of course, and it will fit nicely into that little purse of yours." Sonny reached into the inside pocket of his jacket, and he handed Jenny an envelope filled with fifty one hundred dollar bills as payment for her part in putting the deal together with Charlie's brother.

Tom and Dave were at the bar. Neither Tom nor Dave had dressed for the let's pretend party. Tom was wearing his usual black T-shirt, black jeans, royal blue and white high-rise converse sneakers, and black horn rim sunglasses. His only concession to the fact that he was at a party was a Frank Sinatra style tuxedo jacket with a silk collar and the sleeves pushed up to his elbow. Dave was wearing a wrinkled white dress shirt hung loose with baggy jeans and what looked like black comfortable beat cop shoes. Sonny always marveled on how Dave always look like he just got out of the shower and had put on the clothes that he had sleep in the night before.

Sonny embraced Tom and slipped him the envelope with five thousand dollars. He also handed Dave an envelope, and Dave casually folded the envelope and stuffed it in his back pocket.

Sonny ordered a Martel's cognac with a soda back from the bartender, took out a Camel's non-filter cigarette and put it in a black ebony cigarette holder, and lit up. The cigarette holder had a crystal filter, and it was the only way he could smoke a non-filter Camel cigarette anymore without getting an upset stomach. He also liked the FDR affectation.

Tom touched Sonny on the shoulder to get his attention and said, "There is a rock of cocaine downstairs on the coffee table in the Captain's quarters the size of your fist. From what I hear, Billy "Trips" smuggled it in."

Dave, who was listening to the conversation laughed and said, "Get this Sonny. He smuggles it in under his cowboy hat. Can you believe that shit? He's got an elaborate smuggling business where he brings in tons of drugs in on freighters and private planes, and he never touches an ounce. Then he walks through customs with a rock of cocaine under his hat that will put him away for ten years. I'll tell you something, Sonny. You hippies are fuckin crazy."

"Ginny and I are going below for a taste," Tom said. "Do you want to join us?"

"I'm cool, Tom. I think I just want to stand here for awhile and take in the view."

"That's cool," Tom said and he and Ginny disappear into the crowd in search of a high.

Sonny took a sip of his Martel, looked at Dave, and said, "You look like hell. Did you just get up?"

"I'm a creature of the night, Sonny. I'm at my peak in a darkly lit after-hours-club where I radiate with the immortality of death, savoring last minute pleasures."

Sonny laughed, and they both leaned back against the bar and took in the sights. To Sonny's right, Peter Tattoo and Larry were standing at the bar talking to Andy Warhol and two of Andy's Superstars, Jackie Curtis and Viva. Viva was a poor little rich girl who always picked up the tab for Andy and starred in his movie F**K. Viva was tall and thin and beautifully emaciated like a prostitute in a Nazi concentration camp; and she was wearing skin tone spiked high heels, skin toned ballerina body tights, and a dark brown mink coat that came down to her thighs like a mini dress. Her bright green eyes were shaded with long false black eye lashes, black eye shadow, and mascara so that she looked like a cross between a kitten, a raccoon, and a pretty girl with pink lips. Jackie Curtis, a transvestite with flaming red lips and flaming red hair frizzed out to the max, was wearing a bright green mini dress with oversized orange and blue dots, angel wing sleeves, and thigh high black leather garter boots with platform heels.

Peter was wearing his Hell's Angel's colors, and he had two coke whores on a silver leash. They were the black and white lesbians that Sonny saw at the Bitter End the other night. Sonny was amused by Larry, who was dressed in a conservative three piece dark brown Perry Ellis suit and looked like a member of the African American branch of the Mafia, the IBM of crime. He was talking to Jackie; and judging by his body language and the expression on his face, he was trying to impress her with his bad boy image. Sonny wondered if Larry knew that he was now in Andy's world of the castrated father and blurred gender identities and sex roles. He wondered if Larry knew that Jackie was not a woman, and Viva went both ways. He wondered if Larry knew that Andy wasn't really Andy.

Andy sent out body doubles and impersonators to lecture at the colleges and universities as him, and he often sent a body double to parties like this that he felt did not deserve his real presence. Andy once told Sonny that it didn't really matter if it was really him or not because he wasn't really Andy Warhol, and his art wasn't really art. So there he was, Andy's doppelganger at the center of the emptiness, the virtual reality symbol of absence and passivity with the well draped superficiality of a fashionable corpse that turned even the most beautiful fabric into a stiff with a wisp of lilac and the shadowy soft spoken vocabulary of skin and bones, the perfect mirror of the times – superficial, commercial, and facile without any depth, an illusion of a delusion enhanced by drugs.

On the helicopter pad, above the emptiness of the bedlam, a band began to play the music of the era. They were the New York Dollars; and they wore heavy make-up, platform shoes, elaborately teased hair, tensile and glitter, silks and satins, leathers and studs with lured red, pink, and green boas and feathers. They played a primitive style of rock and roll that ridiculed the hopes and dreams of the 60s and glorified self-destruction as they screamed,

> *"Hey suicide baby.*
> *Do what you want.*

You can be a daredevil,
And fly above the clouds with no parachute on,
Climb the Himalayas,
Hang from the edge,
Stare down the bomb and kill anyone you want.
Hey suicide baby,
Fuck everyone.
Do what you want.
Do it. Do it, baby.
You got nothing to lose.
You're immortal now."

These screams of hopeless freedom penetrated the caverns of New York; and the city lights like synapses of its brain formed an astrological constellation that projected into the future like a horoscope. In that future, Sonny saw large segments of Brooklyn, Queens, and the Bronx plowed over; and at the edge of this barren land, Sonny saw what seemed to be a scene from a World War II movie – whole sections of New York City and Long Island looked like they had been bombed out, only fragments of buildings were still standing amidst rubble, walls and interiors exposed, stairways to nowhere.

Where there were once beautiful wealthy homes and cozy suburbs, there were now homes abandoned and in disrepair with shattered windows and lawns full of weeds. Dead playthings were strewn here and there. A swing-set laid belly up, its legs straight up in the air like a dead household pet. An early colonial mansion was stripped of all its furniture; and the walls were barren, cracked with plaster torn away revealing the skeleton of a dead house. Men, women, and children were sleeping on the floor, ragged squatters who lived in the abandoned home. One child was tied to a post so that it would not crawl off and fall through one of the holes in the floor.

They all seemed to be buried in a death like sleep that was their only escape from the wretchedness about them. The sole source of light and heat was the fire burning in an old fireplace, the marble face cracked, exposing the raw crumbling mass. Over the fire a beat up old kettle was suspended on a rod; and a young girl, wearing a down coat torn in many places and repaired with duck-tape, was kneeling on one knee and tending the kettle of watery soup. Sonny could hear the girl counting as she placed beans in separate piles, and he realized that the girl couldn't count past ten. She merely repeated the first ten numbers over and over again until she got confused. Then she tried to even out the piles by sight as the shadows of the fire danced across the floor and the kettle formed a bulbous caldron of despair that consumed the room in darkness.

In Manhattan the Metropolitan Museum of Art was boarded up, and Central Park was all fenced in. It looked like it was a prison for the homeless who lived in the cages like animals. The large bronze statues of *Alice in Wonderland* and the *Mad Hatter* in Central Park were being lit up by red flames emerging from steel drums burning firewood for the poor to warm themselves by. The massive towers of Manhattan were no longer ablaze with light. They were now dark silhouettes that glowed iridescently like a horse fly revealing bridges and walkways that connected the rooftops of the old city to the floor of the new city that was like a spider web. Lower Manhattan was flooded. The streets were made of floating pontoons, and the Battery was a sinking Venice of Concrete. The vision faded, and he once again was looking at a city of lights and the Statue of Liberty and the golden glow of her torch, but he had to wonder. Was he witnessing the beginning of the end? Was the Dark Ages of global corporate feudalism coming? Was that what he saw?

Chapter Four

The next day, Sonny drove upstate by way of Route 17. He drove over hillsides where north sky blue touched evergreen and new leaves of oak and spruce and birch waved in the cool flow of the gentle curves of the road. Once past that forever shopping mall called New Jersey, the countryside was beautiful. The highway cut through the Adirondack Mountains where dynamite and bulldozers sculptured pink, orange, and beige stone. Foothills sloped like tides into the valley where the Delaware and the Susquehanna River flowed over boulders and pebbles and fallen trees, beaver dams and fishing eddies, Calcoon and Skinner's Falls.

Sonny had made this run so many times that he could do it with his eyes closed through blankets of snow, icy roads in a storm, billows of snow caking all; but today the sun was bright and brought out the warmth and color of Upstate New York. Sonny savored the light, the color, and the life. He took nothing for granted. In this part of the country winter was not far beyond the new coat of white paint and the stacks of firewood growing on the side of the house. Sonny put an album by Aerosmith on the tape player; and he listened to the rock and roll pistons, the lead guitar soaring over elevated freeways. He flowed with the music of *Dream On* and Aerosmith singing;

> *Sing, sing with me,*
> *Sing for the year.*
> *Sing for the laughter,*
> *And sing for the tear.*
> *Sing with me.*
> *It's just for today.*
> *Maybe tomorrow,*
> *The God Lord'll take you way.*

Soon Sonny was traveling backcountry roads where plowed fields and old clapboard barns began to appear. The earth was turned over and sprouting green; mud oozed out along the edges like frozen waves of dirty water. Stones jolted steel as a pickup truck pulled into a drive and dogs ran around the splattered tires and children chased each other through clean sheets tracked up with bird's feet flapping in the wind. Sonny could smell the six packs of beer.

As he neared Ithaca, the sun was setting on junk cars, worn out piles of tires, an Agway store, Betty's Grocery, an apple orchard where blossoms were rose colored in the lavender sky. A yellow barn with a stone foundation cast purple shadows and windows glowing like campfires began to appear in the growing darkness. Streetlights appeared as he entered the city.

Sonny pulled into college town and parked in front of the Royal Palms Tavern. The yellow adobe facade had two large circular windows on each side of the door, and a large neon palm tree glowed yellow above the entranceway. Across the street Johnny's Big Red Bar & Grill sign glowed in the neon image of a big red bear, the nickname and symbolic mascot for Cornell University. Johnny's and the Royal Palms met in orange shadows and red and yellow flashes reflecting off multicolored cars blending in with the commercial glow of Sam's College Town Store and the neon white of the UniDeli.

The interior of the Royal Palms was a collage of student abuse and talismanic images of growing up from one generation to another. The 50s black vinyl booths had been patched over and over again, and white cotton stuffing stuck out of the more recent tears in the vinyl. Pictures, hand painted by college age students in the state of drug-induced adolescence, littered the multi-colored squares of Styrofoam on the hung ceiling. Sonny had done one of the squares when he was in college. It was a picture of man looking up God's rear end and seeing a mirror and his own image in it. The caption read, *"Behold, The Infinite Point of the Universe."* One of the walls was covered with a mural of all types of human-like-dogs drinking at the bar. Real dogs hung around the bar or were lounging on the floor that was covered with layers upon layers of stained and worn marble linoleum.

The dogs spotted Sonny before his friends did. Sonny petted Oz, a white fluffy Samoyed. Dunbar rubbed up against Sonny's leg, and Happy smelled his boots and began to wag her tail. Above the scarred and carved dark oak bar was hanging a rowing oar given to the owner by the 1960 rowing team that won the World Cup Regatta. Along the back bar was a glass mirror with etched pictures of shapely women drinking out of champagne glasses. The columns that supported the shelves of liquor were surfaced with miniature glass squares that reflected the drunken light. In the back room, a pool player with his cue stick in hand was leaning against empty beer cases stacked against dark brown wall; and he was staring at the intensely lit billiard table as another player broke the rack spaying brightly colored billiard balls all over the table. On the jukebox Paul Simon was singing,

> *"When you're down and out*
> *When you're on the street*
> *When evening falls so hard*
> *I will comfort you*
> *I'll take your part*
> *When darkness comes*
> *And pain is all around*
> *Like a bridge over troubled waters*
> *I will lay me down*
> *Like a bridge over troubled waters*
> *I will lay me down."*

Sonny saw Jimmy and Big Lou standing near the entranceway. Jimmy was a short stocky man with long sandy brown hair, a drooping full mustache, and bangs like a sheep dog. He was wearing baggy jeans, work boots, and a white T-shirt splattered with what looked like paint, dirt, and motor oil so as to artfully spell out, *"The Ugly Brothers and Company."*

Jimmy noticed Sonny and greeted him warmly then asked, "How long are you here for?"

"I don't know, Jimmy, at least for a month and maybe more. So, what's been happening, man?"

Jimmy laughed his nanny goat laugh and gulped his words like most country people do in Upstate New York; and, in-between his country "well" and the rest of the sentence, he took a swig of beer and said, "Louie and I caught some pretty nice trout today. Yep..." He nodded his head over and over again. "Some pretty nice trout. We've been eating those suckers up all day long and drinkin Louie's homemade apple brandy."

Lou, who wore Billy Holly styled black horn rim glass, was six foot five; and he had a scraggly long black beard and unkempt long black hair. He too was wearing an oil and grease splattered Ugly Brother's T-shirt; and he was still wearing his hip high fishing boots over his loose fitting jeans. Lou's eyes were his most disconcerting feature. Lou had the wild eyes of a Vietnam War veteran who had seen and done too much killing, but that all went away when he smiled and revealed that he had one comical front tooth missing.

"Yep," Lou said, 'you sure missed one hell of a cook out."

"Yep," Jimmy said, "and you should taste Louie's apple brandy." Jimmy nodded his head over and over again. "Yep, you should taste Louie's apple brandy. Yep. Yep."

Jimmy continued to nod his head until all those, "Yeps," like a dog barking got through to Lou who said, "Yeah, I got a jug outside in the truck."

Jimmy smiled, winked at Sonny, and then said, "Well, that's one hell of an idea, Lou. What are we waiting for?"

They walked out of the bar and over to Lou's 1952 Ford pickup truck with chrome monster teeth. It was painted dark Coventry green and looked like it was in mint condition. Lou pulled a jug of chilled apple brandy out of the cooler, and they passed it back and forth. The brandy tasted great to Sonny. It was dry, clear; and judging from the way Jimmy and Louie laughed, it could knock you silly.

Sonny handed the jug to Lou and said, "This stuff is dynamite."

"Yep, we got nine kinds of apples in there and most of them came from the family farm."

Sonny pointed at the T-shirts, "So who are The Ugly Brothers and Company?"

"Well…when Louie and me are not fishing, and we're not working on our cars, we're putting up sheet rock; and I mean putting up sheet rock. You remember how I taught you?"

"Sure."

"Well, it was all wrong."

"Thanks a lot, buddy."

"No, I mean it was all right, and that's why it was all wrong."

"I don't understand."

Jimmy smiled and said, "Well, you come to work with Louie and me this time, and we'll show you how to do it all wrong, but I'll tell you one fuckin thing. We'll have those suckers up fast." Jimmy took another swig of the apple brandy. "Yep, you should see how the Ugly Brothers do it. Nothin right about what we're doin, just fast. It's the American way, Sonny." Jimmy smiled.

Oz, Jimmy's dog, wagged his tail.

Lou belched.

Sonny smiled at the absurdity of the caricatures. Jimmy was a Ph.D. student in engineering who was doing research in solar energy before he dropped out to join the

Greenpeace Movement; and Lou came from a gentile old Ithaca farm family, and he was an undergraduate student at Cornell in Agriculture before he dropped out and was drafted. Now who were they?

Sonny took another swig from the jug and laughed, "So this is it, salt of the earth, working class heroes, limited narrative, and minimalist dialogue?"

Lou farted, and they all burst out laughing, and Sonny said, "Come on, I need a beer to chase down this fire water."

They walked back into the bar, and Sonny bought drinks for Lou and Jimmy; and then he saw Wable, Robin, Bear Claw, and Katmandu Willie at the end of the bar. Wable was tall with dusty blond hair, and he saw the world through faded blue jean eyes that seemed to have just told you a joke about yourself, and you just didn't get it. He was wearing hand-me-down clothes, but it didn't matter to him. Life to Wable was a room full of toys that he played with, and the twelve year old inside of him had hunkered down and refused to grow up because there was nothing to grow too. According to Wable, America was belly up. Strip away all the pretensions and hypocrisy; and it was an absurdist comedy, or as he said it, "His only salvation was that he was the green banana in a rapidly dying culture."

Robin Hathaway was standing next to Wable at the bar; and he was wearing a bright yellow T-shirt, British army knee length shorts with large cargo pockets, hiking boots, and a John Deere cap to hide a severely receding hairline. He maximized the rest of his dark auburn brown hair by wearing it in a ponytail, and his beard was well trimmed, Van Gogh style so as to give him a scholarly look.

Robin was the son of a famous professor at Cornell, and he graduated from Cornell as an English and Language major. When Sonny asked Robin why he hadn't followed in his father's footsteps, Robin said, "I can think in five different languages and nothing I learned at Cornell made sense except in Mandarin Chinese."

Sonny smiled to himself at the many personality changes Robin had gone through over the time that he knew him. He was Robin Crabtree in Height Ashbury reciting nonsensical poetry at the coffee shops; and the more he pulled his lines out of his ass, the more they loved it. In New York City he was Robin Fardash, and he went to all of the Warhol parties and painted the toilet seats between crotches and arches of pee. Sonny went to the opening where they hung Robin's toilet seats; but then Robin had a nervous breakdown. Even at Bellevue Hospital he tried to convince them that he was someone else. To the shrinks he was Robin Hathaway, the paranoid; but to himself, he was Robin Hathaway with a multiple personality disorder. They cured Robin Hathaway, the paranoid; and they let Robin Hathaway and his multiple personalities escape disguised as Robin Hathaway the cured. Then one night, as Robin told it, he grew weary of all the characters that he had created; and he wrote them all down on a slip of paper, tore them up, and threw them in the wastepaper basket; and he became Robin Hathaway singular, first person, future tense. Now he taught English in a high school in Harlem, and he was voted Teacher of the Year every year by the students.

Randy Faramonte, who they called Bear Claw, was pouring himself another glass of beer from the pitcher on the bar. Bear Claw, a robust bear of a man, grew up in Ithaca; and he went to the Industrial and Labor Relations School at Cornell. When he graduated, he joined the marines and went to Vietnam. Halfway through his second tour of duty he refused to kill anymore. Having already won the Bronze Stare for bravery, the Marine Corp brass didn't want to court martial him for fear of what the media would do with the story; so they turned him into a medic and sent him out on the most dangerous missions. They told him that he was never coming back, but he did come home. Now he was a union organizer in the tradition of Eugene Debbs and the Wobblies, and he was organizing service industry workers. He must have come here from work because he was still wearing his polyester suit. The jacket had been thrown over a chair and the sleeves of his white dress shirt were rolled up revealing a tattoo on his arm that read, *"Never Hip A Lame."* Bear Claw was talking to Robin, and when he smiled he flashed a gold tooth that made him look like a Barbary Coast pirate.

Sitting on a barstool next to the Bear Claw was Katmandu Willie. Katmandu Willie was a working class kid who dropped out of high school. He was always in a hurry; and he totaled three cars before he was eighteen; but pot slowed him down; and for the first time in his life, he stopped long enough to really look around. He began to listen, and he began to realize how incredible life was even in the smallest things. Then he got what a poor boy like him would never get, a passport. He traveled to Turkey, Afghanistan, India, and Nepal on bum checks and credit card scams. In India he hyperventilated hash in a shack looking up at a mountain, and he saw Vishnu. In Katmandu, he saw Buddha smiling through the clouds of opium in a death house; and he climbed the Himalayas. The last thing that Sonny heard was that he came home, and he went out to the Far West from the Far East to ride horses and meditate on his inner light, the kick of a Colt 45, the Buddha in every grain of sand, and a cactus that looked like an Indian shaman praying to a lone wolf howling in the pale moonlight amidst absolute silence and billions upon billions of stars.

Bear Claw saw Sonny, and he called to him to join them. Sonny was greeted warmly by everyone, and as he sat down on the barstool Wable said, "Hey, Sonny, you came back home just in time. "We've got a big game Sunday and I put your name on the roster."

"What roster?" Sonny asked.

"The Truckers."

"Softball," Sonny asked.

"This is our year," Wable said. "All we need is a money ballplayer, and you're it. You're going to be our DH."

"Gee, Wable, I don't know how long I'm going to be here."

"You ain't going anywhere. We play National Cash this Sunday for the league championship, and you're playing. I want you to concentrate on line drives, a nice even level swing."

"Are you the coach, Wable?"

"Neah, I'm Catfish Wable, the pitcher. Robin is Twinkle Toes the Terrible, and he's playing shortstop. The Claw, when he's not on the road, is the backstop. Katmandu is playing right field. Crotch plays center field and pitches. Super Co-op is on third. I don't think you know him. He's a member of the Sunshine Farm Commune that Tikey founded.

Super Co-op's OK, a good fielder, but he could use a little less veggies and a little more meat on his bat. Big Ben is our utility player, Ben wrote a rock musical recently that is six hours long, and he wants to sing and play all the parts. We told him that he has to stop playing with himself and play with us. I think it's therapeutic. Joe Fenton is playing left field. He's Siddhartha now. No shit, man. He has an ashram on Aurora Street, and he's teaching us how to breath rhythmically when we are up to bat so we can see the universe in a soft ball."

Wable saw Andy, the bartender approaching them to see if they wanted more drinks, and Wable said, "Our real weakness is second base. We might have to move Robin to second base and try Irish Drew at short."

"Who is Irish Drew?" Sonny asked.

"Some asshole," Robin said, "who thinks his name is some sort of alliteration and a reference to an obscure Irish poet. A literature major I suppose with vain aspirations of becoming a writer, a bumbling babbling one if we were to judge his writing by how well he catches a baseball."

Andy, who cut his hair in the style of Elvis and rolled up his pack of non filter Camel cigarettes in the sleeve of his white T-shirt in the style of James Dean in *Rebel Without a Cause*, stood on the other side of the bar taking it all in, tapping his finger on the bar, waiting for them to get through shitting on him. Finally, he said, "Fuck you guys."

Wable looked at Andy derisively and said, "If I ordered another drink, do you think you could handle it; or are you going to bobble that too, Irish Drew?" Wable drew out the Irish Drew like it was some sort of rotgut whiskey.

Sonny laughed and pointed at Andy and said, "This is Irish Drew?"

Irish Drew juggled the drinks, snatched their money up like he was fielding a ball, and gave them the finger as he moved away.

Sonny laughed and said, "Is Tikey playing?"

"He's playing first," Wable said. "He's probably our best hitter."

"How's the farm doing?" Sonny asked.

"The commune's doing great," the Bear Claw said. "Everything they grow is organic, even the feed; and they grow specialty items like fresh herbs that they sell to the gourmet stores and food markets in New York City. Do you know how much thistles are going for an ounce? I'm telling you, man, you're in the wrong business, Sonny. The bad news is that Tike broke up with his old lady."

"Why?" Sonny asked.

"I guess he came home one night and found her in bed with his best friend."

"Who?"

"Gene."

"From Trumansburg?"

"Yep."

"Didn't he play for the Truckers a couple of years ago?" Sonny asked.

"Yeah," the Claw said, "but he's playing for the Rongovian Embassy now, and he's turned from buddy to buddy fucker with the change of uniform."

"What about the twins?" Sonny asked.

Bear Claw shrugged. "I don't know. They're twins so I guess they can split them up."

Robin laughed and said, "It's the perfect solution to the modern marriage. Alter everyone's genetic code so that everyone has twins. Then when the inevitable happens, they just take one each."

Sonny laughed. "That's funny, Robin."

"Where are you staying, Sonny?" Wable asked.

"Right now, nowhere."

"You can crash at Club Sleeze if you want."

"Sounds good, Wable."

"Joe's got a room upstairs that he wants to rent," Robin said.

"Really? Where's Joe?"

Robin gestured towards the rear of the bar. "He's out back. They're having a horseshoe tournament out there."

"Who's playing?" Sonny asked.

"Tonight it's the Royal Palms against Twietmann's, Robin said."

"I have to see this." Sonny walked to the back of the bar, past the pool table and out into the backyard of the Royal Palms. From the rear, the Royal Palms looked like a stack of beer cases ready to fall over. The horseshoe pits were flooded with light. Weeds hung over a chain link fence, and several picnic tables were off to the side and a bunch of people were sitting there watching the game. Joe was at one of the picnic tables. With his horn rim sunglasses and his slicked back ducks ass haircut, Joe looked like the Mafia representative to The Farm Bureau.

Sonny sat down next to Joe, "Hey, Joe."

"Hey, Sonny."

They watched the horseshoe match. Andy's brother Ben and Bill Hill were playing for the Royal Palms. They looked like pink and purple Easter chicks compared to the old rosters from Twietmann's. Ben was trying to out redneck the rednecks as he stood around kickin up dirt and lookin like he had a bag of shit it in his pants. Finally, one of the guys from Twietmann's stuck out his beer belly and let the horseshoe fly. It flipped a couple of times, and then Sonny heard the sound of the horseshoe ringing the stake.

Bill and the other player from Twietmann's stood there with a horseshoe in one hand and a beer in the other staring into the pit. Sonny could hear the grass growing. Finally, the tall lanky player from Twietmann's picked up the horseshoe and shouted, "Twietmann's one, the Royal Palms zero."

Sonny listened to everyone bantering back and forth. At one point Gump shouted from the sidelines. "Hey, Ben, why don't you loosen up those suspenders. You sound like a Jew's harp."

Sonny laughed, it was true; Ben was twanging it up a bit. In fact, everyone was playing up his farmer's role in this horseshit tournament, everybody except Bill. Bill just seemed happy to be shooting shoes with the boys and drinkin beer. Bill was a Vietnam War veteran who came back from the war and enrolled in the Cornell Law School with the intent of becoming a civil rights defender and a public interest advocate of the poor. Recently he discovered that he was dying from a bone cancer caused by Agent Orange, so he didn't seem to be caught up in the theatrical part of the game. He seemed to be happy just being alive and tossing the shoe, watching it go flip flop in the floodlights then plop down hard in the dirt as it slid towards the stake pushing up clouds of dirt coming to rest.

"That-a-way, Bill!"

Bill took a swig of the cold bottle of beer perspiring

in his hand. He looked satisfied. The horseshoe swung back and forth in the other hand like a weighted pendulum as the Grateful Dead sang,

"Goddamn, well I declare, have you seen the like?
Their walls are built of cannonballs,
Their motto is don't tread on me.
Come hear Uncle John's band playing to the tide,
Come with me, or go alone,
He's come to take his children home.
It's the same story the crow told me;
It's the only one he knows.
 Like the morning sun you come
And like the wind you go.
Ain't no time to hate, barely time to wait,
We, oh, what I want to know,
Where does the time go?"

Sonny turned to Joe and said, "Joe, I hear you have an apartment for rent upstairs."

"Yes, Sonny, I do. It needs some work though."

"That's not a problem. I'll do the work. It will be good for me."

"I'll give you the first month's rent free plus pay for the materials if you fix it up nice for me."

"It's a deal, Joe."

"Don't you want to see what it looks like before you decide?" Joe asked.

"Hey, Joe, this is me. I know what it looks like. It looks like shit."

Joe laughed and said, "Yeah, I guess you're right, but

it could look really nice if you fixed it up." Joe laughed again. "I think I'll wait until you fix it up before I decide how much I'll charge you. If it looks really good, I'll charge you a hundred twenty five a month."

"It's a deal. Where's the key?"

Joe fished through his pockets and pulled out a key ring. He pulled a key off the ring of keys and handed it to Sonny then smiled and said, "Welcome home."

"Thanks Joe." In the background Sonny heard the crowd cheer. Bill finally threw his last horseshoe. Sonny went inside and on the jukebox Don McLean was singing,

"Bye, bye Miss American Pie.
Drove my Chevy to the levy,
But the levy was dry.
And them good old boys were drinkin whiskey in
Rye,
Singin,
This will be the day that I die."

The song made Sonny sad. Everyone here seemed to be playing at being working class heroes and giving the work-a-day-life a fourth dimension, but could they hold out against the dominate narrative that was intent on destroying all traces of the 60s by controlling all the major media and eliminating all the spaces between the lines so that there would be no alternative story to retreat to and therefore no meaning. Would these parts that they were so playfully playing at become their lives? Would the stage lights slowly dim until they forgot who they were and that the revolution was about where authorship and authority resides and whose story this is, theirs or ours. In the end, would they be like the guy at the bar wearing work boots with steal toes looking blankly at his glass of beer and then blankly at the TV that he can't hear because the music is too loud.

On Sonny's way through the crowd, someone grabbed him around the waist from behind and hugged him. He turned around. It was Heather Johnson. Heather had flaming red hair that was long and wild and sweaty from partying all day and swimming in the bikini bathing suit that she was wearing underneath a damp white cutoff T-shirt and shorts that hung loosely at her hips. Her face was a little puffed up from drinking too much today; but her clear blue eyes, the easy smile, the perfect white teeth, and even features gave her the appearance of the All American girl from Middle America in a Colgate Toothpaste Ad. Heather's face, however, belied the fact that Heather had been a member of the Weathermen, and Sonny had heard that she was with the Sandinistas in Nicaragua. Heather was an old friend, and Sonny hugged her and asked, "You came for the funeral?"

"Wouldn't miss it. I'm on vacation; and I'm staying with Annie who is living in a yurt that she built. We bath in her pond, run around naked, and have intercourse with her goats; or, at least, that's what the neighbors say."

Heather laughed and said, "She's so out there, Sonny. She wants to be totally self-sufficient. She has her own smoke house and underground root storage cellar where she stores vegetable and fruit preserves from her garden and apple orchard. She made the dandelion wine that we got bombed on today."

"She's going to live there in the winter?" Sonny asked.

"She says that she's going to build a log cabin all on

her own." Heather laughed. "She has a book on it. I told her that she can come live with me and camp out in front of my fireplace, and I'll surround her with plants and flowers."

"Where do you live?" Sonny asked. "What have you been doing? Are you wanted? Is the FBI going to burst in here at any moment? Should I be somewhere else?"

Heather laughed and said, "No, as far as I know, I'm not wanted by anyone."

Sonny put his arm around her affectionately and said, "I want you."

"Get out of here, Sonny. You want every woman in the world. Tall, small, fat and skinny, it doesn't matter to you. You love women. That's one of the things that I love about you."

Sonny laughed. "That's not so. Women are great sorceresses, all of them; and I'm a willing participant; so I don't see them as tall, small, fat, or skinny. I see them as stately, petite, voluptuous, and lithe."

The both laughed and Sonny asked, "So what are you doing? Where are you living?"

"I'm working for Amnesty International, and I'm living in Washington."

"I saw Miranda in New York City," Sonny said.

"I know. She told me. She still is in love you, you know."

Miranda and Heather had been close friends in graduate school; and they were part of a tight knit group of women student activists and feminists that Sonny use to call *The Sick Sisters*; but, no matter how close they all were, Sonny didn't want to talk to Heather about Miranda because he felt a lecture coming on; so he changed the subject.

"What about Jan? Have you heard from her?" Sonny asked

"Jan wrote me a letter about six months ago. She's a big editor in New York now for one of those chic new glossy sea level magazines. She's in line to become the editor-in-chief."

"Good for her. She once told me that her biggest handicap in life was the fact that she had been raised to be the prize, and she was right. She is beautiful, smart, personable, and she has a wonderful sense of humor. Some rich asshole would have loved to snatch her up and made her a trophy for the rest of her life. I'm glad to see that she's doing what she wants to do. Is she married?"

"No. She's not married, but she says she's beginning to suffer growing pains every time she sees a baby."

Sonny laughed and then said, "How about Marge?"

"Marge is dead, Sonny. She committed suicide last year."

"Oh, no," Sonny felt true grief. Marge had been like a sister to him. "God, I don't know anyone who was more kind hearted than Marge. She had such hopes and dreams for everyone. What happened?"

"I think she died of a broken heart, another casualty of the war against cruelty and oppression in a country where love is a victim and rape is the standard of living for women. God, I hate this country," Heather said. "I can't wait for the guillotines to appear so I can play Madame Lafarge to these sons of a bitches who run this country."

Heather had tears in her eyes. Sonny hugged her and whispered, "Someday."

Heather wiped her eyes, smiled, and said, "You look

great, Sonny. I ask people what you been doing, and they just shrug. So what have you been doing?"

Sonny shrugged, and Heather laughed then she kissed him on the cheek and whispered, "You be careful, Sonny. If you ever need any help, call me. Anything. I'm a lawyer, you know." She pulled away and looked at him as if she wanted to take a picture, but then Heidi Rosen came up to her and gave Heather a big hug. Heidi had not seen her for years.

"I'll see you at the funeral," Sonny said. "We'll give the old girl a good send off."

Heather looked like she wanted to ask Sonny something more, something personal; but Heidi was demanding all of her attention; so Sonny returned to where Wable, Robin, The Claw, and Katmandu and sitting and announced, "I've rented the apartment off of Joe."

"Far out," Robin said.

"I'm going to get my shit out of the car before it gets stolen."

"Listen, man," Wable said. "There's probably no bed up there, so why don't you crash at Club Sleeze. Take the guest suite. It's all yours," he said with a flourish; but put the "Do Not Disturb" sign on the door before you go to sleep."

Sonny laughed and said, "Thanks, Wabs." I'll see you later."

Sonny left the bar, and he took the stairway to the second floor. The apartment that Sonny was looking for was at the head of the stairs. He opened the door, turned on the light, and fortunately the light switch had a dimmer which Sonny immediately turned down. The place was a mess. There was debris all around. The sink had a broken drain with a pail underneath. The stove was greasy, and Sonny didn't dare to look into the refrigerator. To cheer himself up, he dimmed the lights a little more. The apartment had been recently sheet rocked and the walls had been recently painted a flat white. The hardwood floors were dusty and scratched up. Sonny turned the lights down again. Now the bathroom looked like it just needed some cleaning, and the floors didn't look so bad. It was going to be fine.

Sonny went down to the car and brought his stuff up to the apartment, and he was getting his overnight kit out of his backpack when he heard someone coming up the stairs. When he turned to see who it was, he saw Heather standing at the door. From the smile on her face and the look in her eyes, he knew what she wanted. He walked over to her and put his arm around her waist, his hand slipping down to her ass that felt like it had been pumping away on a bicycle seat for miles, firm and round and responsive as he ran his fingers up and down the crease of her ass.

Heather grabbed Sonny's bulging cock through his pants then ran her finger up and down the zipper on his pants and said, "I never got to say goodbye, Sonny."

Sonny slipped his fingers up and under her shorts and bathing suit, and she was dripping wet and her skin was burning from the sun that may have ignited her desires. Sonny took her hand, her love juices on his fingers, and led her into the room. He unrolled his blond sheepskin rug and placed it on the floor; and when he turned around, Heather had already taken off her T-shirt and shorts; and she was unfastening her bikini top that was made of a glittering gold and silver and brown knit that unraveled to reveal beautiful firm voluptuous breasts. Heather pulled down her thong style bikini bottom that seemed just to fall away in a pool of glitter; and she rolled around in the rug then spreading her legs to receive Sonny who buried himself in her naked flesh and the smell of Cayuga Lake, Annie's pond, cattails and crushed flowers, pine needles, burnt fire wood, burning ambers, dandelions wine, saliva, and semen.

Heather made love like a woman who had not made love for a long while, her passion all pent up into a wildness that needed a release. As she wrapped herself around him, she kept telling him to fuck her harder and harder until she started to scream with a passion that seemed to hurt her at the same time it gave her boundless joy. When Sonny thought it was over, she went down on him, mouthing him until his cock bulged again with desire; and then she laid back ready for him to enter her; but first he teased her like she had teased him with her lips, sucking on her tits, licking her nipples until they were as hard as his dick; and then he entered her, this time slowly drawing it in and out, longer and longer, until she seemed to be going into a trance, her eye lids fluttering. Sonny felt her let go, letting him into a place deep inside of her; and they both came.

Heather started to cry. Sonny was alarmed. He thought somehow he had hurt her. "What's the matter, Heather? Did I do something wrong?"

Heath slipped out from under Sonny, and she hugged him and said, "No, Sonny, you didn't do anything wrong. Quite the opposite, it was beautiful; but it's all breaking up; and we're all going in our own directions. I wanted this because I don't know if we'll ever see each other again. I want to remember us like this." Heather kissed him, and then got up and put on her clothes. Sonny watched her a bit confused as she went to the door and said, "I love you, Sonny."

"I love you too."

"I know, but you're not in love with me. I don't think I'm in love with you either." She shrugged. "I could say that you know where I am; and I'm always there for you; and we'll be friends for life; but, somehow, it never works out that way; and I don't know why."

"Hey," Sonny said and smiled. "You're my mouthpiece and what a mouth piece. Wow. You're my lawyer for life."

Heather laughed then said, "If you need me, Sonny, you know where I am. Call me." Heather turned and walked down the stairs, her bare feet almost noiseless as she disappeared.

Sonny thought about just going to sleep right there on the rug, but he knew he would be sore as hell tomorrow if he slept on the floor. Sonny got up; and he decided to take the shortcut to Club Sleaze; so he grabbed his overnight bag, a towel, a change of clothing, and his sleeping bag; and he climbed out of the window in the hallway and walked onto the flat rooftop of the adjacent building. The stars were out and the moon was bright and full. He could hear the loud music and the crowd below at The Palms. The lead singer for Pink Floyd was shouting.

> *"We don't need no education*
> *We don't need no thought control*
> *No dark sarcasm in the classroom*
> *Teacher leave them kids alone*
> *Hey! Teachers! Leave them kids alone!*
> *All in all it's just another brick in the wall."*

Sonny climbed onto the porch of Club Sleaze and entered through the window and then walked through the darkness out into the light of the living room. Club Sleaze was pretty much as he remembered it. It had cheaply paneled walls that didn't look like much more than cardboard pictures of wood, and there were a couple of couches and chairs with the stuffing kicked out of them. The steel office desks that were once manned by activists organizing demonstrations and voter registration were pushed against the wall and were now stacked with old pamphlets, handouts, books, and an old hand cranked printer that once churned out flyers. The walls were covered with posters.

One was a black and white poster created for the Vietnam Day Committee announcing the October 16th demonstration in Ithaca and throughout the country. It consisted simply of a fist held up and extended into the air and a caption that read, *Resist!* Another poster announced the 1967 Demonstration in Detroit and listed its demands. *Elections are a Hoax - US out of South East Asia and the Middle East - End Oppression of Women - Cops Out of the Ghettos - Free Political Prisoners.*

On another wall was a poster with a black and white picture of an Indian woman and her child surrounded by the silhouettes of Union soldiers aiming their rifles and bayonets at them. The caption read, *We Remember Wounded Knee,* and in the bathroom, above the toilet, was a poster of the black silhouettes of women holding hands marching up a mountainside and holding a flag bearing the symbol for the female sex and a caption that read,

"We Celebrate the Women's Struggle. We Celebrate the People's Victory. The mountain is only so high. Our capacity is without limits. The stars move, our will is unshakable."

On the bathroom floor were stacks and stacks of Playboy magazines, the best collection in town. Sonny chuckled and thought to himself, "Well, nobody said that we were mature. We were just children dreaming of love not war."

In the sixties, Club Sleaze was the main office for the underground in Ithaca and a stronghold of the student revolution and the counter culture that spilled out of the university classrooms into the streets then graduated to the countryside and later spread throughout the land, but it still clung to the origins of its original idea, the womb that it came from – stillborn. Club Sleaze was still known in the underground as the place to go; but more often, now, it was just a crash pad for anyone who didn't have a home or was too drunk or stoned to drive. The motto of Club Sleaze was written on the wall above the entranceway, *"What Goes Around, Comes Around."*

Sonny opened up the refrigerator. There was a six-pack of beer in there and a pot of peeled potatoes. Sonny pulled out a can of beer and popped the top. He looked for a garbage can, but he soon realized that he was standing in it. Actually the garbage cans were in the corner of the room, but they overflowed onto the kitchen counter piled high with empty beer cans and dirty plates spiced with bits and pieces of food. The moldy pie with cigarette butts pouring out from underneath the crust was the most appetizing, and the kitchen sink looked like a pile of junk someone had tried to bury in a swamp. Sonny was sorry that he had opened up a can of beer, now he was part of the problem for which there was no solution but to take out the garbage.

Sonny put the pop-top in his pocket, and he went into the living room. God, I don't know how Wable can live like this, he thought to himself as he turned on the TV that had a rabbit ear antenna for reception. A grainy picture of black and white and gray dancing dots came on the screen that made him feel as if the news was coming to him from the twilight zone. The news show was reporting on the Senate Select Committee Hearings on Watergate. A Nixon aide had revealed that Nixon had secretly put microphones in the Oval Office and all of his conversations had been recorded. An image of Nixon's face appeared on the screen; and as Sonny put the dots together, it became a black and white mosaic of a paranoid schizophrenic who saw his own evil in others and saw conspiracies everywhere when he was conspiring against all. As Sonny watched Nixon stare through two black dots at the all-seeing God of TV and the surveillance tapes, he wondered if Nixon knew what he had become. Was that why he was compelled to record it all? Did the son of Quakers want to bear witness to the enemy within?

Sonny changed the channel to *Laugh In*, took a sip of beer, and he was about to sit down on the couch when he looked down and saw, "Dunbar!"

Dunbar, Wable's dog, wagged his tail a couple of times as if to wave. He eyed Sonny suspiciously.

"Don't worry Dunbar, first come, first serve. The couch is yours." Sonny sat down on the other couch, and Dunbar stretched out and curled back up into a ball. Sonny drank his beer and watched Dunbar watching him. Dogs were special in Ithaca. Anabel Taylor, years ago, left all her money to Cornell University with one stipulation. You couldn't throw a dog out of any building on campus. Now dogs ran free all over Ithaca, and freshmen picked up their puppies with their beanies, and little old ladies beat dogcatchers with brooms.

"Dunbar, what's it like to be a sacred cow?" Sonny asked.

Dunbar groaned and buried his nose in the couch and began chewing on a spot that probably was the smell of a five-year-old hamburger. Sonny watched Dunbar roll over on his back and stick his nose in some of the exposed stuffing that was shaped like a cloud coming out of the couch. Dunbar moaned and put his paws up in the air. His eyes were closed. He was in doggy heaven smelling who knows what, maybe the smell of jelly doughnuts in a pretty girl's hand.

Sonny tried to watch Laugh In, but he was so tired that he couldn't focus, so he got up and turned the television off. He went into the bedroom, spread his sleeping bag out over the bed then flopped on the bed and immediately fell asleep.

The next morning, the clear crisp air poured through the window like a cold shower of oxygen; and it woke Sonny. Beams of light bounced off the walls and settled like a pool of golden water across the floor. The dust rose like dew into a misty fog.

Sonny sat up and rubbed his eyes then walked into the living room. Lou was crashed out on one couch. Jack Mack was crashed out on the other couch, and Big Zeke was passed out on the mattress in the middle of the floor.

Sonny very carefully moved their feet and silently tied their shoestrings together. As a final touch he tied Jack's foot to Big Zeke's foot. They formed a dangling rope of legs across the space between the two couches. The way Sonny saw it; Wable would walk out of the bedroom and head for the toilet. He would trip over Jack and Lou's feet and fall on Zeke and Jack, and Lou would fall on both of them. Sonny laughed all the way down the stairs. Out on the street, he walked to the UniDeli for a cup of coffee. Once there he planned out his day and read the sports section of *The New York Post*.

In the early part of the day, he scrubbed his apartment clean, and then he drove over to the U-Rental and got himself a floor sander. Sonny had enough money to live just about anywhere he wanted to live in Ithaca; but it wasn't a good idea to flash money when you had no visible means of support; and, for the most part, Sonny had very little interest in money and luxury items. When Josh gave him the money he earned, he would put it in his safety deposit box and go on living as he had always lived, modestly and with good taste. Working on this beat up old apartment wasn't a chore to him at all. He loved to take abused and neglected things and give new life to them.

Around noon he took a break and decided to take a walk in the gorge. As he walked down the steps to the gorge, he could hear the roar of the falls; and his thoughts of New York City were washed away by the sight of the water cascading down a rocky precipice. The sharp edges of the rocks gleamed like crystal, and the water felt like it was flowing through his veins. It was great to be back in Ithaca, walking down this path, the light reflecting off the water, his remembrances.

He sat down on a natural bench surrounded by an amphitheater of stone where words and sounds echoed. He remembered when he was a young undergraduate at Cornell, and he would come here to sit alone, hidden, and let his mind roam freely around in the world of words, taking each letter and following its line, trying to get a feeling for the spells it cast, the words it wove itself into, trying to find the source of light in the lines of sound, the vision in language, words whirling into reeling lines of light weaving into flashing luminous patterns of trans-magic, flares from the spinning whirls, weaving spells, creating visions out of words, the light playing off the leaves like so many pages, the rock-like-objects punctuated by shadows, parables nestled in the wind, birds chirping.

From where he was sitting he could look up to the edge of the gorge and see Beak's Peak. It was from there that Beak had tried to crash, soaring over the edge one night after speeding on drugs for three days. Chucky Wells, the Bear Claw, and Sonny had descended into the gorge looking for Beak. It was like descending into the Inferno at night. The sound of the water felt like blood gushing through the gorged out earth. They could hear Wable shouting from above for Beak. They looked up. Three quarters of the way up the side of the gorge was a dark recession. It looked like a ledge, so they climbed up the side of the gorge to take a look, feeling for a body as they climbed. When they reached the gaping darkness they called for Beak.

"Beak, are you there? Beak, it's OK. It's the Claw. Beak?"

They heard the rushing of feet as if Beak was running

over treetops. They felt him soar over their heads. Sonny and the Claw simultaneously stood up and reached out. Chucky grabbed hold of both of them. They all flew off into darkness. He saw the period and the end through the silence fly, the point grow into night. Whose dying vision, his or mine?

By the time Sonny realized that Beak may have taken all three of them with him, they tumbled and fell into a dirt slide coming to a halt tangled up in the branches of a fallen tree. They were all alive, no broken bones, a few cuts and bruises; but they survived the crash.

The next day, Wable painted a white X to mark the spot where Beak had landed. "It gives people something to shoot for," Wable said as he climbed back out of the gorge with his paintbrush and can of white paint. From that day on the spot was known as Beak's Peak. Sonny thought about Marge and how she committed suicide. There were so many casualties in the civil war that never happened. He thought about Miranda and how they broke up.

Sonny remembered the day that he broke up with Miranda. It was near the end when the 60s were over and everyone was crashing or looking for a safe place to land. Sonny remembered hanging out with Robin and Bear Claw at Moorie's, a bar situated on one of the steep hills that led up to the Cornell campus "far above Cayuga's waters" as the school song said. The owner of Moorie's had a pragmatic approach to owning a bar in college town. He had a great location in the middle of a magnificent ice carving that had melted away after the Ice Age and left behind the hills, the gorges, the falls, and the lake below; so his philosophy was to keep it simple and cheap – a bar made of two-by-fours, plywood with a mahogany veneer, a Formica bar top, heavy barstools that would not fall over easily, sturdy chairs and tables, and booze. Plastic Tiffany style lights that he got for free from the beer salesman hung from the ceiling advertising Budweiser beer, and a bright yellow neon sign that scrolled out the name of Miller High Life hung from the front window along with a picture of a Bicardi Rum bottle in an ice blue glacial setting, sparkling and glowing from the back light like a wedding ring for alcoholics.

Beyond the pure funk, the feature of Moorie's that Sonny liked best were the large picture windows on both sides of the entranceway that looked out at Eddy Street and the Eddy Street Gate. The Eddy Street Gate was the original gateway to Cornell, and it was a stone archway covered with ivy that had a quote carved across the stone archway by Ezra Cornell, the original founder of the university, that read, *"So enter that daily thou mayest become more learned and thoughtful."* Above the quotation someone had painted in subway style bright red graffiti letters, *"Leave and Learn."*

Near the gate was a grass slope where the students, young townies, and a splattering of adults and faculty members gathered to sun themselves and read or drink beer or wine out of a bottle in a paper bag to be passed around in the communal setting that they called, People's Park in Ithaca. From the slope they could look out at the city and the lake below, or watch one another go up and down the street to and from the campus and in and out of stores – the Italian carry out for a sub or pizza or pasta; the Greek restaurant that featured Popeye pizza with feta cheese; the shoe store that sold leather sandals, sneakers, and boots to the college kids and Florsheim shoes for everyone else; the laundry mat where you could find everything you wanted to know on the bulletin board; and the small grocery store whose main consumer products were beer, soda, toothpaste, Tampon's, toilet paper, and cigarettes, no matches. Or they could watch students going in and out of old worn down ill repaired homes, some classics that were built in the 19th century and converted into pre-trashed apartment buildings with false Styrofoam ceilings, drafty windows, worn out linoleum, wall-to-wall cheap carpets, and pre-stained old appliances and toilet fixtures.

All up and down the street neon signs formed a babel of consumerism; and beyond the babel, along the edge of college town, was the gorge, the falls, and Beak's Peak. Sonny and Miranda lived on this street. They lived across the street from Moorie's and the slope. Sonny's favorite time was late at night when all the neon signs were turned off, and everyone went home to sleep, and the streets were silent except for the sound of the falls echoing through the gorge calling to him.

The day they broke up, Moories was packed with people, and there was a feminist rally outside on the slope that was spilling out onto the street. One speaker after another was extolling their sisters to throw off the yoke of oppression; and the speeches were intermingled with music by an all women's rock bank called, No Men Allowed, who were singing, *"I got my own electric guitar now, baby, and you can't shout me down."*

Sonny was looking out Moorie's window at it all, and he saw the Shuffler shuffling by. The Shuffler was a brilliant chemist who had taken one too many acid trips on an acid that he made in his own lab. The Shuffler believed that the earth was going to crack when we sucked out all the oil, and solar energy would not be our salvation. Light would become just another form of capitalist currency; and the rich would eventually suck up all the light and heat; and in the shadows of the giant solar satellites, large segments of the population would live in perpetual darkness and freeze to death. Eventually, we would destroy ourselves completely because the human species was a failed experiment and consciousness was the original sin. The Shuffler was wearing a T-shirt that said, *Think and Die*, and on the jukebox Blind Faith was singing,

> *"Come down off your throne*
> *And leave your body alone*
> *Somebody must change*
> *You are the reason*
> *I've been waiting so long*
> *Somebody holds the key*
> *Well, I'm near the end*
> *And I just ain't got the time*
> *Oh, and I'm wasted*
> *And I can't find my way home"*

While Sonny was watching the Shuffler shuffle pass the window very slowly balancing his head like a jumbo egg ready to fall to the pavement in a Humpty-Dumpty tragedy, Katmandu Willie came into Morrie's and joined Robin, Bear Claw, and Sonny at the table. As the door to Morrie's swung open and closed, the voices of women outside could be heard shouting, "Freedom Now."

Sonny laughed and pointed at Katmandu Willie and

said, "I was just thinking about the degeneracy of values, and look who appears like the genie in a bottle of codeine cough syrup."

Willie grabbed The Claw's bottle of beer, took a swig, and said, "What the fuck are you guys doing in here. There are hundreds of chicks out there ready to be fucked."

Robin corrected him. "The operative term, Willie, is "relate". Haven't you read your Lysistrata?"

"OK, then, let's go relate."

Robin laughed and said, "You know. I was sitting next to Katmandu Willie at the bar the other day; and he was talking to this chick; and he said to her that he went to Katmandu to see a guru; and the guru said to him that, "Life is nothing but a fountain."

Robin looked confused then said, "What the fuck does that mean, Willie?"

"I was explaining to her how when I make love the female becomes the Goddess Sakti and that in the tantra-yoga-asama of Kundalini one must rise as one must fall in the cosmic fusion of polarities, and it is in this heightened state of sexual awareness that we, for a moment, experience Nirvana as a perpetual orgasm."

"Jesus, Willie," Bear Claw said, "where did you learn all that bullshit, in Katmandu?"

"No, I read it in a book, but it seems to work. I get Kundalined a lot, man."

They all laughed, and Robin got up and said, "I'm with Willie. Let's go relate and participate in the bacchanal gathering of the witches. As they say in French, La vie Boheme."

Bear Claw raised his glass and said, "Here's to free love. It's one hell of a shot in the arm for the working class man."

They all raised their glasses and toasted, "To free love."

As Sonny got up from the table, he saw Wable get up from his seat at the bar and approach two college students who were leaving Morrie's. "I don't mean to bother you," Wable said, "but I'm collecting for the Dunbar Fund. I don't know if you know who Dunbar is?"

Wable showed them a jar with a slot in the top. There was some money in the jar and a picture of Dunbar pasted to the glass peering pathetically up at the two college students from the picture, one of his legs was in a cast.

"He doesn't have a job," Wable said, "and I thought maybe you might consider contributing a little to his fund. It will go towards his doctor bills, dog food, etc."

Robin shouted, "It's a scam, man. Make him show you the dog."

One of the students had his hands in his pocket and was about to pull out some money when the other student laughed and said, "Let's see the dog."

"Ye of little faith," Wable said, and he shouted for Dunbar who was hiding under a table. Dunbar came out and peeked around the bar, no broken leg. He saw the jar, and he began to limp. Wable walked to the door and opened it up and said, "Dunbar, I want you to go out there and find me a pretty kitty."

Dunbar took off out the door running, and Wable turned to the crowd, shrugged and said, "It's a miracle." He then looked over to Sonny, Bear Claw, Robin, and Katman Willie and said, "It's time to go hunting, Boys."

Sonny could see that Miranda was about to speak, so he stood up and said, "I'm going outside too."

"Jolly good," Robin said, "Let us all go and relate."

They all left Moorie's and joined the demonstration. Miranda was standing in front of their apartment building where the band had set up their equipment to play, and she was using one of the band's microphones to speak to the growing number of demonstrators that filled the street and the slope.

"The feminist movement," she said, "is not about the male world of adolescent competition and winners and losers or a class of people who live above the law and are networked into a web of power and greed that has no bounds, an amoral world where pathological personalities survive by ruthlessly destroying and feeding off of the lives of others with an insatiable hunger that has lost its flavor in the transformation from the human to the sociopath. We see these monsters in lush restaurants eating small portions from large plates, picking at their food as they conspire to consume the indigestible.

Too often women have embraced their oppressors or emulated the male role model and become equal participants in an oppressive society that, at its extreme, comes together in one identity, the criminally insane who lurk in our streets and roam the corridors of Wall Street and stand astride our largest corporations like muggers and rapists.

Nor are we about a society where working class Americans, who work at dead end jobs, have to look long and hard to find someone worse off then themselves so that they too can declare themselves winners. This is the role of the homeless in a heartless society. This is not what the feminist movement is all about. We as women need to lead the revolution against a society that believes that death and destruction are manly virtues and love and care and empathy for our fellow human beings is feminine and weak. We need to rise up and affirm the power of life against death and restore the eternal balance of Mother Nature because we, as women, are most qualified to care for our country and our global family and lead America into a new age."

The demonstrators burst out in cheers and applause, and Katmandu Willie shouted in Sonny's ear so that he could hear him. "Do you know what she's talking about?"

"In your terms or mine," Sonny asked.

Katmandu Willie shrugged. "Whatever way it makes sense."

"She's saying that it is bad enough that half the population in America are assholes; but if women embrace male role models of success, we will have a country full of assholes." Sonny laughed and said, "It's about the unmeaning of America."

Katmandu Willie laughed and said, "I dig," then he pointed into the crowd and said, "Look whose here."

Dunbar was back in front of Morrie's, wagging his tail, looking for Wable. He had a pretty girl with him. He looked in the window of Morrie's. No Wable. He turned around and corralled the girl again just as Wable came out of the crowd on the run and embraced his long lost friend. Dunbar licked his face. The girl smiled. Wable patted Dunbar on the head and expressed his eternal gratitude. He was on one knee; and in no time, he had the girl laughing as Wable paused between lines from time to time to have Dunbar do a few tricks.

Sonny watched Wable, Dunbar, and the girl go off into the crowd of people. The speeches stopped and the band began to play again. Soon after that Eban Sinclair came up to Sonny, Robin, Willie and The Claw and said, "Peace, brothers."

"Look who we got here, Sonny," Katmandu Willie said. "It's Little Eban MBA."

Willie didn't like Eban. Willie thought that Eban had been a police informant during the takeover of Willard Straight Hall by members of the Afro-American Society at Cornell University on parent's weekend, April 19, 1969. The takeover of the dining and recreational hall turned into the first armed standoff on an American university campus. The National Guard were brought in, the national media appeared, and the takeover ended with a picture of the black activists emerging from the building armed with shotguns and rifles and a promise by the administration of amnesty, an African American Studies Program, and an increase in minority enrollment in the university. Over the door of the entranceway to Willard Straight Hall that the armed militants had marched through in triumph was a banner that read, *Welcome Parents.*

Sonny didn't know if Eban was an informant; but he did know that Eban had first been a member of SNCC, then SDS, then the Weathermen, and more recently The Gay Rights Liberation Movement, and now he had just been admitted into the Cornell University School of Business Administration. Sonny remembered back to People's Park when Eban was one of the first students to throw a bottle at the cops and may have been instrumental in provoking the violence. Maybe he was an informer and an agent provocateur or maybe Miranda was right. He was just an asshole.

"Hey, Bro," Eban said to Sonny, "I need a favor."

"What's that, Eban?"

"I want you to talk to Miranda about allowing me to speak at the rally."

"Why me?"

"She's your girlfriend, and I thought you might have an in with her, so to speak. She doesn't like me."

"I know. She told me that media monsters like you and Jerry Rubin fucked up the movement. The networks saw you coming and said, 'Hey, let's turn the spotlight on these guys. They'll make assholes out of everyone.' "

"She said that?"

"Yes, and she also said that all you want is that microphone in your hand. That's your cock. You're not a political revolutionary. You're a public exhibitionist."

"Fuck her. I'm going to speak whether she likes it or not."

"I don't think so." Sonny turned to Katmandu Willie and said, "Willie, if little Eban Sinclair tries to whip out his dick and talk into it, hit him in the head with a bottle."

Eban turned to Katmandu Willie and said, "Willie, you wouldn't do that to me, would you?"

Willie shrugged and said, "Hey, Eban, life is nothing but a fountain."

Eban nodded, contemplating what Willie said, gave Willie a weary glance then walked away. A few moments later, black and white police patrol cars appeared with their red lights flashing; and Sonny watched the Police Chief and four other cops approach the band. The Police Chief talked to the bandleader who shrugged then took the microphone and said, "People, we've just been told by the police that we have to stop playing."

The crowd booed and jeered, but the band started to

pack up their instruments. Then Sonny saw Miranda arguing with the police chief.

"We have a permit. This is perfectly legal." She then showed him the permit.

The Police Chief barely looked at it before he handed it back to her and said, "You don't have a permit to be a public nuisance and disturb the peace. We've received several complaints, and we want you to disperse."

"I want to see the complaints. They have to be in writing. That's the law."

"Listen, young lady," the police chief said, "If you don't break this up, I'm going to arrest you and your friends here."

"Go ahead," Miranda said. "We have our rights, and we're not moving." Miranda sat down and all the women around her did the same.

The Police Chief turned to two of the cops, and he was about to order them to arrest Miranda when the Claw picked up an African bongo drum, sat on the edge of the sidewalk, and began to pound away on it.

The Police Chief and the two cops started to walk through the crowd towards the Claw. Eban with a smile on his face grabbed the microphone and said, "Comrades, the streets belong to the people, not cars."

Sonny saw Katmandu Willie in the crowd. He had a bottle of beer in his hand. "Oh, no," Sonny said as he watched Willie throw the beer bottle at Eban; but he missed him and hit the Police Chief on the shoulder.

The Police Chief turned around, angry, and he shouted to his men, "All right, that's it, let's clear this out." He pulled out his handcuffs, and he was walking toward

Miranda to arrest her. At the same time he was calling for reinforcements.

Sonny ran, grabbed Miranda, and shouted, "Run!"

They ran through the crowd that closed in behind them, and they ran through the gateway and up the pathway to College Ave. Sonny and Miranda stopped. The cops had not followed them. They were both out of breath. They could see other people running and they could hear police sirens.

Miranda was furious. "Look at what you have done," she shouted. "You and your friends have ruined everything. Look at you. You're drunk and stoned, and you call your self a revolutionary? You're nothing but an alcoholic and a drug addict."

Sonny searched his mind to call her the worse thing he could possibly call her, and then he said, "And you're nothing but a fuckin liberal."

Well that did it. Miranda hauled off and slapped him as hard as she could and shouted, "We're through!" and she walked away.

Sonny watched Miranda walk away. He hesitated and thought about chasing after her; but then he thought about what she called him and said, "Fuck her;" and he ran back down the pathway into the bedlam where he saw a cop swing his billy club. Many of the women were fighting along with the male students who had been there as spectators or as supporters of the women. Sonny heard more sirens, and he saw the sheriff's cars appearing, more cops, fists thrown, screams, shouts, crying. The townies that were on the slope now came charging down. Someone in one of the apartments turned their stereo on full blast as the Claw kept banging away on the bongo drums, and The Rolling Stones sang,

> *"Hey!*
> *Said my name is called disturbance*
> *I'll shout and scream, I'll kill the king,*
> *I'll rail at all his servants.*
> *Well, what can a poor boy do,*
> *Except to sing for a rock n roll band*
> *Cause in sleepy London town*
> *There's no place for a street fighting man*
> *No."*

Tear gas came out, windows were broken, and a police car was turned over. Sonny ran through the tear gas and smoke, pushing through the people around the Claw who were protecting him from the police.

The Claw was in Vietnam. Shells were falling all around him. He heard the shouts and screams of war. He was trying to sew up a Vietnamese child who had been hit by a shell. The Claw's hands were full of blood. He kept whispering to the soundless staring child. "We're going to make it, baby. We're going to make it."

He drew the string through the wound, and he was ready to cut it like an umbilical cord when he looked into the boy's lifeless eyes. The Claw looked at his hands, and he dropped the end of the string. "Oh God!" he shouted as he began to beat the earth with his hands. He felt like he was inside a bomb. He felt that if he stopped beating the ground, his heart would stop.

Sonny grabbed him and shouted above the chaos,

"Come on, Claw, there's nothing here worth fighting for anymore.

Robin appeared and helped Sonny drag the Claw away as The Claw shouted, "Arrest me. I killed people. I killed trees. I killed flowers. I killed the fuckin sky and the sun and the moon, and I did it for my country." The Claw began to sing, *God Bless, America.*

Chapter Five

The next few days Sonny worked on his apartment. He painted the apartment's walls with flat white paint and sanded and varnished the floors. He then went out and bought a trundle bed, a Sony Trinitron color TV, a stereo system, some houseplants, and a white Peruvian Indian spread with orange and russet brown geometric patterns that turned into temple gods and Inca birds of Paradise. He threw his white sheepskin rug on the floor, opened up his orange canvas lounge chair with chrome supports and light oak armrests, and hung a begonia with pink flowers and a baby's breath plant that had delicate white flowers that looked like a bridal veil in the windows. It was great to have a home again and not just a hotel room. Crashing at Club Sleeze had awakened all his fears of being homeless again. Even now with all the money that he had hoarded in his safe deposit box, he still had recurring nightmares about wondering the streets of New York City and bits and pieces of other places that he had lived.

It was a gray and black world without any other colors or light; and when he went to places that he thought he lived, there would be other people living there. When he went looking for friends, somewhere to stay that night, he had no idea where they were; and if he did encounter them, they would just disappear leaving him alone and lost again with his concrete bed, the night growing darker and colder. Only once in his dreams did he feel like he found his way home through the darkness.

In the dream, he found his father's bar; and when he walked in, it was full of color and music and people laughing and talking and having a good time. His father was behind the bar, and he was happy too; and when he saw Sonny, he smiled and asked him where he had been and then he said, "You look hungry. You should go in the kitchen and get something to eat."

"I'm tired, Dad," Sonny said.

His father handed him the key to the upstairs apartment where they lived and said, "Go on upstairs then and get some sleep." It was as simple as that, and it was the happiest dream that he ever had.

Sonny looked around the room, and he felt like there was more to do. Above the desk whose work surface was made up of a simple rectangular sheet of smoked glass supported by wood saw horses painted bright green, he hung up a portrait of a Seneca Indian Chief painted in the early 1800s on an animal hide. He put his oatmeal colored canvas directors chair with an oak frame in front of his desk, and he hung his compound bow on the wall next to the bookshelf that he would fill with books that he wanted to read. He was about to straighten out the spread on the trundle bed when he remembered Miranda laughing at him saying that he was like a little old lady, always picking things up and putting them in their place. He smiled when he remembered picking up her sketches that were strewn all over the floor and putting them in a neat pile. Miranda was mad as hell, and they had a big fight over the difference between being messy and randomness. Sonny looked at the alarm clock next to the bed and realized that it was time to go to the funeral. He was nervous. He would see Miranda today, and he wondered if she would be alone.

Sonny put on a light gray silk T-shirt, light washed out indigo boot-cut Levi blue jeans, well-worn handmade tan cowboy boots, and a wide brimmed dark leather cowboy hat with a black and white, tan and gray eagle's feather in the headband.

Sonny went into the bathroom and picked up the bathroom towel that was draped over the edge of the sink, folded it, and put it on the towel rack. He looked at himself in the mirror, and then he put on his silver mirror-like-pilot sunglasses to hide his wariness. Sonny could smell the fresh air coming through the window caressing the smell of the begonias and the baby's breath flowers hanging in the windows; and he felt like he could sleep for a week; but he hated to sleep, he hated his dreams. Nothing good ever happened in his dreams, so it must be reality. Sonny took one last look in the mirror to make sure that he was there and then left his studio apartment for the funeral.

Sonny drove to the Sunshine Farm Commune where the funeral was being held. The commune supported five families, and it was part of a communal farm network that supported a local food co-op and a free food kitchen for the poor and the homeless. Modest log homes were cut out of the woodlands that bordered the hundred acre farm; and at the end of the main road, he could see the original two hundred year old two story white colonial farmhouse that was in the shadow of a giant walnut tree that was probably as old as the house. Orange tiger lilies and blue and yellow irises bordered the house, and red begonias hung from the porch. In the background, beyond the two blossoming dogwood trees, a pathway led to the edge of a wooded gorge with falls that cascaded like giant steps down into Treman State Park.

Sonny found a place to park; and as he walked along the road, he noticed that the fields along the road had been fenced off by garlands, ribbons, and flowers; and he was being channeled through a cartoon flaming archway that welcomed him in bold red and yellow letters to *Hell's Paradise*. As he walked through the archway, he felt like he was walking through a field of flowers and fire. The impression was created by brightly colored plywood cutouts shaped like giant flowers and flames, a commingling of Paradise and Hell that was sprouting and bursting into a photo gallery of the 60s like buds sharing seeds, their roots burning like fuses disappearing and reappearing like a serpent winding its way through the tree of life.

Growing amidst the gardens of flowers and fires and photos were trees bearing the forbidden fruits of knowledge and sensuous pleasure. A naked woman and man entwined formed the roots and trunk and limbs of the trees, their long hair forming the branches upon which hung books and record albums spinning in the breeze like planets forming orbits of musical spheres and a multi-verse of words.

When Sonny looked up he could see on the branches overhead – *One Flew Over The Cuckoo's Nest; Plant This Book; The Doors of Perception; The Bell Jar; The Howling;* and *The Fall* intertwined with *Bridge Over Troubled Waters; Beggar's Banquet; Revolution; Déjà Vu;* and *Cheap*

Thrills. A Sign nearby warned the travelers through *Hell's Paradise* not to pick the forbidden fruit.

In the first garden patch of hope and despair that Sonny came upon, there was a flowering photo of Myles Horten who was the founder of the Highlander School located in the Appalachian Mountains of Tennessee. The Highlanders became a major training center for Southern community activists and labor organizers; and it was at the Highlanders Center that an old slave spiritual was transformed by Zalphon Horton and Pete Seager into *"We Shall Overcome,"* a song that would become the national anthem for the civil rights movement.

The next photo was a picture of Rosa Parks who took part in workshops at the Highlanders Folk School before she climbed into a segregated Cleveland Avenue bus on December 1st 1955 in Montgomery, Alabama; and she refused to sit in the back of the bus. From the window of the bus she could see a Nativity scene on the lawn of an all-white-Baptist-church that faced a historical town square where slaves had been sold. All about her, store windows were lit up with Christmas lights; and the words of the song, *"I'm Dreaming of a White Christmas"* floated across the square like snowflakes.

Next to Rosa was a picture of Eli Baker, the inspiration behind SNCC, an organization that rejected the idea of charismatic leaders who got off the Freedom Train when they made it to the suburbs or were invited to the White House. She believed in empowering people at the grassroots level where poor southern sharecroppers would have to take on responsibility for themselves rather than relying on outsiders and "The Lawd" as she called Martin Luther King.

"Let the People Decide" became SNCC's battle cry, a call to arms that echoed through the inflamed photos of black men, women, and children marching on City Hall in Birmingham, Alabama in 1963 where police dogs mauled marchers; and men, women, and children were thrown to the pavement and hurled against the wall, helpless as they were being washed away like street litter by the powerful blasts of water coming from fire hoses being manned by members of the Birmingham Fire Department. At the same time, thousands of black school children, some barely older than six, were being herded off into school buses to learn their lesson in jail, their American history textbook being the prison bars and the spaces in between the lines of the National Anthem where the true story of America was written in the tears of their children.

Next to the picture of the children was a photo of a quarter of a million black and white Americans marching from the Washington Monument to the Lincoln Memorial and a photo of Martin Luther King giving his famous speech in which he declared that he had a dream for America, an America free of racism, a dream of a united America in which children of all races were allowed to dream of a new future of harmony and love, a dream that was being consumed by the fires of Hell all in black and white.

One black and white photo was of an FBI poster in bold white letters with a black background that read, MISSING: CALL THE FBI; and below that notice and call for help, were pictures of an eighteen year old black boy named James Channey and two white CORE organizers, Michael Schwerner and Andrew Goodman, all members of the Mississippi Summer Project for voters registration. In another black and white photo was a picture of the dead bodies of these three missing boys found laid out in the shape of a cross under tons of bulldozed mud, shot dead at point blank range by members of the Ku Klux Klan. Their only crime was that they believed that in America everyone should have a right to vote; and near the dead bodies of the boys was another black and white photo of Addie Mae Collins, a fourteen years old girl who liked her new white dress with a bow in the back; Carole Robertson, a fourteen years old girl who liked her hair in pigtails; Cynthia Wesley, a fourteen years old girl who liked strawberry ice cream best; and Denise Mc Nair, an eleven years old girl who liked to play with her dolls – all blown away by a bomb while putting on their choir robes in the 16th Street Baptist Church in Birmingham, Alabama.

Amidst the leaves of flame and the garden of profusion turned into a conflagration of flowering fire was a photo of John Kennedy, his body slumped over his belief that the future belonged to the youth of America who would explore new frontiers of American greatness. This dream was blown away along with his belief that the American system was essentially sound and only needed incremental change, just a little tweak here and a little tweak there, adjust the cross hairs, pull the trigger, and, bang, the problem is gone. Below the photo was a quote from JFK.

> *"Let the word go forth from this time and place, to friend and foe alike, that the torch has been passed to a new generation of Americans."*

In the next garden patch there were photos of the

student uprisings and the antiwar movement. One photo was a picture of Mario Savio with a bullhorn in his hand standing on the rooftop of a police patrol car near Sather Gate at the entranceway to the University of California at Berkeley. Savio, surrounded by thousands of students, was demanding free speech on campus and the release of Jack Weinberg, who was sitting in the patrol car handcuffed and arrested for violating the campus wide ban on organizing politically on campus. When the University tried to discipline Mario Savio and other students for participating in the demonstration, the students revolted; and a seemingly minor incident ignited into the beginnings of a major uprising nationwide against the cold efficiency of the knowledge industry and the assembly line style education.

The uprising at Berkeley was pictured in photos of thousands of students demonstrating in Sproul Plaza and occupying the administrative building where they were conducting sit-ins and teach-in on topics like *Students and Their Civil Liberties, Racism and Sexism in the Class Room, Vietnam and the Funding of Military Research on Campus, Bad Living Conditions, Lack of Choice in the Curriculum,* and *The Corporate Takeover of Higher Education in America.*

During that occupation, one photo captured Joan Baez singing, "*This land is my land. This land is your land,*" with the local police providing the Greek chorus in the first mass invasion of an American campus where eight hundred students were arrested. One male student was captured by a camera being carried away by the police with a sign pinned on his chest that read, "*I'm a CU student. Please don't bend, fold, spindle, or mutilate.*"

Mario Savio, who had participated in the Summer of

Freedom in Mississippi, was like many young student activists. They had learned to organize in the South as political activists and volunteers in the civil rights movement, and now they brought their organizational skills and inspiration back North to organize the free speech movement on campus. Many of the student activists believed that by appealing to the scholarly ideals of the faculty and the Enlightenment traditions of American education they could be the agents of change, and they could turn the educational institutions of America into a nexus of democratic reform, but these ideals were shattered over and over again in places like Columbia University.

In 1967 at Columbia University, after repeated appeals to the university and calls for a public hearing were met with indifference and placebos by the administration, students took over five buildings at the university in protest against class ranking as a standard for determining a student's draft status, the channeling of students into defense related jobs and professions so as to maintain their deferment, military research and recruitment on campus, and *"Gym Crow,"* the name they called the segregated gymnasium being built by the university on public land at Morningside Park.

Once again the message was clear, and it was beaten into the student's heads with bully clubs and baton-like-flashlights by the Tactical Force Units of the New York City Police Department who were evicting them from Low Library. In one photo, a female student was being dragged by her hair down the marble stairs of the library. Blood and lipstick were smearing her face where she was bashed in the mouth, and her skirt was push up over her waist revealing her pure white panties like a church girl in a sadomasochistic pornographic movie. Another student was being dragged down the stairs feet first, his head bouncing against the stone steps. Over and over again the lesson was being pounded into them. Their privileged position in society was conditioned upon their willingness to be well paid and well trained slaves to the system. Revolt and they would be treated as no better than the sharecroppers in Mississippi and the three boys buried in the mud bank in Mississippi by the Ku Klux Klan

Amidst this class in 101 Institutional Violence was a photo of the front page of an issue of *Rat Subterranean News*. It was a black and white and red sketch of Low Library during the student take over. The Roman Pantheon-like-dome of the library was replaced by a black Nazi war helmet with a red swastika painted on the side. The caption read, *"Heil Columbia."* Next to that photo, amidst the flowers and flames, was a picture of a twelve-foot statue of the Goddess Minerva seated in a Klismos chair with lamps at the ends of the armatures symbolizing Wisdom and Teaching. The statue stood on a marble and granite base in the middle of the stairway leading up to Low Library and its Ionic columns and entranceway. The goddess's arms were out stretched, a scepter in her right hand and an open bible resting on her lap. Chiseled on the base of the statue in Roman letters was the name of the goddess, *"Alma Mater,"* meaning in Latin, *"Nourishing Mother."* Hanging from her outstretched hands like a ripped and torn gown was a banner that read, *"Raped by Cops."*

Out of the conflagration and the flowering also came photos of the March on the Pentagon in 1967 where thousands of people marched from the Washington Monument to the Lincoln Memorial and then on to the Pentagon. It was the first time the counter culture openly confronted the establishment at the seat of American power; and it was a picture of an American melting pot of resistance boiling over and pouring out students from every part of the country - liberals, radicals, black nationalists, women's groups, veterans of the Vietnam War, ordinary working class people, and hippies dressed as witches, warlocks, holy men, prophets, and saints. Abbie Hoffman was there trying to levitate the Pentagon and rid it of its evil spirits as a young girl with golden hair that radiated in the sun stuck a yellow daisy into the muzzle of an M-14 combat rifle being held by a Army soldier whose bayonet was aimed at her breasts.

Another photo captured the police attacking the demonstrators in the dark when the campers were transforming their draft cards into burning candles and singing,

> *"Silent Night, holy night,*
> *All is calm, all is bright,*
> *Round yon Virgin Mother and Child,*
> *Holy Infant so tender and mild,*
> *Sleep in heavenly peace,*
> *Sleep in heavenly peace."*

In the photo, a spotlight went on; and it exposed a cop beating a young girl mercilessly. When the cop realized that the light was on him and his picture was being taken, he raised his bully club above his head in triumph, the girl crumbled at his feet, symbolizing all the women who had betrayed their men in Vietnam, unfaithful whores who had abandoned their place in the home. Below that picture was a poem by the poet Robert Lowell, one of the speakers at the march.

Pity the planet all joy gone.
From this sweet volcanic cone,
Peace to our children when they fall
In small war on the heel of small
War until the end of time
To police the earth, a ghost
Orbiting forever lost
In our monotonous sublime.

Next to the poem was a photo of Shulamith Firestone and Ellan Wiles, the founders of the Redstockings feminist organization. Below their photo was an excerpt from their manifesto.

"We are considered inferior kind, whose only purpose is to enhance men's lines. Our humanity is denied. Male supremacy is the oldest most basic form of domination. All other forms of exploitation and oppression; racism, capitalism, imperialism, etc. are extensions of male supremacy, men's domination of women, and a few men dominate the rest."

Next to the quote was a photo of five women who called themselves *"Women Against Daddy Warbucks;"* and in that photo, they were running into one of the thirteen Manhattan draft boards they invaded, stealing thousands of draft files plus the "1" and "A" keys off of the typewriters. In another photo, a covenant from WITCHS, (Women Inspired to Commit Her Story) appeared on Wall Street to pit their ancient magic against the evil power of the Financial District, "*The Center of the Imperial Phallic Society.*"

Also amidst this garden was a profusion of brightly colorful photos of People's Park and the students planting flowers, shrubs, trees, and sod. The light danced on the darkness and created a Dionysian aura, as nature's children turned an abandoned lot owned by the university filled with garbage and debris into an acre of Eden with flowers everywhere, brick walkways, organic gardens, a children's playground, and a bandstand for concerts. The sun seemed to cast a halo over everyone, the park glowing like it had been blessed. In contrast were black and white photos of bulldozers plowing over all the colors of Paradise, the emerald green grass and the bright purple and orange and yellow flowers, the bright red of the sandbox splintered and broken, and the bright yellow arms and legs of the swing being swallowed up by the darkness. In another black and white photo the teargas swirled and slithered about like a black ghost-like-serpent as sheriff's deputies in gas masks and riot helmets fired shotguns loaded with lethal buck shot at point blank rang injuring over a hundred students and killing James Rector.

The next photo was a picture of thousands of National Guard troops occupying Berkeley, an American city, and camping out in the remains of People's Park. The only color in the black and white photo was the drab olive green and brown of the soldier's uniforms, their equipment, and the metal monsters that looked like they were covered with mold. Next to the photo of the invading army was a photo of the front page of the Berkeley Tribe with a quotation from Ronald Reagan that said in bold red letters,

"If it takes a BLOODBATH let's get it over with. No more appeasement."

That photo was paired with a cartoon of Mickey mouse wearing a Ronald Reagan watch followed by a photo that captured the moment when thirty thousand people came marching down Telegraph Street towards People's Park to confront the National Guard, the sheriff's department, and the local police with Flower Power.

A local traffic cop at one of the intersections had flowers in his hair; and a soldier with a flower in the muzzle of his rifle was waving it at the marchers like a white flag. It was like everyone was a child again, like a twelve year old that had won a baseball game, like the child who opened a Christmas present and it was exactly what she wanted but better, like children in mass gobbling up ice cream and cake with lots of frosting at a birthday party, and like the laughter of a child who tried to run away and was swept up by a parent and hugged. The last photo in the sequence was a photo that captured the moment when Miranda, riding on the back of Sonny's motorcycle, saw Ronnie holding up the battle helmet with a tulip planted in it. She was pointing into the crowd, and Sonny was smiling like he has never smiled since.

There were so many good things being done then. Civil rights, the student campus revolt, and the antiwar movement were just a part of it. This was illustrated by the next garden that was blooming with flower dedicated to the women's movement. One photo was a picture of the front page of *Women's LibRATion*. On the front page was a profile picture of Emma Goodman framed with melting chains. Her hair was in a bun; and she was wearing wire rim glasses as she read from one of her own books, *"It Begins in Women's Souls."* Next to Emma's solitary and dreamy countenance was a photo of the march down New York City's Fifth Avenue that was called for by NOW as part of the Women's Strike for Equality. One banner read *"Sisterhood is Powerful"* and another said, *"Anatomy is not Destiny."*

Next to that photo were pictures of women protesting the Miss America pageant at the Atlantic City boardwalk in September 1968. In one picture the women are auctioning off a dummy of Miss America – *"The Murder Mascot"* who entertains the troops with her pure white nakedness as the symbol of American "consume-her-ism." In another picture, the protesters were crowning their own candidate, a live sheep who was being auctioned off as the perfect sacrifice to male dominance.

Also enveloped in the flowers and flames were photos of secretaries and working women on Madison Avenue throwing down their bras from the towering office buildings to be thrown in he "Freedom Trash Can" along with *Good House Keeping Magazine*, dish towels, steno pads, girdles, high heel shoes, and the makeup that turned them into caged birds of Paradise; and in another photo a women's group named Bread and Roses, upset by an announcement by a radio station in Boston that they were looking for "chicks" as typists, invaded the radio station and handed the station manager eight baby chickens.

The final photo in the garden was a photo of Ti-Grace Atkinson addressing a meeting of NOW in which she proposed that all hierarchy be eliminated from the organization and that they should abolish all offices or spread them around. Like the original founders of SNCC, and SDS, she wanted to see participatory democracy and noted that in the feminist movement there was a division between "those who want women to have the opportunity to be oppressors too, and those who wanted to destroy oppression."

Across the path from the garden that celebrated the feminist movement was the communal garden where free health clinics that served the poor and the millions of Americans without health insurance sprouted throughout the country. There were photos of volunteers and hippies panhandling on the streets so as not to rely on grants that brought establishment rules, fee schedules, and the requirement to send bills to patients who were homeless. One of the photos was of the Bear Claw working at the Grassroots Free Clinic putting a cast on the arm of a child who was holding a basketball in his other hand. The Claw had just told the child a joke, and they were laughing.

Also blossoming in the communal garden were the free schools that believed in freedom and responsibility and that democracy had to be lived as well as taught. Next to the flowering free schools were the free legal aid clinics and law communes that handled cases for political activists, civil rights groups, union organizations, poor tenants in rent disputes, and citizens against commercial high rise development that threatened to plow over their neighborhoods. They also handled cases involving conscientious objectors to the war, young students and working class kids who were charged with avoiding the draft or going AWOL, and soldiers who were being prosecuted for protesting the war or disobeying an unlawful order while serving in the military.

In the midst of this garden of communal abundance

were photos of the food co-ops that believed that food was a basic right and should not be sold for profit. One photo showed volunteers going door-to-door selling food stamps to raise the initial capital to start the co-op. The food stamps could be redeemed later for food at the co-op. Another photo showed volunteers cleaning out what had to be an abandoned automotive garage; and in the next photo, all the grease and dirt and debris were gone and in its place was a colorful photo of an old fashion grocery store with barrels of grains and herbs, fresh organic vegetables and fruits, and an odd collection of refrigerators and coolers labeled Cheese, Dairy, and Poultry. On the wall was a sign that read, *"We Want You To Spend Less, Not More",* and in the bookrack was *The Handbook of Homemade Power* that read,

> *"Alternative Energy Sources that you can put in use now. Heat your home with the sun! Use the wind to make electricity! Power a shop, house, or farm with a water wheel! Run natural gas appliances – even your car – on methane that you can produce yourself! Cook on a wood-burning stove! Yes, there are answers to the energy crisis, and this book tells you how to make them work for you."*

At the heart of the garden of the communal movements were photos of the Diggers gathered around a eucalyptus tree at the Panhandle in Haight Ashbury giving out free food. There were crates of apples, bread cooked in coffee cans, and ten-gallon milk containers of Digger stew, all to be handed out to the homeless and the abandoned and run-a-way children of America. A manifesto nailed to a tree spelled out the Digger's philosophy.

Do Your Thing.
Do It For Free.
Do It For Love.
We Can't Fail!

Sonny stopped to take it all in, the hope and dream that fundamental change in America would come from the growth of grassroots organizations and institutions in each and every community, the workplace, the school room, and the home, that all the diverse movements were related; and as they were nurtured in the fertile ground of the counter culture, they would consolidate and grow into a powerful national movement. They believed that if they lived the dream, the dream would come true. Sonny thought back to when he got a glimpse of what it would be like when all their dreams came together at the threshold of reality.

On October 15th 1969 the Moratorium to End the War in Vietnam was conducted throughout the United States. Hundreds of colleges and high schools were closed; millions of Americans wore black armbands; and people from all walks of life joined the marches, rallies, vigils, and teach-ins. On November 15th, as a participant in this moratorium, Sonny went to the largest peaceful antiwar demonstration in American history. Washington was an impressionistic painting where it changed form depending on how far or near you came to the truth. That day, for a moment, it was the sun that radiated all and reflected on beauty and the symbols of enlightenment. It was patches of color that turned into sail boats playing in the light of the Potomac River and the reflections of the tree lined parks and magnolias – the natural setting for the Imperial style of Rome, the columns, the architraves, the pediments, and the marble men formed in stone. It was the Washington Monument piercing the sky, a mass of masonry thrusting upward into a needle's point, a dot to mark the spot. It was the piles of stones that made up the Capitol and its geometric forms, all the columns and the domes created by the Masonic temple makers that hid the mysteries in riddles. Is the strength in the straight line that is never there? I upon I, individual pillars working together in harmony and balance carrying the burdens of time, defying gravity as they raise each generation tier upon tier, time curving in upon itself in a dome, a globe, a point where a string, a simple heartbeat, a line perfectly formed can hold up the weight of the universe.

That day, in the midst of all the Masonic magic, one million Americans stood as one; and for a moment Sonny understood what Jefferson meant by "We the People" because at that moment we were of one heart, one mind, one vision. We were we, and we were the giant that could defeat the Leviathan. Then it was gone; and it was only the beginning.

Sonny believed with all his heart that the children of the 60s were on the edge of a new age that would have nurtured our evolution into a quantum world of consciousness where each of us would make up the billions of alternative universes, the stars that would come together in a cosmos of humankind at the center of creation and the origins of reality. If this country had not killed its children's dreams and the youth of a nation, we could have led it into a Renaissance of Democracy, a new Golden Age of Pericles and made America the beacon of light for the rest of the world far into the future.

Sonny felt a deep sadness when he exited the photo gallery; but then he entered a rainbow archway into *Hippie Heaven;* and he saw the thousands of children of the 60s laughing and dancing. Many of the women wore halter-tops that exposed their navels and youthful stomachs, or they wore skintight tank tops without a bra. When the halter-tops or tank tops were worn with low slung, skin tight, bell-bottom-pants that flared out to cover their feet, they looked like mutated mermaids swimming in a sea of testosterone and estrogen, water clashing against rock and roll. There were many other mutations at the funeral as well. There were hybrids of cowboys and Indians wearing all sorts of combinations of patched colorful jeans and raw hide leather jackets, leather skin tight bell bottoms and moccasins, cowboy hats and colorful headbands, eagle feathers and war paint forming Hindu hieroglyphs on bare chests. They also wore clothes emblematic of manual labor – painter's white overalls with splashes of color that were an impressionistic abstract painting of all the houses in Ithaca, and bandanas in every color worn like crowns of perspiration. In the shadows were the black on black of anarchy and Trotskyite wire rim glasses worn by well-read anti-intellectual revolutionaries. There were also all kinds of floral mutations and exotic hybrids of male and female seeds, sexy silk and gauzy dresses and flowing gowns designed for a summer garden party. The more militant feminists wore leather motorcycle jackets, and one girl was wearing a World War Two aviator's cap and goggles. The witches wore hooded capes embroidered with pentagons and hexagons that conjured up

Hell's Angels and heavenly nymphs in velvet angel sleeved dresses and bare feet or short-shorts or cut-off jeans with wreaths of flowers and glitter in their hair and painted flowers on their cheeks. All in all, they were a phantasmagoria of the human psyche walking on free fall.

Sonny saw Big Lou and Jimmy barbecuing a whole pig. Big Louie was wearing a formal dinner jacket with tails, a Superman T-shirt, a top hat, jeans, and size fourteen Red Wing work boots. Jimmy, who was pouring beer over the pig as it rotated on the spit, was wearing his Ugly Brother's T-shirt, kaki Bermuda shorts, and combat boots. On his head he wore a large brimmed straw Panama hat with a brightly colored feather head band, and he had painted flowers on his cheeks to add to the incongruity.

Hamburgers and hotdogs were sizzling on a large grill next to the kegs of beer that were foaming, head after head; and the tables were full of a cornucopia of food. Out in the field, many people were dancing to Bad Company singing,

> *"It's all part of my rock & roll fantasy.*
> *It's all part of my rock & roll dream."*

Sonny watched the dancers; and as the lead guitar reached its high end, soaring hands reached for the sun, and the drummer beat them down again. Some of the women seemed to be sowing the field with their dance, seducing the crops to grow. Many were just rock and rolling any which way, stirring up memories of when they were one. Rock and roll was their tribal music and it vibrated through the sinews of their being. Sonny gave himself up to the music, the collective rhythms and tones that resonated through them all; and he became part of the hypnotic power of the mass that made sacred and real the spellbound, the simple words of truth that spoke the language of a generation, and the metaphors of sound that went beyond words to pure feelings, our common humanity, and our bonds with nature. Sonny listened to Doobie Brothers sing,

> *"Oh , Oh, listen to the music*
> *Don't you feel it growin', day by day*
> *People getting ready for the news*
> *Some are happy, some are sad*
> *Oh, we got to let the music play"*

Someone tapped Sonny on the back, and he turned around. It was Miranda. Sonny had forgotten how beautiful her emerald green eyes were and how much he loved her auburn red hair that whirled into golden flames in the sun. Miranda was wearing a black silk tank top shirt, white silk shorts, cowboy boots, and a black silk aviator style jacket with a flaming red, gold, purple, and green dragon on the back. Sonny could see her nipples through her silk shirt; and he loved her plump lips, the way they looked slightly parted, open.

Miranda smiled, and her smile overwhelmed her face as she said, "I've missed you so much."

Sonny hugged her as if his life depended on it and whispered, "I love you too." It was as simple as that.

Miranda took his hand and said, "Come on. Let's take a walk in the gorge."

They walked past the giant walnut tree then the dogwood trees with blossoms of pink and white flowers, and they entered the forest pathway to the falls and the gorge that had been seeded with wild flowers native to the region. It was alive with color. There were clusters of yellow Hawkweed that formed shredded bursts of light growing out of white wooly clouds, and white Queen Anne's Lace mingled with sprays of lavender and purple Bull Thistle that were protected by porcupine leaves. White Trillium with yellow stamens peeked out of the forest depth, and bright red Cardinal Flowers looked like splashes of fire while yellow Trout Lilacs swam in the sun along the forest floor. The pathway led to the falls that flowed through the gorge that ended in a precipice where the water fell over two hundred feet into a witch's caldron of rainbow droplets and mist like diamonds and pearls.

They stood near the edge amidst White Star Flowers and Yellow Sun Drops with petals like wings. Miranda turned to Sonny and her emerald green eyes seemed to reflect the jeweled mist, the forest, the quivering light reflecting off of the leaves that made her seem impressionistic, almost ethereal. It was as if she was not real but an apparition of colors and shapes that emerged out of the natural beauty around her. Sonny could feel her pulse throbbing in his hand or was it his? He listened to the water make its way to fall after fall, life flowing down, fluid and lucid, taking form around unforgiving reality, disappearing into the earth and reappearing as giant trees, leaves, and flowers, our very being roaring and misting but still flowing on. In the midst of all this beauty, could there still be death? Was there a beginning and an end; or did it just flow on reborn with every fall, forgetting all the worn out ways it left behind?

Sonny felt the warmth of Miranda's smile, the sun. He was burning with desire for her. He drew her to him and felt the substance of passion, the moist roundness of her lips, open, receptive, words being formed in tongues of flame. The flow of life was rushing through their bodies. He felt like they were becoming one another, being draw into the earth, the air, and the branches of the trees reaching upward to the sun.

"I got lost, Miranda," Sonny said. "Then I lost you, and when I went to find you, you were gone."

Miranda kissed him lightly on the lips and caressed his face as if to make sure he was real, and said, "I thought you left me. I didn't know where you were."

"I know."

Miranda walked over to a ledge overlooking the falls and sat down, her legs dangling in the air; and Sonny joined her. "You went to Kenya. What was that like?" Sonny asked.

"It was great. The training was difficult, something like boot camp, I guess. The typical day started at 7:00 AM with a physical training and conditioning program then classes in Kenyan geography, economics, social mores, and politics. Stuff like that. We also studied first aid and disease prevention, but our main focus for Kenya was teacher training. Anyway, we finished up about 10:00 PM at night, and we did this for fourteen weeks, then two week at a tropical training camp in Puerto Rico; and from there we got shipped off to Kenya. Fortunately, unlike a lot of countries, the Kenyans wanted us. The country desperately needed teachers, so we were greeted with open arms."

"What were the living conditions like?"

Miranda smiled and said, "I wish I could say that we really roughed it; and I was a real frontier woman; but, actually, we were quite comfortable. We did have to dig our own outdoor latrines, which I never got quite used to; but we lived in well-screened bungalows with outdoor shower stalls; and we had small gas stoves, refrigerators, and gas lamps. But, what was special about Kenya was not our accommodations or the land itself, though it was quite beautiful and breathtaking at times. It was the people. They truly lived a communal life of cooperation and sharing, Sonny. They were warm and friendly, and they had a sense of empathy that made them sensitive to your slightest moods. They could read your feelings in the slightest gesture or facial expression, and they would be open and honest in their feelings towards you. It was such a refreshing change from our life here as solitary cats. For example, one day I was feeling sad, homesick, and I was missing you. It was morning, and I was sitting on the steps outside the bungalow drinking a cup of coffee. One of the mothers of the children that I taught came up to me, looked at me as if I were one of her children and said, 'Miranda, why are you so unhappy, today?' And then she hugged me."

Miranda laughed. "They thought I was a spinster."

Sonny laughed. "Why?"

"Because I was skinny by their standards, and I was twenty one, and I wasn't married. They also considered us all white, even the African Americans who came with us. And sometimes they laughed at us; and I never got the joke; but despite some of the cultural differences that never quite got bridged, they were truly grateful for what we did; and I have to believe that we did some good. All in all though, I think I learned more from them than they learned from me. Though they were not educated in our sense, there was much wisdom there that we lack. For example, much of their education comes from proverbs that are passed on from generation to generation; and these proverbs expresses their collective wisdom over time;

whereas, we, despite all our formal and specialized education, are always fresh and new, passing on nothing; therefore, we are always children without a history or parents or a home. We leave everything behind."

"So what are you doing now?" Sonny asked. "Marge told me that you are working with a feminist group."

"I am. We advise women on their abortion rights, health issues, birth control, and other issues related to women."

"Like NOW?"

"No, not like NOW. NOW focuses on women's rights, legislation, and legal action, stuff like that. We believe that if women are going to be truly free we need to free them of all the myths and images and feelings of bondage and submission that they have been programmed with since childhood. For example, I work as a moderator in consciousness raising sessions." Miranda smiled and said, "But enough of me, Sonny. Tell me about everything you've been doing."

Sonny told her. He started with the day he woke up in a blanket of snow, homeless; and then he told her everything. When he was done Miranda looked into his eyes, and Sonny couldn't read the expression on her face. Was it shock, pity, disapproval, concern, amusement, admiration, love, or was it just plain disappointment?

Miranda hugged him and said, "Oh, Sonny, you've created a hell around yourself. I should have known how serious it was when I saw Dante's. Why? You haven't done anything wrong. You didn't lose the revolution. In fact, it isn't even lost. It's just begun." She looked deeper into his eyes. "You said you wanted to understand your father and love him. Do you understand him now?"

"Yes."

"Do you love him?"

"Yes."

"Do you think he would want you to do this?"

Sonny thought for a moment and said, "No."

"OK, then why are you doing it? Do you need the money? Are you homeless and desperate?"

"No, I have lots of money. I don't know how much. I just put it in a safe deposit box, and I never look at it. I also hide it in all different kinds of places, in books and stuff; but then I can't remember where I hid it. I'm sort of like a demented squirrel."

"No, it seems to me that you are having a fabulously creative and self destructive temper tantrum." Miranda grabbed his hand, "Sonny, you have to stop this. You're a visionary, and we need you. I need you."

Miranda thought for a moment, looked closely at Sonny again and said, "You know, you never had faith in us. You never had faith in me. You were always afraid that I was cheating on you, that I was going to leave you, and that I didn't love you. You didn't even have faith in you. We're the nucleus of love, Sonny. If we can't keep it together, we can't keep anything together or hope to change anything for the better for anyone. Love is a leap of faith, Sonny."

Miranda stood up and took her clothes off and said, "Come on. Take your clothes off."

Sonny was confused, but he followed her instructions happily. Miranda was so beautiful when she was naked.

"Come here," Miranda said.

Sonny joined her on the ledge. She kissed him, grabbed his hand and said, "If you jump with me, I'll love you forever."

Sonny looked over the edge of the falls to the water below. It had to be at least a two hundred foot drop. He had swum in the pool of water below; and it was deep; but there were huge, jagged, glacial rocks along the edge. He tried to remember how far they went out. He turned to Miranda and said, "You're kidding."

"No. You once told me that you were the greatest broken field runner of all times and that nobody could touch you, but not this time. There is no running away."

Miranda stepped back to get a running start. "Are you with me?"

Sonny stood there looking at her; and without thinking, lines from Dante's Inferno came to his lips.

> "Oh splendor of the living light eternal!
> What man has paled beneath Parnassus shade
> Or drunk the limpid water of its fount,
> Who would not seem to have a mind encumbered
> Should he but endeavor to portray you
> As there you stood, revealed in open air,
> With heavenly harmony your only veil?"

Sonny took Miranda's hand and said, "Let's go," and Miranda and Sonny leaped off of the edge feet first disappearing into the diamonds and pearls, the mist like stars. Sonny's hands and arms flew upward in the air as he hit the water going deeper and deeper into the layers upon layers of evolution until he touched the claws of the glacial age where it stopped before it retreated from the sun. At that moment, in a burst of light, Sonny had a revelation that consciousness was new to the universe; and we are it.

Sonny burst through the surface of the water and inhaled the air like the bubbles of fine champagne. He looked around, and he found Miranda threading water nearby and smiling at him. "I do," Sonny said.

Miranda hugged him and said, "Me too. Oh, my God. What a rush. Come on."

They swam to a place behind the falls where the multicolored mist and refracted light seemed to be trying to form a rainbow, and they made love like teenagers, coming together almost instantaneously, Miranda in multiple orgasms, pulsing, and Sonny to the roar of the falls.

As they walked back up the trail to where they left their clothes, Sonny said, "You know what is wrong with science, Miranda?"

"What's that?"

"They imagine that the universe is as boring as they are."

Miranda and Sonny dressed and walked back up the trail to the party. By the time they reached the party, it was dark; and the night sky was full of stars that seemed to be raining little sparks of light that turned into swarms of fire flies. It was magical. Even the scattered bonfires seemed like faded suns, dreams from far out places. The dancers looked like ghosts, silhouettes in the moonlight appearing and disappearing in the flames of the bonfire as the band Boffalongo was on stage singing.

> *We like our fun and we never fight*
> *You can't dance and stay uptight*
> *It's a supernatural delight*
> *Everybody was dancing in the moonlight.*

Dancing in the moonlight
Everybody's feeling warm and bright
It's such a fine and natural sight
Everybody's dancing in the moonlight.

When the music stopped, a black coffin with the "60s" printed on the side in bold red letters was brought on stage; and Sonny listened to one person after another go up to the microphone and give their eulogy to the sixties. Each was a spark from what once was a blazing flame. In the sixties, America erupted into a multi-verse of dreams, a profusion of visions. There were so many stars like leaves of grass, nature reclaiming its own from the sterile order of concrete; but now that generation's dreams were dying, disappearing in the night. Sonny was watching the American Dream fade, campfires going out, stars reduced to a single flame, ambers.

Mozart's Requiem began to play, a sorrowful dirge filling the darkness with a grander darkness that gave darkness form; but then several stage spots cast bright white lights on the coffin of the 60s. The lid of the coffin opened slowly, and a golden baseball bat began to emerge from the coffin like a hard on. Then the lid flew open, and Wable stood up in the coffin with the golden bat in his hand waving it over his head and shouting, "Beat National Cash! Beat National Cash!"

All the people at the funeral joined in the chant, and "Beat National Cash!" echoed through the darkness. The funeral was over and the resurrection had begun.

Miranda gently slipped her arm in Sonny's arm and said, "Come on, Sonny, let's go home."

National Cash

Sonny and Miranda walked to his car, and in the background the Who were singing,

> I'm free – I'm free,
> And freedom tastes of reality,
> I'm free – I'm free
> And I'm waiting for you to follow me.

> If I told you what it takes
> To reach the highest high,
> You'd laugh and say "nothing's that simple'
> But you've been told many times before
> Messiahs pointed to the door
> And no one had the guts to leave the temple!

> I'm free – I'm free
> And freedom tastes of reality
> I'm free – I'm free
> And I'm waiting for you to follow me.

> Chorus:
> How can we follow?
> How can we follow?

As Sonny and Miranda drove away, Sonny said, "They're not going to get away with killing the sixties."

"Why not?" Miranda asked.

"Because you can't kill your children and their dreams and get away with it. The ancient Greeks knew that. Sooner or later the Furies will come."

Miranda's apartment was on University Avenue in an old beautiful Victorian apartment house with many pillared porches, layer upon layer like a wedding cake that overlooked the town and looked like it was about ready to fall apart or down into the valley, half painted, half not, the warped boards and white siding rippled in the silver light of the full moon. Sonny loved what Miranda did with her apartment. The ceilings were high; the windows were floor to ceiling; and the floors and trim were a darkly varnished oak that contrasted well with the pearl white walls. The moonlight poured across a love seat and Sonny recognized the philodendron from her room in Berkeley. It was standing on an antique Victorian pedestal, its leaf like hands caressing the dark green embroidered love seat that looked like it was worn from years of nestling in front of a ceramic and carved oak fireplace. There was a chill in the night, so Miranda lit a fire, and its glow filled the room. Above the fireplace hung a large circular canvas painted in bright orange like a setting sun.

Miranda then lit a desk lamp on her worktable where pencils and charcoal sketches and an IBM typewriter shared space with splashes of color, brushes, tubes of oil paint, and water colors of every hue and pigmentation, all the elements of life in color. On an easel nearby was a half finished painting of the Swedish ivy hanging in the bay window, light pouring through the blinds forming planes of light and darkness.

"Are you hungry?" Miranda asked.

Sonny realized that that he hadn't eaten all day. "I'm starving."

Miranda went into the kitchen, and Sonny followed

her. "Can I help?" he asked.

Miranda reached up on her tiptoes to a shelf in a kitchen cabinet and pulled down a bottle of red wine. As she was uncorking it she said, "Let me get organized, and then you can help me chop chop." She poured a glass of French merlot for Sonny, then clicked glasses and said, "To us."

"To us."

Miranda took a sip of her wine and said, "Did you like the photo gallery?"

"Very much so."

"Billy Benedetto did it. I told him to go see Dante's, and he came back raving about it. I think you inspired Hell's Paradise."

"That's cool."

"That's cool? I worked like hell with him on that."

"No, no. I mean it was wonderful. I can see your hand in it. You took the edges off, and made it cherub like in its ridicule of mortality. I liked that. That's what I love about all your art. It's profound in its innocence and simplicity, like a child pointing at something wondrous."

Miranda laughed, and said, "OK, that's a lot better. Now get out of here so I can get this meal together. Put on some music. Relax. I'll call you when I need you. I hope you like Kenyan."

"I've always liked your cooking, Miranda. You put the damnedest concoctions together, but they all taste good."

"That's because I'm an artist. Now get out of here so that I can improvise. And put on some music. The record player is in the living room."

Sonny went into the living room, and he found the stereo system on one of the wall shelves that were staggered so as to create geometrically pleasing lines and planes. Next to the book shelves was a tropical plant that looked like a fan; and above the plant was a large oil painting that was made up of several canvases layered and shaped so as to create a three-dimensional image of brightly colored brush strokes freeing themselves of the conventional geometry of the traditional canvas. It was bright and cheery and liberating. Albums were strewn about the floor. Sonny picked out a Leonard Cowen and a Joni Mitchell album, two of Miranda's favorites; and then he sat down on the love seat in front of the fire, sipped his wine, and listened to Leonard Cohen sing,

> *And just when you mean to tell her*
> *You have no love to give her*
> *She gets you on her wavelength*
> *You've always been her lover*
> *And you want to travel with her*
> *And you want to travel blind*
> *And you know she will trust you*
> *For you've touched her perfect body*
> *With your mind.*

Sonny sat in front of the fire for a while listening to the music, but he was restless, and his mind was full of ideas and possibilities. He couldn't sit still, so got up and walked back into the kitchen.

The kitchen was 50s modern with white metal cabinets that had chrome handles, some missing. The Hot Point electric stove had a control panel that looked like the dashboard on a nineteen fifties Cadillac with tail fins - lots of knobs, push buttons, and a large round clock with chrome trim that looked like a speedometer that didn't work. The refrigerator, also art deco in style, had rounded edges, a huge chrome handle, and the brand name, General Electric, scrolled in large chrome letters across the door, some askew and dented. The floor was covered with faded green linoleum, and the walls were a faded blue. The kitchen table was an art deco style table from the 50s with a steel frame and a chrome finish and a yellow faded Formica table top with chrome trim that had lost its sheen. The matching chairs had yellow vinyl padded seats and back rests, and when he put his hand on one of the back rests, he noticed that it was loose in its steel and chrome frame. He looked more closely, and he saw that a bolt was loose. He could fix that.

Miranda was browning chicken in a frying pan; and there was what looked to be a soup or a thin sauce simmering in a pot. Exotic looking ingredients were arranged like an artist's palate on the workspace next to the cutting board.

"You know, Miranda, I think I've got the answer. I've been thinking about it for a long time, and I think I know where the movement went wrong and what we need to do."

Miranda put the spatula down, took a sip of her wine, and said, "I'm listening."

"Well, the way I see it, if we're going to win a revolution, our revolution has to be deeply rooted in the ideals of our culture, or we get what they got in the Soviet Union and China. The Communist Party in Russia replaced the old aristocracy; and in China, the party replaced the old Mandarin class. The old boss is the new boss the same as the old boss. But, in the United States, we do have an ideal that is deeply rooted in our culture. It is essentially a revolutionary concept as old as this country, and that ideal is democracy pure and simple, but it doesn't exist. It's a myth, a lie. And that lie is the underbelly of the system. We don't live in a democracy. At its best, the US is a watered down version of democracy. At its worse, there are no real choices to make or issues to be resolved in an election because all the important issues have been bought and sold before the election even begins."

Sonny poured himself more wine, tasted it, and continued. "Democratic institutions in this country have been corrupted by big money interests, global corporations, and the major economic organizations and professionals that serve these interests. They have done this through campaign funding, the lobbying of Congress, the control of revolving door regulatory boards, and the ownership of most media and informational systems in this country. In fact, the actual casting of ballots has become a meaningless formal ritual designed to ratify the selection of candidates who have already won the one-dollar-one-vote fund raising contest."

Miranda smiled and said, "You're preaching to the choir, Sonny. Our organization broke away from NOW because it wasn't democratic enough, and it was too leadership driven. In fact, many of us recommended that our leaders should be chosen by lottery."

"I know, Miranda, but one of the points I want to make is that one of the fatal flaws of the revolution was that we didn't believe in the American people. Sure, SDS, SNCC, and the communalists reached out to working class people and believed in direct and participatory democracy; but, to often, we gave up on it too easily; or we never believed in it at all. Too often we thought that we were morally superior, that we were smarter than everyone else, that we had the answers when we didn't; and when we assumed that, we became just another deluded elitist group contending for power, authority, and authorship of the collective narrative. But, if we return to a core principle of democracy; and we see that how we make our decisions is as important as the decisions that we make; then, we will see that we already have significant models and the tools for implementing true democracy available to us, right now."

As Sonny was talking, he was being enveloped in the exotic smells coming from the pots and frying pans mingled with the smells of Miranda. Sonny pointed to one of the pots, "What's that?"

"Fruit palm soup."

Sonny put his finger in the soup and tasted it. "Hum. Interesting. What are these?"

"Cassava fonts and this is fufu."

Sonny could smell the coconut in Miranda's hair mingled with the smells of…"What are these? Are they green bananas?"

"No, they're plantains and they're for cooking. They're firmer than what we call bananas, and they don't get mushy when you cook them."

Sonny grabbed Miranda's hand and had her touch the bulge in his pants and the erection that was getting harder and harder. "Like this?"

"Sonny!"

He then smiled and touched her nipples. "And these? What are these? What do they taste like?"

Miranda gently pushed Sonny away and said, "Oh, no you don't. You're not going to make me burn my stew. We were talking about the tools of democracy, I believe."

Sonny laughed, "OK, back to the revolution. What I was saying is that in over twenty states we have, in one form or another, an initiative, referendum, and recall voting process where we can make our own laws, repeal laws, and fire the son-of-a-bitches if they don't do their job. If we're going to start a democracy movement in this country, what we first need to do is establish a grassroots movement that will implement this process in every city, county, and state; and then we fight out and discuss all the critical issues in every one of those forums, in every one of those cities, counties, and states until we surround Washington with an alternative government and a public discourse that will express the true will of the people. We demand a national initiative, referendum, and recall; and once we accomplish that, we will have taken a major step forward towards realizing a truly functional political democracy; or, at least, we will have established an effective check and balance against a dysfunctional representative system that often does not represent the interests of the people and only represents the interests of big money and special interest groups. That's phase one. What do you think?"

"I think you're going to hear the classic Madisonian argument that our Constitution protects us from majority rule and that too much democracy is not a good thing, and we have to protect our individual rights and freedoms against the tyranny of the majority and mob rule."

"Well, first of all, our civil liberties and individual rights are protected under the Constitution. That won't change, and it hasn't changed in states that have this process. As for mob rule, if you're looking for the mob, you won't find it amongst the people. You'll find the mob on Wall Street, in the boardrooms of global corporations, and in Washington. Christ, I thought my dad was the Devil when I was a boy; but, now, as I look back, he was an angel compared to these monsters. At least my dad drank his whiskey straight. He had no pretensions as to who he was and what he did. These son-of-a bitches murder millions of people and cause untold suffering for millions more, and they don't go to the Big House. They go to the White House."

"No, Miranda. That Madisonian stuff is all elitist bullshit. We have a lot of research and data on the process, almost a hundred years; and the research shows that when people vote on an initiative, referendum, or recall; they are reasonably well informed. Also, an initiative or referendum or recall is not an opinion poll where people just get to shoot off their mouths without any responsibility for the consequences. Initiatives and referendums and recalls are news. The more important they are, the more they are covered. There are news articles, opinion pieces, debates, and forums. They're the subjects of conversation among peer groups and pamphlets are distributed as part of the process in some states. For example, in California, the arguments for and against the proposition are presented by representatives of each of the opposing sides in a pamphlet; and the pamphlets are sent to all the voters. If we were to legislate that all TV networks and radio stations have to provide free airtime at prime time for the representatives of the opposing views in a proposition, it would go a long ways in leveling the playing field. It would be the price that the media would have to pay for using the people's airwaves."

"But..." Sonny took a sip of wine and continued. "Here's what I found most remarkable about the process. No matter how you break down the voting – gender, religion, economic class, education, or race – everyone ends up winning half the time. That's a .500 batting average, and that's great when you think about it. The way the system works now, we don't even get up to the plate."

Miranda reached up to one of the cabinets. Sonny loved to watch her. Miranda had the most beautiful ass in the world. When she turned around with what looked like a small bag of saffron, Sonny kissed her; but Miranda once again pushed him away, tossed a couple of pinches of the herb in the pot, and said, "You said that was phase one. Is there a phase two?"

"Yes. Phase Two takes us to the next stage of America's evolution to true democracy. Phase Two is premised on the self evident truth that we can't call our selves a democratic country or a free people if we only vote a few times a year from year to year; and, essentially, elect dictators for limited terms of office; and the rest of the time, we work in an authoritarian workplace where we have no civil liberties, no right to vote for our leaders or determine our own economic futures. So, phase two is the creation of an economic democracy in America."

"How are you going to do that?"

"My idea is to turn capitalism on its head; and I guess I would call it, America Incorporated. Basically, the American people would go into business with themselves. Through their government and an Economic Executive Board elected directly by the people and subject to a recall, the American people would invest in and create employee owned and managed businesses. They would, essentially, buy into a fifty percent share of the business; and, as partners in the enterprise, the employees and the American people would decide together how the business will be run and how it will both serve the interests of the employees and the public good."

Sonny stopped to pour himself more wine, lit a cigarette, and paused for a moment to collect his thoughts, then said, "Now, here is what I think is one of the more interesting parts of the plan. The profits don't go to the government. Each registered voter would have an individual investment account, and the profits would go into that. If the employee/owners and citizen/investors decide to use some of the profits for capital improvements, then the money invested would be considered a loan by the employees and the American people to the enterprise; and they would have to be paid interest like any bank. The irony is that by turning capitalism on its head we create Marx's workless society because as workers become wealthy enough to not work anymore, new worker/owners will take their place; and they, in turn, will work themselves out of a job. In the end, people will work at what they want to work at and that is what we call play."

"Like People's Park," Miranda said as she sat on Sonny's lap and put her arm around his shoulder.

Sonny smiled. "Yes, like People's Park."

Miranda put both arms around his neck and put her head against his, their hair intermingling, dark brown and auburn red with golden lights, and she said, "So, you have been working. You haven't been wasting all your time being an outlaw and a cowboy."

Sonny shrugged, "Sort of. I've been working at the New

School Library, taking some notes; but there's so much more to do. I haven't written a word, and a lot of the time I feel like it is hopeless and nobody cares anymore, but I can't get these ideas out of my head. I feel that I've found a way to cut the Gordian knot and unravel the labyrinth of lies with a truth whose time has come."

Miranda hugged Sonny, kissed him on the cheek, and said, "Come on. I've got an idea. This stew is going to simmer slowly for a half hour or more. Come with me."

Miranda led Sonny to her worktable, sat him in front of her typewriter, put a stack of typing paper next to the typewriter, and said; "Write."

Miranda left Sonny staring at the typewriter. He realized that he hadn't written anything in two years. He touched one key like a piano player would do, then another and another until he was playing the typewriter again. He stopped and looked over what he had written. Some of it looked like nonsense, incoherent babble, but some it was good. He took one of Miranda's pencils and bracketed some lines and added some notes. Then he stared at the typewriter again.

Miranda, who was sketching in front of the fire, got up and went through one of her files. She pulled out a sheet of typewriter paper and handed it to Sonny to read then went back to the love seat in front of the fire to sketch.

Sonny picked up the sheet of typewritten paper and read. It was an excerpt from a book written by Carrie Chapman Catt and Nettie R. Shuler entitled *Woman Suffrage and Politics* that was written in 1926.

"To get the word "male" in effect out of the

Constitution cost the women of the country fifty-two years of pauseless campaigning. During that time they were forced to conduct 56 campaigns of referenda to male voters; 480 campaigns to get legislatures to submit suffrage amendments to voters; 47 campaigns to get state constitutional conventions to write woman suffrage into state constitutions; 277 campaigns to get state party conventions to include woman suffrage planks; 30 campaigns to get presidential party conventions to adopt woman suffrage planks in party platforms; and 19 campaigns with 19 successive Congresses."

Sonny shouted to Miranda who had gone into the kitchen, "OK. I've got it." He then went back to work typing. From time to time he would wad up a sheet of typewriter paper and throw it over his shoulder to add to Miranda's litter and splashes.

Miranda came back into the room and looked over his shoulder. "How is it going?"

"I think I've got the first sentence. He took a red pencil and underlined it.

Miranda read it. "Not bad, Sonny. In fact, it's great. It says it all. Come on, dinner is ready."

Miranda went back into the kitchen to finish up, and Sonny straightened out his papers, picked up his glass of wine, and went into the living room to see what Miranda had sketched. He picked up the sketchbook from the love seat, and he saw that Miranda had been working on a sketch of him typing at her worktable. Letters and numbers were being transformed into people like ghosts streaming from the pages, taking shape. There were splashes of color here and there to indicate that something was coming to life.

Sonny heard Miranda shout, "Come on, Sonny. Dinner is ready."

Miranda and Sonny ate dinner at the kitchen table, and the dinner was different but delicious, unlike anything that Sonny had eaten before. At dinner they talked about everything. They talked about going back to graduate school together. Sonny talked about the new technology, and how he could foresee people voting by phone and the computer Internet systems that were being developed. He talked about Western Civilization going full circle and America returning to the Golden Age of Pericles, the Athens of the future on a national scale. This time everyone will be free, and we will unleash powers and energies that the world has never seen before. America will become the greatest country in history, the last truly great nation state that will usher in a new age that will set the standards for a global society. Miranda talked about art and a book she read by Susan Langer and how art explored the frontiers of reality in form and color. They talked on and on and though they disagreed on many things, they didn't disagree on one. They were a party of two and that was a beginning.

By the time Miranda and Sonny finished dinner it was nearly midnight. Miranda was in the bathroom, and Sonny was in her bedroom. There was a window over her platform bed; and Sonny could look out over the city lights that looked like a constellation in the night, the full moon a light orange glow. There was a ficus tree near the bed; and on the other side of the room, an unfinished ash wood dresser and hanging above it was an oval gold gilded mirror. An oil painting that Sonny recognized as Miranda's work covered most of one wall. It was a painting of three women with ochre skin and green shadows who wore toga style dresses of bright red, orange, and violet with one breast bare, like a mother suckling her children. The women were picking red mangos from a mango tree with leaves like green feathers flying everywhere in a golden light that peaked through the tropical forest.

Sonny undressed and fell onto the bed and the white down feathered comforter that Sonny recognized from Berkeley. The sheets were lavender and smelled of iris perfume. Miranda was in the bathroom brushing her teeth. She then rubbed her body with a combination of coconut, sweet almond, and eucalyptus oil. When she was finished, her body glowed. Miranda looked in the mirror, and she liked what she saw, being in love made her feel beautiful. Miranda slipped on a pink silk thong that made her feel sexy and a white silk T-shirt that made her nipples hard. She touched her vagina with her fingers. She was wet, very wet. On the record player Joni Mitchell was singing, *"Help me. I think I'm falling;"* and Miranda touched the back of her ears commingling her love juices with the fragrant oils; and she giggled at the pure eroticism of her magic potion.

Miranda left the bathroom, and she entered the bedroom where Sonny was lying naked underneath the lavender sheets. As Miranda laid down next to Sonny ready to make love, Sonny said, "Miranda, when I had that near death experience called love today, I had an epiphany. I think I know why things are the way they are and what they could be and why; but more important, I think I know who we are and what we're doing here."

Miranda laughed and said, "That's all?"

"No, listen to me. For billions and billions of years the universe has blindly bumped into itself, learning from experience, its senses growing from touch to smell to the vibrating harmony and dissonance of sound, color, then consciousness, visions of the past and the future, remembering itself and projecting itself into the future with every possibility. What I'm saying is that everything falls in place when you realize that consciousness is new to the universe, and we are it. We are the universe's mind. We are everything and everyone that has ever existed. We are the universe discovering itself, and the world around us is our mirror."

"That's fantastic, Sonny," Miranda said. "What a vision." Then she smiled and said, "Let me see if I'm clear on this. When I look at you, I'm looking into the mirror; but, first, before I could see, I sort of bumped into you and then we began to touch, like this."

Sonny smiled and said, "Yes," as Miranda crawled on top of him, and they began to feel each other up.

"And then," Miranda said, "We smelled each other, like this." Miranda caressed his whole body with her hair like she was painting him with breezes; and he smelled the coconut oil, palm leaves, eucalyptus, mango fruit, almonds, and desire.

"Now," Miranda said, "I want you to close your eye and then open them when I say, 'And then there was light.'"

Sonny closed his eyes, and when he heard Miranda give him the command, he opened his eyes and saw that she was completely naked, posing for him in all her beauty like she was swallowing the light. Sonny wanted desperately to make love to her, but when he tried to draw Miranda near him so that he could enter her, Miranda stopped him and said, "You forgot one thing."

"What's that?"

"You forgot about us tasting each other."

Miranda began to lick him all over like she was devouring him, like the mango fruit; and then she put his penis in her mouth, and Sonny moaned. His universe had become all tongues and mouths. Miranda straddled him and put her breast in his mouth for him to suck; and when he was finished feasting, Sonny turned her over and pulled down her panties playing with them up and down her legs and about her knees, tying her in a woven silken skin, soft words slipping off of sheer weaving lines, naked she smiled when they came together at the edge of reality where infinite possibilities meet random chance and cause and effect relationships become the table upon which we throw our genetic dice, two black holes dancing around each other drawing the cosmos into the mystery where a star is born.

Chapter Six

Sonny woke up invigorated, and he and Miranda drove to Stewart Park for the Trucker's game against National Cash. Sonny pulled up along side of Tikey's 1946 Ford truck. On a flatbed Tikey had built a miniature geodesic dome with a window popping out of the top like a turret. Beside Tikey's truck was an old U.S. mail delivery truck painted over with camouflage paint, a jet airplane canopy as a skylight. Sonny spotted the Claw's four-wheel drive truck riddled with shrapnel size rust spots. His left fender had almost rusted away and hung tied with ropes to the side panel. The rear window of the cabin was totally shattered and the side windows were cracked and mended with masking tape. When it rained the Claw kept his vision clear by pulling at a coat hanger that made the windshield wipers work. The only thing that really worked on the Claw's truck was the motor. Yes, the Truckers and their trucks were all there, junks still on the road with time rusting out the parts, the Truckers clinging to their own, like dogs clinging to a bone.

Miranda hugged Sonny, kissed him, and then said, "Break a leg," and sent him on his way to play his part in the living theater of Trucker baseball.

Sonny walked over to the softball field lined with great oaks and saplings. The Ithacans was all there ready to play their role as fans and as just plain town folk and Doctors of Philosophy, hippies and freaks, and hippie freak farmers, carpenters and painters each wearing their badges of courage – a hammer dangling from the side, a ruler in the back pocket, paint splattered pants, work boots, a fly and sleepy eyes, girls all bright and sun tanned. Everyone was just standing or sitting around on the grass drinking beer, bullshitting, looking at the lake, strolling over to the shore to feed the ducks as sailboats breezed by and an ostrich called from the mini-zoo while his nearby neighbor, the lama, was chewing his carrots oblivious to the play; and a doe peeked through the trees, curious.

Sonny walked by the National Cash bench. The team was dressed in full uniforms with red, white and blue pin-strips. They all cut their hair like they mowed their lawns, all trim and flat and neat with a little red around the collar from riding on their mini-tractors. The Truckers, unlike National Cash, had only a T-shirt for a uniform, a black T-shirt with flowing round sensuous letters spelling out Truckers in sliver and gray with a touch of chrome and a sprinkle of stars. Along with his Trucker T-shirt, Sonny was wearing a red bandana, flared jeans with holes in the knees, red baseball shoes, and his aviator styled sunglasses with mirrored lenses.

As Sonny walked to the Trucker's bench, Dunbar leapt in front of Sonny and snatched a soft ball in the air. Several of the other dogs were waiting for ground balls, barking. Robin was feeding the dogs the ball. Sonny saw Tikey all nervous, up tight, shaking his legs from time to time to get the kinks out. Krotch was walking around in circles probably imagining that he was spinning around and running for the ball, executing an over the shoulder catch just like he and Tikey practiced in Ithaca's never-ending-winter, shagging snowballs, drinking beer, dreaming of summer.

Sonny spotted Jack Mack, the coach of the Truckers. Sonny and Jack had been at Cornell together. Cornell, at the time, required all male students in their freshmen and sophomore years to participate in the Reserve Officer's Training Corp. Participation involved wearing a uniform, going through inspection to make sure you were clean cut, polished, and buttoned down; and then they marched around Barton Hall, a cavernous Gothic style armory. During one inspection, a student-let's-pretend-officer berated Jack for his slovenliness and ordered him to cut his hair and shave his beard. Jack told him to "Go fuck himself."

During Jack's court martial he was given a chance to recant; and he responded with a resounding, "No;" so Jack was court-martialed and thrown out of Cornell with his Kerouac under his arm, an extra pair of underwear and socks stuffed in his coat, and his thumb out, going down the road in search of America. Jack was one of the thousands and then millions of young people who said, no, to the values of the fifties; but there he stood with his hands in his back pocket, holding up his ass as he looked over the field checking out his hangover. As he swayed back and forth, Jack looked to both sides to see if anyone noticed; then he hunched his shoulders and hid his eyes behind his wire rim glasses and his leather poolroom visor; and he headed back to the bench to hide in the crowd.

"Hi, coach," Sonny shouted.

Jack jerked back in surprise, but then he recognized Sonny and put on his official coaching face as he drew in his chin and came to attention. Jack looked sternly at Sonny through slightly askew glasses and said, "I see you're late in reporting to the team."

"Hey, Coach, if you had read my contract you would have noticed that it explicitly stated that I didn't have to show up before you needed me."

Jack smiled then put on his coaching face again. His eyes seemed to be screaming, 'Oh God, what a hangover I have!' But he merely nodded and said, "Very good. Carry on."

Sonny went off to play catch, bat the ball, and bullshit with the boys. Jack mumbled for infield practice several times, but no one heard him. He looked around meekly then reached into his pocket and pulled out some chewing tobacco, stuffed it in his mouth, and chewed a bit. Then he drew up his courage, threw back his shoulders, spread his legs, and shoved his hands in his back pockets in a classic Jack Mack pose, and spit out a gob of tobacco and shouted out, "Katmandu, get out there and hit infield."

On cue the bats came banging out of the bag clashing to the ground, and the Truckers ran onto the field for infield practice. Co-op, who looked like a bearded Viking in a snow storm of dust, wore a black mouth guard; and when he smiled, he looked like a toothless protector of the hot corner against all shots. Robin, who was wearing his gold sneakers, a golden glove, a Trucker T-shirt, shorts, and a John Deere hat, was at shortstop looking at himself in a pocket mirror, admiring his Van Gogh beard. Irish Dew was at second, jumpy and nervous. Tikey was on first; and with his bandanna hanging down his neck like a tongue dangling, he looked like he was about to commit some horrible sex crime like winning. The Claw was catching, and they were all waiting for the ball, but it never came. Irish Dew finally toppled over. The Claw threw down his catcher's mitt and shouted, "Well, come on, Katman, if you're going to come, come, man. We're waiting on you."

Katmandu Willie was leaning on his bat talking to a pretty girl who was all starry-eyed playing her part as a fan.

Jack barked.

Dunbar barked.

Everyone barked.

Katmandu Willie walked to the plate and got down to business. He methodically peppered the ball around the infield, trying not to make the plays too hard, building up their confidence, and creating the drama; but finally Tikey booted one. He kicked the dirt. The boys gave him encouragement. "You're the one, Tikey. You're the one."

Katmandu Willie had the ball. Tikey looked like the fate of the world hinged on the outcome of the next play.

"All right, Tikey," Willie shouted. "This is the big one." Tikey waited. He pounded his mitt. He was on his toes. Willie drove one to him and shouted, "Bring it home. Bring it home." Tikey snagged it and winged it to the plate and Willie shouted, "He's out."

Jack was right on the line and on the field. He waved everyone in, and the team trotted off the field leaving Jack alone for a moment on the mound. Then Jack saw Joey Siddhartha still in center field in a lotus position, meditating. Joe had been a Navy Seal, trained as an assassin; and he had seen his best friend who was in the water with him eaten alive by a shark. Joe had found peace in Buddhism, and now he was meditating on being a twelve year old again when life was all wonder and baseball was everything. When he heard Jack shouting for him to come on home, Joey waved. He got up, put his

Yankee baseball cap on, picked up his glove, and then reached into his pocket and took out a piece of Double Bubble gun and popped it into his mouth. Joe savored the fabulous sweetness of it all then ran off the field.

Jack waited until Joey Siddhartha crossed home plate and rejoined his team. Then Jack looked over at the National Cash team, spit out some chewing tobacco onto the pitcher's mound, and walked off the field, much like he walked out of Cornell, shoulders back, proud to be a rebel.

On cue, Art the Dart Wilson sauntered up to the plate. Art was the umpire. He weighed about two hundred and eighty pounds and had arms as big as most men's legs. He was the perfect umpire for a Trucker game. He was black and bad and loved to laugh. Art liked his position of authority. He liked being the man, deciding who's out, who's safe, what's foul or fair.

The Truckers started in on Art as soon as he came to the plate. "Hey look," the Claw shouted, "Art's going in for color toning. Look how his dark blue T-shirt matches the color of his skin. Expecting a beating today, Art?"

Art turned and waved a huge finger at the bench. "Black and blue's the color of your skin if you fuck with the Dart today."

"Hey, Art," Robin shouted, "I have a new shipment of porno from Atlantic City."

Art's face lit up. "No shit," he said then bent over to brush the plate.

"That's right, Art," Robin shouted. "And one of the girls looks like you. Her ass covers two pages of the centerfold."

Art straightened up and stuck out his ass as he straightened his pants. He looked at the Truckers and just smiled. He knew he was going to fuck the Truckers at least once in the game, and the Truckers knew it too. Art took his position behind the plate, straitened his pants again, adjusted his cap and shouted, "Play ball."

The Truckers took the field, but the pitcher's mound was empty. Art was looking around for Wable when he heard the sound of a helicopter. The helicopter came in low over the field and hovered over the pitcher's mound. Hundreds of balloons came floating down from the helicopter with a Trucker baseball card attached to each one, the stars descending to the ground. Tikey was sliding into home with his work shoes still on. Krotch, the right fielder, was hot with his Hawaiian tropical shirt open at the chest, curls pouring out of the leaves and over the bandanna. He seemed to be saying as he smiled, "Ain't I pretty." Irish Dew was looking tough with a pack of Camels rolled up in his T-shirt, and Tony Lett was smiling with a bat in his hand. Below his picture were his stats: Batting Average – 529, Times at Bat – 17, Hits - 9, Home runs – 1, RBIs – 4. Tony could never quite break into the starting line-up. He said it was because he was black. Jack said it was because he was good looking. But all differences aside, they were floating down side-by-side now. Behind Jack was Co-op with an ear of corn sticking out of his Agway overalls. Robin was a Hall of Famer and still active using a giant dildo as a bat; and Bad Ball, the team statistician, was scratching her head staring into the statistics book with a pencil in her hand. Batting Average – 987, At Bats – 376, Hits – 82, Home runs – 599, RBIs – 1248. Dunbar was right behind her wearing Wable's baseball hat and sunglasses. The Wonder Beast of the East autographed his card with a paw print, and the card informed the fans that

Dunbar was the first player ever voted Fielder of the Year by both his teammates and the SPCA.

The helicopter descended to the mound turning the infield into a dust bowl. Out of the clouds came Wable wearing a red and white baseball cap and mirrored sunglasses with his usual Trucker uniform. The cheerleaders rushed to the helicopter waving their pompons followed by five hundred cheering fans. The cheerleaders were dressed liked 50's cheerleader with teased hair and deep red lipstick, black and purple pompoms, black knit sweaters with *Truckers* in bold purple letters, and short pleated skirts with white ankle socks and black sneakers. A poster nailed to a tree near the field advertised their special appearance.

> *The Renowned Ugly Sisters, The Greatest Cheerleaders in the World Featuring Fat Melody, Toothpick Annie, Barbara The Warsaw Butcher, and Pamela The Bearded Poetess.*

The last thing the spectators wanted to see was Fat Melody doing a cartwheel, but that was the first thing she did as she flipped over and plopped to the ground and shouted with her arms spread wide, "Truckers! Truckers! Truckers!"

In the background, her sisters jumped in the air striking classic cheerleader poses, shouting along with her, stirring up the fans, who like a Greek chorus picked up on the chant. It was then that Sonny realized that the Bearded Poetess was Miranda wearing a fake beard. "Oh, my God," he said to himself, once more amazed by the many faces of the girl he loved.

The Claw, who was standing on home plate, pointed his finger at the National Cash team and roared, "Today we're serious, mother fucker."

Stinky Wales, who coached National Cash, watched from the sidelines. Stinky used to coach the Truckers but gave up on them, got married, gave up dope, bought a house, and didn't hang out anymore. When he joined National Cash he went after proven athletes, ex-high school baseball stars with a resume and a steady job. National Cash cleaned their uniforms for every game, but today with all the dust blown up by the helicopter, they were dirty before the game started.

Stinky was handed a Trucker Hall of Fame Card with Weasel "Stinky" Wales on his knees begging to come back to the fold. A reporter for the local TV station caught Stinky looking at his card, and he asked him what he thought of the Truckers. Stinky looked straight into the camera, smiled, and said, "The Truckers are the best fourth place team in the Western Hemisphere." The cheers for the Truckers rang in Stinky's ear. He turned to see that Wable had struck out the first batter, and he painfully watched Wable retire the sides.

As Wable walked to the sidelines he was asked by the reporter for the TV station what the secret was to his success. Wable stood before the TV camera with his hands on his hips and mirrored the field in his sunglasses. "I attribute my success to this years crop of home grown. I think most of the guys feel the same way."

Stinky Wales the deserter and betrayer of the counterculture and all that the Truckers held holy watched the Truckers bat around. By the time his team ran off the field, the Truckers were ahead 4 – 0. Stinky looked at his baseball card again and threw it away in disgust, "Never!"

He looked at his team. Their heads were down. "Come on, you assholes, snap out of it," he shouted. "The Truckers stink, and you act like you're playing the New York Yankees."

National Cash did begin to snap out of it. They scored three runs and blanked the Truckers in the bottom of the second inning. In the top of the third, National Cash chipped away at the Truckers, and they had a man on third with two outs. Stinky had his best hitter up, and he smelled a run. He smiled at the Truckers who looked worried and tired. Wable was sweating on the mound, and the psych was gone. The batter lined one down the third baseline over Co-op's head. Stinky instinctively jumped up in the air. It's a hit! While Stinky was still in the air, he saw Dunbar come from nowhere and leap up and catch the ball in his mouth. Stinky came down stunned.

"Dunbar."

The umpire called time out. Stinky raced out onto the field. Jack, with his head down in embarrassment and his hands in his back pockets, walked slowly to the mound where the umpire was standing. Stinky was screaming to his base runners telling them to keep on running. Dunbar gave the ball to Wable, and he ran home with it. Art the Dart shouted time out again, and Art, Jack, Stinky, Wable, and Dunbar converged at home plate. All the dogs were running around in the infield waiting to play, barking for the ball. Finally the field was cleared, and Art ruled the hit a single and the man on third scored. Stinky protested claiming that if Dunbar hadn't interfered with the ball the hit could have gone for extra bases.

Art shrugged and said, "It's just one of those things, Stinky."

Stinky jumped up and down and shouted, "It's not just one of those things. Dunbar's a better fuckin fielder than anyone of these assholes on the Trucker team. I demand that he be ejected from the ball park."

Art looked at Wable and said, "Wable, can you put Dunbar in your truck?"

"Come on Stinky," Wable said.

"Fuck you, Wable. I'm not going to lose this game to a dog."

Wable looked at Dunbar and threw him the ball. Dunbar snagged it. "It's yours, Dunbar," he said. "You earned it."

Wable led Dunbar away as Dunbar meekly looked from side to side wondering if he had done anything wrong. The ball was there, and no one was going to catch it. He smelled fear on the field, and now it was gone. He was cheered up by the applause from the fans, but he knew the ball game was over for him. He obediently jumped up on the driver's seat as Wable closed the door.

Wable shouted over his shoulder as he walked away, "Nice game, Dunbar."

Dunbar was encouraged. Wable was pleased. There'll be other games, other plays, but not today. All he could do now was stick his nose through the crack in the window and watch the game, smell the excitement, drool on his souvenir ball.

Wable walked back to the mound. He looked around, then turned to his infield and said, "Let's get this one out for Dunbar."

National Cash

The first pitch was a balloon ball that the hitter went for and popped up. The score was tied 4 – 4. God damn it, Stinky thought, Dunbar broke the momentum. If only Good Dog was alive. Dunbar would never get away with that shit. Good Dog would kick his ass. Stinky dreamt of walking down the street and spotting Dunbar with Good Dog at his side. "Look whose here, Dunbar."

At the crack of the bat Good Dog and Dunbar disappeared and Stinky saw Tikey sail one over the right fielder's head giving Tikey's children something to remember him by. Tikey jumped up and down on home plate just to make sure he'd nailed down his place in Trucker history. Fortunately for National Cash the Claw, Wable, and Katmandu all got home run fever, and they all popped up. The score was 5 – 4 Truckers in the bottom of the fourth, and the Truckers held on to the lead spending most of the time in the dirt, but they dug out the grounders, and Super Co-op came out of the bushes with a fly ball to kill a rally, but in the top of the seventh the bottom fell out.

Krotch missed one of those one hand spectacular catches that he was dreaming about all winter. He looked down at the ball in disbelief. He tried to pick it off the ground, and he missed it. By the time he picked up the ball the base runner was heading for third. Krotch relayed it to Robin. The batter rounded third and was heading home. Robin caught the ball and threw it home. It was going to be close.

The batter slid.

Claw snagged the ball.

The Claw and the batter collided, and Art the Dart shouted, "Safe!"

Irish Dew ran home from second base. He jumped up and down poking Art with his finger protesting the call. Wable almost in tears was kicking up diamond dust all around them, and Tikey was skipping around the clouds of dust as if he had a hotfoot. But Art just smiled, and said, "Pay back's a bitch," and walked away.

National Cash was ahead 6 – 5. The Truckers retired the remaining batters, and it was the bottom of the seventh and final inning. Tony Lett pitched hit for the Claw and led off with a single. Wable flied out and advanced Tony to second. Joey singled, and there was a man on first and third. A pop up by Krotch broke the momentum and knocked the air out of the Trucker's balloon. It was two out, a man on first and third, and Jack called a time out.

Jack walked up to Sonny and said, "OK, Sonny, I want you to pitch hit for Wable. Get a hit, man."

Sonny said, "Is it in the script, Jack?"

Jack nodded.

Sonny smiled and said, "Don't worry Jack. If it's in the script, I'll do my part."

When Sonny stepped up to home plate, Jack was surrounded by protesting players.

"Jack, what are you doing?"

"Are you crazy?"

"He hasn't had enough game time."

Jack stood silently, jaw set. He had made up his mind.

For Sonny this was home to him. He loved living on the edge. It was the only peace he ever knew, the calm of giving himself up to the game. Sonny had been studying Jaws, the National Cash pitcher; and he knew that Jaws liked to throw away the first two pitches to eager hitters. Given the situation, Jaws had to figure that Sonny was eager. As Sonny stood at the plate, behind him he could hear,

"Hit a home run."

"Wait on it."

"What the hell is he doing there?"

"Get a single."

"You're the one."

"Jack, you lost the game for us."

Sonny let the first pitch go by.

"Ball one."

"That away."

"This is going to be the one."

Jaws floated a high lofter. As he watched the ball, Sonny's hands gripped the bat tighter and tighter. He could hear in the foreground.

"Swing! Swing!"

The ball hit the plate.

"Ball two."

"Good eye. Good eye."

The chatter was dying down. Jaws got set. He stood there for a moment then delivered the pitch. His arm came across his body. The pitch was going to come inside out. Sonny waited. It was going to be a little too low for him.

"Strike one." Silence. Two balls and one strike. Sonny figured that this could be the one. Jaws delivered a quick pitch. Is it inside, or isn't it? He wondered, and he waited, and he watched it go by. It was really close. He stepped back and looked at Art.

"Ball three."

All right, Jaws won't waste a walk on him, he thought.

He doesn't even know if I can hit or not. I have two pitches to go. I have him, if I can only concentrate and watch that ball into the bat, feel the impact, and follow through. Sonny stepped to the plate and the last thought in his mind before facing Jaws was forget everything that you've ever learned.

Jack watched Sonny hit a perfect line drive into center field. He felt the crowd explode behind him. Thank god, his gamble worked. Jack watched Tony Lett cross home plate, but then he saw Wable waving Joey on to third base! Jack could only stand there and watch in horror. He thought he had complete control of the game; but now, on Wable's whim, anything could happen. The throw from centerfield looked right on the money. Joey, seeing the fear in Wable's eyes, dove headfirst. At one point he was three feet off the ground heading for hard ground. The ball, the bag, Joey, and the third baseman met at the same time.

Out of the cloud of dust emerged Art the Dart shouting, "Safe!"

Jack sighed in relief. Sonny was happy on first base. He felt like a hero. The score was tied with a man on first and third. Robin hit the first pitch. Joey scored from third. The fans filled the field. That's it. The Truckers won!

Sonny was on second base watching the celebration, enjoying the moment, the play, the feeling of friendship and love. He watched the children jump up and down taking over the field for themselves trying to recreate the moments of greatness, imagining themselves as Truckers of the future. The Truckers of today were hugging each other in joy. Sonny was happy. This was fun. It was guerilla-theater and a hometown soap opera all at once. He wondered if anyone got the story.

National Cash

Miranda came up to him and grabbed his arm. She wasn't wearing her beard, and she was smiling up at him.

"Why didn't you tell me that you were going to be an Ugly Sister?" Sonny asked.

"It was a surprise."

"You were great," Sonny said, and he put his arm around her.

Mirranda, on her tiptoes kissed him on the cheek and said, "You were great too. You're my hero. You won."

Sonny laughed and said, "Well, it's a beginning."

Epilogue

Sonny didn't go back to New York City for another trip; and, now, after many years, he was standing at the same window in the Chelsea Hotel as he did in 1973. He had finally found a publisher for the first book that he had written, the book that he started in this room.

Now he was back in New York with Miranda and his son, Julian; and he had just come back from his publisher's office where he signed a contract for his book. When Miranda and Julian came back from Toys R Us, they would go home. There was nothing here for him anymore. The city had changed so much. He saw it as soon as the doorman opened the plate glass door into the lobby of the Chelsea. All the old paintings that overflowed with rebellion were gone. The lobby had been given a complete make over. The old lady was wearing a brand new silk gown, and she was wearing her jewels again. Even Sonny's old room was now an eclectic gem of different period pieces with modern touches in her setting. The old white Victorian marble fireplace was restored, and the French provincial furniture with muted velvet cushions was offset by a rich burgundy carpet, an art deco vanity, and a light brown leather couch. The room was painted with a rich creamy color and trimmed with high gloss paint that accented the high ceilings, the decorative friezes, and the moldings. Light was pouring through the floor to ceiling French windows that opened up to the ornate black wrought-iron balcony.

On the surface it was quite beautiful, but he could see that the old lady was not happy being made up to be what she wasn't anymore. When Sonny inhaled deeply, he could smell the decay behind the makeup, the smell of all the many lives she had lived there, the faded hopes and dreams covered over by a new layer of mildew resistant paint. Sonny felt sad. This was not the New York City that he had grown up in. Manhattan was now only a city for the rich. There was no middle class, and there was no lower class. Even the Bowery had been gentrified, and the poor and the homeless had been swept away like garbage and dumped in the boroughs like the rest of the servant class that only came to the city to serve their betters. All that remained to be done was to build a wall around Manhattan and pull the drawbridge up at night.

Sonny finished packing, and the last thing he put in his travel bag was a copy of his manuscript. He opened it up and read the first line that he had written the night of the funeral for the 60s in Miranda's apartment.

"Democracy is a revolution that has never been won."

As Sonny zipped up his travel bag, Julian burst in the room followed by Miranda. "Dad, Dad, look at this." Julian took a box out of the Toys R Us shopping bag.

Miranda was smiling. She kissed Sonny on the check and said, "Hi, Honey."

"Look Dad."

Sonny held the box in his hand. It was some sort of gun set.

"What is it?"

"It's a laser gun. There are two of them. They fire laser beams; and if they hit you, this thing that you wear on your chest flashes red; and you're dead."

"Wow."

"That's what I said. And you know something else?"

"What's that?"

"We went up the back stairs, and there are ghosts there. Come on. I'll show you."

Sonny turned to Miranda, "You ready to go?"

"Sure, go ahead with him. I just have a few things to pack, and I'll meet you down stairs in the lobby."

Sonny grabbed his travel bag, and Julian took his backpack and the bag with his laser gun set in it. They left the room and walked down the back stairs. It was as he remembered it, the paintings on the walls and the doors of perception that led to alternative universes. He saw the rebellious painting that once hung in the lobby, the colors and shapes that tried to break out of the canvas to form a new reality.

"Do you hear them, Dad?

Yes, he did hear the ghosts as he had before, their echoes swirling up and down the stairwell, but now he understood them.

"What are they saying, Dad?"

Sonny smiled. *"Power to the People."*